The Courtship of Cade Kolby

LORI COPELAND

THE COURTSHIP OF CADE KOLBY

WHEELER
PUBLISHING, INC.
ROCKLAND, MA

★ AN AMERICAN COMPANY ★

Published in Large Print by arrangement with Avon Books, a division of The Hearst Corporation in the United States and Canada.

Wheeler Large Print Book Series.

Set in 16 pt Plantin.

Library of Congress Cataloging-in-Publication Data

Copeland, Lori.
   The courtship of Cade Kolby / Lori Copeland.
      p. (large print) cm.(Wheeler large print book series)
   ISBN 1-56895-627-4 (softcover)
   1. Large type books. I. Title. II. Series
[PS3553.O6336C68   1999]
813'.54—dc21   98-46991
                                                       CIP

Chapter 1

Winterborn, Kansas
1885

"**W**ell, I'll be damned. Cade Kolby, showin' up after seventeen years as if he hadn't been gone a day." Sawyer Gayford shifted in his chair to watch the town's famous native son ride in.

Roy Baker, editor of the *Winterborn News*, elbowed the dust from the front window of the barbershop and craned his neck to look out. "Never saw anything like it. Look at him. You'd swear he didn't know he was the most feared bounty hunter in Kansas."

"There's your headline this week, Roy," Sawyer said.

Roy snorted. "This *week*? Cade coming home will be news for months to come."

"Well, Kolby left as a boy, but he's coming back a man." Walt Mews motioned for Roy to sit back down in the barber chair. "Looks like he's been rode hard and put away wet."

Sawyer spat tobacco juice out the open front door. "Heard tell he's shot and killed ten men."

"Some say twenty," Roy said.

Walt snipped the final bits of hair around Roy's ear. "More like fifty." Then he shook out the barber cape. Reaching into his pocket, he plucked out a coin and flipped it to Roy. "You win. I bet he wouldn't come."

"I knew he would." Roy chuckled, pocketing

1

the windfall. "Mac and Senda raised him right."

"Humph. He's ornery, if you ask me. Run him off once with a shotgun for tying my cats' tails together," Sawyer complained. "Nearly killed each other afore I got 'em untied."

"He was full of piss and vinegar, all right." Walt looked out the front door.

Adolescent boys playing marbles around the hitching post abandoned their shiny agates and shooters and raced to watch the arrival of Winterborn's most notorious citizen.

"He wasn't all that bad as a kid," Walt mused. "When my Edna hurt her back, he showed up to weed her rose garden. Then he sat a spell with her to eat the sugar cookies she baked him. Seems like he was a right thoughtful young'un."

Sawyer grunted. "The boy's made hisself quite a reputation."

"The missus don't hold with all that killin', but I say a man's got to do what he's got to do." Walt closed the shop's door. He'd stayed open longer than usual, and Edna would have supper waiting. "I say he's doing folks a service. A man with a price on his head expects trouble."

Roy snickered. "Zoe's been in a snit, thinking he wasn't going to show up. Been ill-tempered as a hornet. The wife sent me over to the store this morning for flour and oatmeal, and Zoe nearly took my head off."

"Hard to believe she was sweet on Cade at one time."

2

Sawyer nodded. "Yeah, you'd think she'da had better sense. She's older than him, ain't she?"

"Not much. Maybe two, three years."

Walt straightened the shelf beside the mirror in front of his barber chair. Bottles of pungent-smelling hair tonics were lined up alongside each customer's personalized mug, painted by Edna Mews's questionably artistic hand. "Zoe's daddy, may his soul rest in peace, would've stripped the hide off Cade if he'd known those two were sweet on each other."

Roy got up to stretch. "He knew; just couldn't do nothin' about it."

"I say it's good Cade left when he did. Zoe might not have married Jim Bradshaw if he'd stayed around," Walt said.

The men looked toward the front window as Cade's brown and white pinto trotted by.

"Wonder how long he's gonna stay?" Roy wondered.

"Just long enough to find his sister's brood a good home, I'll wager," Walt answered, patting his pocket. "I got a silver dollar says he's not planning to raise those kids. Men like Kolby don't stay anywhere long."

"Times are hard. Won't be easy to find a family eager to take on four extra mouths to feed," Sawyer said.

"I heard Zoe wants the kids, but I don't know how she thinks she could take care of 'em," Roy said. "Jim left her all those debts when he died, and she can't keep the wolf from the door as it is."

Walt polished his spectacles with a cloth, his eyes still following the rider. "I heard she's got some real financial woes with the store. That little woman's seen her share of trouble."

Roy scratched his head. "It'll be interestin' to see how she and Cade take to each other after all these years."

Sawyer chuckled as he got up and put on his old battered hat. "Yep, real interestin'."

A grin played at the corners of Cade's mouth as he rode through town. Winterborn hadn't changed.

There's Old Man Thompson looking out the Land Office window, checking his watch like he has some place to be. Walt's looking out the barbershop window, making bets with the other men. He laughed, thinking about how he and Ben Pointer had often snuck Walt's *Police Gazette* out of the shop and read it behind the livery.

Bet my last silver dollar that same row of mugs with Edna's silly pictures is still next to the mirror in front of Walt's chair. His grin widened when he thought of those mugs. Bless her heart, no one thought of Edna as an artist except Edna.

Milly Mason's millinery boutique was still above the barbershop. Ladies favored the outside entrance to avoid the "unsavory" atmosphere of Walt's shop below. The men's salty language and racy reading material had put a bloom on many a sensitive cheek.

4

Unless someone had struck gold, very few in town could afford Milly's fancy Eastern hats, and it appeared that seventeen years hadn't changed her clientele.

Nodding, Cade graciously doffed his hat to a couple of well-dressed ladies about to enter the millinery.

The image of his mother ogling Milly's hats weighed heavily on his mind. Senda Kolby wasn't able to afford the ribbons from one of Milly's bonnets, much less the whole fine creation. But she never complained. As she said, she prayed for the best, expected the worst, and thanked God for what he gave her.

Cade's grin faded. He could afford a hundred bonnets now, but Mama wasn't around to enjoy them. Regret hit him hard. Word of his folks' death had reached him six weeks after their burial. Pa had died from a farm accident; Mama, a month later, from pneumonia.

The mare picked her way slowly down Main Street, approaching Ben Pointer's blacksmith shop and livery stable. The sign over the door said Ben would shoe horses and oxen, sharpen plows, and repair farm implements.

"Ben Pointer and *Sons*" registered in his mind. Ben was just a couple of years older than he was. Did he have boys big enough to help? Well, hell. Seventeen years—a lot could happen in that time.

The jail came into sight. Was Pop Winslow still sheriff? Was he still handing out peppermints? Memories gripped Cade, deepening the ache like a branding iron hot in his belly. He'd known coming back wasn't going to be easy. He just hadn't expected it to be this hard.

Up ahead, the old swing he and his sister, Addy, had played on still hung next to the windmill. Worn and frayed, the rope swayed loosely in the late summer breeze.

Memories rushed back, and he blinked hard to clear the mist from his eyes. Him and Addy, playing at the jail as youngsters, diving into the swimming hole—God, Addy *dead*. Only thirty-six years old, and she was gone. Distance and years had failed to dim the closeness they shared. He might not have gotten back home as often as he should have, but he'd always known she was there. Each night as he'd gone to sleep in a cold bedroll before a waning campfire, he'd taken comfort in the thought that he had people who cared: Mama, Pa, Addy—a family waiting for him, when or if he came back. Somehow it had made the lonely days and nights more tolerable.

Now Mama and Pa were gone. Addy was gone. Winterborn wasn't home anymore; it was just a town of bittersweet memories.

With the corner of his eye, he caught a glimpse of a red-headed woman entering the drugstore. His quickening heartbeat caught him off guard; for a moment he thought it was Zoe. It wasn't, though, and he settled back in the saddle.

His grin resurfaced. Now *there* was a woman. Visions of a cloud of red hair, damp and tangled after lovemaking, caused a twinge in his groin. Seventeen years, and he still hadn't met a woman to match her.

Her message the previous week had been curt: get himself to Winterborn, now.

She was probably mad as hell at him, and he wouldn't blame her. When he'd ridden off seventeen years ago, he'd made promises he'd never kept. He'd meant to come back, eventually. But after so many years passed, with just as many outlaws looking for him as he was for them, he'd figured it was better just to keep going. If it weren't for the dire circumstances, he wouldn't be here now.

Reining his horse to a halt, Cade eyed the Bradshaw General Store, located down the street past the butcher shop. It looked almost the same; there was only one difference.

The mare shied, her tail swishing away a pesky fly as he stared at the sign creaking in the breeze above the store. The *Winterborn News* had moved into the upstairs, where the sleeping rooms had been. Addy had written that Zoe had taken over the store after her husband's death and was living in the quarters behind it. Most likely that's where he'd find the children. He squirmed, dreading the thought of facing Zoe after all these years. He'd sooner fight a wildcat bare-handed.

Red. She'd always be Red to him.

He chuckled. Helluva woman.

Procrastinating, he shifted in the saddle. What the *hell* was he doing here? What did he know about raising kids? No one would care if he missed another funeral. He didn't have to come back to Winterborn in order to grieve over his sister's death.

He'd ridden more than a hundred miles, and for what? To order a coffin and see that a fitting hole was dug? The kids couldn't stay with him; he had unfinished business. He and Hart McGill had played cat and mouse for six months, and the chase was no longer a grudge match. It was a death sentence. Before it was over, either he or McGill would be in the ground.

Leather creaked as he leaned back in the saddle and mentally cursed Addy for leaving her kids in his care.

Children's laughter caught his attention. Four boys and three girls played in front of the store, rolling a large hoop with a stick. Were some of them Addy's kids? How old were they now? He couldn't remember. He'd never seen them, let alone kept up with their birthdays.

Nudging the mare's flanks, he rode on. Red wasn't going to like his coming back and disrupting her life. But then, he had a strong hunch there wasn't much she did like about him anymore.

"Brody Wiseman, come away from the window."

"Uncle Cade is comin'. I can see him—"

"Brody!"

"Golly, Zoe." Jamming the rest of a biscuit into his mouth, the ten-year-old boy turned away. "*Someone's* comin', and I bet it's him."

8

Zoe wiped sweat from her forehead as she cleared the supper dishes. The heat was suffocating. Flies buzzed around the screen in the back door, attracted by the aroma of the evening's cabbage, and the small window barely allowed ventilation. Jim had thought the three rooms behind the store were sufficient as living quarters. She had agreed—for two people. Not for five and three pets.

A tight knot coiled in the pit of her stomach. So, Cade had gotten her message. He was finally back. The last time she'd seen him, he'd kissed her good-bye and said he was going in search of a wanted man who had a twenty-five-dollar bounty on his head. He wouldn't be gone long, he said. She didn't know what his conception of "long" was. In seventeen years, she'd gotten a few sketchy letters, a smashed box of fancy chocolates from New Orleans, and a Christmas doll with two broken legs and a cracked face.

His gifts were meaningless, except for the locket he had slipped around her neck before he left. Her fingers touched the small oval resting in the hollow of her bosom. She'd wanted *him*. She'd wanted to hear his voice and feel the heat of his kiss, the warmth of his arms—not eat smashed chocolates and sleep cuddling a doll with broken legs.

Over the years, she'd grieved for him until she could grieve no more. She'd given him her virginity. He'd pledged everlasting love and said nothing would ever separate them.

Nothing except a man with a bounty on his head.

As the years had rolled by, she'd stopped believing he'd ever come home—except in a pine box, maybe. Addy had told her he was just sowing wild oats, that he'd be back someday. Well, she didn't have his sister's faith. She had finally stopped looking out the window.

But now he was back. And how would she handle it? Her hand slipped to her stomach, recalling the pain and loss she'd faced alone. She wasn't the young, foolish girl of seventeen years ago. His coming back now changed nothing.

Cade Kolby was a stranger, a cold-blooded predator. It was only a matter of time before someone with a faster draw killed him, and once, she told herself, that would have suited her just fine.

Brody shuffled over to the table and sat down, staring at the sugar bowl. Since Addy's and John's deaths, he had been quiet and withdrawn. Where was the lively youngster Brody had been a few short weeks ago?

"I know it's him." The boy laid his head down on the table.

Of course it was *him*. Who else would be late for their sister's funeral? Damnation! Why, after all these years, did she want to run and look outside like one of the kids? Had he aged? Was he still as good-looking as the devil and twice as ornery?

"He won't get here any sooner by you looking out the window," she told Brody. "Besides, it's not polite to stare."

Zoe's nerves were raw. Over the past few

weeks, her orderly life had turned chaotic. Brody's and Will's bedrolls filled one corner of the kitchen. The children's scattered belongings so cluttered the three rooms that she could barely walk through them. And the children's pet dog and cat came and went, inside and out, adding to the confusion.

Sleep was just a fond memory. Little Missy insisted on sharing her bed, and the five-year-old had elbows like witching sticks.

Scooping up Will's dirty shirt, Zoe carried it to the bedroom off the kitchen, tripping over eight-year-old Holly's pallet at the foot of the bed. Stacks of clean children's clothes were piled around the disheveled room. The place looked like a hovel, but at least she felt like she had a family now.

If Cade wasn't going to keep his sister's kids himself, then *she* would. She had toyed with the thought from the beginning. Finding the money to clothe and feed them wouldn't be easy, but she could pinch a penny harder. In addition to the washing and ironing she took in, she would see if someone could use any bookkeeping services. She prided herself on being very good with figures.

She had sent for Cade only because it was Addy's dying wish. She didn't need his interference, not now, not after all these years. But for some insane reason, Addy had wanted her brother to be responsible for her children's welfare—a natural choice if Cade had been like most brothers, but he wasn't. He was...Cade.

Even though Zoe had been like a sister to

Addy and an aunt to the children, Addy had been adamant. "Send for Cade. Make *him* decide who gets my babies."

It was unlikely that he would stay in Winterborn and raise them, and Zoe would die before she saw him take them on the road with him. Nor would she allow him to give them to complete strangers. He had little choice but to let her keep them. John's Aunt Laticia was the only other relative the children had, and she was much too elderly to assume their care.

Zoe remembered how John had teased the children by threatening to send them to Aunt Laticia if they didn't behave. The photograph of the old lady on Addy's and John's dresser portrayed a stern, no-nonsense matron sitting straight as a poker, with a stiff white ruffled collar that looked as if it were the only thing holding her head up.

Zoe had visited with the matriarch on the rare occasions when she came to town to see her nephew and his family. Aunt Laticia wasn't as bad as her picture suggested, but no one could convince the children of that. They hid under their beds half the time she was there. Addy admonished John for making the children afraid of his aunt, but he only laughed and said he was half scared of her himself.

"When can I look?" Brody asked.

"When he gets here. It might not even be him." But Zoe knew it was. The quiver in the pit of her stomach told her so.

Stepping to the mirror, she tidied her

unruly hair. Why was red hair always so frizzy and hard to control? Dark circles under her eyes reflected the difficult past few days. Addy's and John's death had been hard. Comforting the children had been harder. They wanted their ma and pa.

The back door banged open, and a breathless Holly came in carrying a basket filled with plump, shiny tomatoes from the garden. Tendrils of dark brown hair were plastered to her sweaty features. "Somebody's comin'."

Little Missy entered the room behind her sister and raced to the window to look out. "Ooooh, he's all *diwty*. Is *that* my Uncle Cwade?"

"Come away from the window, Missy, and wash your hands." Zoe adjusted the starched curtain. Frowning, she moistened the tip of a dish towel with her tongue and wiped an imaginary speck off the already glistening pane.

At the sound of running feet thundering through the store, she folded the dish towel neatly and hung it on a peg. "Will? Is that you?"

"Zoe, come quick! He's here! I heard Mr. Mallard say 'There's that little pissant, Cade Kolby'!"

Good heavens. It seemed that Herschel Mallard hadn't forgotten that silly incident years ago when Cade had put a bonnet on one of his prize bulls. She hid a grin. The animal had looked pretty silly as it ran through town with Herschel chasing it.

Zoe heard Will open the front door and race outside. Shoving his chair back from the table, Brody jumped up and ran after him, craning his neck to get a closer look at his uncle.

Holly's and Missy's eyes were as round as saucers. Clutching rag dolls to their breasts, the two girls strained to see.

"It's all right, girls." Zoe reached for their hands, getting a firm grip. "Your Uncle Cade won't bite." At least not little girls, she thought, recalling their last night in the barn.

Lifting her chin, she took a deep breath. She likened the moment to pulling a tooth: painful, but necessary.

She released her breath and walked out through the store.

Chapter 2

Zoe lifted a hand to shade her eyes against the westerly sun. As her gaze focused, her heart sank and her mouth dropped open. No wonder Missy had said "oooohhh." His appearance was disgraceful. Long, reddish-brown hair and a week's growth of beard made him look downright sinister. She could see why he struck fear in the hearts of wanted men. He was leaner, meaner, and more blatantly male than she remembered.

Yet, beneath the trail grime, he was still as handsome as ever. The years had treated him kindly.

Heat spread through her lower body like warm molasses. She suddenly felt hot, intensely hot, then cold. She knew why she had never forgotten him. Damn his worthless hide. He was unforgettable.

She reminded herself to breathe as his mouth turned up in a faint, breathlessly sexy smile.

"Hello, Red."

Here it was, the moment she'd been dreading from the day she'd sent the wire, and already she was reacting to him as if she were a smitten schoolgirl.

"You need a shave," she said, ignoring the mischief in his eyes as he leisurely perused her.

"I see you've still got your red curls."

Stiffening her spine, she looked away. She'd eat dirt before she'd let him know she'd been waiting seventeen long years for him to come home. "Your watch stop, Cade?"

His slow, devil-may-care smile did little to temper her foul mood. "I kept in touch, didn't I?"

"Three letters in seventeen years? That's your idea of keeping in touch?"

He scratched his beard and changed the subject. "Can't remember the last time I shaved. Must have been somewhere between here and Wichita."

Appalled by his lack of sensitivity, she shook her head. Seventeen years, three months, and four days since that last night in his daddy's barn. The memory had never left her, but *he* couldn't remember the last time he shaved. "Well, at least you made it," she said, turning to go back into the store.

Brody grabbed her arm and stopped her.

His eyes silently pleaded with her for civility. The boy wanted her to invite the long-awaited uncle in. For his sake, she thought—only for Brody's sake. Swallowing her pride, she turned back to find Cade's eyes still on her.

"Come on, Red. You thought I wouldn't come?"

"You didn't for John and Addy's wedding."

"Marrying and burying are two different things."

His steady, midnight-blue gaze impaled her, and the invisible hand around her throat tightened. "Well, you missed the burying, too. We've already laid your sister and brother-in-law to rest."

If she hadn't loved Addy so much, she would have felt a measure of satisfaction at his discomfort. He deserved her cold shoulder, but with the children looking on, it was hard to refuse him simple courtesy.

"I came as soon as I got your message."

She lifted her chin. "I wasn't sure you'd get it. You're the only person I know who uses a saloon as an address."

So like him to miss the important things. Always chasing the almighty dollar and leaving responsibility to others. He might be hurting inside, but so was she.

When she glanced back, he was still looking at her. A smile played at the corners of his mouth. "What happened to your freckles?" he asked.

"I outgrew them." Just as he'd outgrown his boyish imperfections, she noted with dismay. She tried not to look at him, but it was impossible.

Hours in the hot sun had colored his skin to a rich, dark hue. A growth of heavy beard with a hint of gray covered once-youthful skin. His shoulders were broader than she remembered. He filled every inch of his mustard-colored duster. Sinewy thighs flexed as he shifted his weight in the saddle, drawing her attention to the tools of his trade. A Colt Peacemaker was strapped to his thigh, and the dying sun glinted off the butt of a Winchester rifle resting in the scabbard attached to the saddle.

Her gaze traveled to his blue denim shirt, open at the collar to reveal a curly thatch of dark chest hair. Beneath a sweat-stained black Stetson, wavy, chestnut-colored hair hung past his shoulders. She told herself to inhale when she realized she was holding her breath again. She was going to drop at his feet in a dead faint if she didn't get control of herself.

The reins rested lightly in his gloved hands as he forced her eyes to meet his.

"You always were the prettiest girl in Kansas."

She refused to look at him. As God was her witness, she would never let him affect her again. But the children—she had to be civil for the children. "You need a bath."

The youngsters gathered in a silent huddle, tongue-tied and fidgety, itching to meet this dark stranger who so favored their mother in looks.

As she watched Cade's eyes move from one waif to the other, Zoe realized too late that she should have checked their appearances.

17

Brody had biscuit crumbs on his upper lip, and one of Holly's stockings bunched around her ankle. The front of Missy's dress was water-spattered, and her braids were escaping their ribbons. Will's nose, in constant need of wiping, was running a stream. Before Zoe could stop him, he swiped the sleeve of his shirt across his face and took care of the problem.

Cade frowned. "Are all these Addy's?"

She nodded. "If you had come home more often, you'd know."

The jingling of Cade's fancy silver spurs caught the children's attention as he swung out of the saddle. Pulling off his gloves, he smiled at the youngest, who cowered behind Zoe's skirt. "What's your name?"

Urging the girls to the forefront, Zoe introduced them. "This is Missy. She's five." She gestured toward her sister. "And Holly. She's eight."

His gaze centered on Holly. "My God," he whispered. "She looks exactly like Addy."

"This is Brody. He's ten and the oldest. And Will is six."

Gathering the youngsters protectively to her, Zoe took a deep breath, then said, "Children, this is your Uncle Cade."

The four pressed farther into her skirt, clearly in awe of the rugged stranger.

She looked at Cade, whose eyes were pleading for help. She stared back. "Addy thought Will favors you."

"Is that good or bad?"

Ignoring his attempt at humor, she shrugged. "She never said."

"How come you're not keeping the kids at Addy's house?"

"The furniture and contents have been burned." When he frowned, she explained. "Because of the fever, the doctor thought it best to destroy all of John's and Addy's belongings.

"Was it the pox?"

"Doc Whitney's not certain, but he didn't want to chance spreading whatever it was. The Wilson family all perished from a similar illness a few months back. Other than John and Addy, there've been no new cases, but Doc's still holding his breath."

Cade took off his hat and hit it against his leg. Dust filtered to the ground. "Losing both parents must be rough on the kids."

"They're doing well, considering."

Several town gawkers had gathered in the street, eyes and ears glued to the home-coming. Lord knew the busybodies were more curious about her and Cade than they were about the children's welfare, Zoe thought. Cade fell into step as she herded the kids back into the store. There was no need for a public spectacle.

As they entered the building, Cade tossed his hat onto the counter. The pungent smell of a round of cheese on the ledge next to the till blended with the aromas of spices, coffee, and dye from the yard goods. Pickles, apples, and soda crackers filled barrels beneath the counter. "Show me where to stash my gear, and I'll wash up for supper. Is that cabbage I smell?"

Zoe never broke stride as she walked toward the living quarters, past the tall shelves of canned goods and cooking utensils, and a table of linens and fancy ribbons. She sidestepped two bushels of fresh vegetables and a bucket of blackberries. "Supper's over, and I have no idea where you're sleeping."

She sounded snappish and meant to. He had no right to march in and assume nothing had changed. *Everything* had changed, especially where he was concerned.

Brody suddenly grabbed Will around the neck and wrestled him to the floor. "Give me back my slingshot. I know you took it!"

"Did not!"

"Did too!"

Will set up a howl as Zoe waded in and broke up the scuffle. "Will did not take your slingshot. I put it away. You've broken two windows and a slop jar this week."

As Brody hung his head, Will punched him in the arm. "See. I told you I didn't take it."

"For heaven's sake, boys! Isn't there enough commotion going on without this? All four of you children go out back and play. Nicely."

Holly glanced at Cade, who was watching the fracas and smiling. "But what if he leaves again?"

"He's not going anyplace," Zoe said. "Go out and make sure the boys don't get their clothes dirty. They've changed twice today already."

"I don't wanna go outside," Missy said, twirling a long blond braid. "Bwody tied my haiw to the pump handle yestewday."

Zoe gave Brody a withering look that made his head dip even lower. "Go, Missy, I want to talk to your Uncle Cade alone. I can assure you, Brody will not tie your hair to anything." She looked at Brody. "Isn't that right?"

He jammed his hands into his pockets. "Yes, ma'am."

The children left in a noisy flurry as Zoe returned to the front of the store. Cade followed close behind her and helped himself to a handful of crackers and a chunk of cheese.

Grinning, he lifted a brow at her playfully. "Make sure they don't get dirty? Isn't that asking a lot of boys?"

"You don't have to do the wash."

"Looks like John and Addy did a good job with the kids."

"They're wonderful children." She watched his face sober.

"Why did Addy leave their welfare up to me?"

She shrugged. "You're the only family left."

"Did Laticia die?"

"No, but she's sixty-five years old. She and Abraham are hardly in a position to raise children."

"Abraham? Is that old black driver still around?"

She nodded. "Still answering Laticia's beck and call."

A glint of humor twinkled in his eyes as he bit into a cracker. "You're a little tense, Red. Boys can't get dirty? No supper, no room? What kind of hospitality is this?"

Grabbing a cloth, she furiously wiped the counter, her patience at an end. "What did you expect, Cade? That you could waltz right back in here, and things would be exactly as they were when you left?"

He slipped a piece of cheese into his mouth. "You're as prickly as a porcupine."

She snapped open a linen table napkin and refolded it. "Would it have hurt you to clean up before you rode into town?"

He grinned, slipping another piece of cheese off the blade of the knife. "You want to draw me a bath?"

Her posture stiffened. "Frank Brighton has a hog trough you're welcome to use." She ignored his laugh and went on wiping the counter.

Swallowing the cheese, he reached for an apple, studying her. "Addy wrote that you married Jim Bradshaw. How come?"

The cleaning cloth hit the counter with a *whack!* "Did you think I'd wait for you forever?"

He took a bite of the apple. "Were you actually waiting for me, Red?"

His tone had dropped seductively, and she turned to look at him. "Would it have made any difference if I had been?"

He didn't have to answer. She knew by his expression it wouldn't. Anger inflamed her— directed not at him, but at herself for being so vulnerable. No matter how often she told herself that seeing him again would make no difference, it did, and she hated it.

"Speaking of forever, didn't we take a blood oath we'd never marry anyone else?" He winked as he reached into a barrel for a

22

pickle. "Looks like I'm the only one who took the vow to heart."

"You have a heart, Cade?"

He laughed again, sat down, and propped his dusty boots on the pickle barrel. "Sarcasm? Not like you, Red."

Years of frustration begged to be released, but she forced the urge aside. The children needed him; their needs were foremost now. She walked past him and shoved his feet to the floor with a noisy jingle of spurs.

"It's late. You need to find yourself someplace to light—other than my pickle barrel."

He got to his feet, shaving off another piece of cheese. "I thought I might bunk in here for a few days."

"You thought wrong."

He swore under his breath and reached for another cracker. "Hell, it's not like we're strangers—"

Whirling, she hurled the rag at him. "I'm *not* nineteen anymore, Cade Kolby!"

He ducked, and the cloth sailed to the floor.

"And don't be saying 'hell' when the children are around!" How dare he come in and act as if he owned the place, and her, too!

When he looked at her as if she'd lost her mind, she grabbed up the cleaning rag and began polishing the counter harder. "And don't think you'll be hanging around here, with me doing *your* wash and cooking *your* meals. Just because I loved Addy doesn't mean you can take advantage of me. Is that clear?" Turning around, she met his glacial stare. A

23

muscle twitched in his jaw. "Don't stand there eating my cheese and looking at me like that."

"You've changed."

"You're darn right I have."

It surprised her when his eyes softened. "Let's try to keep this civil," he said. His tone was cajoling, soft...dangerous.

"Don't call me Red."

"That's your name, isn't it?"

"Not to you, it isn't."

"All right. Mrs. Bradshaw, is it?"

"Zoe."

He nodded. "Zoe." He sliced off another hunk of cheese. "So, what do you want me to do, Zoe? Jump off a cliff? If you're mad because I didn't come back right away, I intended to come back for you."

"When? When exactly did you plan to come back for me?" She wasn't amused by the twinkle in his eye. If he found the situation funny, then he had a misplaced sense of humor.

"I'm back now, aren't I?"

Oh, he was infuriating. A woman would be a fool to fall for his ways, but she felt herself warming. *Stop—now!* her common sense screamed.

She stored the rag under the counter. "You made a long, useless ride if you've come back for me. You best be thinking about the kids."

"That's why I'm here. Tell me what you want me to do." He reached into a jar for a stick of peppermint candy.

She watched his tongue run around its sticky sweetness as his gaze focused on her.

When she frowned, he took the stick out of his mouth. "How much?"

"Ten cents."

Digging into his pocket, he fished out a coin and flipped it to her. "Highway robbery. I buy them in Wichita for a penny a stick."

She smiled. "I charge a penny to anyone but you. How long do you plan to stay?"

"As long as it takes."

He walked around the counter, and she backed away, realizing what he was about to do. "Cade, I forbid you to try anything foolish—"

He caught her around the waist and pulled her up close. The warmth of his breath on her cheek was devastating.

"Calm down, wildcat." She squirmed, and he pulled her tighter against him. "You have a right to be angry. I'm sorry; I apologize. How about a hello kiss for an old friend?"

For one insane moment, she actually considered letting him kiss her. She wanted it, fool that she was. No matter how many times she'd told herself he would have no effect on her, he could still make her weak in the knees. Every fiber of her body wanted him, yet also warned her against him as his lips inched closer.

She suddenly clamped her jaw shut and turned her face away. He was so near that she felt the scratch of his beard against her cheek. "Sorry. You're seventeen years too late."

He smiled. "Come on, Red, let's not fight."

Oh, how easy it would be to give in. Goose bumps rose on her arms as his hands slipped to the small of her back. He was more persuasive than she remembered, more incredibly appealing.

Touching his tongue to her ear, he whispered, "One kiss, Red, for old times' sake."

She freed herself, picked up his hat, and jammed it on his head. Planting both hands in the middle of his chest, she backed him toward the doorway. "Get yourself cleaned up, then come back to see the kids. And don't wait *seventeen* years to do it." She jerked her bodice into place. "And don't expect me to be here when you get back. I'll have Gracie oversee your visits. Make your decision about the kids and leave, Cade. The sooner the better."

He stumbled backward, cursing as she slammed the door in his face.

She slid the bolt home, then, on second thought, jerked the door back open and snatched the cheese out of his hand. She banged the door shut again and jerked down the Closed for Business shade, hoping he'd get the message.

Chapter 3

Chalmer Winslow was polishing his sheriff's badge with the kerchief tied around his neck when Cade pushed open the jail door.

"Hey, Pop." He walked in, grinning. "Good to see you."

As a kid, Cade had hung around the jail a

lot. There wasn't a lot of law-breaking in Winterborn, so parents allowed their children to play there while they tended business. Pop had never had kids of his own, which was why he took to all the youngsters, handing out peppermint candy when they came to visit.

"Well, well. Cade Kolby." The old man got up to shake hands. "Heard you were coming back." Chuckling, he studied Cade from head to toe. "You've grown up a bit."

Cade clasped Pop's hand affectionately. "I was *born* taller than you, but you look about the same. A little less hair," he teased. Actually, the last time Cade had seen him, the sheriff had been thirty pounds lighter, with fewer wrinkles.

"Hell, I'm falling apart, but at sixty-eight, who's complaining?" He smoothed his mustache with his forefinger, then rubbed the bald spot on top of his head.

"I thought you might have turned in your badge by now."

"Been looking for someone to take over as sheriff, but so far no luck." An even wider grin split Pop's face. "Look at you." He squeezed Cade's arm. "All muscled up. Hard to believe you were that tall, scrawny whippersnapper who used to come in here, nosing into everything."

Cade glanced at the empty cell. "You really going to give all this up? What could be so hard about being sheriff in Winterborn?"

Pop laughed. "Around here? Chicken thieves are about it. Oh, and there was that bank robbery a couple years ago that got Zoe's husband killed."

"Addy wrote me about that. Zoe must have taken it pretty hard."

"You know Zoe. Can't tell how she's feeling."

Cade rubbed his shoulder. She hadn't had any trouble expressing herself a few minutes ago. His gaze roamed the small room. The jail hadn't changed. It had the same battered wooden desk, potbellied stove, a couple of straight-backed chairs, and one cell that, if things were still as they'd been before, wasn't used much.

Sitting down again at his desk, Pop propped up his feet and crossed his arms at the back of his neck. "So. Heard you got Luke Biglow."

Cade straddled a chair and sat down. "Luke and I bumped into each other around San Antonio a few months ago."

"Heard the reward was mighty hefty."

"Some people are worth more dead than alive."

"Tell me about it. Look at this." Pop held up a handful of wanted posters. "Half my time's spent nailing these up around town."

Cade took the notices from him and leafed through them, handing them back without comment.

Pop's features sobered. "Sure sorry about Addy and John. Sad for those young'uns. Zoe's had her hands full lately."

"Maybe that's why she's in such a foul mood. She just threw me out of her store."

"She did? And you lookin' so pretty." Pop winked. "How long you stayin'?"

"Don't know."

"You plan on raising the kids? If not, there's

28

an Amish couple out near Salina that might be interested. But, you know, the Brightons sure do want 'em."

"The Brightons? Frank and Helen? Aren't they a little old to take on four youngsters?"

"Not Frank and Helen. They're close to seventy now. Frank's youngest boy and his wife, Seth and Bonnie. They got three of their own, but they want more. Seth's building another room on and said he wants to have a whole houseful. Seems he talked to Addy and John about adopting the kids before they died, but Addy insisted that you make the decision."

Cade got up and moved to the window. Why would Addy do that? He looked at the town where he'd spent his youth. Seventeen years—in some ways, it seemed like a hundred. No wonder he was so tired.

"I can't keep them, Pop. I know that's what Addy hoped I'd do, but I can't."

Pop dropped his feet to the floor and leaned forward. "I guess it's a jolt to have four kids dropped into your lap."

Cade watched a wagon pull up in front of Zoe's store. "They'll need a better home than I can give them."

"I think a lot of you, boy, but I have a tendency to agree. Those kids need some stability in their lives. You don't stay in one place long enough to fry an egg, let alone raise a family."

Cade took off his hat and ran his fingers through his hair. Pop was right. His home was a campfire and a bedroll. Children needed schooling, a roof over their heads, clean clothes, and three meals a day. What did he know about rearing kids? What did he know about family life, period?

"It'd be hard for a man with your reputation to settle down even if he set his mind to it," Pop said. "Some no-good always tryin' to get you before you get them."

Cade ran his hand across the back of his neck. "The time isn't right for me to settle down. I've got a personal score to settle. Hart McGill. Heard of him?"

"McGill? Who hasn't? Him and his brothers have terrorized half of Kansas. There ain't a woman safe around any of 'em. What's he done to you?"

"He shot and killed my best friend."

"What for?"

"Because I shot his baby brother."

"That'll do it every time."

Cade returned to the chair and sat down. "Someday I'm going to settle down, Pop, have my own kids and my own little piece of land. But that's not in the immediate future. You're right; there's always someone out there looking for a fight. I don't want to bring trouble to Winterborn." He owed that much to his family's memory.

Pop nodded, looking past Cade to the posters on the wall. "There're some mean cusses out there, all right. But where could you go to escape them?"

"I won't. My past will follow me wherever I go, but someday I'm going to be too old for this and I'll have to quit. I've got a pretty good nest egg put away; I wouldn't be hurting for money. Maybe get a place down by the border..." Cade's voice trailed off.

"Mexico? Ain't far enough, son. You'd still have to watch your back."

Cade knew that. He just didn't like to think about it. "I'm going to need a place to sleep tonight, Pop."

Pop raised his brows. "That ain't all you need. You could use a barber. Walt's raised his prices for a shave and haircut. He's got a gun to our head, but we have to pay it. The baths out back don't come cheap, either."

Cade laughed. "No matter what the price, I've got to pay it. Zoe won't let me near the kids until I get cleaned up. I suppose Glori-Lee's still renting rooms?"

"Not as many as she used to. It's all she can do to keep up with the café. Anyway, she's full up, I heard. You can come home with me or take the bunk upstairs. It ain't much—just a cot and a washstand. You'd have to take your meals elsewhere, but seeing as how you're not going to be around too long, it won't matter."

"I got the impression Zoe wants me to wrap up my business pretty quick. Meanwhile, she'll expect me to spend time with the kids."

"It's not going to be easy. I don't know anywhere you can keep them with you. 'Course, there's John's and Addy's house, but it's empty. If Glori-Lee *had* a room available, it wouldn't be big enough to cuss a cat in, and my place can't accommodate the five of you."

"I won't be here long enough to set up

housekeeping. My stay in Winterborn will be brief. So far McGill doesn't know where I am, and I want to keep it that way."

"Where's he think you are?"

"Hearsay has it I'm heading for St. Louis. That should buy me a month or so, but I don't plan to stay that long."

"Well, I'll help you all I can. You want to come home with me?"

"The bunk upstairs is fine." Zoe would have to keep the kids until he could make arrangements for their adoption. "I don't want to stay with you, anyway. You snore too loud."

Pop cackled. "Don't you be spreadin' a rumor like that, boy!"

"Rumor? When Addy and I used to play in here, you'd be reared back in your chair, raising the roof."

Pop heaved his bulk out of the seat, put his arm around Cade's shoulders, and walked him to the door. "You square-dance?"

"You asking?"

"Still full of it, aren't you? There's a dance over at the hall every Saturday night. I know it ain't proper for you to come tomorrow night, so soon after Addy's death, but keep it in mind. You could ask Zoe. You two used to be sweet on each other, didn't you?"

Cade smiled. He'd be the last person Zoe would dance with, judging by the way she'd acted earlier.

He hadn't lied to her. He'd been so busy collecting rewards, he hadn't realized twelve years had passed. Then Addy's letter had come, saying Zoe was about to marry Jim Bradshaw, owner of the town's general store. He'd wanted to come home and stop her. She was his. She had always been his for as long as he could remember. But he'd been closing in on the most wanted man in the territory. He couldn't stop and turn back.

As it had happened, he didn't get his man, but Zoe got hers. The next letter from Addy described the wedding. All the whiskey in Kansas hadn't been able to blot out the loss he'd felt. Why hadn't he gone back? He'd loved her. Was it the endless quest for money? No, he had all the money he wanted, and he wasn't wallowing in contentment.

He shoved the thoughts aside. Why dredge up ancient history? He couldn't turn back the hands of time; he couldn't change a thing.

He put his hat on. "I don't know about the dance, Pop. I'm a little rusty."

"Oh? I thought dodging bullets kept a man pretty nimble."

Cade poked Pop in his fat belly. "You should've been dodging those biscuits and gravy."

Pop patted his stomach. "I've worked hard to get this. Got to have strength for sheriffin' in Winterborn."

"Guess you're right about a haircut. I'll stow my gear upstairs; then I'll go see Walt."

Sniffing the air, Pop added, "Don't forget the bath. You smell worse than a polecat. No wonder Zoe threw you out."

The men parted at the front door. Pop reached into his shirt pocket for a peppermint.

"Here you go, boy. Something to sweeten you up."

As Cade caught the piece of hard candy in midair, he suddenly felt like a kid again. He thought of the times he and Addy had scrambled after the peppermint treats. Grief blinded him as the reason for his homecoming sliced razor-sharp, deep through his gut. Addy was dead, and four kids needed a home.

A light breeze from the open door turned the blades of the overhead fan in Bradshaw General Store. Zoe was standing on a ladder dusting the top shelf of canned goods when the Mayor's wife came in. Next to Addy, Gracie Willis was Zoe's closest friend, despite the twenty years' difference in their ages. Gracie, with her silver hair and cheerful nature, was as young in mind and spirit as a schoolgirl.

Giving a cobweb a final swipe, Zoe turned with a smile. "Morning, Gracie. You're out and about early today." Gracie usually did her shopping in the afternoon.

"Didn't sleep well last night," Gracie conceded. "Kept seeing Addy wasted away to nothing, lying there in a pine box next to John—I can't get her out of my mind." She took a handkerchief from her handbag and wiped her nose. "I'm sorry; I know you miss her, too."

The emotion in Gracie's voice brought a knot to Zoe's throat. She took a deep breath, willing herself not to cry. She'd about cried herself out. "Losing Addy is going to take some getting used to, all right. We were together nearly every day of our lives. The longest we were apart was when Jim took me to Wichita on that buying trip three years ago."

During Addy's and John's illness, she'd gone to their house three times a day, fed and bathed them, washed their sweat-drenched bedclothes, and watched them die a slow death. There was nothing anyone could do but try to make them comfortable. The fear in their voices as they agonized over the children's welfare still haunted her.

When she closed her eyes, she saw Addy's worried face and felt her fevered hand in hers. She heard her weak voice pleading with her to take care of the kids until Cade came home. Cade—Addy's faith in him had never wavered.

Drying her eyes, Zoe watched Gracie inspect fresh ears of corn heaped in a bushel basket beside the counter. "Heard about your visitor yesterday," Gracie said.

Climbing off the ladder, Zoe tucked the dust cloth into the waistband of her apron. "I expect everyone in town's heard about him."

"How does it feel to see him after all these years?"

"Never thought much about it," Zoe lied.

Gracie looked up from a china teapot she was examining. "You were real smitten with Cade Kolby when you were young."

"Was I? I don't remember."

"I wish his mother had lived to see this day." Gracie sighed. "Senda was proud of her boy, though she didn't approve of his occupation." She dropped three ears of corn into her basket. "Lawrence was talking about Cade just this morning. Surprised he turned out as good as he did."

"If you call bounty-hunting good."

"Senda and Mac were fine people, just dirt-poor. Most of us have to watch our pennies, but after Mac got sick, that family lived hand-to-mouth. Cade wanted things better for his folks. That was evident when he quit school to work for Clarence Redding, rest his soul. He chopped wood and hauled hay fourteen hours a day for whatever Clarence saw fit to give him."

"I understand why Cade took to bounty-hunting; I just don't approve of it." Zoe frowned as she rearranged bags of sugar. "He used to look at Pop's Wanted posters all the time and talk about what he'd do if he had money. It really didn't surprise me when he didn't come back." She'd been hurt, but not surprised. "What really surprises me is that he's still alive. I thought he'd have been gunned down by now."

"He sure made things easier for Mac and Senda. Not a month went by without Cade sending money home. Senda didn't have to worry anymore about making ends meet. Just before she died, Cade sent her a brand new Home Comfort cookstove. Law, I was so envious I thought I'd die. Had a warming oven twice the size of mine.

"I never tasted anything so good as that first pan of cornbread Senda baked." Gracie giggled. "We ate the whole pan between us. Mac came in and asked what smelled so good, and Senda told him she'd ruined the cornbread and thrown it out to the hogs."

A burst of giggles escaped Zoe. "I miss Senda." Her merriment slowly faded. "She was like a mother to me."

"I always thought it was good the way the Kolbys took you under their wing after your ma died. I know it wasn't easy on you, being an only child and your pa being gone so much."

"Pa worked himself into an early grave for me. Selling Bibles was a hard way to make a living, but he never complained. But I did get lonely. I guess that's why my years with Jim were so good. He was always here, and home and family meant a lot to him."

"Yes, it's a shame you two never had children."

The thought pained Zoe. Jim would have liked to have had many, but he'd known it would never happen.

Gracie glanced around the store. "Where *is* Cade this morning? Thought he'd be here with the kids."

"He's been here and gone. The children are out back playing. They didn't want to go with him today. I think they're a little scared of him."

"Well, I'm disappointed."

"I told him you would supervise his visits with the children. I have other things to tend to—"

"Zoe Bradshaw! I'll do no such thing. It

37

won't hurt you to spend some time with him yourself—not that I don't want to see him. Walt said it took an hour and a half to get him shaved, barbered, and cleaned up. May saw him ride into town and said he was as good-looking as ever, even with all the trail dust." Gracie turned. "Is he?"

"Looks the same to me." When he'd shown up that morning, clean-shaven, hair cut to a respectable length, wearing fresh clothes and smelling of Edna Mews's homemade soap, she'd had to remind herself to stay calm. But when he'd helped himself to the biscuits and jam without being invited, she'd snatched the biscuit away and given him a tongue-lashing, reminding him that Glori-Lee served breakfast at seven.

"Didn't notice he's changed a bit, huh?" Gracie dropped a tin of peaches into her shopping basket. "May says he's a fine figure of a man. Strange you missed that."

"Sorry, didn't notice."

"Goodness, I think you've been taking Reverend Munson's 'shalt-nots' too much to heart."

Zoe busied herself rearranging a display of cast-iron skillets, refusing to rise to the bait. Cade was a perfect "shalt-not." He was a fine-looking man, but who wanted someone who was here today and gone tomorrow? There was more to a man than the way he looked. Her husband had not only been hand-some; they'd shared the same values. He'd been there when she needed him.

Pausing before the rutabagas, Gracie tested

one for firmness. "So you didn't notice? 'Thou shalt not lie.' That's what the Good Book says."

Finally Zoe couldn't stand it anymore. "All right!" she blurted out. "Yes, he's so good-looking it makes my teeth ache. Is that what you want to hear?"

"If that's how you feel." Gracie dropped the vegetable into her basket and moved to the linens.

"So he's matured. He's still Cade."

Perusing the shelves, Gracie mused, "Refresh my memory on why that's so disturbing. What's wrong with him? Pop says he goes out of his way to bring a man in alive."

Zoe hardened herself to Gracie's words. Whether he brought them in dead or alive, he collected money on other people's miseries. "They're not *always* alive, are they? If you want to quote the 'shalt-nots,' don't forget 'Thou shalt not kill.'"

Gracie dropped the pillowcase she was holding. "He's just doing what the law requires, no more. You know as well as I do: outlaws have to be stopped."

"There are marshals and sheriffs for that."

Gracie moved to a shelf on the far side of the store and called over her shoulder, "Is he going to keep the children?"

"I doubt it. That would mean settling down, and I can't picture that."

Gracie examined a jar of fancy jelly. "How much?"

"Fifty cents. You ask that every week."

"I keep hoping you'll lower the price."

"Can't. It comes all the way from Kansas City."

Gracie set the jar back on the shelf. "Lawrence thinks Cade will probably find a good home for the children and move on."

A dark premonition flooded Zoe. Of course he'd move on. Didn't he always? "It's hard to believe he'd give away his own flesh and blood."

"Well, to be fair, he can't take them with him."

"He'd have to give up bounty-hunting."

"Give up bounty-hunting? Lawrence says a man can't just walk away from something like that, especially a man with Cade's reputation. There's no telling how many he's angered.

"Lawrence's cousin was a bounty hunter," she went on. "He always sat with his back to the wall when he came to visit. Slept with one eye open and his gun under his pillow. I remember telling Lawrence it must be sad to be always looking over your shoulder. No sane man would involve innocent children in that way of life."

Zoe stared out the front window, trying to imagine Cade as a father, let alone a "sane" one. It was like trying to imagine Reverend Munson bounty-hunting.

What *was* going to happen to the children? She was a second mother to them. If Cade took them away from Winterborn, it would break her heart, yet she knew it was his right.

"There are always the Brightons," Gracie offered. "They'd give the children a good home, and you know how much Bonnie wants them. It would be a shame to take them away from everything they've ever known."

Sighing again, Zoe walked behind the counter. "Nothing against the Brightons, but I think they'd be better off with me. Good heavens, Gracie, they're children, not sacks of flour."

Gracie frowned. "You can't keep them. Why, you're barely holding on now. How could you think of taking on the responsibility of raising four young children by yourself? Those kids need a father."

Zoe's chin came up. "And a mother."

"Then maybe you and Cade ought to give those children a home." Gracie quirked a brow. "Have you thought about that?"

"It's out of the question, and you're out of your mind!" Zoe turned her back and straightened the coffee bin.

"My, my, aren't we huffy today?" Grinning, Gracie picked up a spool of ribbon. "I don't think it's such a cockamamie idea. Cade is single, you're widowed—why do you suppose he never married?"

"I didn't ask." Weary of the subject, Zoe grabbed the jar of fancy jelly. "Here. You can have it for thirty-five cents."

"Bribery? I like that in a person." Gracie dropped the jar into her basket and turned to squeeze the melons. "Is he going to be taking his meals here?"

Writing Gracie's purchases on a pad, Zoe kept her temper in check. Gracie was trying her best to ruffle her feathers, but it wasn't going to work. She was on to her tactics.

"Gracie, you didn't come here to shop. You're here to be nosy. Okay: no, Cade will not be taking his meals with us. His coming back has not sent me into a girlish titter, nor do I lie awake nights pining over lost love. His return to Winterborn will not change my life, other than to make it easier. When he rides out in a few days, which he no doubt will, I don't think I will even notice, other than to wave good-bye to the children, should he choose to keep them. There. Have I answered all your questions?"

A smile crept over the older woman's face. Sampling a cracker, she mused, "These are a little stale. Would you sell them for half price? Lawrence does so love soda crackers."

Zoe scooped up a bagful and stuck it into Gracie's basket. "Here. My gift to the mayor. Will that be all?"

Moving to a stack of yarn, Gracie said, "Hate to miss the dance tonight, but I don't think it's proper for us to go so soon after Addy's death—even though I promised her I wouldn't mourn for more than a week. What about the checkers game Thursday night? You think Addy would mind? She never missed one until she got sick."

"She told me she didn't want us missing anything—and she said for you to keep a close eye on May Wilks. She cheats."

"No!" Gracie exclaimed, turning toward Zoe.

"Addy saw her king her own checker. Twice."

"Why, imagine! A woman her age cheating

at checkers." Shaking her head, Gracie dropped baking soda and brown sugar into her basket on the way back to the counter. "Now that we're on the subject, I've had my suspicions about Willa Baker."

Zoe totaled the purchases, shaking her head. "Willa doesn't cheat. She's just forgetful."

"She's also the champion and as sly as a fox. I say she bears watching."

Zoe handed the bill to her. "Two dollars and fifty cents."

Leaning close, Gracie whispered, "You've shorted yourself. You know I was just trying to get a rise out of you, asking for bargains. I'll pay full price for the jelly, and the crackers are perfectly fresh." Straightening, she sobered. "That's your problem, dear heart. You are too giving. No wonder you're going broke."

"A little off the jelly and free crackers aren't going to change my financial situation."

Unfortunately, the store ledger contained more debts than Zoe had assets, but she couldn't deny credit to needy families. Times were hard. When the gristmill closed down last year, many a man was caught unawares. She didn't intend to sit by and watch children go hungry. When desperate neighbors came to her looking for credit to feed their families, how could she refuse? Jim had never turned anyone away; she didn't have the heart to start now.

"Jim was the most caring man in the world," Gracie sympathized, "but he was a poor money manager. His daddy was the same way."

Trying to shake off the feeling of impending

doom, Zoe wrapped Gracie's purchases. "I'm falling farther behind every day."

"And you think you can feed four kids and keep them clothed?"

"I'll do what I have to."

"You thought any more about selling out? Frank Lovell wants your store. He's not my favorite person, but he's got the money to buy it."

"Where would I go? I have no family."

"It's a shame Addy and John couldn't have helped with the kids' expenses, but after the mill closed, John could barely feed his family. If they'd asked, Cade could have helped them out."

"The last thing John or Addy would have done was ask Cade or anyone else for money," Zoe said.

"Well, you know Lawrence and I will help if we can. We've got a little set aside, if you need it."

"Thanks, Gracie, I appreciate it, but that isn't the answer. Things are tight, but when that shipment of yard goods comes in, I'll make a decent profit—enough to see me through another couple of months." After that, she didn't know what would happen, but the last thing she wanted was for Cade to know about her shaky financial situation.

She handed Gracie her purchases. "I know I can count on you."

"And I know you. You're like Addy and John. Pride will keep you from ever asking for help."

"I have no desire to be a martyr. Don't

worry; I'll ask if I need it. Just don't mention it to Cade."

"You don't think you can keep something like this quiet in Winterborn, do you?"

"I'll only have to keep my money troubles from Cade for a week or two. He won't be around any longer."

As the door closed behind Gracie a moment later, Zoe climbed back up the ladder to finish cleaning.

She hoped she never had to ask friends for money, but with suppliers breathing down her neck, and her being two months behind on the bank payments, she couldn't hold out much longer. She was already taking in washing and ironing. When would she find the time to do anything more? She dusted harder, blinking back tears. Taking charity wasn't something she liked to consider, not any more than losing the children was. She couldn't trust Cade to be sensible. Heaven knows she had enough reasons to believe he wouldn't be. Would he do the right thing and let her have the children? Ha! He'd never done the right thing in his life.

Still, maybe he understood how limited his options were.

He was thoughtless, true, but he had only two choices: give the children away or raise them himself. His lifestyle prevented him from keeping them. That left the first choice.

Only one thing was clear in her mind. Those children were hers. If he refused to recognize it, he would be in for the fight of his life.

Chapter 4

Cade opened his eyes Sunday morning to the sound of rain dripping off the eaves. A damp-smelling breeze ruffled the rumpled curtain at the open window, and he stared at the dingy, water-stained ceiling. Thunder and lightning had kept him awake most of the night, and the heavy downpour had left a puddle in the middle of the warped pine floor.

He rolled his tongue around his lips and shuddered. Glori-Lee's bacon and collard greens had tasted considerably better last night.

He stretched full-length, recoiling as his feet encountered soggy bed linens. The old roof was leaky as a sieve. Poking a foot out from under the sheet, he closed his eyes again. If he'd wanted this kind of misery, he could have slept outside.

Cade put off getting up and lay listening to the sounds of the awakening town.

The church bell rang in the distance, calling to morning worshipers. The smell of frying bacon and fresh coffee drifted to him, and he inhaled, smiling when he heard the unmistakablly shrill voice of Hattie Thompson shouting to Woodall that he was going to be late for church. No doubt, Woodall was dallying over the *News* as he finished his morning ritual.

Funny how everything had changed, but nothing was different.

For no reason at all, a childhood incident

popped into Cade's mind—the time he and Addy had sneaked some of Mama's syllabub at Christmas time. Pa would have skinned them alive if he'd known how his children had gotten roaring drunk in the barn loft on that delightful holiday drink made of cream mixed with wine and brandy. He grinned. Zoe had refused to be a party to the nonsense. She'd stayed sober and covered for them, telling his folks that they were sick from eating too much sweet potato pie and had gone to bed early.

He sobered. They had paid dearly for that syllabub; his temples still throbbed just thinking about the miserable thumping headache he'd had the next day.

Zoe had blackmailed him, making him answer to her for a full week. He'd rolled out of bed before dawn in the biting January cold and waded through snow up to his hips to gather eggs and muck out her daddy's barn.

He shifted his hip on the thin mattress. It hadn't been so bad, though. Zoe had brought him cinnamon rolls fresh from the oven and steaming cups of black coffee. They'd sat in the warmth of the barn stalls, surrounded by dry hay and milking pails, and talked for hours. There wasn't anything he couldn't tell her in those days. They knew everything there was to know about each other.

He consciously forced a shift in his thoughts. What was he going to do about the kids? "Addy," he whispered, "why would you pick me, of all people, to decide their future? Why didn't you just give them to the Brightons? Pop said Seth and Bonnie would give them a good home and proper upbringing. Why drag me into a situation I can't fix?"

Rolling out of bed, he sat on the edge of the bunk and scratched his head. He smelled like a French whorehouse with all that soap and shampoo Walt had used on him Friday night. He shook his head, trying to dilute the smell of Edna's fancy bar soap. He didn't know what she made it with, but the flowery scent stuck to him like a burr.

He got up and dressed, strapping his gun belt around his waist. Sidestepping the rain puddle, he moved to the battered washstand and poured water from a chipped pitcher into a pottery bowl.

He lathered his face with soap, then reached for the straight razor. He couldn't believe he was shaving again. Twice in one week. He never thought about it when he was on the trail. Because of Red and the kids, he now had to worry about his appearance. His hand froze when an almost imperceptible sound caught his attention. From the open doorway behind him came an indistinct rustle.

With intentional calmness, he lifted the razor with his left hand, letting his right slide to his gun. He stared back at his reflection in the mirror and shifted slightly so he could see the open doorway.

Four small children stood there, staring at him as if he were the boogeyman.

The tension subsided, and his hand casually dropped from the holster. Setting down the razor and picking up the soap mug, he whipped up a rich lather, pretending to be oblivious to his early morning visitors.

Brody stood straight as an oak, twisting his hat in his hands. Red jelly rimmed Will's upper lip, and he held a biscuit in his hand. Holly's and Missy's wide eyes sized him up.

He found the intense scrutiny amusing. Should he break the ice and let them know he saw them, or should he allow them to look their fill until their curiosity was satisfied?

Drawing the razor over his lathered cheek, he talked to his image in the mirror. "Well, Cade, your sister's left you a passel of fine-looking children."

Will quickly covered his mouth to stifle a giggle. Brody elbowed him sharply. Holly's face turned as red as a hot poker, and Missy buried her head in her sister's side.

Tapping the razor on the rim of the bowl, Cade continued talking to himself. "A man would be right proud to have kids like that."

He bent closer to the mirror to shave under his nose, then down his left cheek. "I'd like nothing better than to stay here in Winterborn and be their pa, but I can't. I travel from town to town and never know where I'll lay my head at night. Good kids like that need roots. They need a ma who can fry chicken, bake biscuits, and tuck them into bed at night."

Sloshing the razor through the water, he paused. "Pop says the Brightons would love to have them. Don't know much about Seth

Brighton, but I heard he's a fine pa to his own kids. Seems to me he'd make a fine pa for Addy's kids."

He smiled when he saw Holly's bottom lip jut out like a sore thumb. Brody didn't look any too happy about the prospect, either. The looks on Will's and Missy's faces pulled at his heartstrings.

Drawing the razor back through the water, Cade said, "I hear Seth's got a fine bunch of ponies at his place. I could talk to him and see if the boys could have a horse of their own."

Brody's and Will's faces momentarily brightened.

"And Bonnie raises those cats. Hear she's got a new litter that're cute as buttons."

Holly and Missy looked vaguely interested.

"Yes." Cade finished shaving and laid the razor aside. He studied the children's reactions in the mirror. "All and all, I'd say the Brightons would make a fine ma and pa for Addy's kids."

Four chins lifted with open hostility. Reaching for Missy's hand, Holly nodded to Brody, who in turn grabbed Will by the collar, and they marched out as soundlessly as they had arrived.

Cade dried his face on the rough towel, glancing toward the empty doorway. Something close to loneliness came over him. He hadn't experienced the feeling often. He wasn't accustomed to needing anyone. His horse and the open road were his family, yet it was as if Addy spoke through Holly's eyes, reminding him he wasn't getting any younger.

A man his age should have namesakes of his own; he needed a reason to come home at night. He should certainly have more than one horse; he should have several, plus more cats than old Bossy could provide milk for.

The kids needed more than ponies and cats. They needed love. He could give them love; what he couldn't give them was permanence.

He'd talk to the Brightons and see if they had enough love and permanence to go around.

Zoe glanced up from her bookkeeping Monday morning to see Cade standing on the back porch. His sudden appearance affected her in an unsettling way, but she assured herself that the strong coffee this morning was the cause of her sudden heart palpitations.

Peering through the screen, she frowned. Early morning was the only time she could work on the store ledgers without interruption. What was he doing here this early? His smile caught her breath, and she hurriedly turned back to the ledger. The numbers seemed to dance before her eyes, and suddenly she couldn't remember what five times seven was. Darn him!

"The children aren't up yet," she said.

"Good. I came to talk to you."

Wonderful. A shoot-out at daybreak—just what she needed. Laying the pencil aside, she got up and unlatched the screen. Sunrise glistened off the early morning dew, scattering diamond patterns across the grass. The honeysuckle growing up the building's back wall perfumed the tiny kitchen.

When he entered the room, she could have sworn the limited space got even smaller. His presence filled every corner as he pulled off his hat and looked around.

Glancing toward Will's and Brody's pallets, he whispered, "Looks like a houseful."

She knew he'd expect a cup of coffee, but she'd had to scrape the can this morning to make her own. There'd be no more coffee for her this month. She sat back down at the table. "What did you want to talk to me about?"

Hooking his hat over the chair back, he took the seat opposite her. "The Brightons."

She totaled a column. "Bonnie and Seth?"

"What kind of people are they?"

"They're good people. You remember Seth's folks, Frank and Helen?"

"I remember the old man being strict. He was quick to take his kids behind the woodshed and use a stick on them."

Her pencil paused in midair as she thought about it. "I don't know that Frank's like that now. He seems to be a reasonable man, and his children are all responsible, hard-working adults."

"Do you think Bonnie and Seth would make a good home for Addy's kids?"

She sipped her coffee, looking at him over the rim of the cup. "Yes, but I don't think that's the best place for them."

52

"Oh?" He glanced toward the stove. "Any more of that coffee?"

"No. This is the last of it."

"The last of it?" He shifted slightly in his chair. "Don't you own a general store?"

"I do, but I have to pay for my coffee just like everybody else."

He reached across the table and took her cup. Their hands touched, and she jerked back as if she'd been burned. He flashed a disarming grin as he took a long sip. When he handed the cup back to her, she deliberately wiped the rim where his lips had been.

He chuckled. "Afraid of me, Red?"

She got up and took her cup to the sink. Wild horses couldn't make her put her mouth where his had been. She wasn't playing games with him. He was trying to evoke memories that were better left alone. "When have I ever been afraid of you?"

"Well, if you're not, the kids are." He turned the ledger she was working on and scanned the long rows of figures. "So far they haven't said a word to me. They can talk, can't they?" He jumped back when she returned to the table and snapped the book shut in his face.

She stuck the ledger into a drawer and pushed it shut. "The children will warm to you in time. They're a little intimidated at the moment."

"I don't have time, Red. How do I get them to open up to me *now*?"

"Give them a few days." An edge of impa-

53

tience crept into her voice. "You surely have a few days, don't you?"

"Very few. But they did come over and watch me shave early yesterday morning."

She opened her mouth, then quickly shut it. It had been the wee hours of the morning when she'd blown out the lamp and gone to bed, after finally finishing Mrs. Penscott's ironing. She mentally groaned when she recalled having slept later than usual and letting the children fend for themselves. They had gone out early and come back wide-eyed, chattering about their uncle's strange behavior and how they'd missed Sunday school and weren't happy about it.

"They didn't know I saw them," Cade added. "I got the feeling that if I'd turned around, I'd have scared them out of their wits."

She turned to the stove and poured hot water into the dishpan, just to give herself something to do. "They thought you were strange, talking to yourself about the Brightons and their supposed ponies and litters of kittens."

"I didn't lie to them. Pop told me Seth and Bonnie have a good-sized farm. He said Seth talked to Addy about adopting the kids a few days before she died."

"He did, but that doesn't mean Addy wanted Seth to have them." She watched his features sober.

"Exactly where *does* Addy want them, Red?"

She scrubbed a pot, bracing herself. "They'd be better off with me."

"With *you*?"

54

The disbelief on his face assured her he'd never considered the option. Before her confidence wavered, she went on. "Apparently, you've decided not to keep them."

"I can't keep them, and I can't believe you'd want them."

She whirled to confront him. "And why not?"

"Hell, Red—you don't have a husband. If Seth and Bonnie take them, they'll have both mother and father."

Tears welled in her eyes, and she cursed her fragile emotions. Fighting the tight knot in her throat, she reminded herself to keep her feelings in check. He knew how to get under her skin, but she wouldn't let him. There was too much at stake to let him intimidate her now.

"No one could love those children more than I do. I was there the day each one was born. I helped deliver Missy and Will; they're like my own. I'm the one who nursed Addy until her last breath, and believe me, Cade, I would never have sent for you if it wasn't your sister's dying wish. Next to you, I'm the closest thing to family the children have, other than John's Aunt Laticia. I won't let you give them away!"

She heard her voice choke with emotion. He'd gotten to her again. How dare he sit there and calmly discuss Addy's children as if they were nothing more than strangers in need of a roof over their heads!

"Won't let me? Aren't you forgetting that I'm their uncle, and I can damn well do what I want?"

The tone of his voice forced her to look at him.

She met his gaze evenly. "You don't *know* them, not one thing about them. How could you? You never once bothered to come home and meet them. Do you think the presents you sent them at Christmas made up for your absence? I don't know what Addy was thinking when she put her children's welfare in your hands—a man who doesn't care whose feelings he steps on."

He didn't waver. "I'm all they've got right now. And I'll decide who raises them."

Wiping her nose, she muttered, "You better make the right choice."

"Look, Red, I'm not trying to hurt you..."

"I don't have a price on my head. Why would you waste time on me?" Her eyes held his, refusing to break contact.

Brody and Will stirred on their pallets. The last thing she wanted was to involve the children in their quarrel. Lowering her voice, she whispered, "Addy's dead, and her children need a home—a home I can give them, a home I *want* to give them. Please don't take them away from me, Cade. There's no reason to uproot them from everything they've known. Let them stay here with me. I can raise them as well as Seth and Bonnie can."

Arms crossed, she stared out the window, watching a sparrow flit in and out, building a nest under the kitchen eaves. At the moment, she envied the bird. The only problem it faced was today. She had years of loneliness ahead of her if Cade took the children or, worse yet, gave them to the Brightons. If that were to happen, she would be relegated to being a doting "aunt," bringing gifts at appropriate occasions but never really sharing in their lives.

When she turned to face him, she saw his anger, as well as...disgust and pity? Please, God, not pity. Not from him.

"I'm not saying you wouldn't love them," he said, "but look around you. How can you take care of them? You're practically walking on kids."

Zoe cringed as he sized up the room, his gaze lingering on the old, worn-out furnishings. She bit her lip, suddenly aware of her faded dress and obvious lack of means. If he were ever to guess just how badly off she was financially, he would never let her have the kids. But she only had to keep her money problems hidden from him for a short time. He wouldn't be around long enough to realize her situation. She'd see to that.

"I know what you're thinking," she said, "that I wouldn't be able to afford them—but things are picking up. As soon as I get the new shipment of yard goods, I'll make a tidy profit."

"Money isn't the only consideration. I can provide you with all the money you'll ever need."

Rinsing a dish, she said softly, "I don't want your money."

"Too dirty for your taste, Red? I wasn't offering you my money. I was talking about the kids. Whoever has them, I'll see that they're taken care of financially. But I want them to have a mother *and* a father. That's what Addy would want."

"So if I had a husband, you'd let me keep them?"

"Do you have someone in mind?"

"No. Merely asking."

"You surely wouldn't marry someone in order to keep the kids. What kind of stability would that give them?"

"There are plenty of men who would welcome a ready-made family."

"Name two."

"Perry Drake and Jake Bledso."

"Drake? The banker?"

"Yes. He's a wonderful man."

"And who is Jake Bledso?"

"A man—a very nice man who bought a farm east of town."

Cade leaned back in his chair. "Funny, I've never heard of Jake Bledso. Maybe I'll bump into him while I'm here."

"Well, you won't. He's...back East on business." Actually, she didn't know Jake. She'd heard Perry say he held the mortgage on the Bledso farm. For all she knew, Jake was married or too old to care, and as far as Perry was concerned, he'd taken her to the Saturday night dance a couple of times, but that was all.

Straightening the sugar bowl, Cade cleared his throat. "I know you mean well, Red, but if Addy wanted you to have the children, she wouldn't have involved me."

She jammed a skillet into the dishpan. "Oh, yes, I forgot who I'm dealing with. Cade Kolby, Prince of Uncles—Prince of Lovers—Prince of—"

He slammed both hands on the table and got up. The warning in his eyes said she'd made her point.

Brody stirred on his pallet, opening one eye. When he spotted Cade, he quickly shut it.

Cade reached for his hat. "I'm taking the kids swimming today. Is that all right with you?"

She shrugged. "Why ask? Addy made you God, not me."

He put his hat on and adjusted it low on his forehead. "See that they're ready in an hour."

Zoe turned and flung a wooden spoon at him as the screen door slammed. The spoon ricocheted off the wire mesh and took a hard bounce onto Brody's pallet.

Brody picked it up, then looked at her. Will lifted a tousled head and rose on an elbow, sleepy-eyed and yawning.

Staring at the screen door, Zoe slowly counted to ten. Clenching her hands into fists, she silently ranted and railed, calling Cade every name under the sun. Throwing a spoon at him had probably lessened her chance of keeping the children, but she didn't care. It was hard to control the anger that simmered inside her, the anger *he* provoked.

Brody and Will were still watching her. For their sake, she would pretend their uncle wasn't the most impossible man on earth. Turning from the door, she met the boys' curious stares brightly.

"Guess what? Uncle Cade is taking you swimming!"

Chapter 5

Cade left the Bradshaw store and walked down the street to the jail. When he opened the door, he found Pop sprawled on the cell bunk, white-faced and moaning.

"What's wrong? Are you sick?"

Pop drew his knees up to his chest with a groan. "Gooseberry pie," he rasped.

Cade entered the cell and knelt beside him. The old man's face was nearly as white as his mustache. "Lord, how much did you eat?"

"Three, maybe four pieces—I lost count."

Cade shook his head sympathetically. "Green-apple quickstep. That's rough."

"Dadburn that May Wilks! She knows better than to let me make a hog out of myself on her pies!" Pop doubled over again.

Cade glanced around the empty office. "Can I do anything to help?"

"Just get out of my way—I'm coming through." Pop hauled himself off the bunk and made a beeline for the back door.

Cade sidestepped his hasty departure. "Maybe next time you need to stop at one piece!"

Moving to the desk, Cade sat down and leafed through the Wanted posters. He laid two aside, knowing he had already collected the rewards on them. Hot bile rose to his throat when Hart McGill's picture came up. He stared at it long and hard. They'd upped the reward another five hundred dollars. The bastard wasn't worth it. He'd kill the son of a bitch for nothing.

When he thought of Owen Cantrell, shot in the back while passing through his own front door, it turned his stomach. Owen had been gunned down for no reason other than because he was Cade's friend. The image of Bess Cantrell, grief-stricken, being carried away from the graveside by her two sons, would stay with Cade for as long as he lived.

Hatred burned inside him.

The poster said McGill had last been seen in Oklahoma, but he knew Hart was holed up in a bordello in Great Bend. A reliable source had told him he'd be there for a few weeks. Cade knew that when it came to pleasure, McGill was in no hurry to leave.

Pushing his anger aside, Cade moved to the window and thought of more pressing matters. If Hart ever got wind that Cade had loved ones in Winterborn, their lives would be worthless. He'd talk to Seth and Bonnie about getting the kids settled as quickly as possible. They didn't belong with Zoe.

The back door opened and Pop returned, carefully easing himself onto the nearest chair and letting out a sigh. "Boy. That was close."

Cade grinned and sat down. "You going to live?" Pop looked pale, his strength obviously drained.

"For a few minutes—never know when the next bout will strike. You come over for any particular reason? Thought you'd be busy with the kids."

"Actually, I did have a reason for stopping by. The roof's leaking like a sieve, and I'm not looking forward to sleeping in a wet bed again. I could move the bunk, but the roof's dripping in so many places that it wouldn't do any good. I can see daylight through the cracks."

"Yeah, I know about the leaks. Just haven't had time, money, or manpower to fix 'em."

"I can see you're not in any shape to fix anything right now. I just hope it doesn't rain again anytime soon."

"How are you and the redhead gettin' along?"

"We're not. I need to finish my business and get out of here."

"Too bad. Zoe needs a man like you—someone who won't let her run roughshod over him. Jim was too patient. Zoe got the best of him at times—" Pop's eyes suddenly widened. "Oops. Nature calls." As he bolted toward the door, he called over his shoulder, "Don't go—I got a favor to ask ya."

Cade browsed through the gun cabinet for several minutes while Pop was gone. He took out a Henry lever-action rifle and examined it. The guns hadn't been used for some time. They needed a good cleaning.

"Whew, doggies!" Pop said, entering the room again. "If I ever look at another piece of gooseberry pie, shoot me."

Cade slipped the Henry back into the cabinet. "You wanted to ask a favor of me?"

"Yeah, I've got some problems over in the next county. I'm not in any shape to go. Thought you might take care of it for me."

"Sure. What'd you need?"

"Hague Pearson got all liquored up a couple of nights ago and got himself shot. Someone needs to go over and bring his body back."

Cade frowned. "Hague Pearson—that old hermit who lived near the county line?"

Pop nodded. "That's the problem. Me and Mooney Adams got a bet going. You remember old Mooney, sheriff of Suffox County?"

"I remember Mooney. Mean son of a bitch, but honest."

"Whoever has the least crime on his record at the end of each year wins a quart of whiskey. We ain't got any crime here in Winterborn, so it's a pretty sure bet I'll win, but Hague could put a kink in the plan. I want you to drive over there and decide exactly where Hague got shot. Mooney says he got shot on our side of the line and dropped dead on his side. I say he got shot in Suffox County. I don't want Hague's death on my record, and Mooney don't want it on his."

"I'm guessing Hague didn't want it on anybody's record."

Pop chuckled. "Don't mean no disrespect. Hague was an ornery sort, but he always let me hunt on his property. I'll see he gets buried proper-like. I'd be much obliged if you'd drive over there and get it sorted out for me."

"Sounds like a damn good way to get shot."

"Naw, Mooney knows he's in the wrong. He's just trying to win that quart of whiskey."

"I'm taking the kids swimming today. Can it wait until tomorrow?"

"Don't see why not. Old Hague ain't goin' anywhere."

"I also want to talk to Seth and Bonnie. Do they live on the old Brighton place north of town?"

Pop nodded. "Yep, you can't miss it. It's just down the road a piece from Frank's and Helen's place."

"I'll stop by and talk to them on the way back tomorrow."

"Want to satisfy yourself they'll make a good home for Addy's kids? They will, you know. Seth's a hard worker."

"So I hear." Cade got up and stretched. "By tomorrow you might feel like taking care of the Suffox County trouble yourself." Cade laughed when Pop's stomach rumbled so loud they both heard it.

"Son, there ain't enough outhouses between here and Suffox County for me to chance it. The rate I'm going, you'd be bringing back my carcass alongside Hague's."

Later that day, Cade leaned against a tree trunk, watching the children play in the water. Their gleeful squeals filled the hot afternoon air. One by one, the oldest three dropped into the cool water from the swinging rope that was knotted to the jutting branch of a walnut tree, while Missy waded along the shore.

Glancing across the stream, he silently conceded he'd missed being home. It was peaceful here. He, Zoe, and Addy had spent hours at the swimming hole as kids.

A hawk cried overhead, drawing his attention. Why had he ever left? Was it the money or the thrill of the chase that interested him? He'd made a lot of money, but what good is money when you're six feet under? The incident near Laredo last month was as close as he'd ever come to dying. The outlaw had been a hair quicker than he had. His hand absently went to the nagging pain in his right shoulder, a reminder that his luck would play out someday.

Missy began to cry, and he shot to his feet. Twigs snapped beneath his boots as he raced to the water's edge. He found Addy's youngest sobbing and holding her bleeding foot.

"What happened, sweetheart?" He picked her up and examined the wound in her toe. A tiny nick oozed a thin trickle of blood.

"Something bit me!"

"Nothing bit you; you stepped on a sharp rock."

"Thwow it away!"

"All right." Still holding her in his arms, he waded into the water and pretended to single out the culprit. "Wait a minute—yes, there it is. Come here, you rascal!" He picked up a rock and hurled it to the opposite bank, laughing when the heroic theatrics brought a giggle of relief from Missy.

"You're going to get in trouble, Uncle Cade," Holly said, giggling and pointing at his wet trousers.

"Yeah," Brody added. "Once Will and I waded through a puddle of water and ruined our shoes. Zoe made us polish 'em for an hour."

"A hunnert hours," Will corrected.

"Maybe she won't notice." Cade waded out of the stream, carried Missy up the embankment, and settled her in a grassy spot. Then he wrapped his handkerchief around the superficial wound.

"It huwts, Uncle Cwade."

Her voice was tiny and sweet. She hadn't spoken directly to him until today. "I know, honey. It'll stop in a minute."

Holly ran up the grassy knoll, breathless. "Should I go get Zoe?"

"No, Missy will be fine." He smiled at the eight-year-old as he held out his hand. "Come here; don't be afraid of me."

Holly hesitated, then walked slowly toward him. After a moment, she sat down beside him, staring. "You look kind of like Ma."

"Think so?"

"Uh-huh. Did you pull Ma's hair like Brody and Will do mine and Missy's?"

He chuckled. "I'm sure I did. Isn't that what brothers are for?"

Will shot out of the water with Brody chasing him. The boys ran up the hill, intentionally shaking water on the girls.

Missy yelled, "Quit it! You'll get my sowe toe wet! Uncle Cwade bandaged it fow me." Cornflower-blue eyes turned in his direction, and Cade heard the voice of an angel say, "Thank you, Uncle Cwade. You'we a good boy."

Will shook water on her again. "He ain't a boy. He's a growed man."

"Yeah," Brody said, eyeing Cade. "He shoots a pistol. I'm gonna shoot a pistol

66

when I learn how." He looked at Cade straight on. "Will you teach me?"

Cade knew the last thing Addy would want was his teaching her child how to use a pistol. "Have you ever shot a gun, son?"

"My pa let me shoot his shotgun one time when he took me squirrel-hunting." He rubbed his shoulder. "It hurt."

Cade turned him in the direction of the water. "You can learn to shoot when you're older. Right now, you're wasting swim time."

"Can I get in the watew again, Uncle Cwade?" Missy held her foot high in the air, waving it.

"Don't know why not." He carefully unwrapped the handkerchief and saw that the bleeding had stopped. "Just don't step on any more sharp rocks."

Holly took hold of her little sister's hand. "I'll watch her, Uncle Cade."

"Thank you, Holly. I'd appreciate it."

As they walked away, Missy turned around and grinned. For the first time, he noticed she was missing a front tooth.

"Are you glad I'm talkin' to you, Uncle Cwade?"

He winked. "Real glad."

The children splashed noisily in the water as he leaned back against a tree. Addy and John must have been proud of their kids. No wonder Zoe wanted them. Who wouldn't?

Settling his hat lower on his forehead, he thought of Zoe and felt touched by her love for his sister's kids. If he hadn't left, would they have married? Would they have had a houseful of kids of their own by now? He dimissed the foolish thoughts. He'd intended to come back and marry her, but she'd never believe it now. She'd made that evident.

Pushing his hat up, he realized it was getting late. The sun was setting, and the children had missed lunch. Zoe would wonder what had happened to them. Before he could call them in, the sound of snapping twigs brought his hand to his holster. He brought up the gun and centered his aim on the intruder.

Zoe froze at the edge of the clearing, her gaze riveted on the weapon. He heard her suck in a deep breath as her face turned tense with cold disapproval.

"Don't ever sneak up on me like that," he said, slipping the Colt back into his holster.

"It's getting late. I was worried." Her voice was chilly with condemnation.

"Sorry—time got away from me."

"Why doesn't that surprise me?" she muttered.

"I heard that, but I've had a peaceful afternoon and I'm feeling generous." He pointed to the ground beside him. "Might as well sit down." He grinned when she seated herself a safe distance from him.

"How are you getting along with them?"

"Good. They're talking to me now. Some, at least."

"That's nice."

"They don't talk much, do they?"

"Wait until they get to know you. They'll talk your leg off," she said. "Better call them in. It's getting late."

Cupping his hands to his mouth, he shouted, "The red-headed boss lady says you've had enough for one day!"

A bevy of groans and complaints was heard as the children sloshed out of the water and trudged up the embankment.

"Hi, Zoe!" Holly said.

"We swimmed all day!" Will grinned from ear to ear.

"Hello, children."

Brody's lips quivered as Zoe wrapped a large towel around him. "Ow! That hurts!" he cried.

Zoe lifted the towel and examined Brody's reddened shoulders. When Will, Holly, and Missy crowded around to see, Cade realized they all looked like cooked lobsters.

"Cade, how long have they been in the sun?"

"I don't know. All afternoon, I guess." He frowned. "A little sun's good for them."

"A *little* sun? They're blistered!"

He pressed a finger to Brody's sunburned skin, leaving a white indentation. "What do you do for this?"

She picked up the kids' strewn clothing and helped Will put on his shirt. "Never mind—I'll take care it. Come along, children. I'll give you a vinegar bath to take the heat out."

"A vinegar bath! Pee-eew!" they chorused.

Cade marveled at how motherly she seemed as she gathered the quivering children and herded them up the embankment. "Hey," he called. "I'm taking them to Glori-Lee's for supper."

"That won't be necessary. I have chicken in the warming oven."

He caught up with her in two long strides. "Sounds good. It's been a long time since I've had a home-cooked meal."

She slowed and let him pass. "Then, by all means, order roast chicken at Glori-Lee's tonight. She's an excellent cook."

He turned around. "Are you saying I'm not invited to eat with the children?"

"That's what I'm saying." She picked up speed and passed him.

He easily caught up with her again. "How long are you going to hold this grudge?"

She walked faster, head down. "How long are you going to be here?"

Grabbing her arm, he stopped her and made her face him. "In that case, it *is* necessary that the children eat with me tonight. How am I going to get acquainted if I don't spend time with them?"

"Why don't you just hold a *gun* to their heads and tell them to like you?"

"A gun? Is that what the cold shoulder's about?"

"I don't hold with killing. You know that; you knew that when you rode out of here seventeen years ago." She jerked away from him, rubbing her arm.

She was spoiling for a fight, but he wasn't going to fall for it. His business here didn't include her. "You're the one who sent for me."

"*Only* because of Addy."

He took her arm again, grasping it tightly.

"Only because of Addy?" Their gazes locked in a heated duel, and he shook his head. "You were never good at lying, Red."

The defiance in her eyes warned him to release her, but he wasn't about to let her go until he settled the matter.

She didn't back down. "Tomorrow, when they've recovered from being burnt alive, you can take them to wherever you're staying and spend time with them."

"That's gracious of you. I'm sleeping over the jail. I have a leaky roof, a cot, and a washstand. All five of us can't get *in* the damn room, let alone socialize."

"That isn't my problem, and don't call me Red, and don't use that vile language in front of the children."

"Dammit," he repeated, "can't we call a truce? I need your help, and you're shutting me out. You have a right to be mad at me, but that's between us. Right now, let's worry about Addy's kids—and I'll talk any way I want to." He glanced at the children, who had wandered ahead, chasing a frog that had appeared in their path.

Zoe stopped and brushed a lock of hair from her cheek. "Damnation. I wish it would rain again and cool things off."

"Watch your language around the children," he mocked. A spasm of irritation crossed her face. "And stop wishing for more rain. I'm not sleeping in a wet bed another night."

"Stay with Pop."

"Pop doesn't feel like company."

71

She turned accusing eyes in his direction. "What's wrong with him?"

"Six pieces of gooseberry pie."

Her cheeks bloated suddenly as if the thought made her sick. A smile started at the corner of her mouth, then quickly faded, and they stood for a moment in awkward silence.

Children's laughter filled the clearing, and Cade considered the situation. He used to have such fun with her; it should be a happy time now. Instead, it was war.

Sighing, she said, "I wish you had been here for the funerals. The children needed a man to lean on."

"I tried. Sorry I didn't make it." He'd ridden like hell to arrive in time—for twenty-four hours straight. If he'd ridden any harder, it would have killed his horse.

"When are you going to talk to the Brightons?" she asked.

"Tomorrow. I'm doing Pop a favor in Suffox County. I'll stop at the Brightons on my way back."

"I wish you wouldn't."

"We've already had this argument. If it would make you feel better, you're welcome to come with me. We can talk to Bonnie and Seth together."

She stared into the distance, her face void of emotion. "I'll fight you on this, Cade."

"Why doesn't *that* surprise me?" Cade watched Will grab the frog, admiring the boy's quickness. "Fight me all you want, Red. You're young—you need to think about

72

remarrying and starting a family of your own. A woman with four kids isn't going to attract a whole hell of a lot of men...with the exception of Jake Bledso and Perry Drake. If those two turn you down, you're out of luck."

He watched her swell with indignation. She needed an explanation as to why he wouldn't give the kids to her, he told himself. This was as good as any—a lot better than the truth.

Will ran back to them and thrust the frog in Cade's face. "Uncle Cade, Uncle Cade, look! I caught him!"

Taking a stumbling step back, Cade dodged the slimy offering. "Don't stick that thing in my face."

"Put the frog back in the water," Zoe ordered.

The disappointed looks on the kids' faces made him want to take the damn frog home with him, but instead he watched them take it to the water's edge and give it its freedom.

"How do you find the heart to ever say no to them?" he asked.

"You have a lot to learn about children."

Taking her by the shoulders, he forced her to look at him. "That's why I intend to spend time with them. The kids and I are eating together tonight, either at Glori-Lee's or your house. You decide."

Zoe pulled away and kicked the dirt. "They're exhausted, burnt to a crisp, and half-starved. What they need is a vinegar bath, supper, and bed."

Missy ran back and tugged at Zoe's dress. "Please—we nevew eat at Glowi-Lee's!"

73

"I want to eat at the café," Will joined in. "I'm not crisp or the other thing you said!"

"We're not 'accosted,'" Holly blurted. Cade wanted to laugh at Holly's mispronunciation but knew that if he so much as smiled, Zoe would slap him silly. "I want to eat with Uncle Cade at Glori-Lee's, too!"

Cade's gaze locked with Zoe's. *Get out of this one gracefully.* "You're outnumbered, so you might as well join us."

She tossed her head. "That would be a waste of money. I have a perfectly good chicken waiting for me."

He glanced at the kids and grinned. "Come on—you prefer a chicken's company to ours?" The kids burst into giggles. Zoe didn't.

"Before the meal's over, a chicken's company will look good, Cade Kolby. Have you ever eaten in public with four children?"

"No, but eating's eating, isn't it?" He winked at the kids. "They're big enough to feed themselves. What's the problem?"

"Fine," she said. "Pick them up in an hour, and may I remind you *again*: the name's Zoe, not Red."

Her sudden acquiescence made him wary, and he felt his smile fade. "Why won't you come with us?"

"I have chores, thank you. Come along, children."

Zoe stalked off as the youngsters hung back, trailing behind her and waving shyly to him. Cade lifted a hand and waved back. Damnation. How hard could feeding four children be?

Cade marched his sunburned brood, reeking of vinegar and smeared with baking-soda paste, into Glori-Lee's café a little past seven. The tall, raw-boned widow, who'd owned the restaurant for over forty years, glanced up and sniffed the air.

"Who tipped over the pickle barrel?"

Cade took off his hat and held it in front of him. "You're a sight for sore eyes, Glori-Lee. You're even better-looking than when I left town."

"You better believe it," she said with a hoarse chuckle.

"You got you a man yet?"

"Been savin' myself for you."

Cade laughed. "You surely can do better than me."

She kissed him on the cheek. "You're too old for me anyway. I got my eye on one of the Pointer boys. He's young enough I can raise him the way I want him."

"You're a fickle woman, Glori-Lee."

Grinning, she motioned him to a large table near the front window. A vase of roses was centered on a freshly ironed red and white checked tablecloth. The savory aroma of pot roast and baking bread coming from the kitchen made his mouth water.

A couple of the male diners smiled at him as the kids fought over the seating arrangments. It was the women who gave him the cold shoulder, holding their napkins to their mouths as if they were protecting themselves from the unsavory bounty hunter.

The children finally took their seats, and Cade sat down at the head of the table, admiring his newly acquired family. Despite their blistered skin and pungent odor, they were a handsome lot.

Daily specials were handwritten on the menu Cade studied, all of them making his stomach knot with hunger. "What do you like to eat?" he asked the children.

"Peach pie," they chorused.

"Pie and what else?" he prompted.

"Cream!"

He thought for a moment. "Don't you usually eat something before having pie?"

"Chocolate cake!" Brody answered.

Cade leaned back in his chair. "Okay, cake and pie it is." He was thinking more along the lines of the roast beef and potatoes, but they ought to know what they wanted to eat. After all, it was a special occasion.

"Peach pie, chocolate cake, and a pitcher of cream," he told Glori-Lee.

The woman frowned. "Have they had their supper?"

"Not yet. We're ordering it now." He'd sometimes eaten sweets for dinner, and it had never killed him.

"Pie and cake!" the kids chorused.

Glori-Lee took the order, then stuck the pencil behind her ear and ambled off toward the kitchen, grumbling, "Zoe ain't goin' to like this."

The smiles on the kids' faces were worth a little tongue-lashing from Zoe. Cade laid his hat on the table. "Well, now. Tell me about yourselves. Got any pets?"

Missy's eyes lit up. "We got a tomcat, Womeo, and Butch. He's ouw dog. And Bud."

"Bud? Who's Bud?"

"Bud lives in a jar," Will explained.

Missy giggled. "He's a bug. He's nice."

Cade lifted his brows. "A nice bug who lives in a jar. Anything else?"

"Nope," Brody answered. "Just Romeo, Butch, and Bud. I wanted a pony, but Zoe says she can't afford to feed anything else."

The statement "can't afford" disturbed him. The general store had been in the Bradshaw family for three generations and should have left Zoe well-off, but from the looks of the place, she wasn't. Her dresses were old and faded, and the furnishings were the same ones Jim's parents had had. She was still using the same old cookstove.

He temporarily put the thought aside. "What about school? What grades are you in?"

Holly volunteered, "Third. Brody's in fifth."

"Guess school will be starting up again before long."

"I might not go back to school," Brody announced.

Holly slapped him on the arm. "Oh, yes, you will. Zoe will make you."

Cade intervened. "You have to go to school, son. To learn things."

Brody scooted forward in his chair. "Ma said you never finished school, and you know stuff."

"You need to know more stuff than I do. Besides, I *had* to quit. My pa got sick, and I had to go to work for a farmer just to put food on our table."

Excited, Will sat up straighter. "You know plenty of stuff. Pa said you're the best there is at shootin' bad guys."

"Yeah," Brody said. "A boy at school said you shoot 'em dead. You hardly ever bring 'em in alive."

Cade frowned, disturbed by the boy's words. He did what was necessary to collect a bounty. He'd always given his prey fair warning, and he'd never shot a man in the back. How could he explain the difference to a child? Some saw his profession as legalized killing. He didn't. He considered it a service.

Holly stared at him with eyes so like Addy's, it was chilling. "Ma said killin's nothin' for a man to be proud of."

"Your ma's right, but there're times when it's necessary."

"Ma said she prayed for you every night, prayed you'd come home and we'd all be a family again."

"We *are* a family," Brody insisted.

"Yeah," Will said. "Can I hold your gun?"

Cade patted the boy's head. "No one holds my gun but me."

Glori-Lee returned with a whole pie, a large cake, and a big pitcher of thick cream.

"Help yourselves, young'uns. Lord a' mighty, I hope you don't get bellyaches."

The children were well-mannered and polite, and Cade felt an uncle's pride as the meal progressed smoothly. He had to admit that a meal of pie, cake, and cream was a change from his usual beans and hardtack.

"I need to ask you kids something. We have to decide where you're going to live."

Missy's face clouded. "We don't want a kitten. We want to live at Zoe's."

Will looked up. "I want a pony, but I want to live at Zoe's, too."

"That's what we need to talk about," Cade said. "If you couldn't live at Zoe's or the Brightons', where would you want to live?" He studied the children's sober looks.

"Not with Aunt Laticia," said all four at the same time.

"What's wrong with your Aunt Laticia?"

Brody put his fork down and stared. "She's scary-lookin'"

Will wrinkled his nose. "And she smells funny."

"We want to live with Zoe *and* you," Holly said. "You're our ma's brother. Ma always said Zoe was like her sister, so that makes her your sister, too, and Ma said brothers and sisters stick together."

Cade cleared his throat. "Even though I'd like that, it isn't possible."

"Why not?" Will asked. "Do you have to go shoot bad guys again?"

"I might, but not until we get you settled." He glanced at Brody and saw him reaching for a third piece of cake. Boys ate a lot more than he remembered.

Licking his fork, Brody said, "Pass the cream, please."

"If you have to go shoot bad guys," Missy said, blinking heavy eyes, "why can't we stay with Zoe?"

Cade could see that the sun, the swimming, and a long day were taking their toll on the little one. Red was right. The kids needed a bed as much as they needed supper.

Will yawned. "Did you shoot that bad guy that shooted Zoe's husband?"

Did I? Cade wondered. He'd shot so many over the years, he'd lost track. If the man had had a bounty on his head, it was likely he'd collected the reward. Most wanted men didn't give up without a fight. It was ironic to think he might have avenged Jim Bradshaw's death without knowing it.

Cade avoided the boy's question and changed the subject. "Finish your supper. You're getting sleepy—look at your little sister. She's already asleep—oh! She's fallen into her pie!" Springing to his feet, he grabbed Missy and lifted her head from the plate, pulling peaches out of her hair.

"Uh-oh." Brody pushed back from the table, doubled over. "My belly hurts."

"Mine, too." Will groaned. "And my skin's on fire!"

Glori-Lee rushed over to help as the children's moans grew louder. Cade was aware of the panic-stricken expressions on the other diners' faces as the complaints escalated.

"These young'uns are in pitiful shape," Glori-Lee scolded. "They need a hefty dose of castor oil, and then their beds." Still grumbling, she wiped Missy's peach-covered face with a dishcloth. "Law, feeding these babies cake and pie and cream—gonna kill 'em."

Cade frowned, hurrying around the table. "Are you all right?" he asked Holly as she got up slowly. Her face was pasty-white, and her balance unsteady.

She shook her head. "I feel kinda sick."

He hoped there were enough bushes along the way home to accommodate his poor judgment. Pie, cake, and cream. He should have known better.

"I need to get them home," he told Glori-Lee.

Shaking her head, she said, "I'm glad I'm not the one to take them back in this condition."

He lifted Missy into his arms and took hold of Holly's hand, trying to herd Brody and Will ahead of him as he left the café. Outside a clap of thunder rattled the sidewalk seconds before the heavens opened.

Glancing up, he frowned. *Hell.* A straight wind whipped the treetops and sent tumbleweeds bouncing haphazardly across Main Street.

Walt Mews shouted hello to him as he locked the barbershop, then made a dash for the livery stable, holding the *Police Gazette* over his head.

Cade glanced toward the Land Office as Woodall Thompson consulted his watch and closed the upstairs window.

Cade cursed the angry pewter sky. Jagged forks of lightning lit up Ben Pointer's metal weather vane as Brody broke for the bushes, Will close on his heels.

Missy whimpered and snuggled her face into his neck. Using his hat as a shield, Cade covered her head, then pulled Holly close and wrapped one side of his vest around her head and shoulders.

"I don't feel good, Uncle Cade," Holly said.

"I know, honey. I'll take you home as soon as the boys"—he glanced at the bushes—"finish up."

Missy snuggled closer, her breath sweet against his face. "I don't want the lightning to get me."

"I'll protect you. Nothing's going to happen to you while Uncle Cade is here."

He winced as the rain came down harder. Another night in a wet bed. Looking up, he let out his breath noisily. Somebody up there sure had it in for him.

Within seconds, he was drenched to the bone, and so were the children. They looked at him, their lips quivering and turning blue. Their noses were sunburned; they were worn out, and their bellies ached. It didn't take a crystal ball to tell him he wasn't cut out for fatherhood.

And he still had to face Red.

Chapter 6

"**Y**ou ordered rain? You got rain." It was Cade's voice.

Zoe held the lamp higher and looked at the sopping assemblage standing at her back door. Cade was holding his hat over Missy's face, and Holly's head was tucked under his vest. Brody and Will were absolutely green around the gills, and there wasn't a dry thread to be seen. Water ran off Cade's hair onto Will's head. Blinking, the boy swiped at the stream.

Cade shifted Missy to his other hip. "Are you going to make us stand out here all night? We're not getting any drier."

Sliding a braided rag rug to the door with her foot, Zoe unlatched the screen. "Wipe your feet." Cade brushed by her and carried Missy into the kitchen. The other kids followed, quickly wiping their shoes on the rug.

"It's stowming, Zoe. I was scawed, but Uncle Cwade didn't let anything happen to me," Missy informed her.

Zoe set down the lamp and took the little girl from Cade. She started to peel off her wet clothes. "Holly, help Will. Brody, get out of your wet things and put them in the sink."

Holly sank to the nearest chair and laid her head on the table. "I don't feel so good."

"Me either," Brody seconded.

Will didn't have to say anything; Zoe could see he was sick just by looking at him. "What did you feed these children?" she asked Cade.

"Supper."

Exasperated, Zoe plucked a slice of peach from Missy's wet hair. "What's this?"

"Supper."

Will groaned. "We ate peach pie and chocolate cake."

"And cream," Brody added. "A great big pitcher of it."

"Oh, Cade!" A vein throbbed in her temple as she watched him lift Missy to the counter and strip off her wet shoes and socks. What would happen if he had full responsibility for them?

Missy reached up to Cade, holding out her arms. He leaned over, and she kissed him on the cheek. Cade looked startled but pleased as he bent and kissed her back. Judging from his expression, it was the first time he'd been embraced by a child.

"We had a good time, didn't we, Uncle Cwade?"

"A very good time."

"You can call me Sunflowew. That's what Pa called me."

He hesitated, then said, "All right. Sunflower it is."

Zoe brushed by him on her way back to the sink. It irked her that even though he was so irresponsible, the children took to him like flies to molasses.

He followed her to the sink. "I made a mistake feeding them all those sweets. I'm sorry. I wasn't thinking—but it was a special occasion."

Rinsing peach juice out of Missy's dress, Zoe grumbled, "Anyone with a lick of sense knows you don't feed kids peach pie, chocolate cake, and cream."

"It's not going to kill the kids to eat what they want once in a while."

"Oh, no? Look at them. They look half dead to me."

He glanced at the children. "Have you forgotten the time Addy and I got into Ma's syllabub?"

"No, and have you forgotten you *thought* you were going die?"

"That's my point. We didn't. And I learned my lesson."

She turned to face him. "What? Not to drink syllabub?"

"No, not to let you catch me."

She wrung out Missy's dress and hung it near the cookstove to dry. "Haven't you got somewhere to go?"

"As a matter of fact, I don't. I haven't been to the jail since this morning, but I can tell you that damn bunk is floating in water."

"Too bad."

"Yes, it is. I'm not sleeping there."

"Then go over to Pop's—serves him right for not fixing that leaky roof months ago."

She shooed the children to the bedroom for their nightclothes and bent over to pick up the wet towels, bumping into a broad wall of warm chest.

Cade smiled as she slid up his length, her senses simmering.

"Will you get out of my way?"

"Can't. Room's too small. No place to go."
He tweaked her nose and she shrugged away.

"I don't want to stay with Pop. He might be contagious."

"Too much gooseberry pie is not contagious."

Brody came out of the bedroom buttoning his nightshirt. "He can sleep with me and Will."

Will jumped up and down. "Yeah! That would be fun!"

"I'll fix you breakfast, Uncle Cade," Holly offered. "I can cook eggs almost as good as Ma."

Missy ran into the kitchen and latched onto her uncle's leg. "I want you to sleep with me and Zoe so we won't be scawed of the stowm."

Patting the child on her head, Cade grinned at Zoe. "Sounds like a good idea to me."

His low, purposely seductive tone made her stiffen. Memories of the night before he had left all those years ago flooded her thoughts. He'd held her in his arms and made love to her until the sun came up. A dull, empty ache gnawed at her soul. She'd been a different person then. Hopefully, she had better sense now; she prayed that her eyes revealed only disapproval. Seeing his lip twitch, she knew he'd gotten the message.

"On second thought, maybe I just better sleep with the boys. Your bed is a little short for me." He eyed Zoe. "And a little cold."

"Uh-uh," Missy said. "It's wawm...weal wawm."

Zoe lifted a brow. Sleep with the boys? That quick, and he'd moved in. Taking her for granted, never thinking she might have enough on her hands as it was. She didn't like it, but there was no point protesting; she was out-numbered.

"No one would get any sleep if you slept with the boys."

Cade grinned. "Then I guess I'll have to sleep with you and Missy after all."

Zoe threw a dirty towel on the table. "You can sleep on the settee in the parlor. Be careful. I keep my mother's figurines in there."

Brody smiled. "We ain't allowed to play in there. Ever."

"On account we might break something," Will added.

"The settee? A little old sofa?" Cade asked.

"You're only going to be here one night." She strode past him, speaking in a low tone. "Don't get too comfortable."

While the children ran to the outhouse and were dosed with castor oil to ease their bellyaches, Zoe rounded up an extra pillow and blankets.

Settling Cade on the settee, she warned again, "Be careful of my figurines." He looked at the assortment of delicate angels, swans, and butterflies displayed on a table to one side of the settee.

"I heard you once. I'm not deaf."

"Just so you understand." She closed the door. A second later she heard the tinkling of glass. Clamping her eyes shut for an instant, she held her breath before yanking the door open.

Cade was on his knees at the table with a

glass swan in his hand. His eyes widened innocently.

"I *caught* it."

Slamming the door shut, she went to bed.

Shutters banged in the wind, battering the old store with the force of a gale. Menacing streaks of lightning lit the room, cracking like an evil, giant whip. Zoe got up several times to put vinegar on the fretful children's sunburned shoulders. She tried to stay calm, but the worsening storm was upsetting.

Sporadic booms of thunder shook the tiny rooms, and she heard can goods falling off the store's shelves. It had been years since a storm like this had raged through Winterborn. She nearly jumped out of her skin when a limb split off the huge oak in the backyard and slammed against the porch. Butch howled and scratched incessantly on the screen, wanting to come in. Romeo's meows escalated to frantic roars. She couldn't remember spending a more miserable night.

Around four o'clock, nerves frazzled, she finally fell exhausted into bed.

After what seemed only a moment, a clap of thunder roused her. She was barely aware of Missy's sliding out of bed and whispering something to Holly. The two girls left the room, and Zoe dropped into a deep sleep.

Toward dawn she rolled over, groping for Missy, and found her side of the bed empty. She shot up and noticed Holly was missing, too.

Donning her robe, she looked out the window toward the outhouse. Maybe they were sick. She groaned when she saw that the outhouse door had blown off and half of the back fence was down.

Alarmed, she stepped into the kitchen, and her heart leapt to her throat when she saw that the boys weren't on their pallets, either. "Brody! Will! Holly! Missy!"

She ran through the kitchen and opened the door to the parlor, coming to an abrupt halt when she saw Cade, the kids, Butch, and Romeo clustered in a heap around the settee, all sound asleep.

Her hand went to her mouth when she saw Bud, the children's pet tarantula, out of his jar, standing right in the middle of Cade's chest.

Missy must have opened the jar again.

Zoe stood for a moment, uncertain what to do. She could let Cade wake naturally and…No, that was mean. She'd wake him quietly without disturbing Bud.

Tiptoeing to the settee, she whispered, "Cade."

He opened one eye and smiled at her. He opened the other eye and came face-to-face with Bud. Jerking upright, he flailed his hands at the tarantula, knocking it into the center of the room.

Zoe was stunned to see how quickly a grown man could catapult to his feet. Before she could explain, he chased the creature around the room, stomping at it with his stocking feet.

Butch sprang to life, barking and leaping

over the end table. His tail caught two of the figurines and sent them to the floor with a crash. Romeo yowled and dug his claws into the settee, trying to get away.

The girls scrambled toward Cade, hanging onto the seat of his long johns Missy squealed, "Quit dancing, Uncle Cwade! You're scawing Bud!"

Cade shouted, "Bud who?"

"Bud, the bug," Zoe yelled.

"The bug?" Cade ceased "dancing" and dropped into a chair. Running a shaky hand through his hair, he let out a breath. "That damn thing is a *pet*?"

Sickened, Zoe slumped to her knees, looking in despair at her broken figurines. She should have known enough to put them away.

Brody and Will raised sleepy heads. "Is it still storming?" Will asked.

Missy ran to Bud and scooped him into the jar. Putting the lid on, she looked at Zoe. "Are you scawed of the stowm too, Wed?"

Zoe struggled to keep a straight face. The very idea of Missy calling her "Red"! She finally burst out laughing, slapping her hands on her knees. "No, Sunflower. The storm's over. I just wondered where you were."

Once the excitement had died down, Zoe carefully picked up the broken pieces of swan and butterfly.

"I'm sorry about your figurines," Cade said, stooping to help.

"It's my own fault. I should have put them away."

"I'll buy you new ones."

"Don't be silly. They're irreplacable."

Zoe kept her eyes averted. The sight of him in his long johns distracted her more than she cared to admit. Who would think a man in his underwear could evoke such provocative feelings—even if he did look pretty silly in stocking feet? "The storm was pretty bad. The backyard has a lot of damage. I haven't looked out front yet."

The children scampered out of the room and ran to the back door. Will hollered, "The outhouse is tore up."

"There's a big limb in the yard!" Holly said.

Zoe and Cade joined the children and surveyed the damage to the back, then walked to the front of the store, where Cade opened the door.

"What's it look like?" Zoe asked, trying to see around him.

"Looks like I'll be sleeping on the settee a couple more days."

"Why?"

Her first glimpse of Main Street answered her question for him. The jail's roof had been completely blown off and was now perched on top of Woodall Thompson's sycamore tree. Surrounding businesses had had shutters blown off; the street was strewn with signs and boards. Ben Pointer and Sons was stuck in Glori-Lee's window box. Mayor Willis was already out surveying the damage.

Cade called to him. "Anybody hurt, Lawrence?"

Zoe was mortified when she saw Lawrence

glance up and do a double take at Cade standing at the door in his long johns and her in her robe.

Lawrence smiled. "Not that I know of—is that you, Cade?"

"Hell of a storm. Anything I can do to help?"

Lawrence nodded. "No hurry—take your time. Don't want to interrupt anything."

Appalled, Zoe yanked Cade back inside and slammed the door. "Why didn't you explain?" she demanded.

"What? That I slept on the settee with the kids, a dog, a cat, and a tarantula?"

"You...!" Wheeling, she marched to the kitchen, knowing the incident would be reported all over town before breakfast.

By eight o'clock, the sounds of hammers and saws rang up and down the street. The storm had done extensive damage; according to the mayor, it would take days to get the town back to normal.

Missy shot in the back door, dancing on her tiptoes. "Uncle Cwade, I gotta *go*!"

Cade looked up from his breakfast plate. "Go where?"

Zoe dished two eggs out of the skillet and put them on Brody's plate. "She needs to use the outhouse."

"It don't have no doow on it. Evewybody will see me!"

Cade scraped his chair back from the table and got up.

Zoe frowned. "Your breakfast will get cold. Can you wait a moment, Missy?"

She danced up and down. "Noooooooo!"

"Give me ten minutes, Sunflower, and I'll have you back in business."

Missy skipped out behind him, and the screen door banged shut. Zoe carried Cade's plate to the warming oven. Raising the window for some air, she paused with her hand in mid-motion when she noticed Cade stripping off his shirt. Powerless to look away, she stood frozen to the spot, drinking in the sight of his bare, muscular back glinting in the morning sun. Sinful images danced in her mind. His once-youthful frame had matured. Sinewy cords rippled as he lifted the heavy outhouse door into place. Looking at him this way aroused her memories of the night that had changed her life forever.

She smiled as Missy held her hands between her legs and jumped on one foot. Cade hoisted Will up on his shoulders to get the fallen limbs off the roof of the outhouse, while Brody and Holly hammered nails into a cross-board on the door. There was no denying it: Cade loved kids. Zoe nearly laughed out loud when he put Will down and chased him around the outhouse. Cade was a kid himself!

Family. This was her family now. Her smile faded when she realized her own flesh and blood could have been helping repair the outhouse. How old would their child have been today? Sixteen? Approaching adulthood—the same age Cade had been when he left. She quickly looked away, swallowing the lump suddenly crowding her throat.

Missy's impatience grew. "Huwwy, Uncle Cwade! Huwwy!"

Cade grabbed a hammer and began pounding. "I'm hurrying, Sunflower—can't you use the bushes?"

Zoe grinned when she heard Missy's indignant gasp—"No!"

In another few minutes, the door to the outhouse had been repaired enough for Missy to seek relief, and within an hour nearly all the broken limbs had been cleared from the yard. Brody, Will, and Holly worked like beavers alongside Cade, while Missy issued orders with the gusto of a calvary officer.

Around noon, Cade stuck his head in the kitchen doorway and called to Zoe, "I'll be at the jail."

She glanced up from the ironing board, her gaze meeting his and catching until she smelled a scorched odor coming from Mrs. Penscott's petticoat. She quickly folded it and put it back in the dirty clothes basket. "Are the children going with you?"

"No, they're going to help Lawrence Willis clear Main Street."

"Tell them not to get in the way."

"You tell them. I don't want Missy to court-martial me."

Crossing the street diagonally, Cade spotted Pop standing in front of the jail assessing the damage.

"Boy, wind took her off slick as a whistle." Pop stared, hands on hips, at bare rafters where once the spare room had been.

"It'll take you awhile to put it back on," Cade agreed.

"Ain't got the money to build it back proper-like."

"The town doesn't have the money for a new roof?"

"Nope. Never thought about having it blown clean off," Pop confessed. "We got enough money to patch it, but not enough to replace the whole durn thing. Suppose we'll just do enough to keep the jail dry and not worry about that room overhead. Hardly ever used it anyway."

"I was sleeping there," Cade reminded him.

Pop's eyes widened. "You weren't in there during the storm, were you?"

"No. By then, the bunk was so wet that I stayed the night with the kids."

Pop chuckled. "The kids?"

"Zoe wasn't crazy about the idea, but she let me sleep on the settee."

"Women. They can be cruel, can't they?"

Cade stuck Pop's hammer and nails in his back pockets, then grabbed a rung of the ladder that was leaning against the building. "Round up a couple of extra hands to help me put on a makeshift roof before it rains again," he said to the sheriff.

"You got time to do this?"

"Hague Pearson will have to wait another day. We need to get this roof on."

"I guess another day's delay won't matter. You be sure and remind Mooney, that Hague's death's on his record, not mine. Don't let him pull one over on you."

"Not many men pull one over on me, Pop."

"Well, I'd go myself, but I got more troubles. I broke out in hives. Can't quit itchin'."

Cade nodded, noting the red lumps on Pop's face. "What did you eat now?"

"Hard tellin'," Pop said, scratching his hip.

"Maybe the Pointer boys will help with the roof. If you've got a minute, can you get them for me?"

As Pop hurried off, Cade climbed the ladder. His "brief" stop in Winterborn was getting longer every day.

Toward dark, Cade's head was throbbing from the ring of hammers driving nails through wood. Signs had been reattached to storefronts and broken windowpanes replaced. It was gratifying to see small children lugging wooden carts through town, picking up scattered branches and other debris. Brody and Will piled their cart high, then hauled it to the end of town and dumped it.

The jail had a roof again, though it was nothing to brag about. The salvaged shingles were old and would probably still leak like a sieve. The overhead sleeping space had been torn down and used to patch a hole in the town hall.

Cade returned to the general store that night sunburned and hungry, and his hands were blistered. The aroma of Zoe's fried chicken made his stomach growl. When he opened the screen door, a fly buzzed inside past him.

Zoe jammed her fists to her hips. "Where'd that fly come from? I told you kids to watch that back door!"

"Don't blame the kids. I let it in."

"Well, shut the door before we have a houseful. I suppose you're hungry."

"I'm worn out, and I don't feel much like going over to Glori-Lee's." Cade watched her eyes soften and knew it was an invitation to eat with them.

"Wash up. Supper'll be ready in a few minutes."

Missy ran around the table and pulled out his chair. "Aftew you wash youw hands, Uncle Cwade, you sit by me."

He stepped toward the sink just as Zoe moved away from the stove. They bumped bottoms, and she spun to face him.

"Sorry," he muttered as she stared at him.

He sat down at the table and took off his hat. Holly had buttered his corn and poured him a huge glass of milk. "Thank you, sweetheart." His gaze focused on Zoe's backside as she slid a pan of biscuits out of the oven and carried it to the table. She still had that little wiggle when she moved. He remembered it well.

Zoe took a seat at the head of the table, and they joined hands, bowing their heads. "Holly, I believe it's your turn."

After grace, Zoe passed the biscuits while

Brody doled himself a hefty portion of potatoes. "When are you going to teach me to shoot a pistol, Uncle Cade?"

Will grinned. "Me, too."

Spooning string beans onto his plate, Cade could feel Zoe's eyes on him. He knew how she felt about guns, so the subject was delicate. "You both need to be older before you shoot a pistol, but I'll show you how to handle a shotgun so it won't kick so hard."

Zoe ladled gravy over her potatoes. "At their age, why do they have to know how to shoot *any* gun?"

"They're boys, Red. Boys turn into men who hunt food for the table—squirrels, rabbits, deer." Cade winked at the boys.

Zoe passed the butter. "I saw that."

Grinning, he reached for a biscuit. "Remind me to have a discussion with you about men being men."

Without looking at him, she said, "I know about men being men." She lowered her head and stared at her plate.

He knew that look on her face; she was talking about him. "What is it with you and guns, Red?"

Brody strained his neck in Cade's direction. "She's been like that ever since Jim got shot in that bank holdup."

Guilt swept over Cade. He felt like an idiot for being so insensitive. "I'm sorry. I'd forgotten about that. Eat your supper, boys. We'll talk about this later."

But he doubted he could ever convince Zoe that he didn't kill just for the sake of killing.

Seth Brighton was mending a harness when Cade drove into his barnyard early Wednesday afternoon.

He swung down from the hired wagon, and the two men shook hands.

"Well, I declare. Cade Kolby." Seth grinned from ear to ear. "We heard you were back." Seth's eyes moved to the wagon bed, where a pine box was securely strapped. "What you got there? A man with a price on his head?"

Cade fell into step with the younger man as they walked toward the house. A couple of towheaded kids played in a dirt pile near the back.

"It's Hague Pearson. He was shot and killed in Suffox County. I'm picking up the body for Pop."

Seth shook his head. "That's too bad. Hague never caused no trouble around here. Stayed to himself."

"That's what I hear. By the way, one of your hogs was out on the road, and one of your sons helped me chase it back in."

"That'd have to be Eddie Lee. He's a big help. Storm blew the fence down, and the hogs got loose," Seth said as they climbed the steps to the porch. "Sure was sorry to hear about John and your sister. They were good people."

"Yes, they were."

"Say, I'll bet you're parched. How 'bout a glass of buttermilk? Got some cooling in the spring." He raised his hands and called to one of the kids, "Jimmy! You go on down and fetch the buttermilk!" He turned back to Cade. "For a boy jist gettin' over the measles, he can run like the wind."

"I can't stay, Seth. The business in Suffox County took longer than I thought, and I still have another place to stop. I'd like to get back before dark, but I wanted to talk to you."

"Then maybe we'll just sit in the shade a spell." Seth ushered him to a chair on one side of the porch. "Sue Ann," he called, "you run in and check on your mama."

Seth settled in the seat next to Cade's. "Guess I know what you're here about."

"Pop said you and your wife were interested in adopting Addy's and John's children."

"We sure are. That's a fine bunch of kids. John and I were friends for a long time."

Jimmy, returning with a jug, ran up on the porch and stood in front of Cade. "Are you Will's and Brody's uncle who shoots bad guys?"

Seth took the jug and set a hand on the boy's shoulder. "You go on back and play, son. Your pa's talking business."

When the boy was out of earshot, Cade said, "I want to get the children settled as soon as possible." As he talked, Cade watched Seth's children playing. They appeared happy and well cared for. Pop was right; the Brightons would provide a good home for the children. He had to make the kids see that. In time they would love it here. Seth and Bonnie could give them what he couldn't: stability.

Seth shifted in his chair. "Be a few weeks before we're able to take them. Bonnie needs to get back on her feet."

Cade frowned. "Is your wife ill?"

"Come down with a fever day before yesterday."

Cade felt uneasy when the young man's face sobered.

"Bonnie's doing poorly today." Seth glanced away. "We're hoping it'll pass, but..."

"Has the doctor looked at her?"

"Sent for him first thing—said he couldn't say if it was serious. We just have to wait." Swallowing hard, he blinked. "I'm taking the kids to my folks this evening. They're going to keep them, just in case..."

"I'm sorry," Cade said.

Seth rubbed his eyes with thumb and forefinger. "Bonnie will feel bad about this, knowing she could have had them right away. She has her heart set on taking Addy's children—and we still mean to take them. It's just gonna have to be put off for a few days...until we see how Bonnie comes along."

"Of course." Cade got up to leave. "Is there anything I can do?"

"No—appreciate your prayers." Seth reached out to shake his hand. "We'll send word the minute Bonnie's up and about again. It shouldn't be too long..." Seth pointed to the south end of the house. "I'm building on. We'll have plenty of room for the young'uns."

Cade nodded. "Let me know if I can help."

"Sure will. Thanks for stopping by."

Chapter 7

It was late afternoon when Cade approached the outskirts of Winterborn. Pausing, he stared at the cemetery entrance. He'd put off visiting his family's graves for as long as he could. He'd avoided cemeteries most of his life since he'd put many a man there himself.

He climbed down from the wagon and leaned down to pick some blossoms from a clump of wild daisies. In the midst of prairie grass and scattered wildflowers, a lone cottonwood shaded the family plots. Addy would have liked knowing she and John were buried near it.

His gaze traveled to the nearby headstones, reading the familiar names of those he had known from childhood, swallowing against the tightness in his throat. When he came to the inscription "Max and Senda Kolby—Together in life, Eternal in death," his vision blurred. Mama's and Pa's graves.

Kneeling, he observed a moment of silence before moving on to Addy's and John's fresh graves, where he laid the handful of daisies among the wilted bouquets left by other mourners. Rising, he removed his hat and tried to remember a prayer. Any prayer. It was hard; he hadn't prayed in a long time.

Shame washed over him. When he was a boy, there hadn't been a Sunday when he wasn't seated next to his mother at the Good Shepherd Baptist Church. Senda Kolby had raised her children with an iron hand and a forgiving heart. She had lived and died by the Ten Commandments, and expected others to do the same. Had she been disappointed in him? Was it her prayers that had kept him alive all these years?

The peacefulness was broken by the call of a meadowlark overhead. He glanced up just as the bird flew away, and he envied its freedom.

A childhood memory of Addy flooded his mind: the vivid picture of his sister as a toddler falling out of a toy wagon, tears running down her dirt-streaked face. He'd led her to the front porch and set her in the swing, wiping her tears with his shirttail.

An emotional half-chuckle escaped him. He had given her his prized slingshot, hoping it would make her feel better.

"Sorry—I'm all out of slingshots," he whispered.

In his estimation, no one had been good enough for his big sister. To Addy's dismay, he had run off more promising suitors than you could shake a stick at.

His gaze shifted to the grave beside Addy's. He wished he'd known John Wiseman. In Addy's letters, she'd praised the man she'd married. Through her words, he had felt her happiness—a happiness that was short-lived.

The crunch of dry buffalo grass caught his attention, and his hand slid to his gun. Then he heard Zoe's voice call out, "It's me, Cade."

Turning, he saw her approaching the graves, carrying a small basket of flowers. She was flushed from the walk, and a few straggling tendrils of hair stuck to her face, which glistened with tiny beads of sweat. He couldn't recall if she'd ever painted herself like some women did. She had a natural beauty. She didn't need kohl or rouge to turn a man's head.

"This is the last place I thought I'd see you today." Setting her basket on the ground, she wiped her forehead with a handkerchief. "The children are looking for you."

"What do they want?"

"Nothing in particular—they're with Pop now. Why are your cheeks wet?"

He turned away. "It's hot here."

She picked up a handful of flowers. "I don't know why men are so embarrassed to cry. It's a natural thing to do under the circumstances.

"I was sweating."

"You were crying," she accused.

His gaze met and held hers. "Do you always have to have the last word?"

"Only when I'm right."

Stepping around him, she laid flowers on Addy's and John's graves, then proceeded to Jim's. Cade felt a pang of envy when he saw her somber expression. Had she loved her husband deeply? He hoped Jim had made her happy. It seemed that all he, Cade, had brought her was misery.

Standing before Jim's headstone, she bowed her head. He wanted to comfort her, but it wasn't his place. He didn't want to add to her pain.

He watched her lay flowers on Jim's grave and her parents' graves, then move to his parents' resting place. She pulled long strands of grass away from their headstone and placed flowers against the simple granite.

"You come here often?" he asked, stepping to her side.

"As often as I can."

"Do you always put flowers on my folks' graves?"

"I guess it's habit. Addy and I used to come here together."

"I appreciate it."

"It's no bother." Straightening, she dusted her hands, glancing at the sun. "It's a scorcher today."

"Hot as hell."

She smiled. "I know—you've been 'sweating.'" He turned to walk away, and she took hold of his arm. "Cade, we need to talk."

"Here?"

She shook her head, and he wondered if she guessed his reluctance to linger in a cemetery.

"We can talk over there," she said, pointing to a tree outside the gate.

Their shoes kicked up puffs of dust, and grasshoppers jumped beside them as they walked the rutted path. The smell of dry hay was thick in the stifling hot air.

Zoe's gaze went to Cade's horse and the hired wagon behind. "I see you picked up Hague."

"Yes, it's been quite a day."

Moving toward the tree, she motioned for him to follow. "Let's rest in the shade."

Sitting on the grass, she leaned back against the tree trunk, fanning herself with her handkerchief.

He took a seat beside her, removed his hat, and hooked it over his knee. "What's on your mind?"

"The children have been so happy since you got here."

"I'm glad."

"Me, too, but my point is, they're getting attached to you."

"Well, it works both ways. I'm getting attached to them."

"They don't want you to leave, you know."

He took a deep breath and released it slowly, choosing his words carefully. "I don't want to hurt the kids." When he looked into her eyes, he saw her misgivings. She didn't trust him. The thought hurt, but he conceded that he *had* neglected his family; it was his own fault. "I'll stay as long as I can, but I do have to move on."

"Why?"

The question was fair enough, and she deserved an answer. How could he tell her about Hart McGill and not upset her? He couldn't.

"Why do you have to go?" she persisted. "If you're so adamant about me not having the kids, why don't you stay here and raise them yourself? Is Winterborn such a bad place?"

"Do you know what would happen to this town if word spread that I was here?"

She sighed. "Trouble."

"'Trouble' is putting it mildly." There were men waiting to jump at the chance to gun him down in public. He wasn't going to subject Winterborn to danger, let alone Zoe and the kids. Coming back had made him realize how much he missed the town: Pop, the old-timers at the barbershop, the smell of cookies baking at Edna Mews's house, young boys playing marbles in the street. He had been one of those boys once. Now his life was an endless succession of dirty cow towns, empty bedrolls, cold beans, and warmed-over coffee. Not much to show for thirty-three years.

He focused on the meadow opposite the road and watched sunflowers bob their heads in the breeze. He couldn't travel far enough to escape the enemies he'd made, but he wasn't going to endanger his loved ones because of them.

The grizzly image of Hart McGill crossed his mind. He couldn't rest until the lowlife was six feet under.

"If you don't plan to keep the kids, then don't stay long, Cade." Zoe wiped her palms on her skirt. "The longer you stay, the harder it will be for them to give you up."

"They won't be giving me up. I'll be back."

She stood and brushed off the back of her skirt, jaw clenched, frustration written on her face. "Where have I heard that before?"

Trying to lighten the mood, he playfully tugged at the hem of her skirt. "Don't get yourself in a snit. I made a promise to an old friend's widow that I'd bring in the man who killed her husband." He winced when he saw the stubborn tilt of her chin that always meant trouble.

"Well, at least you've started keeping promises."

"You know what? I'm getting a little tired of your sass." He grinned when impatience flared in her eyes.

"Is that right? Well, let me tell you what I'm tired of—"

He reached up, took her hand, and pulled her down beside him, mocking her wide-eyed countenance.

"Cade Kolby, stop manhandling me."

Leaning close, he whispered against her ear, "You big enough to stop me?"

She stiffened and tried to pull away from him, but his arm slid around her waist and held her immobile.

"Don't think you're going to kiss me," she declared.

"How else am I going to shut you up?" He gently flipped her on her back, resting his bulk on top of her. He smiled at the surprise in her eyes, then lowered his mouth to take hers. He had forgotten how sweet she tasted, how intoxicating she smelled—how good she felt. A soft moan escaped her throat when his tongue sought entry. He felt her yielding, and the old fire surfaced—the white-hot heat that only she aroused in him.

Too many years had passed since they had been together like this. Her body felt familiar but more mature. Youthful breasts were now womanly, rounded and full, pressing against his chest. He wanted to unfasten her buttons and taste her tender flesh. Throwing caution to the wind, he peeled back the fabric of her dress, his hand seeking the rose-scented fullness spilling from her chemise.

Immediately he knew he had gone too far. Her delicate fingers clamped around his ear like a bear trap.

She pushed against his chest. Her words escaped through clenched teeth. "I *said*, don't think you're going to kiss me."

Rolling off her, he sat up.

"Now," she said, rebuttoning her bodice, "answer my question."

She might be calmly fastening her dress, but her shaking hand and the blush on her cheek told him he still had a strong effect on her. "I forgot the question."

"When exactly are you leaving?" she repeated.

Getting to his feet, he rubbed feeling back into his ear. "As soon as I see the children settled."

She stood and faced him. "Those children should be mine, Cade."

"Do you remember how lonely you were as a girl, with no mother? Your pa was gone most the time. Is that the kind of life you want for the children?"

"Of course not, but I wouldn't be gone. I would be here every day to see to their needs."

"I remember how happy Addy and I were, growing up with both a mother and father. I want that for Addy's kids, and I think that's what she would want."

Zoe's eyes misted as she fumbled for her handkerchief. He reached for her hand and gently rubbed the back of it with his thumb. "This isn't easy. I'm not trying to hurt you. I'm trying to do what I think is best for all concerned."

Seth and Bonnie were fine people and would do right by the children, he told himself. As soon as Bonnie was well, the kids would go there to live. No use telling Zoe about Bonnie right now, though. He'd wait until she was in a better mood.

Zoe reached for her basket. "You're the most impossible man on earth!"

As Cade watched her walk briskly down the road, her backside flouncing with every determined step, he shook his head. Such sass. His grin widened. That's what he liked about her.

"I don't think so," he yelled, slipping his hat back on. "I've met worse." Hell, he'd *been* worse. She just didn't know it.

Whirling, she flung her basket at him. Without missing a step, she marched on.

He thumbed his hat to the back of his head and took a deep breath. Sparring with Red made him feel like a kid again.

He sobered. It wasn't the kid in him that had reacted to that kiss, though. There had been other women over the years, but none had aroused feelings in him like she did. One harmless kiss had stirred something primitive in him, a drive and desire he couldn't satisfy. The sooner he moved on, the better for all concerned.

Cade delivered Hague's body to Pop, convinced him the death would not be counted against Winterborn's record, and took back the hired wagon before returning to Zoe's. By now it was dark. He'd missed supper at Glori-Lee's by an hour, and he assumed he'd go to bed hungry.

Bonnie Brighton's sudden illness shadowed his thoughts. Bonnie could be bedridden for weeks. Even worse, she might not recover at all. If the fever proved to be the same as John's and Addy's...He'd seen the unspoken fear in Seth's eyes. Only time would tell, but time was the one commodity he didn't have. He had days, at most. Hart McGill wasn't a fool; it wouldn't take him long to discover that Cade Kolby wasn't anywhere near St. Louis.

Butch barked as Cade rounded the back of the store. Cade called the dog's name, and the mutt bounded over, eager for Cade's rough caresses.

The door opened and Missy peeked out, breaking into a smile. "I'm glad you'we home, Uncle Cwade. We kept suppew wawm for you."

Supper warm for him? God, it had been years since anyone had kept supper warm for him.

He smiled at the angel with the cornflower-blue eyes. "You did?"

Missy nodded, then jumped up and down. "He's home, Zoe! He's home!"

Brody, Will, and Holly joined Missy in the kitchen. Zoe came in, pushing a lock of hair out of her face. As the children dragged Cade to the table, she reached into the warming oven and took out a plate of food. Holly ran to pour a glass of milk, while Missy buttered a thick wedge of cornbread and laid it on his plate. Brody hung over his shoulder, talking about the frogs he'd caught.

111

Cade was overwhelmed by all the attention. As Zoe set the plate in front of him, he said, "I expected to go to bed without supper."

"It's not much," she warned. "Just beans and cornbread."

Just beans and cornbread. At eight o'clock at night, with his not having eaten since early morning, it looked like turkey and dressing. He dug in, aware of the eyes suddenly focused on him.

His fork slowed as he glanced up and met Holly's disapproving gaze. Crossing her arms, she shook her head.

He lifted his brows. "What?"

Leaning over, Missy whispered, "You haven't *pwayed*."

"Prayed?" He glanced at Zoe.

"Blessed the food," she offered.

Stunned, he asked, "Me?"

"You're the one eating, aren't you?"

He bowed his head and clasped his hands together as he had long ago. But that was all he could remember to do. Missy edged closer, and he looked at her out of the corner of his eye. "What do I say?"

"Just say, thank you fow the food, God, and thank you fow my family."

He glanced up and met Zoe's amused eyes. Bowing his head, he prayed, "Thank you for the food, God, and thank you for...my family." The words felt strange on his lips.

The warmth of the kitchen surrounded him as he ate. Brody wanted to know all about his day, so Cade explained about the trip to Suffox County. Will, Missy, and Holly

112

huddled close to the table, listening with rapt attention.

Will's eyes became as big as saucers. "Did you shooted a bad guy today?"

Cade patted the boy's head. "No, I didn't shoot anyone."

Zoe brought her sewing to the table and darned socks, smiling at the children's occasional bursts of laughter. Cade told of how he and Eddie Lee Brighton had chased a pig down the road trying to recapture it.

"Maddy had to stand guard over Hague's body while I chased that porker on foot for better than twenty minutes, until I wore her down." Cade laughed. "Must have run off four pork chops and a side of bacon before she gave in."

Zoe glanced up at the mention of Maddy.

"Did some lady go with you?" Brody asked.

"No." He looked at the children and winked. "Maddy's my horse. Short for Madeleine. Named her after a woman I knew in Wichita. Feisty little filly..." His gaze caught Zoe's and she looked away, biting off a piece of thread sharply.

When the clock struck nine, Zoe laid her mending aside. "It's bedtime."

The children complied without argument. In a flurry of commotion, the boys ran to make up their pallets. The girls disappeared into the bedroom, returning to Cade a few moments later for good-night kisses.

After the children had gone to bed, Zoe bustled around the kitchen, putting away dishes. Leaning back in his chair, Cade watched the way the lamplight shone on her hair. Her lithe figure hadn't changed much. Her waist was still so tiny he could span it with two hands.

"What did Seth and Bonnie say when you stopped by?" Her voice was soft, hesitant.

He'd deliberately avoided the subject, but it was open now and she had to know.

"How well do you know Bonnie?"

Zoe trimmed the lamp. "Not well. I see her occasionally at social functions and church. She stays to herself most of the time."

"She wasn't raised around here?"

"No, near St. Louis. Why?"

"Bonnie's come down with a fever."

Zoe almost dropped a cup. "Why didn't you tell me this afternoon?"

"There's nothing we can do. You seem to have enough to worry about. Besides, I wanted to wait until you were in a better mood. It doesn't change anything. As soon as she gets better..."

"The fever!" Zoe's hand went to her throat.

"No one knows for sure how serious it is, but she's pretty sick."

"That's terrible...what does that mean for the children?"

"Frank and Helen have taken them—"

"Not Seth and Bonnie's children. These children."

Getting up from the table, Cade carried his plate to the sink. "For the moment, it means I'll be in Winterborn a few days longer than I intended."

"But, Cade, if Bonnie has come down with the same fever that killed John and Addy—"

"We don't know that. In a few days, Bonnie

114

will either be better or worse. We'll look at the situation then."

"Cade—"

"No, Zoe." He answered her question before she asked. "I said, Bonnie's illness doesn't change anything. It merely delays things."

When he saw her face cloud with resentment, he reached out and tweaked her nose. "Thank you for holding supper for me," he said gently. "It's been a long time since I've tasted any-thing that good."

The dirty look she gave him before she walked out of the room made him wonder if it would be even longer before he sat at her table again.

He looked up and saw Holly standing in the doorway. "Hi, sweetie. I thought you'd be asleep by now."

The child walked over to him and put her arms around his neck. "Don't be mad at Zoe. She's just tired."

Cade squeezed her against him. "I could never be mad at Zoe, sweetheart. Don't ever worry about that. Hey, I could use some help feeding Maddy tomorrow. Why don't you go into the store in the morning and get a carrot? I'll bet she'd love that."

The girl's eyes brightened. "Can I give it to her?"

"Sure can."

The next morning, after they put down fresh hay, Cade lifted Holly up and sat her on the

115

side of the stall so she could pet Maddy's mane.

"She sure loves carrots, huh, Uncle Cade?"

"I think she loves you, too."

"Someday I'm going to have a horse like Maddy."

Cade patted her hand. "I like seeing you smile. I know it's been rough on you guys lately."

Holly's eyes misted. "I miss Ma and Pa. Ma was always laughin' and singin'."

Cade lifted her down and hugged her close. "I know, sweetie. I miss my ma, too. I guess we always will, but it gets easier. They wouldn't want us to be sad." He tilted her face up with his finger. "Let's see that happy face again."

Her lips trembled just before they turned up in a sweet smile. "I love you, Uncle Cade."

He swallowed hard. "I love you, too."

May Wilks's laugh was shrill enough to wake the dead. Once May got going, folks as far as Suffox County could hear her high-pitched, mirthful squeals and intermittent snorts.

"King me!" May stacked Gracie's checkers in her growing pile and laughed until tears rolled down her cheeks. Though Gracie had just lost the game, she wound up laughing as hard as May.

Zoe found herself joining in, giggling along with Willa and Gracie. If they were given a king's ransom, they wouldn't be able to say what was so funny.

"Oh, my." Gracie wiped tears from her

eyes as she got up. "I think it's time for cake and coffee. Too bad Edna can't be here to get in on the fun."

May glanced up. "Where is Edna tonight?"

"She spent the day helping Walt clean the barbershop. Said she was just too tuckered to play checkers tonight."

Arranging her black pieces for a new game, Zoe smiled and asked, "Can I help with the refreshments?"

"You can cut the cake. It's rum raisin. You hear that, May?" Gracie winked at Zoe. "I baked it fresh this morning."

Zoe grinned. May couldn't hold her rum raisin cake—at least, not Gracie's. The mayor's wife had a heavy hand with the rum bottle. Last time May had eaten the cake, Lawrence had had to hitch up the buggy and drive her home.

May never looked up as she put another "won" mark in her column. "Just a small piece, Gracie. Farley says I've been eating too much lately."

"That Farley." Gracie laughed, waving her hand. "Anything my brother says should be taken with a grain of salt." Zoe followed Gracie into the kitchen, leaving Willa and May to squabble over their scores.

Gracie's kitchen smelled of perking coffee and rum. Grandmother Willis's hand-cro-cheted white tablecloth adorned the large, round, oak pedestal table sitting near the bay window. A fresh bouquet of snapdragons from the flower garden had been set in the midst of the Willises' best china. The white oak cabinets were polished to a sheen, and Gracie's Stanley cookstove was the talk of the town.

Zoe breathed a sigh of envy. Someday she hoped to have a house just like this one. She lifted the cake cover and sniffed. "How much rum did you put in this time?"

"I made it the way Lawrence likes it." Gracie giggled. "May likes it that way, too."

"Do you think she won that last game fair and square?"

"Well, she may be married to my brother, but that doesn't prevent me from keeping a close eye on her."

Zoe laughed. "I haven't beat her very many times, but I haven't seen her cheat."

While Gracie filled the creamer, Zoe cut thin slices of cake and arranged them on china plates.

"I've been dying to talk to you all day." Gracie looked up from the cream pitcher and grinned. "What's this about Cade moving in with you? Lawrence said he saw him there the morning after the storm."

Zoe felt her face burn. She wiped a bit of gooey burnt-sugar frosting off the knife and tasted it. "He didn't 'move in' with me. The jail roof had a leak in it."

"Lawrence says there *are* no sleeping quarters over the jail anymore."

"I'm afraid the children want Cade to stay with us, but that's impossible."

"Well, there's always Pop. His place is small, but he could put up one more."

"Pop's under the weather."

"Edna said he ate eight pieces of gooseberry pie at the social. That's enough to fell an elephant," said Gracie, replenishing the sugar bowl.

Zoe smiled. "Cade said he ate six. No telling how many he actually ate, but then he broke out in hives. I guess he's had a miserable few days."

Gracie poured coffee into the server, wiping up stray drips with a clean cloth. "Don't suppose Glori-Lee can help. She's closed off half her rooms since she hurt her back last spring."

Arranging the china on a tray, Zoe pressed her lips together. She didn't know what she was going to do now that he had no place to go. He was ill-equipped for fatherhood, and one would think, after the café incident, he'd know enough to leave child-rearing to her.

"Is he sleeping in the kitchen? Land's sake, you can hardly move around in there the way it is."

"In the parlor. It's all very proper. I could hardly turn away the children's uncle without explaining the reason to them, and I didn't want to get into that. But, yes, it is crowded."

Not only crowded—it was much too close for comfort. She couldn't avoid Cade if she wanted to. This morning she'd been caught off guard when she walked out of the bedroom and found him bare-chested, shaving at the sink. She'd caught herself staring. And he'd noticed. She'd pretended not to let it bother her, but he wasn't fooled. He took his sweet time putting his shirt on, his mischievous eyes never leaving hers. She wasn't about to back down, so she just stared a hole right through him.

Zoe shivered against the goosebumps, recalling the effect he still had on her as she licked the knife and put it in the dishpan. "It's nice to see the children smiling again. When I left this evening, Cade was on the floor wrestling with Brody and Will. You should have heard Holly and Missy giggling. Gracie, they haven't done that in weeks."

"So they're really taking to him?"

"Yes, but Cade has told me he doesn't intend to raise them himself. I'm afraid if they get much closer, he'll only break their hearts when he leaves, and they've already had enough sorrow in their young lives. By the way, Cade stopped at the Brightons' to talk about the children. Bonnie has come down with the fever."

"Oh, no!" Gracie said. "Like Addy and John?"

"They don't know. Seth's worried sick, but Doc Whitney says they'll have to wait a few days and see. I thought I'd take dinner to them tomorrow and ask if there's anything I can do."

"What about *their* young'uns?"

"Seth took them to Frank's and Helen's, just in case the fever's contagious."

Gracie paused and studied Zoe. "What's that got to do with Cade's plans to let the Brightons adopt the kids?"

Zoe shrugged. "Not that I wish ill health on anyone, but it buys me some time. I'm going to do my best to convince Cade to let me adopt the kids. They're so much a part of me already."

"You're hell-bent on keeping them, aren't you?"

"I've always wanted them, but I did what Addy asked. I sent for Cade. Now I wish I hadn't. I thought surely he would give them to me if he wasn't going to keep them himself."

"Why does he object to your having them? Is it your lack of money?"

"He doesn't know my financial situation. He says he wants the children to have a mother *and* a father, but I think he's just being stubborn."

Gracie raised her brows.

"Don't start speculating," Zoe chided. "I just mean things are strained between us right now. He wouldn't let me have them if I were married to the richest man in Kansas."

"He said that?"

"Not so many words—oh, he said I needed to marry and get on with my life and have my *own* family."

"You should."

"Those kids *are* my family." Tears stung her eyes. *They're the only children I can ever have.* She threw a spoon into the sink. "I don't understand why Addy didn't give them to me in the first place."

"Hmmm," Gracie mused. "A body would swear she was trying to get you and Cade together. After all, other than John and the children, you were the two people she loved the most."

"That's crazy. Even Addy wouldn't do something that far-fetched." But privately, Zoe wouldn't put it beyond Addy to have thought that if Cade came back, it could be the same as before. Yet Zoe had gained enough sense to realize that loving him was like loving the wind.

Willa's voice resounded from the parlor. "May Wilks! Where did that third king come from?"

May's hyena-like laughing snorts filled the parlor.

Zoe and Gracie broke into giggles over May's antics. Why, Zoe wasn't sure.

"Sounds like there's going to be a tiff," Gracie said. "We'd better get the cake and coffee in there."

Zoe backed out the kitchen door balancing the tray of cake with one hand, four white linen napkins tucked under her chin. "Gracie, promise me you won't mention my financial situation to anyone."

Gracie laughed. "Have you ever known me to gossip?"

"Only since I was born." She grinned. "I don't know what you did before that."

Chapter 8

After the supper dishes were cleared away, Brody came into the kitchen. "It's Saturday night, Zoe. Are we going to the dance?"

Cade was on the back porch, cleaning his saddle. He glanced up as Brody made the inquiry.

Zoe folded the dishcloth and hung it up to dry. "Not tonight; you need to go to bed early. We missed Sunday school last week, and I don't want that to happen again."

It was the first Sunday she'd ever missed. Ironing until the wee hours of the morning was taking its toll. If only the new yard goods would arrive, she wouldn't have to take in extra work. She had enough orders already to make her bank payments through the coming winter months.

Holly looked out the window. "The lights are on at the dance hall."

"I know, dear," Zoe said, thinking Holly had held up remarkably well during her parents' illness and death. "Perhaps we'll go next week."

"I'll bet Mr. Drake will be there," Holly added.

"Mr. Drake will understand."

Brody snagged Will around the neck, noisily kissing him on the cheek. "Ohhh, Zoe, you're so preeetty with your long red hair!"

Will giggled and kissed Brody back. "Oh, Perrry, you're so strong and handsome."

"Boys!" Zoe admonished.

"Are you talking about Perry Drake?" Cade called.

Zoe felt heat rising to her cheeks. She saw Cade watching them through the screen and wished he hadn't heard the boys' teasing. He would make more out of it than it was. Perry had taken her to the Saturday night dance a couple of times, but it was nothing, really.

"Did he ever marry Jenny Parson?"

"Yes, Jim and I considered them our best friends." Zoe put a skillet away. "Jenny died of snakebite a month before Jim was killed." She ventured a glance toward Cade.

"So," he said, holding her gaze, "you and Perry sweet on each other?"

She slammed the cabinet door shut. "Don't pay any attention to the boys." As bank president, Perry was kept busy, and Lord knows she had no time to socialize. Gracie thought Perry would make a suitable companion for her, but there was no love interest on her part.

Holly moved to the table. "It's gettin' dark. Want me to light the lamp?"

"Why don't we use candles tonight?" Zoe suggested. There was barely enough oil left to last the month. She had to be more sparing with it. No coffee, no lamp oil—how soon would it be before Cade noticed?

"We can't see good with candles," Brody complained.

"We can't see *well* with candles," Zoe corrected.

"So? Want me to light the lamp?"

"A candle will do, Brody. Thank you."

"We haven't been to a Saturday dance for a long time," Holly said. "Not since Ma and Pa got sick."

Zoe realized fun was a thing of the past for all of them. "I'll tell you what I'll do. After baths, I'll play the phonograph, and we can have our own dance."

"Oh, yeah!" Missy said. "Ouw own dance!"

Brody brought in the wooden tub, and Zoe

put water on the stove to heat, then hung a curtain to allow each bather privacy. She noticed that Cade stayed on the porch, keeping a safe distance from all the commotion.

By eight o'clock, the kids were spanking clean, their hair washed and smelling of New England rum, a solution Zoe was sure kept the hair shiny and free from disease.

Cade grumbled, consenting to a bath but refusing to put rum on his hair. "I'll drink it, but I'm not wearing it," he said.

Afterward, he refilled the tub with clean water, then disappeared into the parlor with the kids.

Zoe bathed in peace, listening to the sound of music coming from the other room. Cade's booming laughter nearly drowned out the strains of "Little Brown Jug" as the kids and he thumped nosily across the floor.

Smiling, she closed her eyes and slid deeper into the hot water. What were the children going to do when Cade left? To his credit, he'd been truthful with them, telling them outright that he couldn't stay. However frank he'd been, though, his departure wouldn't be any less painful for the children. At times she wondered if they fully understood the implications of his leaving, and that they could be living with another family soon. She dreaded the emptiness she would feel once they were gone.

Picking up the sponge, she lathered her arms, shoving her gloominess aside. Judging by the racket coming from the parlor, the children were having too much fun for her to be having maudlin thoughts. She smiled when she thought how just a few short weeks ago she'd lived a life of solitude—evenings when you could hear a pin drop, it was so quiet.

Wincing when she heard Butch bark and Romeo yowl, she hoped her mother's priceless figurines were surviving the rowdy goings-on in the next room. Unfortunately, when Cade had moved in, so had the animals.

She stood up, reached for a towel, and dried off. Tying the sash of her robe, she poked her head into the parlor and smiled when she saw Missy standing on top of Cade's feet, dancing to the strains of "I'll Take You Home Again, Kathleen."

The boys were dancing together, arm in arm, mocking Cade and Missy. They pranced around the room, making faces at each other and having a good time.

Holly sat on the settee, hands folded, seemingly awaiting a turn around the dance floor with her uncle. Butch and Romeo lay on the floor next to her feet, their eyes following the dancers.

Cade had never looked more masterful or graceful as he glided around the floor clasping Missy's tiny hand in his large one. Zoe felt an uncharacteristic pang of envy. When, where, and with *whom* had he learned such niceties? In whose parlor had he last danced so elegantly? Whose hand had he been holding at the time? She doubted it was a five-year-old's.

Suddenly Cade looked up, smiling at her. "Care to join the fun, Red?"

She pulled the collar of her robe higher around her neck. "I don't think so."

"Come on," he coaxed. "The boys need a few dancing lessons." His eyes motioned toward Brody and Will, who were stumbling over each other's feet.

"Come on, Wed, it's fun," Missy encouraged.

"Well." Zoe stood for a moment, debating the advisability, then quickly decided it couldn't hurt. The children needed a little diversion.

After scooting the table of figurines to a safe corner, she held out her hand to Will. "May I have this dance, kind sir?"

Will's face turned beet-red, his gaze shifting to the ceiling in an effort to appear nonchalant, but he eventually walked self-consciously into her arms.

The phonograph played, and the dancing couples swirled to the music. Holly took her turn with Cade, and Missy made Brody dance with her.

When the music ended, the dancers were laughing and breathless. Zoe and Cade collapsed in nearby chairs, and Brody hurried over to rewind the phonograph.

Zoe held up her hand to stop him. "Brody, it's getting late."

"Just once more," Holly pleaded.

Missy grabbed hold of Cade's hand and pulled him to his feet. "I want to dance with you again."

He turned to Zoe and winked. "Women. They just can't get enough of me."

Zoe had no trouble seeing why. "Really?"

She winked back. "There's no accounting for good taste."

His eyes said, "Touché," and they both broke into friendly grins.

The music played on. For the next half hour, Cade took turns dancing with Holly and Missy. The young girls' faces were flushed, their eyes sparkling with delight.

As the clock chimed nine-thirty, Zoe put a halt to the festivities.

"No more—it's way past bedtime."

Holly and Missy showered Cade's cheeks with kisses. "It's the best dance we ever went to," Holly proclaimed. "The very best!"

The girls scampered off to bed, humming the strains of "I'll Take You Home Again, Kathleen" under their breaths.

Will shuffled off toward the kitchen, grumbling, "I hate dancing with Brody."

Brody shoved him on his way out. "I hate dancing with you, too."

"Boys, stop bickering. I'll be in shortly to hear your prayers."

Reaching for the candle, Zoe turned to Cade. "I left clean sheets beside the pillow and blanket."

"Thank you. I'll manage."

Her face burned as his gaze skimmed her. "Good night."

She let Butch and Romeo out and then listened to the boys' prayers, touched when they asked God to make their Uncle Cade stay. The girls' prayers were the same. It was too late to worry about them getting attached to him. They already were.

Just as Zoe was about to drift off to sleep, she heard the faint sound of music coming from the parlor. She got out of bed quietly so as not to disturb the girls and slipped into her robe. She peered around the corner and saw a flickering light. Had she forgotten to snuff a candle?

"Cade," she called softly. When he didn't answer, she left the bedroom and padded into the parlor. There wasn't one candle burning; there were several.

He's lit every candle I own!

Inside the doorway, a strong arm caught her around the waist and pulled her into the room.

"I believe this is our dance."

She struggled to free herself from his grasp, his low, seductive voice affecting her good sense. "Aren't you worn out from dancing with all your 'women'?"

Drawing her closer, he whispered, "Ah, fair lady, I have yet to dance with the prettiest one of all."

She wrenched her arm free and wet her fingers to extinguish a candle or two, but he stopped her.

"You look beautiful in candlelight."

"You don't." Candlelight only made him more handsome.

"Ah, such a tart-tongued wench."

She squirmed against his embrace, but her struggles were in vain. All she could do was settle into his arms. His warm breath brushed her temple as they swayed to the strains of a waltz. What was she doing? Dancing half-clothed in a candlelit parlor with a man who threatened her resolve was more than dangerous. It was insane.

He smelled clean and soapy. Her fingers itched to touch his hair, but she didn't. Once she touched him intimately, she would never stop. Everything about him was familiar, and so hopelessly wrong.

Resting her head on his chest, she listened to his steady heartbeat. "This is crazy, Cade."

"We're only dancing."

"You know it's more than dancing. What do you want from me? You've already won the children's hearts. Can't you let me be?"

Cade tightened his hold. "Can't we just enjoy a dance together? Must every move I make toward you mean something significant? I'm simply enjoying a beautiful woman's company."

"We could enjoy the moment, but for what purpose?" she whispered.

"For old times."

"Old times? You don't remember a thing about 'old times'—admit it."

"I remember more than you think."

Her eyes closed as she struggled with her feelings. Did he remember every breath, every word, every vow? Apparently not. "There was a time when we both thought we meant something to each other," she said, and felt his lips brush her hair.

"We were so young, Red. Our lives are different now. My life can't include a family, even if that's what I wanted."

"You talk as if there's some evil force waiting for you at the outskirts of town."

She watched him smile, and her heart sank. He wasn't smiling because he was happy; he was confirming her words. She'd seen that expression on his face before. It was his way of telling her bad news.

"Give up bounty-hunting—now, before it's too late," she pleaded. "You have all the money you could ever need. Can't you find it in your heart to make a home for Addy's children? That's what she desperately wanted."

He stepped back, catching her hands to his chest. Their gazes locked in the flickering candlelight. "Listen to me, Red. I could give it up right now, this moment, and nothing would change. I'll always have to guard my back. Do you think I want that for Addy's kids? Do you want them to have to watch their backs, too? The enemies I deal with don't give a damn. They'd just as soon gun the kids down as they would me."

Sickened, she jerked away. "Killing. Always killing."

"That's what bounty-hunting's about. Occasionally it requires killing."

Her fists balled into tight knots of anger because the life he chose was one that would eventually destroy him. "The Good Book says 'Thou shalt not kill.'"

"Sometimes circumstances say otherwise."

She turned to go, suddenly unable to breathe. The situation was hopeless. When would she accept that he was a man hardened in his ways?

Pausing in the doorway, she said quietly, "I hope you leave soon."

• • •

Monday morning, Zoe was in the kitchen ironing the wealthy Mrs. Penscott's expensive petticoats when she heard the tinkling bell over the front door. Gracie ran through the store and on into the back rooms, breathlessly blurting, "Have you heard? Pop broke his leg."

Mouth agape, Zoe set the iron on the stove. "No. When?"

"Saturday night at the dance. I thought maybe someone told you at church yesterday. Sorry Lawrence and I missed the services. We just plain overslept."

"No. No one said a thing, but I left right after the sermon. The kids wanted to get back and go fishing with Cade. What happened?"

Gracie snickered. "Pop allemanded left when he should have allemanded right. He nearly took poor Clara Simms down with him."

Zoe's hand flew to her mouth to cover her amusement. The mental image of Pop and the puritanical Sunday school teacher sprawled in the middle of the dance floor tickled her.

"Was she hurt?"

"Just embarrassed. Her crinoline flew up over her head and got hooked on that silly comb she always wears. It took two of us to get it untangled." Gracie put her packages on the table and helped herself to lemonade. "Pop didn't know he'd broken anything until he tried to get up. Lucky thing Doc Whitney was there. He took Pop over to his office and set his leg right then."

Zoe walked to the front window of the store and looked up the street to the jail. "The kids and Cade went over early this morning to see Pop. I'm surprised they haven't come back and told me."

"They're probably too busy waiting on him. You know Pop. He likes attention."

"Don't all men?" She stripped off her apron as she hurried behind the counter. "I'll take him some nut bread. That should make him feel better."

Gracie sat down on a stool and propped her feet up on a nearby barrel. "I'm going to sit here and finish my lemonade." She shuddered and puckered her lips. "Good heavens, it's tart. You out of sugar?"

"Just running a little low. While you're at it, finish the ironing." Zoe slipped two loaves of sweet bread into a wicker basket and covered them with a towel.

"The kids are attached to Cade's hip." Gracie said as Zoe scurried past her. "You see one, you see the other."

"I know. That's what worries me. Watch the store for me. I'll be back in a minute," she called over her shoulder as she walked out the door.

Crossing the street, she spotted Will running from post to post, ripping down Wanted posters.

"Will," she hollered, "what are you doing?"

Will hung his head and held the posters behind his back as she approached. "Nuthin'."

"You're doing something." She tried to

see around him. "What's that behind your back?"

"Nuthin'."

"Will," she scolded.

He twisted the toe of his shoe in the dirt.

"William Wiseman?"

He slowly brought the posters forward and handed them to her. Her brows lifted in question. "What is this all about? You know better than to destroy public property."

Teary-eyed, he jutted out his bottom lip. "If there wasn't any bad guys to be shooted, Uncle Cade would stay here with us."

Her shoulders dropped as she knelt to console him. His wrenching sobs broke her heart.

"He told...us...he...had...to go get...a bad guy. That's...why...he can't...keep us."

Her anger surfaced. Cade could have been a little more tactful. She'd like to wring his neck like a Sunday chicken!

"Even if he does go, he'll come back."

"No, he won't." Will sobbed. "Mama said he never does."

Zoe took the towel off the sweet bread and used it to dab at the little boy's tears. "Well, let's not worry about it now. Uncle Cade is here, and I don't think he's going after bad guys any time soon. Now, I want you to take these posters to Pop and tell him you're sorry for pulling them down."

"And tell him I won't do it again."

"That's my sweet boy." She kissed him on the cheek and watched proudly as he marched into the jail, carrying the posters.

After folding the cloth, she laid it in the

basket and proceeded slowly, giving Will time to complete his apology before she arrived. She also didn't want to be around Cade any more than necessary. Living with him was difficult enough.

She was a fool to allow him to get so close so quick. The flame between them was as strong as ever, and it frightened her. Why wasn't he fat and bald like Frank Lovell? Why didn't he reek of mothballs and stale cigar smoke like Frank Lovell? Heaven knew she wouldn't have a hard time resisting him then.

Her jaw firmed. This time, Cade wasn't dealing with a lovesick girl. This time he was dealing with a woman who knew the difference between love and pure old sinful lust.

She let herself into the jail. It was so crowded, there was barely standing room. Two tittering young ladies had cornered Cade. She did a double take. Judy Farnsworth? When had she started dressing like a strumpet? The low-cut bodice on her red satin dress revealed enough bosom for two girls! Zoe wondered if her mother knew she was out in public in that garb.

She recognized the striking brunette with Judy as Edna Mews's niece, Susan Tetherton. Just a short time ago, Susan had been in pigtails and overalls, playing marbles with the boys. Well, she wasn't playing marbles today.

Zoe forced herself to smile when she heard Susan say, "Cade Kolby, I've heard about you all my life, but Aunt Edna never told me you were so downright handsome." Susan leaned in close and spread her palm across

135

Cade's broad chest, her yellow dress shimmering with every move.

Another silly giggle came from Judy's painted lips. "Told you, Susan. Told you he was tall and positively breathtaking." She twirled a section of his hair around her slender, ring-clad finger while she breathed deeply and pulled her shoulders back, bringing her breasts up closer to his eye level.

Zoe glanced at Pop and the children, who were sitting behind his desk, gorging themselves on cookies.

"Hi, Zoe," Brody called. "Want a cookie? Judy and Susan baked them for Uncle Cade. They're good."

Closing the door, Zoe set the basket on the corner of the desk next to Pop's propped-up leg. "Brody, don't talk with your mouth full." She looked at Pop sympathetically. "How are you doing?"

"Ain't worth a plugged nickel."

"Did Will apologize for taking down the posters?"

"Yeah." Pop laughed, ruffling the boy's hair. "He sure likes his uncle. Can't see the attraction myself. How 'bout you?"

Missy hopped out of Pop's lap. "Zoe, my belly huwts again."

Cade excused himself from the young women and, grinning, scooped Missy up onto his shoulder. "Before Zoe gets mad at us, tell her I said 'only one cookie.'"

"He did. He did, Zoe," Holly confirmed. "I only got one, too."

"Brody had four," Will said.

Brody hung his head, withholding comment.

Pop lifted his splinted leg and eased it to the floor. "They'll live. Here, Zoe, try a piece of Edna's rhubarb pie. Woman talks a lot, but she sure can cook."

Zoe smiled. "I thought you'd have sworn off pie by now."

Judy and Susan flashed their dimpled smiles toward Cade. Their fresh beauty and bouncing curls were a sharp contrast to Zoe's own faded calico dress and wayward hair, frizzed from leaning over a washboard doing the never-ending laundry. Her gaze moved to Cade, and she wondered if he was making the same comparison.

She turned back to Pop. "I won't stay—just wanted to check on you. I thought you might enjoy some of my nut bread."

"That's real hospitable of you." He leaned forward and sniffed the basket. "You gotta try some of this, Cade. She makes the best nut bread in town."

Cade reached over and accepted a piece. "You don't have to tell me. Everything she cooks is good."

Loud voices outside the jail interrupted them.

Pop tried to get up but fell back in his chair. "What in the tarnation's going on out there?"

The door flew open and Zoe saw Cade's right hand automatically go for his gun, while his left hand moved her to safety behind him. Warmth flooded her when she realized he was protecting her.

The stagecoach driver, white-faced and grimy with dust, ran in, barely able to talk. "The stage has been robbed!" Catching his breath, he collapsed onto the nearest chair. "Four men. Looked like the Nelson gang, but cain't be sure." The man dropped his head and covered his face with hands that trembled like leaves in a storm. His knuckles were skinned and bleeding, his shirt torn.

"Good grief, Troy!" Pop exclaimed.

"Anyone killed?" Cade stepped to the door and looked out.

"No, but we shore thought we were goners." Troy Becker accepted a cup of water from Zoe, nodding his thanks.

She glanced outside to see a group of curious onlookers converging on the jail. "You're about to have company, Pop."

"Has something happened to the stage?" Walt Mews asked as he burst in. "I saw it coming into town like a scalded cat. My shipment of hair tonic from Boston is on it."

"It ain't no more." The stage driver got up, set his cup on the desk, and looked wild-eyed at Walt. "It's gone, along with Mrs. Bradshaw's yard goods."

Zoe groaned. "Oh, no! The whole shipment?"

"It ain't my fault. They come outta nowhere!" Troy exclaimed. "Never saw nothin' like it!"

Cade stepped forward. "Exactly what happened, Troy?"

"I was approachin' Rider's Pass when all of a sudden, here they come. At first I thought it was Injuns, the way they were whoopin' and

138

hollerin', but then I seen they was white men. They grabbed the money sack and, before they left, took every bottle of your tonic, Walt, poured it all over Mrs. Bradshaw's cloth, and smashed the bottles. Didn't see the sense of that—but that's what they did. You never saw such a mess in all your life."

Zoe took hope. "You mean my shipment is still out there in the road?" Maybe she could salvage part of it. She *had* to salvage part of it. It meant financial ruin if she didn't.

The driver met her expectant expression. "You could say that."

Cade frowned. "What do you mean? Is it there or not?"

"It's there, all right, but I don't think she'd want it. The horses didn't take kindly to the stink of that tonic. They got all excited and tromped on it." He looked at Zoe. "I hate to tell you, but that ain't all they did on it."

"Oh, dear." Heartsick, Zoe sank onto a chair. This was the end. Without the money the yard goods would bring, she was bankrupt.

Cade frowned. "Is the fabric that important to you, Red?"

"Very important," she admitted, hoping her desperate tone didn't reveal her financial woes.

Struggling to get out of his chair, Pop fumed, "Just when something excitin' happens, I got a broke leg and can't do a thing about it."

"Stay where you are, Pop," Cade said. "I'll take care of it."

"Cade!" Zoe protested, following him to the

gun cabinet. The men of the Nelson gang were hardened criminals. She reminded herself that he was used to chasing outlaws across the country, but she wasn't used to seeing it firsthand.

"Better send someone out there to clean up the mess," Pop warned. "Don't let the trail get cold before you form a posse."

Cade glanced at Zoe. "I'll be gone awhile. You'd better take the kids home and stay there in case there's trouble."

Zoe frowned. "Trouble?" She hadn't wanted him back in her life, but she didn't want him dead, either. Her eyes searched his for a sign of assurance. Trouble might be commonplace to him, but it was foreign to Winterborn, and to her.

He grasped her shoulders and turned her toward the door. "Take the kids and go home. I'll be back as soon as I can."

Before she could protest, he solicited help from several of the men, then doled out rifles.

"Go home, Zoe," he ordered.

She started to argue, then clamped her mouth shut. Hurrying the children out the door, she glanced back as the small office quickly emptied, the young girls tittering with excitement. She was angry with Cade for getting involved. That's all the children needed: for Cade to get shot.

The posse formed and decided on a plan of action. Zoe waited for Cade at the hitching post. As he was about to mount up, she reached out to him.

"Cade, this is insane!"

"Someone has to go."

"But—"

"Didn't you say those yard goods were important to you?"

"Yes, but it sounds like they're already ruined."

"I'll salvage what I can." Cinching the saddle tighter, he said, "Take the kids home and stay there."

She grabbed his arm. "If you insist on doing this, promise me you'll be careful." Her breath caught in her throat when his deep-blue eyes met hers. She thought she saw the hint of a smile at the corners of his mouth.

"Worried about me, Red? I thought you didn't care."

Frowning, she backed off, crossing her arms. "Don't be silly. I'm thinking of the children."

He swung up onto the mare. "You worry too much."

She gave him an irritated glance and noticed his face sober at her concerned look.

"I promise—I'll be careful. I'm thinking of the kids, too." Reining his horse to the right, he tipped his hat and rode off.

This was one promise she prayed he kept.

Chapter 9

Cade patted Maddy's neck, his stomach tightening as he took in the stinking wreckage. Flies buzzed around piles of fresh horse manure scattered over the bolts of once-colorful cotton. Broken bottles lay everywhere. Cade glanced at Walt Mews and saw him wrinkle his nose in disgust. There was nothing left of his hair tonic to salvage.

Zoe Bradshaw's yard goods had picked a hell of time to show up at the junction between Suffox and Miller Counties. Rider's Pass was nothing more than a narrow bend in the road, obscured by a heavy thicket of elm, hackberry, and tangled underbrush—the ideal site for an ambush.

Red would throw a fit if she were here to see her fancy bolts of cloth in this condition. Covering his nose with a gloved hand, Cade reined Maddy aside. It would take a better man than him to sort through the mess.

"Walt, you take your men and ride south. Roy, take a couple of men and go west. Ben, take your boys and head east. I'll ride north. Let's meet at the jail around sundown—and be careful. We don't know who we're up against."

The posse wheeled their horses and galloped off in a boiling cloud of dust.

Cade prodded Maddy up the road, wondering how much the lost the shipment would set Zoe back. He didn't know her financial situation, but from what he'd seen, he was sure it wasn't good.

The sound of rolling wagon wheels caught his attention, and he moved a safe distance into the brush. He watched the bend in the road as the pounding of hoofs grew louder, and then a buckboard whipped wildly toward him.

As the wagon flew by, he noted that the driver was slumped over in the seat. He gave Maddy her head, and she galloped after the lead horses. "Come on, girl," he yelled, putting his spurs to her flanks.

Maddy gained on the wagon, her longer stride and lean body a definite advantage over the stocky quarter horse team.

"Easy, girl," Cade assured her as they paced the two out-of-control horses. Leaning to his right, he grabbed one of the flapping reins and pulled back. "Whoa! Whoa there!"

The rig ground to a halt, and Code drew his gun, dismounting to check on the driver. If this was a McGill set-up, he was ready for him. He cautiously stepped on a spoke of the wheel and hopped into the wagon. Pointing the barrel of the gun, he called, "You there!" Realizing the man was unconscious, Cade holstered his gun and searched the man's neck for a pulse.

A young woman was lying on a blanket in the back. He stepped over the seat and knelt beside her. Putting a hand on either side of her head, he stilled her tossing and turning. She was burning with fever.

"Who are you?"

"Sick..." she rasped. "Where's Bruce?"

He noticed the wedding band on her finger and assumed the driver was her husband. "He's here. I'm going to get you to the doctor."

"Bruce...sick...need help."

Cade stepped back over the seat to rouse the unconscious young man. "Wake up." He shook the driver's shoulders, and the man moaned as Cade pulled him upright. "Are you with me, boy?" The young man's head lolled to one side.

"Hell." Cade glanced around, half expecting lightning to strike him dead. If one more thing went wrong, he was as good as six feet under. Pop and his broken leg, Bonnie stricken with the fever, Zoe on his back to give her the kids and get out of town. One delay after the other, and now he was chasing nobodies without prices on their heads when he should have left Winterborn days ago.

A cold bedroll, a lonesome trail, and hardtack were beginning to sound good. And he wouldn't have to shave or get a haircut if he didn't want to.

He stepped into the wagon bed, lifted the unconscious man into his arms, and laid him next to the woman, then whistled for Maddy. After tying her reins to the back of the buckboard, he climbed into the driver's seat and clucked to the team.

Zoe glanced up from sweeping the front porch when she heard the rumble of a wagon coming into town. People scattered for cover as the buckboard wheeled toward Doc Whitney's office at a fast trot.

Her mouth dropped open when Cade jumped down from the rig and bounded up the steps two at a time. He pounded his fists on the doctor's door. Why was he back so soon? Had one of the posse been shot? She threw down the broom and ran to the office. "What do you want with Doc?" she asked, trying to catch her breath.

"I've got two sick people here." Cade motioned to the back of the wagon. "Do you know them?"

Her eyes focused on the prostrate couple. "It's Bruce and Ida Evans—what's wrong with them?"

"Don't know, but they're delirious with fever. I found their team running wild about an hour ago. They need Doc's help. Where is he?"

Zoe shook her head as the stench of chewing tobacco caught her attention. She turned as Old Man Gayford walked up and spit, then wiped his mouth on his sleeve. "Sawyer, do you know where Doc is?" she asked.

"Went home 'bout two hours ago. Said he was feeling poorly."

Cade muttered under his breath. "Hell." He slapped his hat against his thigh with one hand and smacked the door with the other. Frustration flashed in his eyes, and Zoe wondered why he was cursing. Doc couldn't help it if he was sick.

"What's wrong?" Glori-Lee called from the café.

Sawyer shouted back, "More sick people!"

Cade turned. "*More*? There's others?"

"Yep." Sawyer spit again. "Clyde Abbott and his oldest boy come down with the fever this morning. Doc told them to stay in bed."

"How poorly is Doc feeling?" Cade asked Sawyer.

"Don't know. He looked a mite peaked when he left. Didn't say nothin', but he was sweatin' like Judas."

"What should I do with Bruce and Ida?"

"Do with them?" Zoe asked. "I don't know what to do with them. That would be up to Doc." She glanced up and down the road. "Take them to the jail for now."

She started back to the store at a run, calling over her shoulder, "I'll get water and sponges." Cade jumped into the wagon, turned it around and headed for the jail.

Zoe rushed into the store. "Holly, you're going to have to watch Missy for awhile. Brody, can you take care of any customers who might come in?" The boy's eyes lit up. Pausing, she pointed at him. "I know what you're thinking and you may have *one* piece of penny candy. No more."

"How do you always know what I'm thinking?"

"I just know."

Holly put her dolls away, walked up to Zoe and tugged on her skirt. "What's going on?"

"Bruce and Ida have the fever." Concerned about the fear she saw in the young girl's eyes, she added, "We don't know if it's the same fever that took your parents." She threw towels and sponges into several buckets and basins. "I'll be at the jail if you need me."

Missy appeared in the doorway, tears welling in her eyes. "Don't die like my ma, Zoe."

"Come here, honey." The child walked over, and Zoe hugged her. "I'm not going to die."

Brody handed his sister a stick of peppermint candy. "You can help me run the store, Missy." He turned to Zoe. "Go on; she'll be all right."

"Thank you, Brody." She touched his cheek, proud of the young man he was becoming.

Her mind spun as she ran up the street, thankful she didn't have to endure another crisis alone. She wished Cade had been here for Addy and John, but he was here now, and she was thankful for whatever help he could give.

When she walked into the jail, Cade looked relieved. He obviously didn't want to handle the situation alone any more than she did. "Where's Pop?" she asked.

"I don't know. I sent Sawyer to find him. If the jail's going to be turned into an infirmary, Pop needs to know."

"What about my yard goods? Can they be salvaged?"

He shook his head. "Sorry."

Zoe rolled up her sleeves. She'd worry about it later. Dealing with bad news was old hat to her by now. She handed Cade a sponge. "You bathe Bruce, and I'll see what I can do for Ida." Her heart went out to the stricken couple who tossed about on the floor of the single cell, calling out to each other. When Ida tried to get up, she restrained her and eased her back to the pillow. "Bruce is right here, Ida. Lie still. The cool water will help. We need to get your fever down."

"Sick...so sick."

"I know...shhh," Zoe soothed. She turned

at the sound of boots scraping across the floor. Sawyer shuffled in with Pop hobbling along on his crutches right behind him, breathing hard.

"What's wrong?" Pop asked. "Someone said the Evanses are sick."

Cade sponged Bruce's forehead with cool water. "We'll have to use the jail for a few days. Doc's sick, and there's no place to put these folks."

"No reason they can't stay here," Pop said. "Cell hasn't been used for years—unless the posse comes up with someone."

"They'll be back at sundown. We'll know then."

"Ain't much chance they'll catch 'em. If it's the Nelson gang, they're probably long gone." He leaned closer to examine the ailing couple. "They look mighty sick."

"Found them on the road earlier. They must have been trying to get to Doc." Cade poured more water into the basin. "Better keep people away, Pop. We don't want this to turn into a full-blown epidemic."

"Yeah, that's a good idea." Pop backed up, maneuvering out of the cell on his crutches. "I'd offer to help, but I'd just be in the way. I'll be at the house if you need me."

"Sawyer, you stand guard at the front door, and don't let anyone come in," Cade ordered.

The old man nodded and stepped outside, hollering, "Stand back. Kolby said no one's to come in. This stuff might be catchin'."

Zoe knew what this new outbreak meant to the town of Winterborn. Again everyone felt

148

the loss of John and Addy, as well as the fear of the fever spreading. She prayed there wouldn't be a panic.

Missy's words echoed in her mind: '*Don't die like my ma*.' When she'd nursed John and Addy, she hadn't given a thought to catching the fever herself. She glanced at Cade. What would happen if they both came down sick? It was too late now; they were already exposed. "Dear Lord, show us mercy," she said under her breath as she sponged the woman's forehead.

Within the hour, she heard Sawyer warning Perry Drake to keep his distance. Standing in the street in front of the jail, Perry called out, "Zoe! Do you need an extra hand?"

Leaving Ida, Zoe stepped outside. She should have known Perry would be one of the first to offer his help. "Thanks for coming. It's Bruce and Ida. Cade brought them in, and Doc's gone home ill."

"Doc was in my office earlier this afternoon. He mentioned he wasn't feeling well."

Biting her lower lip, Zoe looked toward the jail. "We were hoping the fever had ended with John and Addy."

Perry reached for her hands. "Is it the same fever?"

"There's no way of knowing, but Bonne Brighton is sick, and Clyde and his boy fell ill this morning. Now it's Bruce and Ida." The concern in Perry's eyes was so typical of him. She glanced toward Cade, who stood in the doorway watching them. The question in his eyes annoyed her. It was none of his busi-

149

ness who she talked to. She sidestepped, moving Perry farther away from the open doorway.

"I left the bank as soon as I heard," Perry said. "This doesn't bode well for the town."

Cade stepped outside, motioning to Zoe. "Ida needs you."

She was certain he was only trying to break up the conversation. What had gotten into him? Years ago, he and Perry had been schoolmates. But she graciously stepped back, saying, "Excuse me, Perry; Ida needs my attention."

He detained her. "Tell me what I can do."

"Find Doc. We'll need quinine, and lots of it."

"Of course. I'll go right away."

Perry gave her hand an affectionate squeeze, and Zoe was aware of the disapproval that crossed Cade's face.

"I'm concerned about you," Perry said. "I don't want you coming down sick."

Other than a lack of sleep, and worries about a pile of ironing big enough to choke a horse, she was fine. "I took care of John and Addy all those weeks. If I were susceptible to the sickness, I'd have gotten it by now."

Zoe returned to the cell as Perry left. Ida was asleep, just as Zoe had left her. Frowning, she turned to Cade. "I thought you said Ida needed me."

It irked her that he wouldn't look at her.

"She *looked* as if she needed you."

Snatching up a water bucket, she walked out of the jail as a buggy rumbled to a stop at the hitching post.

"Uh-oh," Sawyer sang out, "got another one. Make room!"

Zoe turned around and marched back in, pulling the remaining blanket from the shelf outside the cell.

Seth Brighton came through the doorway carrying Bonnie, his face ashen. "Somebody's got to help her. She's talkin' out of her head."

Zoe motioned to Cade. "Shove the desk aside to make room for another pallet." It was going to be a long night.

Around sundown, Zoe heard the beleaguered posse ride in. Sawyer's voice filtered into the jail as he yelled for the men to ride on.

"What's wrong?" Roy Baker called.

"The whole town's come down with the fever!" Sawyer shouted.

The whole town? Zoe shook her head. Sawyer would incite mass hysteria.

Cade rose to his feet. "I'll have a word with him. Maybe he should be a little less blunt."

Bruce moaned, twisting on his pallet.

Rubbing the back of her neck, Zoe straightened, working the kinks out. As she watched Cade open the door and leave the room, Gracie came in carrying a large tray of food.

"Gracie, you're a Godsend," Zoe confessed.

"It's nothing—just chicken broth for the sick and beef stew for the healthy."

"You shouldn't be here. We don't know what we're fighting."

151

"Nonsense. I want to help." Gracie set down the tray, glancing at the patients. "My, they're a pitiful lot. Any change?"

"None. Maybe if we get a little broth into their stomachs, it will help." But when Gracie picked up a spoon, Zoe stopped her. "Go outside. Cade and I will do it."

"Law, I'm as capable as anybody—"

"Outside!" Zoe ordered.

Gracie kept talking as she hurriedly unloaded the tray. "I've checked on the children, and they're fine. Stopped by the store just before I came, and Brody had everything under control. They can spend the night with me. That'll be one worry off your mind."

"That won't be necessary. I'll be going back to the store in a little while." She was relieved when Cade returned.

"Are you sure? I'd enjoy their company."

"It would be helpful if you'd feed them supper, but I want them with me."

Gracie left, and Zoe turned to Cade. "Looks like it's just you and me."

"What do I need to do?"

"You need to change your attitude. You were rude to Perry."

"I thought you said there was nothing between you two."

"We're friends."

"That's not what he thinks."

"How do you know what he thinks?"

"I'm a man."

Her lips thinned. Yes, he certainly was a man; she couldn't argue with that. But watching him minister to Bruce had allowed her to see a side of him she'd forgotten existed. A strong compulsion came over her to reach out, touch him—She gave herself a mental slap. He was also a man who acted like a jealous suitor but wanted no kindred responsibility.

She spooned warm broth into Ida's mouth, then tended to Bonnie.

Laying her hand on Seth's shoulder, Zoe said, "You need to go home and get some rest. We'll send someone for you if there's any change."

"Maybe I'd better. I've got chores to do."

Seth leaned down and kissed his wife. Zoe prayed it wouldn't be for the last time.

Later, Zoe sat against the outside of the building, tipping her chin up and closing her eyes as she ate cold stew. Her back hurt, and she had a blinding headache. "I need to check on the children," she told Cade.

He poured a cup of coffee and handed it to her. "You should have let Gracie take them for the night."

She sighed, lifting the back of her hair to let her neck catch the faint breeze. "I want them with me. I want to keep a close eye on them and be ready in case they come down sick."

"There's no reason you can't go home and stay there," Cade said. "I'll take care of things here. For sure, we don't want the children near here."

"You'll need help now that there are three sick people. I'll go see about the children and then come back." She ignored the flare of impatience in his eyes.

"Don't you think one of us should try to stay healthy?"

"Of course; you're right. I've already been exposed. You go stay with the children, and I'll look after the patients."

"I'm as likely to get it as you are, and I don't know anything about taking care of kids or running your store."

Nor can you iron, she thought resentfully, remembering the bushel basket of ironing waiting for her in the kitchen. It wouldn't keep until the Evanses and Bonnie Brighton got better, and the bank payment was due next week. Besides, it wouldn't do any good to protest; the look in Cade's eyes promised an argument.

Cade pitched the remains of his coffee to the ground. "It's settled. I'll stay, and you'll go home. If we can keep the fever contained, the crisis should be over in a few days."

"You two argue over the silliest things," Sawyer butted in, stepping out of the shadows and spitting a stream of tobacco juice. "You go, I go. What difference does it make who goes?"

"Why don't *you* go, Sawyer?" Cade said. "Come back in the morning if you want to help."

Zoe guessed the old man took the hint, because he abruptly left in a huff.

Bone-tired, she watched Cade study the rim of his cup. Sympathy washed over her as she noticed the lines of weariness around his eyes. If he'd thought his visit to Winterborn would be brief and uncomplicated, he was mistaken. Would the new cases of fever further delay his departure?

Zoe glanced up to see Perry Drake's buggy bowling into town. She rose to her feet. "Thank goodness. Here's Perry with Doc now."

The buggy rolled to a halt in front of the jail, and Perry jumped out. "Hold on, Doc. I'll give you a hand."

"Stop all this infernal fussing!" the wiry, white-haired doctor blustered. "I have a slight temperature—nothing to be concerned about. I'll be as good as new by morning." As he stepped down from the carriage, he crumpled to the ground in a dead faint.

"Cade!" Zoe shouted, alarmed.

Cade leapt forward and helped Perry lift the older man. Supporting the doctor's slight frame between them, they carried the ailing physician into the jail.

Zoe was close on Cade's heels to lay out a fourth pallet. She helped the men settle Doc on the makeshift bed, then stood back as Cade loosened the patient's string tie and unbuttoned his shirt.

Perry straightened. "Someone needs to ride out and tell Doc's wife he's sick. We're keeping him here."

"You do that, Drake." Cade took off the doctor's shoes and set them aside.

The room suddenly seemed unusually tight as Zoe watched the two men size each other up. What next? Were they going to engage in fisticuffs?

"Zoe needs my help," Perry announced. "You

need a breather, and Pop needs you elsewhere."

Zoe winced when Cade's eyes narrowed. He stepped to the door and opened it.

"Get out of here, Drake, before you catch something."

"Cade!" Zoe was appalled at his lack of manners. As Perry slipped his arm through hers, she apologized, "I'm sorry, Perry. It's been a difficult day. We appreciate your offer of help, but we don't want you to be unnecessarily exposed."

She felt a blush heat her cheeks when Perry leaned over and whispered in her ear, "I'll stop by later to walk you home." She smiled, wondering why he was suddenly so attentive. He was acting as if their relationship were closer than it really was.

Zoe knew they were headed for trouble when Cade planted his imposing frame next to the doorway, crossed his arms over his chest, and waited for Perry to leave.

When she detected a slight quiver in Perry's arm, her temper flared. How dare Cade attempt to intimidate her friend! The tactic might work on a man with a price on his head, but Cade certainly didn't frighten Perry.

Pausing in the doorway, she said her good-byes, at the same time intentionally mashing the top of Cade's left boot with her foot. It pleased her to see the annoyed expression on his set features.

"Thank you, Perry, for offering to walk me home, but I'll need to stay late now that there are four patients. I'll stop by the bank tomorrow."

"I'll look forward to that."

She smiled as Perry leaned forward and attempted to kiss her on the cheek. He missed by a good two inches when Cade jerked his boot out from under her shoe and knocked her off balance. He then took hold of her arm, pulled her back into the room, and closed the door.

Zoe whirled around, jerking free of his grasp. "You're an insensitive *clod*. We may need Perry's help!"

"You may. *I* won't."

Tossing him a dirty look, she was about to reprimand him for his boorish behavior, but Doc mumbled something about being thirsty.

She poured the doctor a glass of water. "I'm going home in a few minutes. Do you have spare long johns?"

"What's wrong with the ones I've got on?"

She realized how her question had sounded. "We need to get the patients' clothes off. I'll boil them first thing in the morning. I have extra gowns for Bonnie and Ida, and I thought you might have clothing for the men."

"Sorry—I travel light."

"Then get the men's clothes off, and I'll bring sheets to wrap them in. Sheets will be easier to keep sterile."

"Do you want me to take off the women's clothes, too?"

"I'm sure you know how, but in this case I'll do it."

She turned and saw him grin. Tension

melted, and they laughed. The graveness of the situation eased, and for once she appreciated his sense of humor, however misplaced.

Gathering up dirty towels, she hated to admit that she liked having him around. "You dunderhead, you always could make me laugh."

"I probably should take offense at that, but I don't know what 'dunderhead' means. I take it, it isn't a term of endearment."

Doc moaned, regaining full consciousness. "Eh...I'm worse than I thought."

Zoe knelt beside him, sponging his feverish brow. "Did you bring any quinine with you?"

"There's a bottle in my bag."

She restrained him when he tried to rise. "I'll get it." She suspected they'd need more than a single bottle of quinine before this was over.

Chapter 10

Zoe was hanging clothes on the line Tuesday morning when Cade rounded the corner. She quickly looked away as he stripped off his shirt and began to wash up at the rain barrel. She tried to focus on her work, but her gaze kept straying in his direction.

"Who's watching the patients?" she asked.

"They're asleep. I thought I'd bring over the dirty sheets and get cleaned up."

She pinned a pair of overalls to the line, feigning indifference to his state of undress, yet she was anything but oblivious to him. Water ran off his chest, trickling through the mat of curly dark hair. Muscles flexed in his bare arms, and she saw the power of the man rather than the boy she'd made love to so long ago. He'd changed in so many ways that at times she wasn't sure she'd ever really known him. She thought she might never understand him, but her body responded to his raw masculinity.

When he caught her gawking, she felt her cheeks flush. Ducking behind a row of billowing sheets, she reminded herself she was thirty-six years old, not one of Winterborn's dewy-eyed schoolgirls hoping to win his attention. Susan and Judy annoyed her. They were shameful in their open pursuit of him. Were he to change his ways and decide to take a wife, he could marry either girl and have a mother for Addy's children in the time it took to say "which one?"

She held a clothespin with her teeth as she leaned over to pick up a wet towel. A twig snapped behind her. The moment she turned, two large hands grasped her around the waist, and she felt her feet leave the ground.

Squealing, she shoved against Cade. With a devilish grin, he laughed, letting her feet dangle in midair. Spitting out the clothespin, she whacked him on the back. "Put me down!"

He pulled her closer. "Widow Bradshaw, I'm ashamed of you. Don't you know it isn't polite to stare at men with their shirts off?"

She was as helpless as a rag doll in his arms. His power far overshadowed her own.

"Put me down, Cade," she repeated. "Brody and Will might see us."

He glanced toward the back of the house, where the boys were playing with the dog. "What if they do? Hasn't anyone told them about the birds and the bees?"

"No, and you are *not* to mention a word to them—do you understand?" She could imagine the version he'd give.

"My promises are conditional," he warned.

His eyes gleamed with a sensuous light that she knew meant trouble, judging by his feisty mood.

She gripped his hard, bare shoulders, trying to push away, but his arms were like corded steel. She struggled to keep her response impersonal. "I don't do anything on a conditional basis."

The smell of sunshine and drying laundry filled her senses as he lowered her until their faces were inches apart.

She turned her head, averting her eyes. "Let me go. I'm hot and sweaty."

Playfully, he pretended to drop her, and she panicked. Instinctively she fastened her arms around his neck.

"Stop it! You're going to drop me." He tightened his grip, seeming to enjoy her dilemma.

"A gentleman would never drop a lady...especially a lady who looks good enough to kiss." His hand slid around her neck. "I'm going to get my face slapped, but I'm going to kiss you."

Swallowing, she licked her lips. He pulled

her tighter against his bare belly, and his closeness unnerved her. "Don't do this, Cade," she pleaded, but her words fell on deaf ears. He brushed his lips across hers and kissed her cheek.

"You taste nice and salty."

She rested her hands on his shoulders, ignoring the suggestive tone of his voice. Her breathing was labored, and she felt helpless and vulnerable.

She stretched the length of her body until the tips of her toes barely touched the ground, and she was still unable to free herself. Specks of water were beaded on his shoulders, but she refrained from brushing them away. She'd forgotten how the feel of his bare skin ignited fires inside her, unquenchable blazes. The memory of the soft brush of chest hairs against her bare breasts taunted her.

His eyes softened, and she anticipated his kiss. She couldn't let it happen, no matter how much she wanted it. One kiss, and the madness would start all over again. But had it ever really ended? It could have been so very good between them, she thought. If he'd only come back—would she have lost their baby? Would it have made any difference if he'd known?

The feel of his body, as he let her torso slip down his, overwhelmed her. Their gazes locked as he released her. Now that she was free, she was reluctant to leave the warmth of his embrace.

Finally she looked away, smoothing her skirt. "Do you think you'll be home for supper?"

"Is that an invitation?"

"I've made an apple cobbler."

"How did you know that's my favorite?"

"I haven't forgotten anything." She kept herself from looking at him.

He crooked his forefinger under her chin and turned her face back to him. "I'll be here," he said in a soft voice. "Doc's better. He took a little of the broth Glori-Lee brought over."

Shrugging free, she said, "Glori-Lee's been wonderful. She and Gracie came by earlier and helped me boil clothing." She picked up a shirt and pinned it to the line. "No new cases during the night?"

"None that I know of. Do you have any idea what we're dealing with?"

"No. What's Doc say?"

"He said it could be influenza or a dozen other ailments."

She sighed as she hung another shirt to the line. "It's the waiting that drives you crazy."

Putting his hands on his hips, he scanned the long rows of wash. "Did all this come from the jail?"

"Not all of it. Some are the children's." She saw him mentally counting the skirts, petticoats, and feminine undergarments. "Well—I'm doing Mrs. Penscott a favor, too. She's down in her back with lumbago." She rolled her eyes heavenward, praying forgiveness for her fib.

"Daisy Penscott? Judge Penscott's widow? You'd think she had enough money to hire her wash done."

"You'd think, wouldn't you?" Wedging a clothespin between his lips, she murmured, "Here, make yourself useful. Hang up Will's long johns for me."

"Mr. Drake will see you now." Mary Beth Peters smiled as she ushered Zoe into the bank president's office later that afternoon.

Perry Drake might be president of the bank, but stout, middle-aged spinster Mary Beth Peters was his able secretary, without whom Zoe doubted Perry would have risen past bank teller. Mary Beth's jolly demeanor was always welcome.

"I was just sick to hear about the yard goods," Mary Beth said. "I had my heart set on a new dress. Are you going to reorder?"

Zoe didn't have the money to order a handkerchief, let alone bolts of fabric. "I haven't decided, Mary Beth."

As the women approached Perry's desk, he got up to shake hands. "Zoe, you've been on my mind. Were you able to get any rest?"

"Yes, Cade stayed at the jail last night."

"That's good."

Perry had kept himself fit and lean—not as muscular as Cade, but distinguished-looking.

Mary Beth excused herself and returned to her desk.

Sitting down, Perry smiled. "I'm glad you stopped by. Are the children with you?"

"Gracie took them home with her this morning. I'm on my way to the jail to relieve Cade."

"Has Cade decided to stay in town for good?"

"No." She saw relief flood his features.

"I asked because there's been talk—him staying at your place..."

"Talk, Perry? I'm surprised you listen to the gossips. The only reason he's staying at my place is because the roof blew off the jail. If it weren't for the fever, he'd be gone by now."

Perry leaned back in his chair, stroking his chin. "Has he found a home for the kids?"

"Not exactly. I'm hoping to keep them myself, even though Cade is dead-set against it." She saw the banker's brows lift. "He thinks I should marry and have my own children."

"He's right. Not many men would want to marry a woman saddled with four children."

Saddled? She stiffened. Since when did Perry view children as a burden?

The bank's big clock chimed the hour, sounding like the Liberty Bell in the awkward silence. Zoe pressed a handkerchief against her cheek, blotting perspiration brought on by the insufferable heat.

"I'd like to talk to you about increasing my loan," Zoe said.

"Again?" Perry ran his finger along the inside of his collar.

She leaned closer, aware that he was embarrassed by the subject. "A small amount— just enough to pay my bills this month. I've lost the yard goods, and I'll need to reorder."

Perry steepled his fingers, gazing at her.

"Would you consider a personal loan? I'm afraid the stockholders won't—without more security..."

She sympathized with his position. It wasn't easy to turn a friend away. The remorse in his eyes was sincere, but little consolation to her. "I wouldn't ask if it weren't absolutely necessary. I've gone over the books and there's no other way. I counted on a profit from those yard goods, and now I'm not only out the price of the order, but I'll have to purchase more."

Perry lowered his voice. "If it were up to me, I'd loan you anything you wanted. I know you're having a difficult time making ends meet, but my hands are tied without additional collateral."

Collateral. Zoe hated the word. She had mortgaged everything she owned, and still it wasn't enough. She fell farther behind every day. Sinking back in her chair, she picked at the corner of her handkerchief.

"If you won't accept my offer," Perry went on, "then perhaps another private party. Frank Lovell is always willing to make loans."

"I'd *never* ask Frank for money." She pictured the town skinflint, who was known for the exorbitant amount he charged. She was tired of him coming around and trying to attract her with his wealth. All the money in the world wouldn't make him appealing. He already owned most everything in Winterborn; let him be happy with that.

"I'd rather lose the store than go to Frank."

"Sell the store, Zoe. To someone."

She had stood to leave, but the seriousness in Perry's tone made her sit again.

"Your loyalty to Jim is admirable," Perry went on, "but you're in trouble because of his inability to handle business matters. Jim was too generous. I don't know anyone in town who went hungry while he was alive."

Zoe sighed. "That's part of my problem. I'm having a hard time saying no now when families counted on Jim for so long to see them through."

"Your problem is those four kids. Give them up, Zoe. You can't afford them."

Perry was a friend and confidant. She usually respected his advice, but not today. "I can't afford to give them up; they're a part of me. I can't imagine them living with strangers."

He got out of his chair, came around his desk, and laid a hand on her shoulder. "You get that silly notion out of your head. Cade will find the kids a good home, and you can get on with your life—maybe remarry. There's still plenty of time to have children."

No, there wasn't. Sadness washed over her. She could have all the time in the world, but there would never be children of her own. The miscarriage seventeen years ago had left her barren.

Her sadness was replaced by biting resentment. Cade owed her Addy's children! Addy had known Zoe couldn't have other children, so *why* hadn't she given them to her?

"The last thing you need is another mouth

to feed." Perry said, "You're working your-self to death taking in washing and ironing, running the store, and looking after Addy's kids. If you sold out to Frank, your worries would be over."

"All the money would go to pay off the bank note."

Perching on the corner of the desk, Perry studied her for a long moment. "I'm sorry. I wish there was something I could do. You know how fond I am of you. If you would con-sider me as a serious suitor—"

Vacating her chair, she moved to the window beside his desk. "Perry, please. You've been a good friend. Let's not spoil the relationship." She watched people go about their daily rou-tine and thought about his offer. No. She could never marry him.

"Is it Cade? Is that who you're waiting for? If so, you'll be an old woman by the time he settles down."

Perry's words interrupted her reverie. She laughed. "Cade? Don't be absurd. I'm not that foolish."

"That's good."

Perry rose to join her at the window. "Speak of the devil, there he is now." They watched as Cade passed by carrying a tray of food from Glori-Lee's.

"For a bounty hunter, he makes an admirable nurse," Perry mused. "How long does he plan to stay?"

"He hasn't said. Bonnie's coming down sick has postponed his departure."

"I hope he moves on soon. This town doesn't need the riffraff his type could bring in."

His words rankled. "I don't approve of his occupation either, but the children's welfare isn't something you can hurry. He has his faults, but he loved Addy and he'll do right by her kids." Her defense of Cade surprised Zoe as much as it did Perry, judging from the shocked look on his face. Cade wasn't an angel, but Perry had no right to judge him. "Addy loved him enough to trust his judgment."

Perry snapped the shade closed. "Addy was blind to his faults."

How could she justify Addy's intentions when she didn't understand them herself?

Sobering, Perry took her by the shoulders. "You know Jim wouldn't want you to be alone or unhappy. He loved you more than life itself."

Her brave front began to slip as he drew her to him and held her close. Leaning into the comfort of his shoulder, she closed her eyes. Somehow his embrace didn't offer what she was looking for. She stepped back, trying to regain her composure. "I'm needed at the jail."

"Wait a minute." Perry returned to his desk and pulled a ledger from the top drawer. "I insist on writing you a personal draft sufficient to see you through the next few months."

Her hand flew to cover his. "I won't hear of it."

"Be reasonable. Your options have run out.

What other choice do you have, if you're intent on keeping the store?"

"I will not impose on my friends for financial help."

She turned around and walked out of the office. She might be broke, but she still had her pride. Not even financial ruin could take that away from her.

"Stand back, Herschel, you cain't come in here!"

Herschel Mallard tried to push past Sawyer, but the old man blocked his way. Zoe, kneeling next to Bonnie, watched as Cade walked over and broke up the tussle. "What do you need, Herschel?"

"One of my bulls is missing."

Cade grinned. "Maybe he's out socializing with the women."

"Ain't no time to be funny, Kolby. That bull cost me a pretty penny. Where's Pop?"

Sawyer butted in. "Pop's laid up with a broken leg."

"Who's takin' care of sheriffin'?" Herschel peered between the two men standing in the doorway. "What's going on here? Is that Doc layin' there?"

Doc raised his head, moaning. "Go away, Herschel. We all got the fever."

Herschel abruptly stepped back. "The fever!"

"And shut the door, Herschel!" Doc called. "That blasted light's blinding me."

Cade glanced at Zoe. "Can you handle

things here while I help Herschel find his bull?"

Zoe nodded and continued to wipe Bonnie's brow.

Cade rode with Herschel to the Mallard farm west of town. The one-room shanty was located on a rocky hillside.

Checking the fencerow, Herschel trailing behind him, Cade found the trouble toward the back end of the pasture.

Herschel swore a blue streak as he viewed the cut wire. "Rustlers."

"Most likely. Has anyone else had trouble lately?"

"Clyde Abbott's brother, Saul, lost some steers a few weeks back. Pop never found them."

Cade stood up, dusting off his knees. "I'll take a look around, but I imagine they're long gone."

Toward dark, Cade rode to Saul Abbott's farm and knocked on the front door. The smell of meat frying drifted from the open window, and his stomach rumbled. It had been hours since breakfast. A young girl a few years older than Holly opened the door. The child was barefoot, her dress faded and threadbare.

"Are your folks home?"

The girl nodded. "They're layin' down, feelin' poorly."

A man appeared in the background, hitching his suspenders over his shoulders. A heavy growth of reddish beard covered his face.

The man squinted, holding up a hand to shade his eyes. "Is that you, Kolby? Heard you was back."

"Hello, Saul. Didn't recognize you for a second. Are you sick?"

"Me and the missus got somethin' bad. I cain't even look at the light without my head feeling like it's gonna explode."

"Herschel said you had some cattle missing."

"Did you find them?"

"No. In fact, one of Herschel's bulls is gone."

"Those no-goods. Sure would like to get my hands on who's doing it."

The little girl pulled on her daddy's sleeve. "I'm cookin' side meat, Pa. Can we invite Mr. Kolby to stay?"

"'Fraid he can have it all, Sis. Your momma and I don't feel much like eatin'."

"How many in your family, Saul?" Saul was around his age, so he could have a whole houseful of kids by now.

"Got three young'uns—two boys and Sis, here. Then me and the missus, 'course."

"Anybody else sick?"

"Not so far." Saul sank into the nearest chair and held his head.

"I think you and Mrs. Abbott should come with me. We have several cases of the fever down at the jail. One of them is Doc."

"I'd argue if I had the strength, but I think maybe you're right. The missus is real bad. Don't want the young'uns gettin' this." Turning to his daughter, he said, "Sis, you go to the barn and get your brothers. You'll have

171

to see after things until me and your ma get back."

Around bedtime, Cade pulled the Abbotts' wagon to a halt in front of the jail. Saul and his wife were lying in the back. Cade helped Mrs. Abbott out as Zoe stepped outside.

"Oh, dear, more?"

Cade nodded. "Two more."

Zoe helped him get Belle Abbott up the steps and into the jail. "I was getting worried," Zoe told Cade. "The children had to take supper with Gracie since you weren't back."

"Don't start on me—I'm tired."

"You've got to take some responsibility for the kids..."

"I'm taking responsibility, and I'll see they're taken care of properly."

"It doesn't have to be *all* your responsibility. If you'd listen to reason—"

Sawyer spat. "Here we go again. Same old tune. 'I want the kids; you can't have 'em.'"

"Look at the situation realistically, Zoe. I've got two more sick people. Stop harping and help me with Belle."

"Harping!"

"Harping," Sawyer confirmed before he spat again.

With a sigh, she returned to the wagon for Saul. "You, too, Saul? I heard that your brother, Clyde, and his boy took to their beds yesterday."

"Haven't seen Clyde since the dance a couple Saturdays ago."

Zoe made room for the two newest patients. Pallets were scooted over, the men's in the cell, the women's in the office. The small building was filled nearly wall to wall.

Doc lifted his head off the pillow. "This is getting out of hand. We're going to have to quarantine the town."

"I think you're right." Zoe wrung out a sponge. "Twenty-four hours, and there have been eight cases that we know of. We have to do something." She turned to Cade. "Frank Lovell rode to Chesterfield today for more quinine. Even paid for it."

"Frank Lovell? The town skinflint turned humanitarian? Hard to believe," Cade said. "Sawyer, we're going to need you to stand guard at the north end of town. I'll get one of the Pointer boys to watch the south. Put up a quarantine notice, and don't let anyone through."

Sawyer nodded. "You'll have to write out the sign. Never learned my letterin'."

Zoe pulled two Wanted posters out of Pop's desk drawer. On their backs, in bold letters, she wrote, "Quarantined. Stay Out."

By the time the moon came up, the town of Winterborn was closed to all outsiders.

"I wonder why none of the children have gotten sick," Zoe said, then took a sip of coffee, leaning against the outside wall of the jail. She closed her eyes. "So far, only adults have been afflicted with the fever. Clyde Abbott's son was the youngest, and he was twenty-one."

"You should be with the kids," Cade said. "There's plenty of help here. Glori-Lee is furnishing the meals. Edna brought over her soap this morning and checks in every few hours." His gaze went to the open doorway. "And Woodall is a pain in the neck."

"He's only being helpful."

Cade smiled. "When I was a kid I thought he was strange, always checking his watch. But look at him. He's standing out front, keeping track of when I need to give the next dose of quinine."

She saw his eyes grow distant and wondered if he was thinking about his life on the trail. Having few friends to come to his aid, and even fewer to care about him—what must that feel like? During her own troubles, she had always had Addy and Gracie. And the townspeople. They were beside her through thick and thin. "Do you ever miss Winterborn?" she asked.

"At times."

"But not enough to come back for good."

He tasted his coffee, and Zoe realized he was ignoring her remark.

"I also used to hate the smell of Edna's fancy soap," he said, "but it's a relief from the fever stench."

She was only half listening. Her body was sore from leaning over. No new cases of fever had been reported during the night. The patients were stable. Bonnie's nose wasn't running as badly, and her sneezing had almost stopped. Except for the slight rash Zoe had noticed while bathing her this morning, she seemed to be rallying. Zoe wanted to think the worst was over, but her life was in a shambles. Because of the quarantine, no one from the outside could get in to shop at the store. The town trade alone wouldn't pay her bills. The bank wouldn't loan her any additional money, and she couldn't take in one more basket of washing and ironing, and still help out at the jail.

She opened her eyes, studying the man beside her. Did Cade sense her frustration? He sat calmly drinking coffee, making mundane conversation. He refused to let her have the children, yet circumstances prevented him from looking for a foster home.

Laying her hand on his arm, she lowered her voice to a whisper since Woodall was within earshot. "Thank you for helping out the way you have. I don't know how I'd have managed without you. I know you didn't expect to stay in town this long."

"I can't go anywhere until I find a place for the kids."

Of course, she reminded herself. He certainly wasn't staying around for *her* sake. "You have a place; you just won't recognize it." She wasn't whispering anymore.

"You're not raising the kids alone."

She stood up and slapped her hands on her hips. "You are the most stubborn human being God ever put on this earth!"

"Sit down, Red. You're causing a scene." His calmness enraged her.

"Hey—you two!" Woodall hollered from across the street. "We've heard this before!" He tapped his watch, pointing to the time. "Quinine!"

Chapter 11

"Get out of my way, old man!" Laticia Wiseman snapped her whip over Sawyer's head.

"Who you callin' old? Why, you're older than dirt yourself." Sawyer grabbed the horse's collar and attempted to turn the rig around. "Cain't come in here." He pointed at the quarantine sign. "Cain't you read?"

Laticia sniffed and looked down her nose at him. "Obviously *you* can't. The sign's upside down, you fool."

Sawyer frowned and turned to stare at the sign tacked to the fence post. He turned back. "There's fever in there. Go home where you come from."

Raising her whip over her head, she warned him again, "Step aside! I've never been sick a day in my life!"

"Don't doubt it," Sawyer grumbled. "Fever'd run fast from the likes of you."

Laticia handed the whip to her driver. "Lash him, Abraham."

Abraham's eyes grew as round as moons. "Oooh now, Miz Laticia, I don' think we ort do that."

"Give me that!" she insisted, grabbing the whip back from Abraham as Sawyer covered his head with his arms. Giving the horse a smart lash to the rump, she set the buggy in motion. The sudden lurch knocked Sawyer aside, throwing him into the ditch. A back wheel caught the quarantine sign and dragged it down the road.

Scrambling to his feet, Sawyer yelled after the departing buggy, "I said you *cain't* go in there!"

Zoe was walking up the street to the jail when the carriage came whipping into town. Jumping out of the way, she gasped when she recognized the children's great-aunt, Laticia.

"Miss Wiseman!" She caught up and ran alongside the buggy. "You're not supposed to be here. We're quarantined!"

"Balderdash! I'll go where I please!"

The elderly black driver tipped his hat to Zoe as the buggy rolled to a stop in front of the general store. Grinning, Abraham set the brake. "How'do, Miz Bradshaw."

Zoe was certain her jaw dropped to the ground. Laticia sat straight as a board in the buggy seat, dressed as if she'd come for a funeral. Her plumed black hat was cocked to one side, and a stiffly starched collar, as black as a raven's wing, encased her long neck like a vise. Black bodice, black skirt, black shoes, black gloves, and a black cane with an ivory head completed her depressing attire. The kids were right to hide from her. Zoe'd forgotten how scary she was.

Laticia glared down her long nose, and Zoe's mind raced with the implications of the unexpected visit. Since Laticia hadn't come for John and Addy's funeral, it was odd that she'd show up now.

"Miss Wiseman, there's fever here. You have to leave now—your well-being is in jeopardy."

"Nonsense. Abraham! Help me off this seat!"

Abraham jumped out of the buggy and extended his arm to the elderly matron. "Now you be careful, Miz Laticia. It's a mite steep getting down."

"Humph. I'm perfectly capable of getting out of a carriage."

As her foot touched the ground, she balanced her weight with the heavy cane, dismissing Abraham with a sharp nod. "Go on over to the livery and wait for me. I have business with Mrs. Bradshaw."

"Yes'm." Abraham shuffled off to the livery as Laticia turned to Zoe.

She felt herself shrinking under Laticia's scrutiny. The woman had eyes like a vulture's and the children were right: she smelled funny, as if her clothes had been stored in a dank wardrobe. "Is there something I can do for you, Miss Wiseman?"

"I came for the children."

Zoe's head snapped up. "What?"

"My nephew John's children. Where are they?"

"They're playing in the back of the store—"

"Get their belongings packed; they're

178

coming with me." The old woman dabbed a handkerchief along her jaw. "Get me a cool drink while you're about it."

Zoe struggled to grasp the meaning of her declaration. She was here for the children? She wanted to take them home with her? Surely she wasn't serious.

"You want them to come for a visit?"

Moving the handkerchief to her upper lip, the old woman frowned. "News of my nephew's death reached me only this morning."

"I'm sorry—I sent word."

The woman raised her cane. "I don't fault you. I've been away visiting acquaintances in Wichita, but I'm back now. I will see to the children."

"That's absurd! Their Uncle Cade is here to see to them."

"Piddytash." Laticia glared. "What does that—that bounty hunter know about children?"

The loathing in her tone made Zoe's skin crawl. What did Laticia know about Cade? Nothing, she'd wager. Drawing herself up straighter, she prepared herself for battle. "Nevertheless, Addy and John left the decision of who would raise the children up to him."

Laticia dismissed the idea with a wave of her cane. "My nephew obviously wasn't thinking rationally before his death. Had he been, he would have left the children in my care." She banged the tip of her cane on the hard-packed dirt road. "Now, off with you! Bring me my greatnieces and nephews! Abraham doesn't like to be out after dark."

"But Miss Wiseman—"

"No buts! Bring those children to me!"

Zoe's cheeks warmed when she realized Laticia's strident words were attracting a crowd. She saw Cade crossing the street toward them and was relieved, but she doubted even he was prepared for Laticia. She held her breath as she watched the elderly lady's demeanor stiffen as he approached.

"Cade Kolby. The prodigal son returns," Laticia scoffed.

Cade glanced at Zoe, and she shrugged. She didn't know what to say. All she could do was hope Cade could intimidate the grouchy old matriach. "Miss Wiseman," Cade began, "are you aware that the town is—"

"Do I look addled? I *know* the town is quarantined. I'll leave as soon as you bring the children. Now do it!"

Cade frowned. "What children?

"John's children."

"*Addy's* children are staying right here."

Laticia whacked the post above his head. "Don't be impertinent with me, young man."

Zoe turned to locate the sudden sound of loud cursing. Sawyer hobbled into town, dragging the quarantine sign with him. "Crazy old woman. Knocked the fence down, drug it halfway to town!"

Zoe lifted her hands, calling a halt to the fiasco. "Everyone calm down. Miss Wiseman, come inside, and we'll discuss the matter over a glass of lemonade."

"Stop wasting my time, young lady. Get the children."

"The kids aren't going anywhere." Cade stepped up on the porch, dodging the old woman's flailing cane as he took her arm and ushered her inside the store. Zoe followed, and the screen door banged shut behind them.

Brody and Will spotted the old woman, jumped to their feet, and bolted toward the back door, screaming.

Zoe blocked their path. "Stop right there!"

"It's her!" Brody shouted, trying to squirm around Zoe.

"It's the old witch!" Will screamed.

Kneeling, Zoe gathered the boys to her, attempting to calm their fears. "Your father's aunt isn't here to harm you." Zoe had never approved of the way John had tormented his children with the picture of Laticia. When they misbehaved, John had pointed to the stern authoritarian, with her angular face, pointy nose, and close-set eyes, warning that he would send the children to his aunt as punishment for their misconduct.

Addy had always gently reminded her husband that Laticia was family and shouldn't be used as a threat, but John's method of discipline, if not exactly fair, had proved infinitely more effective than a hickory switch. The children regarded their great-aunt as Lucifer—a very unpleasant, musty-smelling evil—and Zoe could see why.

"Boys, say hello to your Great-Aunt Laticia," Zoe prodded. Their mouths fell open, but no sound came out. "Girls," she called. No answer. "Girls! Are you in here?"

Zoe guided the boys to chairs at the table. "Sit here while I find your sisters." She poured a glass of lemonade for Laticia. "Please sit down, Miss Wiseman. I'm sure you'd like a rest after your trip."

"I'm not here to socialize." The elderly matron wrapped her gnarled fingers around the glass and took a long, noisy gulp. Her lips curled, and Zoe cringed.

"Not enough sugar. Nobody knows how to make lemonade anymore."

"Sit down, Laticia." Cade pulled out a chair for her. "What is this about the children going with you?"

"Miss Wiseman, to you." She squinted her eyes at him. "You were always underfoot when you were young, and you haven't changed one bit. Never could figure out how you and Addy were kin. *She* seemed rather level-headed."

Zoe heard Cade swear under his breath as he poured lemonade for the boys. She cleared her throat. "Do you know where the girls are, Cade?"

"I haven't seen them. I've been trying to talk Doc out of going home."

"Doc went home?"

"He said he'd feel better there. Said he was worried about his dogs."

Zoe shook her head, scooped up a stack of clean towels from the kitchen counter, and walked into the bedroom to put them away. She needed a moment alone. Her gaze centered on a huge lump in her bedspread. Butch! That dog had gotten into her bed again. She set the towels on a shelf and yanked back the spread, ready to chastise the family pet.

Holly and Missy, heads down, huddled together in the middle of the bed. "What are you doing under there?" Zoe whispered. "Aunt Laticia is here to see you."

The girls grabbed her around the waist and clung tight. "No, Zoe. Tell her we're sick," Holly pleaded.

"Tell hew we wan away," Missy cried.

She gathered the girls to her. "Girls, there is nothing to be afraid of. She loves you. She's just—she's just..."

"Smelly?" Holly said.

"I was going to say 'different.' She's different." She *was* smelly, too, but Zoe couldn't encourage that line of thought.

She returned to the kitchen with the girls in tow to find Laticia and Cade embroiled in a heated debate. Seating Holly and Missy beside their stone-faced brothers, she turned to Laticia. "More lemonade, Miss Wiseman?"

The woman handed Zoe her empty glass. "The children should be with family. The Brightons may be fine people, but they're not family."

"There is another alternative," Zoe offered, glancing at Cade as she poured. "One that I wish you would seriously consider."

"And what might that be?" Laticia's hostile look gave Zoe chills.

"Let me have them."

"Humph! Haven't you been listening? I said *family* should have them. You're not family." Laticia's stare intensified. "You need to get yourself another husband and have your own babies."

Zoe refused to look at Cade. She didn't want to see that "keep quiet" look on his face. She was sick of everyone telling her to have her own babies. Didn't they know that if she could, she would have had a dozen by now? No, they didn't know. No one knew.

"You're absolutely right, Laticia," Cade said. "The kids should be with family. I'm family, and I will keep them."

Zoe lifted her brows.

Cade squared his shoulders and crossed his arms over his chest. "Until things settle down here."

"And then what?" the old woman demanded.

"That's my problem. There's no reason for you to stay in town. Have Abraham take you home."

Laticia's cane came down with a loud thud against the floor. All four children jumped a good foot off their seats.

"I'll stay in this town as long as I want, young man. It'll take more than the likes of you to make me leave." She whirled to look at the children, giving each one a good once-over. "You, there." She pointed to Holly. "Come here and give your aunt a kiss."

Laticia tapped an arthritic finger against her cheek, and Zoe nodded for Holly to comply. The girl slowly got up from her chair and walked stiff-legged toward the old woman. She stayed as far away as she could while still bending to reach her aunt's cheek. Zoe felt sick. Holly's face was twisted up like a corkscrew, as were the other children's while they watched.

Coming to their rescue, Zoe suggested, "Children, why don't you take a glass of lemonade over to the livery for Abraham? He's probably very thirsty by now."

"Yeah!" Brody yelled, jumping up from the table. "Mighty thirsty!"

The other three scrambled to see who could get out the door the fastest while Brody quickly grabbed up the pitcher of lemonade.

"Don't stay too long." Zoe noted that they paid little attention to her instruction. She turned back to Laticia. It was apparent that she didn't plan on leaving without the children. "Perhaps I can make arrangements with Gracie Willis for you to stay the night in her guest room."

"Gracie who?" Laticia snapped.

"The mayor's wife," Zoe said, watching Laticia's face scrunch up.

"Oh, yes. Gracie. The mayor's wife." The spinster ran pointed fingernails through the sides of her gray hair, then patted it into place. "Yes, I believe I could be comfortable at the mayor's house."

"Well, then. I'll run over and let Gracie know to expect you—shortly." Zoe put her hand on Cade's shoulder for strength. "Would you mind taking Miss Wiseman's things to Gracie's?"

Before he could protest, Laticia butted in. "Don't have 'things.' Don't need 'things.' I got what I have on. I don't plan on doing anything to get dirty."

185

Zoe squelched a fleeting thought. She would love to catch Laticia out of those clothes so she could launder them. Laundry. Heavens! She had all those sheets from the patients to wash tonight!

"Gracie, I'm sorry to ask, but I don't have any room for her to stay with me."

"It's no trouble, dear. One night with Laticia Wiseman won't kill us." Gracie laughed as she set out the coffee service.

"I'm not so sure. She's pretty domineering."

"You left Cade alone with her?"

"Serves him right." Zoe grinned. "Maybe she'll put the fear of God in him."

Gracie laughed again, and Zoe joined her. "What else could happen, Gracie? From the minute Cade got here, it's been one disaster after another. I'm barely keeping up with the laundry. Thank heavens you and Glori-Lee are feeding the sick. I don't know if I'd have the time—or the food, for that matter. I've run out of produce, but it doesn't make much difference. No one's buying anything." She leaned back in her chair. "Oh, Gracie, what am I going to do? If Miss Wiseman takes those kids, I won't be able to bear it. They're scared to death of her."

Gracie frowned. "I never approved of John's shenanigans. It wasn't right of him to frighten those kids like that."

Zoe sighed, reaching for the creamer. "I'm glad Addy didn't have to witness this. Do you realize Laticia is the children's only relative, other than Cade? If anything were to happen to him—" She couldn't finish the thought. It was too disturbing.

"How'd she get past the quarantine?"

"She made Abraham drive right through. Sawyer said they tried to run him down." Zoe studied her cup. "Of course, the next time Sawyer tells it, he'll say they would have run him down and *killed* him."

Gracie laid her head back and laughed heartily. "I'll bet Sawyer was fit to be tied." Her laughter dwindled to a smile. "Abraham. Is that old black driver of Laticia's still alive? I thought about him just the other day. Wondered what that old woman would do without him."

Zoe took a sip from her cup. "He takes good care of her. I never understood how he stays so pleasant and soft-spoken. Over the years, when Laticia visited John and Addy, Abraham has always been a gracious old gentleman.

"Do you know," Zoe continued, "Laticia's daddy gave Abraham to her when she was just a girl? Even with slaves being free and all, Abraham went right on waiting on those folks like they were his own family."

Gracie chuckled.

"Laticia is fortunate to have him," Zoe went on, "but neither one should be raising children at their ages."

"I'll tell you something," said Gracie. "Abraham is wiser than anyone gives him credit for. If you stop and think, he's the only one who knows how to keep 'Miz Laticia' in line."

Zoe raised one brow. "How do you mean?"

"Ever hear him say, 'Now, Miz Laticia, we ort not do that,' or 'We ort not think that way'?"

Zoe nodded.

"Ever see Laticia do what she said she would after Abraham warned her not to?"

Zoe shook her head.

Gracie slapped her thighs with both hands. "I should say not. He's the only one who knows how to handle her."

"Hmmm." Zoe bit into another cookie. "Maybe I'll have a little talk with Abraham. Perhaps he can make Laticia see how foolish it would be for her to take the children. Her health won't hold out forever. If she were to get sick, Abraham couldn't take care of all of them."

Gracie patted Zoe's hand. "The way to Laticia is through Abraham. Yes, I'd say a talk *is* in order. And soon."

Zoe said her good-byes and thanked Gracie for letting Laticia stay the night. She cringed when she caught sight of Lawrence's expression and realized he wasn't happy about his cranky houseguest. He disappeared into the parlor with a book and large decanter of cherry brandy.

On her way back to the store, Zoe stopped by the livery to pick up the children and have a brief chat with Abraham.

"Oh, Miz Bradshaw, I don' think Miz Laticia would pay me no mind should I say somethin' about those young'uns. She pretty well set her hat for 'em. Said we need somethin' to look after—fill in the time o' day."

Zoe covered the black man's hand with hers. "Abraham, a woman her age has no business raising four young children. What Laticia needs is a pet—maybe a pretty cat."

Abraham crowed. "Now, that would be a mite easier on me, Miz Bradshaw. A nice quiet cat." His gaze roamed the stable. "Saw one here a minute ago. Right friendly. Black. Reminded me of Miz Laticia."

Zoe hugged the old man affectionately, taking solace in his soft, chocolate-colored eyes. "You're a good man, Abraham."

"Yes'm. You go on home now—don't be frettin' no mo'."

Zoe looked around the rustic stable. "I wish there was a better place for you to sleep."

"I be jist fine, Miz Bradshaw. Jist fine."

After supper, Zoe ironed for an hour, then wandered onto the back porch for a breath of fresh air. It was the first moment she could call her own since early dawn. She held a glass of water to her neck and savored the coolness against her flushed skin. She was just wondering how Cade was doing with the patients when he rounded the building.

She sucked in her breath. His mere presence made her wobbly-kneed, and she quickly sat down before she fell down.

"What are you doing over here?" she asked. She could see his tired features in the moonlight.

"I got the night off. Seth is staying at the jail."

Patting the step beside her, she motioned for him to sit. The past few days had been no picnic for him, either. What must he be thinking? Was he counting the hours until he could ride off, leaving behind a responsibility that was foreign to him?

Sinking to the wooden step, he took off his hat, then leaned back, his eyes sliding over her with easy familiarity. "You get prettier every day. Anyone ever tell you that?"

"Only men who are in sore need of spectacles."

Resting back on his forearms, he gazed up at the star-studded sky. "You're supposed to say, 'Why, thank you, sir, how you do go on.'"

She made a face. "Do you ever have a serious thought?"

"Not often. At least, not until lately."

Tree frogs sang near the livery pond. Moonlight filtered through the branches of the old oak standing in the backyard.

"Do you ever wonder what it would be like to live a normal life, Cade?"

"I wonder—occasionally." Sitting up, he ran his fingers through his hair. "Don't change the subject. You're a beautiful woman. Take the compliment or leave it."

"Put in such romantic terms, how can I refuse?" Her dress was water-stained, her flyaway hair a disgrace. She hadn't had time to look in the mirror for—what? Days? She must be a ravishing sight indeed. But then, he'd always thought her pretty. That was still nice to know.

"Have you eaten?" she asked.

"Glori-Lee brought extra food to the jail tonight. I skipped the peach pie and cream."

"Kids weaned you from that, huh?" She shivered. Once the sun went down, it cooled quickly.

Slipping to the step above her, Cade gathered Zoe close. Shifting slightly, she sought to escape, but he held her firmly. After awhile, she stopped struggling. There had been a time when she'd considered his intimate gestures as natural as drawing the next breath.

"Cold?" he asked.

No, she thought, shaking her head. Anything but cold. Comfortable, yes. Far too comfortable for a woman determined to keep her distance.

Leaning closer, he sniffed her hair. His breath, warm against her cheek, sent shivers up her spine.

"How do you always manage to smell so good?" he asked. "Like lemon and French soap."

"And what would you know about French soap?"

He nuzzled her neck. "I know that I like the smell."

"Cade, please." She tried to move away, but he refused to let her.

"You smell nothing like Laticia. What is that stench on her?"

Zoe giggled. "She's always smelled like that."

"I know, but what is it?"

"Mothballs, maybe? Who would have the nerve to ask?"

His fingers found her funnybone and tickled it.

Squirming, she giggled, hating herself. *Stop it, Zoe! Get up and go inside. It's insane to sit here, letting him tickle you and responding like a smitten fool!*

She twisted away, distancing herself from his searching hands. He smiled, clearly flirting with her.

"If you're not cold, I could use some warming up."

Zoe sucked in a long breath, then relaxed as he scooted closer and drew her back to him. It was insane, but she couldn't say she didn't like it. If nothing else, they'd shared young love and almost a child. She sighed regretfully. They were friends now, and she'd have to settle for that. She didn't have to make anything personal out of it. Laying her head back against his shoulder, she looked at the stars.

"Admit it," she said. "You're getting attached to the children."

"I've never said I wasn't."

It was true. He might not openly express his affection, but his eyes gave him away. Each time Missy or Holly climbed into his lap, he was theirs for the taking.

"They adore you, you know."

"They're good kids."

I adored you, once. So much so, I thought I would die when you didn't come back. She blinked back tears, reminding herself the past was the past. Painful though it was, the time had come to bury it. "How are things at the jail tonight?"

"No new cases in twenty-four hours. Since Doc left, there's a little more stepping room."

"The sickness is peculiar. Addy and John were as sick as the others, but they continued to get sicker. Bruce's and Ida's fevers are down. They're eating a little, and except for a rash on their faces, they've stopped complaining."

He rubbed his hands briskly up and down, warming her arms. "I think it's Edna's soap."

"Why?"

"Bonnie swears it's giving her a rash, too."

His fingers eased to her shoulders, massaging them. Her bones turned to liquid as he gently worked the tension out of her neck.

"You're tight. Relax, Red."

His low, suggestive baritone aroused feelings she had considered long-dormant. She and Jim had had a satisfactory marriage bed. She hadn't thought she missed a man's touch so much until now.

"You work too hard."

Sensitive understanding mixed with just the right amount of pity: the combination was deadly. Did he know what he was doing? How easy it would be to fall prey to his tenderness. His fingers worked magic through her weary muscles. Every bone in her body hurt. She'd like nothing better than to lean into his calm assurance and stay there for the rest of her life.

He lifted the small chain around her neck. "Is this the locket I gave you?"

She pushed his hand away. "I wear it out of habit."

His mouth brushed her ear. "I could buy you one made of real gold."

"I like this one. You gave this to me the night you left."

"And you've kept it all these years?"

"I keep a lot of things, Cade. Don't read anything into it." Changing the subject, she murmured, "I'm sorry you've had to stay so long."

"Don't be. I'm not. I like being an uncle to the kids. Too bad it took Addy's death for me to see that."

She almost felt sorry for him—maybe because she was tired and weak, needing his comfort and support more than she wanted to admit. He'd been thrust headfirst into a chaotic situation: losing his sister, gaining four children, and becoming a nurse and surrogate sherriff, all in a matter of days. He was holding up well, considering. "I wouldn't blame you if you walked out and never came back."

"I did that once and regretted it."

Smiling, she sighed. She was bone-tired. She'd close her eyes for just a moment; then she'd feel better. His touch was heavenly. As he stroked and kneaded the tension out of her body, things didn't seem nearly as bad as they had an hour ago. The patients were improving, she had only a half bushel of ironing left, and tomorrow—well, tomorrow was a new day....

She drifted off to sleep against his chest, unaware that he picked her up and carried her into the house a few moments later.

Chapter 12

When Cade opened the door to the jail the next morning, Zoe was bent over Bonnie, adjusting her pillow. The purpose of his visit deserted him as his gaze focused on her slim, shapely bottom.

The unexplained need to make love to her was so powerful he could taste it. Holding her in his arms last night had been a difficult act of self-control. How could he tell her he wanted her in his bed?

Cade cleared his throat, hoping to clear his mind as well. "Why didn't you wake me?"

She tucked a strand of hair behind her ear. "You were sleeping so soundly, I didn't want to disturb you."

He glanced toward the patients. "Any change?"

"They all ate a good breakfast."

"Are *you* okay?" he asked, knowing very well she wasn't.

"I'm fine. What about you?"

He grinned. "I've seen better days."

Zoe sighed. "I hope Gracie keeps Laticia occupied for a few hours."

"Laticia's bluffing. She's not going to take the children."

"You can't be sure of that."

"She won't. She may be a blood relative, but no one in his right mind would give her custody of four small children."

Zoe looked away, grousing under her breath. "This could all be taken care of by nightfall.

If you'd agree to let me have them, Richard Moyer could have adoption papers drawn up in a matter of hours."

"Who's Richard Moyer?"

"Town attorney. He could settle this matter if you'd only be reasonable."

"You forget, Mrs. Bradshaw—'reasonable' isn't my strong suit."

"The longer Laticia stays, the more upset the children will be."

"They're bright kids. They know I'm not going to leave them where they won't be happy."

"How could they possibly know that?" Her eyes reminded him of his past record.

"Because I told them." He softened his tone to reassure her. "I haven't broken a promise yet, have I?"

Sawyer stopped Cade as he started across the street.

"Hey, hold up there, Kolby!"

Cade turned, wondering if the watchdog ever slept. "Need something?"

The old man approached, his jaw bulging with his chew. Spitting, he took off his hat and squared his shoulders. Thin strands of grayish hair poked out around his head in various directions.

"I want a badge." The old man twisted his hat in his blue-veined hands. Age spots dotted the weathered skin.

"What kind of a badge?"

"One that'll give me some authority. If

I'm supposed to keep people outta here, I got to have some respect. Did you see how that old crone Wiseman treated me yesterday?"

"Laticia Wiseman isn't known for her manners."

"It don't matter! She cain't knock me in a ditch and tear down my quarantine sign and not pay the piper!"

"And you think a badge would lend you credibility?"

Sawyer nodded. "Yeah, yeah. That's what we want—some of that credible stuff. Somebody's got to keep the law! The law's the law! No dang female is above it!"

"All right. Stop by the store later and I'll make you a deputy badge."

The old man's face beamed in a tobacco-stained grin. He nodded, his hair waving. "Thank ya."

A gnat flitted overhead as Cade tipped his chair back, propped his boots on the kitchen table, and laid the stack of Wanted posters on his chest. A thick ham sandwich and Zoe's bread-and-butter pickles rested peacefully in his stomach.

Clasping his hands behind his neck, he listened to Missy playing with her dolls at the front of the store. A smile touched the corners of his mouth when he heard her say, "Dolly, you sit here, and Bud, you sit here."

As long as she kept the damn tarantula in its jar, he wasn't going to complain.

Stretching, he yawned, flexing his fingers

above his head. With the other kids at the livery with Abraham, the house was unusually quiet. It gave him time to think.

McGill would soon tire of his idle time and come looking for him. The longer he pushed his luck, the more he was putting the kids in danger. Now this damn Laticia business—what was he going to do about her? Bonnie wasn't out of the woods by a long shot. Should he forget the Brightons and talk to that Amish couple near Saline, the ones Pop had heard about? McGill would never find them there.

Was that the bell over the door? He sat up, listening as the tinkling drifted to him. No, Missy was playing with some sort of toy.

Since the outbreak of fever, Zoe's business was down to nothing. Edna had stopped by earlier for ten cents worth of brown sugar; thirty minutes had passed before he could get loose from her. Then Pop had dropped by to announce that, due to the illness, he was canceling Saturday night's dance until further notice. Cade smiled. *Too bad, Drake. Guess you won't get to dance with Zoe after all.*

Patting his stomach, he lay back again, closing his eyes. Seconds later, his soft snores filled the small kitchen.

"You're going to weally like Uncle Cwade, Bud. He didn't mean to scawe you the othew mowning," Missy whispered through the holes in the jar lid as she walked into the kitchen. "He said he would play with me *any* time I want."

She gave the jar a shake. "Awe you awake,

Bud?" Peering through the glass, she sighed. "Hope you'we not getting that fevew. Zoe will have to stick that old twinine down youw fwoat." She adjusted the basket of doll dishes and cookies over her arm. "You got a fwoat, Bud?"

As she passed Cade's chair, she paused. "Ooooh, Uncle Cwade is sleeping." She quietly set the basket on the table, standing and staring at her uncle for a long moment.

Shrugging her shoulders, she unscrewed the lid, carefully lifted Bud from his bed, and placed him on Cade's chest. "You stay thewe, Bud, while I get things weady for ouw tea pawty."

She busied herself preparing the table. She spread a napkin down to serve as a tablecloth, then arranged three tiny cups and saucers around the edge. A stack of ginger cookies completed the tea service before she stepped back to admire her work. Nudging Cade's knee, she whispered, "Uncle Cwade?"

Cade stirred. "Hmmm?"

Missy tiptoed closer and patted his cheek. "Wake up, Uncle Cwade. It's time for ouw tea pawty."

"Mumphm." Cade brushed the air, smacking his lips.

"Uncle Caaade. Wake uuuup."

Cade opened one eye and smiled when he saw the intruder.

Missy smiled, waving.

Cade's gaze slid down, and his eyes widened at the sight of Bud sitting in the middle of his chest. The tarantula's hairy front legs flexed as if he wanted to grab Cade. How come every time he woke up, that damn spider was on his chest! He stared, deciding they'd both be fine if Bud stayed put.

Then Bud started creeping toward his face. Whoa, Nelly! Cade jerked his feet off the table, the sudden movement causing the legs of the chair to fly out from under him. He hit the floor with a jarring crash, sure his back was broken.

Bud scurried across the floor and disappeared around the corner.

Missy stomped her foot. "Uncle Cwade! You'we *scawing* Bud again."

"Missy, you're going to have to keep that damn thing in its jar!" Cade swiped at his chest, shuddering. Seventeen years on the trail, and he'd never once woken up to a sight like that!

Putting her hands on her hips, Missy regarded him sternly. "Zoe's gonna be awfully put out when she *heaws* you'we using bad *wowds* in *fwont* of me."

Bud rounded the corner, skittering across the plank floor.

Missy ran and scooped him back into his jar. "It's all *wight.* Uncle Cwade likes you. He's not mean! He won't *scawe* you again."

"I scared *him*? Missy, that's a tarantula!"

"Uh-uh." She puffed. "He's Bud, my bug."

Cade righted his chair and sank down in it. "I'm sorry, sweetheart. It's just that Bud is—"

"Fuzzy?"

"Yeah—hell yes. That, too." He raked his fingers through his hair and leaned back to catch his breath as Missy screwed the lid on Bud's jar.

"He pwobably needs to west awhile," she said. "He's tuckewed." She pushed the jar just under Cade's nose. "Say you're sowwy, Uncle Cwade."

"Sorry?" he asked. "To Bud?"

Her blue eyes pleaded with him.

"Sorry...Bud." Cade couldn't believe he was apologizing to a damned tarantula.

Missy climbed up on his lap and put her arms around his neck. "It's all wight, Uncle Cwade." She planted a big, noisy kiss on his cheek. "Bud's not mad at you."

How she knew that, Cade couldn't fathom, and he didn't care. He only knew how nice it felt to be hugged by a child.

Missy brushed her hand across his cheek. "Are you weddy for ouw tea pawty?"

He grinned, playing along with her. "A cup of tea would be refreshing, my dear."

"Okay, and aftew we eat, I'll fix youw haiw real pwetty." Missy scrambled from his lap to tend to her hostess's duties. She poured pretend-tea into their cups.

He raised his brows. "My hair, dearest? Is there something wrong with my curly locks?"

Missy giggled. "It looks pwetty shameful, *Miss* Kolby."

"Oh, dash," he trilled. "Then by all means, Miss Wiseman, do something with it. Make me the envy of all Winterborn."

He picked up his teacup, little finger crooked, and took a loud, slurpy sip, soliciting another round of giggles from Missy.

As she busied herself, he thumbed through the Wanted posters and resumed reading. Missy stood on a box behind his chair, carefully rearranging his hair.

"If you had long haiw like you did when you fiwst come hewe, I could bwaid it fow you. Zoe showed me how to make a bwaid with stwips of wags she makes wugs with." She combed and combed. "But I can still make it look pwetty."

"Uh-huh, that's nice," Cade said absently, his attention focused on one particular poster. Hart McGill—the son of a bitch.

He glanced up as the bell over the front door jingled. Shelby Moore came into the store and walked back to the kitchen. Moore looked as if he'd run the six miles from town, wheezing the way he was.

"Afternoon, Shelby," Cade greeted.

Shelby started to return the greeting, but his gaze shot straight to the ceiling, which puzzled Cade.

"Hello, Mistew Moowe." Missy wedged her tongue between her lips as she meticulously fashioned Cade's "coif."

"Afternoon, Missy. Where's Zoe?"

"At the jail looking aftew sick people."

"How did you get past Sawyer and the quarantine?" Cade asked.

Shelby looked blank. "What quarantine?"

"The town's quarantined. Sawyer is supposed to be turning people away. It's the fever." A lot of good it had done to give Sawyer "credibility".

"I didn't use the road; I took the back fields. Who's got the fever?"

Cade told him, and Shelby shook his head.

"I'll be statin' my business and leavin'."

Cade's gaze followed Moore's to the ceiling again, puzzled by his preoccupation with it. Seeing nothing unusual, he asked, "What brings you out in this heat?"

"Lookin' for Pop. Found a dead bull near my place. Think it might belong to Herschel Mallard. Pop needs to come check it before I clear away the carcass."

"I'm taking care of Pop's business for a few days. Guess you heard he broke his leg the other night?"

"Hadn't heard that."

Shelby's eyes darted around the room, refusing to meet his. Cade wondered if he had trouble focusing.

"I'd sooner Pop take care of the matter."

Cade frowned. "I can handle it, Shelby—" He glanced at the ceiling again. "You see something up there I don't?"

Shelby lowered his gaze to study his shoes. "Where's Pop?"

"At his place." Cade got up from his seat. "Give me a minute to find someone to look after Missy, and I'll check on the bull."

Shelby cleared his throat. "Don't mean no disrespect, Kolby, but I druther Pop do it, if he can a'tall." He looked down at his feet, swallowing. "Don't think a man with pink bows in his hair got any business sheriffin'."

Cade glanced at himself in the mirror, his

eyes widening at the sight of five stiff pony-
tails standing out from his scalp, each tied with
a lopsided pink bow. He yanked the bows
loose and slapped his hat on his head. "Missy,
I'm going to have to leave you with Gracie while
I ride out with Mr. Moore to see about stolen
cattle."

Missy grabbed Bud's jar and held it close
to her chest. "No, no, Uncle Cwade! We can't
go to Gwacie's. Aunt Waticia is thewe!"

Her big, fearful blue eyes tugged at his
heart. "Glori-Lee could probably use someone
to help sweep out the restaurant."

Missy's face brightened. "Me and Bud can
do that."

"I think Bud would be more comfortable
staying here."

"Nooo, Aunt Waticia might come and get
him and take him home with hew."

"I don't think so, Sunflower. I can promise
Aunt Laticia will not take Bud home."

Missy's bottom lip jutted out and big tears
puddled in her eyes. *How could anyone ever say
no to her?* "Okay, take him."

Glori-Lee was sitting on her front step fanning herself when Cade brought Missy, skip-
ping at his side, over to the café.

"Bringing you some help, Glori-Lee. Zoe's
at the jail, the other kids are at the livery, and
I've got business to attend to."

"I can always use more help," she said,
smiling up at him.

"I shouldn't be too long. I'm going out to Shelby's place to see about a dead bull."

"Take your time. Folks are in too much hurry nowadays. Need to slow down a mite." Glori-Lee patted the step beside her. "Come up and sit a spell, Missy. I see you got Bud with you. He's lookin' mighty spiffy today."

Missy climbed the steps and sat down, positioning Bud's jar between her and the café owner. As Cade turned to go get Maddy, Missy waved. "Huwwy back, Uncle Cwade! Me and Bud will be waiting fow you!"

"Shelby, are you sure this is Herschel Mallard's bull?" Cade squatted by the decomposed carcass, his handkerchief covering his nose.

"That's Samson, all right," Shelby said. "I'd know him anywhere. See that chip outta his hind hoof? Herschel bragged about it. Thought it made the bull something special."

Cade stood up, dusting dirt off his hands. "Looks like it was shot. If it was someone looking for meat, they'd have butchered it, not left it to rot."

"I 'spect it's that dadburned Nelson gang—same ones who made such a mess at Rider's Pass. I tell you, Kolby, someone needs to string them up by their heels."

"I'll take a look around." It could be the work of a dozen or more penny-ante gangs. Most times they were more troublesome than dangerous, but Cade could see how they'd keep

205

the farmers on edge. This was a prize bull, which meant the gang knew their cattle.

"I'd come with you, but I've got hay to put up before rain moves in."

"Go on with your work, Shelby. I'll look into it."

Shelby nodded, then spurred his horse into a gallop.

Giving Maddy her head, Cade picked his way up the road. There was no sign of the criminal. Whoever had shot the bull had covered his tracks.

It was midafternoon when he stopped by Herschel's to tell him about the bull. He found the farmer walking behind a plow, furrowing his field for winter planting.

"Someone's got to put a stop to this." Herschel took off his sweat-stained hat and mopped his head. "I had a right good sum invested in that bull."

"Shelby said he'd dispose of the carcass for you."

"Tell him much obliged."

The sun was low when Cade started back to town. No one in the area had seen or heard anything unusual. Pop would have to follow up on the incident when his leg healed.

Reining in at a stream, Cade dismounted and let Maddy drink, then leaned down and cupped both hands to fill them with water. A movement on the bank caught the corner of his eye.

Maddy suddenly reared. Cade grabbed for the reins, but the horse reared again, knocking him into the shallow water. Springing to his feet, he drew and fired. Pieces of rattler exploded, throwing bits of meat into the air. The headless snake thrashed about on the ground in its death throes. Maddy surged away and galloped off.

Cade put two fingers to his mouth and whistled, but the horse was long gone. Walking out of the water, he kicked the snake carcass into the grass. Maddy hated snakes—and he wasn't overly fond of them himself. He sat down under a tree to wait. Maddy was bound to come back once she calmed down.

An hour passed, and Cade felt himself getting drowsy. A dull ache in the back of his head was becoming annoying. Tipping his hat over his face, he dozed, knowing the horse would wake him when she returned.

When he next opened his eyes, it was pitch-dark. The headache at the base of his skull was sharper, and he felt chilled. Sitting up, he looked around. He ran a hand over the back of his neck, surprised at how hot he felt even while he was shivering.

"Maddy?"

Cade whistled again. No familiar whinny came to him. Leaning back against the tree, he studied the rising full moon. He'd left town hours ago; Red had to be worried about him.

He got to his feet and stretched, trying to work out the kinks. He was getting old. Every bone in his body hurt, and it was a good three-to-four-hour walk back to town.

Settling his hat lower, he started out. If he got his hands on that horse right now, a snake would be the least of her problems.

Zoe opened and closed the front door for the tenth time that evening. Where *was* he? It was nearing nine o'clock, and he still wasn't home. How long could it take to check on one dead bull?

It was just as well Gracie had canceled the weekly checker game because of Laticia's visit. Zoe was too worried about Cade to have enjoyed the evening.

"Have you run out on me again?" she whispered tightly. It didn't do any good to tell herself she didn't care. It wasn't the children who would be disappointed.

"But I don't want to go to bed without kissing Uncle Cwade good night," whimpered Missy, sitting at the kitchen table with her brothers and sister and her great-aunt.

Hiding her concern, Zoe smiled. "I'll make certain he kisses you the moment he gets here."

"But *whewe* is he? He's 'posed to be back by now. It's dawk out thewe!"

"He'll be back," Brody promised, coming over and opening the back door. He looked out again. "He probably ate supper with Shelby."

"Yeah, that's it," Will said. "Mr. Moore made Uncle Cade eat supper with him."

"It that it, Zoe? Is that why Uncle Cwade isn't back yet?"

"I'm sure that's it." As Missy's face brightened, Zoe coaxed, "Now, scoot—let me tuck you into bed."

With a scowl, Laticia spooned the last of Zoe's sugar into her coffee cup. "And just what makes you so sure he'll be back?" The plumage on her black hat bobbled as she talked. "Have you ever known him to keep his word?"

Missy began to cry.

"Miss Wiseman, why don't you go into the parlor where it's more comfortable? I'll put Missy to bed; then we'll visit."

Zoe could have throttled Laticia for planting ideas in Missy's head. The child was fretful enough. Zoe wished she had not extended Laticia an invitation to eat supper with them, but how was she to know Cade would ride off at noon and fail to return? Ooooh—where was he?

"It's an hour past my bedtime," Laticia complained. "Fetch Abraham and have him take me back to the Willises."

"Brody, please go to the livery and tell Abraham to bring the carriage."

Brody skipped out to do as he was told.

"Mark my words," Laticia warned, "even if that Kolby boy comes back, it won't change a thing. I'm taking the children with me in the morning. He's unreliable and doesn't have a wife to help care for them. He has no business with them." She stood and walked through the store to the front door, pausing on the threshold to confront Zoe, who'd followed her. "You're foolish to think you can ever count on him. He's probably in Missouri by now."

Zoe refused to let the old woman upset her. She had no idea what was keeping Cade, but her instinct told her he wasn't in Missouri.

Oh, dear Moses, had he met up with one of his enemies? Her knees went weak. Had someone waylaid him on the road? Was he lying somewhere in a ditch right now, bloodied, unable to move?

"I'm sure he'll be here any moment." Zoe took a deep breath, trying to control her sudden trembling. "It is so like Shelby to insist that Cade stay for supper."

"If it hadn't been for Abraham's stomach being queasy, we'd be gone by now," Laticia said. "All that rich food you've been feeding us. No one knows how to fix chicken anymore. A body can't eat it without getting sick."

If Laticia had dyspepsia, it wasn't the chicken's fault, Zoe told herself. Laticia had gorged on five pieces, along with mashed potatoes, gravy, and three ears of corn. She'd barely had room for the cherry cobbler, she'd declared, but she'd managed to put away two servings, anyway.

"Are you feeling poorly, Miss Wiseman?"

"Not me." The matron burped. "Never been sick a day in my life. But Abraham—now, he's got a delicate constitution."

"Maybe he'd like a little baking soda to settle his stomach."

Laticia held up a bony hand. "I'll see to Abraham's needs. Don't want a fuss made over him."

Zoe smiled to herself. Abraham wasn't sick; he was stalling. Bless his dear heart.

But poor Lawrence Willis—Zoe wondered if he would ever speak to her again.

Abraham soon arrived with the carriage. After Laticia left and the children were in bed, Zoe picked up her sewing basket and went into the parlor. She cranked up the phonograph. The music made her feel sad, but also close to Cade. They'd danced to this tune.

She glanced toward the darkened window. Where was he? Was Laticia right? Had he ridden off, never to be heard from again? She cursed herself for telling him she wouldn't blame him if he rode away and never came back.

After darning every sock in the basket, she put her sewing aside and changed the cylinder on the phonograph. For the hundredth time, she glanced at the mantel clock. Two in the morning. She walked to the window and pulled the curtain aside. The moon was as bright as day.

The sound of a horse's hooves broke into her thoughts, and she bolted to the back door. "Cade? Is that you?"

Riderless, Maddy stopped to graze beneath the oak tree, and Zoe looked up and down the backyard. There was no one but Maddy. *Please, no. Not Cade, not now.* Shelby said he was tracking down the Nelson gang. *Oh Cade, you fool. Why did you go alone?* A sob caught in her throat and choked her.

"Zoe?"

She turned, startled. "Holly—what are you doing up?"

The girl rubbed her eyes while Zoe walked

her into the parlor and sat her down on the settee. She didn't want her to see Maddy. Holly's gaze traveled to the stack of bedclothes in the corner of the room. Cade's.

"Is Uncle Cade sleeping at the jail tonight? Is that why he didn't come home?"

Zoe didn't want to lie to the child, but neither did she want her to be any more upset than she already was. "No, Seth is staying over there so I can be with you. Uncle Cade is taking care of Pop's business."

Holly's eyes drooped closed. "He'll be here soon?"

Zoe's gaze drifted to the open window. "Soon."

"I can't sleep," Will said, coming into the room. "It's too noisy."

Zoe patted the seat cushion. "Sit next to Holly and me."

Piling onto the settee with them, Will mumbled, "Brody snores."

"Brody always snores. Why does it bother you tonight?" Holly said, pushing her brother away from her.

Zoe held out her arm, inviting Will to sit on the other side of her. As she held the two children close, she thought about what would happen if Cade didn't come back. Laticia would take them. As much as she herself loved them, she wasn't their blood kin. *Oh, Cade! How could you do this to me?* She felt her arms tighten. She wouldn't let them go. She'd run away with them before she'd give them up to Laticia Wiseman—run as far and as fast as she could go with the children, and hunt

212

Cade down, and—and—what? What would she do? Nothing. If Cade didn't come back, there wasn't a blessed thing she could do. The children would be lost to her forever.

Brody appeared in the parlor doorway, his hair standing on end. "Is it morning?"

"No. Go back to bed," Will grumbled.

"I can be up if you can."

"Brody, sit here," Zoe said. "I'll get us some cookies. I think we could use a treat."

Holly lifted her head and peered at her sleepily. "Now? In the middle of the night?"

Brody's eyes brightened. "Honest?"

"Honest." Addy might be rolling over in her grave, but darn it, dying from a treat in the middle of the night was better than dying of worry.

Zoe returned with the cookies just as Missy came into the parlor, clutching the jar housing Bud. "Bud's scawed."

Zoe smiled. "What's Bud got to be scared about?"

"He wants Uncle Cwade to pwotect him."

"From what?"

"Aunt Waticia."

Zoe patted her lap, and Missy climbed up. "I think we need to talk about Aunt Laticia." Missy settled herself, and Holly and Will scooted closer. "Laticia isn't here to harm you, and she wouldn't harm Bud—most especially not Bud."

"Where's Uncle Cwade? I want Uncle Cwade."

"Shhh—here, have a cookie. Let's have a party and think of happy things."

"Uncle Cwade makes me happy."

Smiling, Zoe hugged her. He'd better have a good excuse when he did show up—a darn good one. Her gaze drifted toward the darkened window again, and she bit her lower lip. *Where are you, Cade?*

The clock struck four. Seated at the kitchen table, Zoe glanced at the settee in the parlor and was relieved to see that the last child had finally fallen back to sleep. Exhaustion had overtaken her, and she was physically sick from worry. Her head ached and her eyes burned. Why had she thought Cade had changed? Hadn't she known better than to count on him? Wasn't getting stung once enough?

She slumped on the kitchen chair, cradling her face in her hands. *Cade, please come back.*

Help. She needed help. From whom? Pop? No, he wasn't any help with a broken leg. Abraham? She'd have Abraham drive her to where Shelby said he'd seen the dead bull. Where was it? She tried to remember what Glori-Lee had told her.

Grabbing her shawl, she left the store and quickly ran to the livery to summon Abraham, then hurried on to Glori-Lee's. Banging on the back door of the café, she called out, "Glori-Lee!" Glori-Lee was always up at this hour to bake biscuits.

The café owner came to the door in her dressing gown, her hair wadded under a brown hairnet. "What in the world—"

"Where did Cade say he was going?"

Glori-Lee thought for a moment. "Why, he didn't say exactly—just somewhere near Shelby's place, then on to Herschel's."

"The kids were up most of the night, so they'll probably sleep late. Can you look in on them for me?"

"You can't go out there by yourself at this time of the morning. Get Walt or Ben—"

"No time. Abraham will drive me."

"In Laticia Wiseman's buggy? Are you crazy?"

"I'm hoping to be back before she finds out."

"I'm hoping you will be, too—the whole town hopes you will, believe me," Glori-Lee stressed.

Five minutes later, Abraham pulled up alongside the café and Zoe climbed in, pointing in the direction she wanted to go.

"You bring a pistol, Miz Bradshaw, in case o' trouble?" he asked.

"No, Abraham, I'm scared of guns."

"Me, too—'specially when I's on the wrong end of one." He pulled a small handgun from his jacket pocket and laid it between them on the buggy seat. Patting it for assurance, he said, "Jist in case o' trouble, Miz Bradshaw, jist in case."

As they passed Sawyer at the edge of town, Zoe yelled, "Have you been here all night?"

Sawyer straightened and pointed to his badge. "It's my job."

"Did Cade ride this way when he left yesterday?"

"Shore did—said something about finding Herchel's bull, dead!"

"Thank you!"

The bright moon cast eerie shadows along the road. The heavy thicket and low underbrush made a perfect cover for outlaws. Zoe found herself resting her hand on the pistol, "jist in case."

They'd ridden more than two miles when Zoe grabbed Abraham's arm.

"Slow down!" She pointed up ahead. "Something's there—at the side of the road."

Abraham squinted. "Shore is. Looks ta be—Oh, Lordy, looks ta be a body, Miz Bradshaw."

Zoe was out of the buggy before it stopped. She ran so hard, she thought her lungs would burst trying to suck in enough air. Even before she reached him, she recognized Cade. When her heart threatened to explode with grief, she reminded herself that if he'd gotten himself killed, he had no one to blame but himself. She wouldn't care—she wouldn't!

Blindly falling to her knees, she sobbed, "Please, no..." Who was she kidding? She'd lay down her life for him. She quickly loosened his shirt collar and felt for a pulse, wilting with relief when the strong, steady beat throbbed against her fingertips. "Abraham, come quick. He's alive!"

With every ounce of strength she could muster, she lifted him to a sitting position. "Cade, can you hear me?" She patted his cheek. "Cade!"

His eyelids fluttered. "Red? So damn tired." He leaned against her breast. "Maddy ran off—"

"I know." Zoe brushed his hair back off his

forehead and felt the heat. Fear constricted her throat as she whispered, "Cade, you're burning up." She turned to Abraham as he came running. "Hurry, Abraham, hurry! We've got to get him into the buggy. He's got the fever!"

Chapter 13

"**I** can't believe you'd go out there alone." Zoe sponged water across Cade's forehead, then fussed with his pallet, which she'd laid beside the others in the jail. "Pop's been worried sick about you. I'll tell him you're back."

He cocked an eye open and groaned. "Were you worried?"

"Only because of the children."

"I like it when you worry about me." Cade took hold of her wrist as a spasm crossed his face. "Can you do something about my headache?"

"If I could, I would. Lie still."

"Come on, Zoe. I'm dying."

"There's not much I can do. You have the same symptoms as everybody else." She crossed his hands on his chest and pulled the blanket up around his neck. "Rest. I don't see how you walked all that way with the fever. I'll have to send for more quinine."

He pulled the blanket over his head. "Damn—eyes hurt—can't stand the light."

"Shhh. Rest."

She checked on the others and found them

sleeping soundly. She would give all she owned to sleep like that. Now that Cade was sick, when would she ever find time to sleep?

She hated herself for thinking the worst of him, although she knew the idea of leaving had to be more appealing by the day. If *she* thought about it, she knew *he* did. Her gaze fell on him. So sick, so frail—not the big, tough bounty hunter anymore, just a sick, vulnerable man. For the first time in his life he needed her, and as much as the thought irritated her, she needed him as well.

Stepping outside the jail, she found Pop hobbling back and forth, his crutches thumping soundly on the packed ground. Sawyer was filling him in on the number of visitors he'd kept from coming into town. "Must'a been fifty or more."

Pop frowned. "Sawyer, there ain't fifty people in the whole county. You cain't count."

Sawyer spat and walked away mumbling, "Wasn't fer me, ever' dern man, woman, and child would have this dadburned fever." He hollered over his shoulder. "I got that credible stuff now! People oughta listen t'me!"

"You got what?" Pop called back.

Zoe smiled. "I think he means 'credibility', Pop. Cade made him a badge."

Pop sighed. "That could be a dangerous thing. Sawyer ain't quite right. He got hit in the head one too many times when he used to box."

"Actually, Sawyer has been a big help, even if he is a little overbearing." Zoe sat down on the new bench the mayor had thoughtfully provided and motioned for Pop to join her. She took a deep breath of the fresh air. "Too bad he didn't have his boxing gloves on when Laticia Wiseman came to town. He had quite a run-in with her."

"Well, who ain't?" Pop said, lowering himself to the bench and carefully stretching his splinted leg out before him. "That woman might mean well, but she can rankle the best of us."

Leaning her head back, Zoe closed her eyes. "She's going to take the children home with her."

"When?"

"She said this morning, if Abraham's up to it."

Pop leaned forward. "Abraham sick?"

"I don't think so. I think he's trying to give me enough time to settle on a course of action, but now that Cade is sick..."

"What's Cade have to say about Laticia wanting the kids?"

"He doesn't intend to let her have them, so I'll have to try and ward her off until he feels better," Zoe explained.

"Well, good luck." Pop rubbed his chin. "Laticia's a determined woman."

"I don't know what I'd have done without Abraham this morning. He helped me find Cade."

Pop lifted himself off the bench and propped the crutches under his arm. "Think I'll go have a visit with Abraham—see if he needs anything."

"He'd like that. He could probably use a

break from the children. They're over there pestering him again."

Pop chuckled. "Those kids are too well-mannered to pester anybody."

Massaging the back of her neck, she smiled. "Tell them to go to Glori-Lee's for dinner. She said she'd feed them for me."

Pop waved his crutch at her and hobbled away.

Later that day, the jail door banged open, startling Zoe. The bowl of broth she was feeding Ida nearly slipped out of her hand, and she grabbed a cloth to wipe up the spills.

"Doc! For heaven's sake, you scared the wits out of me." She rose as he glowered at her, his face puffy, red blotches covering his skin in various patches. "Are you okay?"

"Hell, no, I'm not okay! Look at me. Look at this rash." He jabbed at his face with his finger. "You have any idea what this is?"

"An allergic reaction to Edna's soap?"

"Measles!"

Zoe's mouth dropped open as the implication slowly sank in. "Measles?"

"*Measles*. We've all got the *measles*."

Relief flooded her, and she dropped to the nearest chair, weak in the knees. Tilting her head back, she began to laugh. "Measles. They've all got the *measles*!" That meant that, most likely, Cade had the measles, not the fever. She was shocked silly by the news.

"I don't find it particularly funny," Doc complained, eyeing her sternly. "Well, maybe it is a little—although measles seems to hit adults real hard."

Bonnie lifted her head off the pillow. "My Jimmy had them a few weeks ago. He wasn't very sick—I never thought much about it."

Doc collapsed into a nearby seat. "With John and Addy dying of the fever, we all just assumed that's what it was."

Bruce sat up on his pallet, blinking sleepily. "But Ida was out of her head with fever."

Doc nodded. "Like I said—it hits adults hard. Some worse than others." He glanced around the room. "Is that Kolby over there?"

Zoe nodded, grinning. "He came down with the fev—measles this morning. I was about to send for more quinine."

"No need now," Doc said. "It'll run its course."

"But why didn't I get them—and Seth? He's been here with Bonnie so often—"

"You both probably had them when you were kids. Makes you immune," Doc informed her. "So, soon as you all feel strong enough, you might as well go on home to recuperate."

"Well, thank the Lord," Bonnie said. She got up to gather her belongings, scratching. The others did the same, complaining but relieved.

When Cade rolled to his feet, Zoe stopped him. "All but you," she corrected. "You're staying right here until your temperature goes down."

Pop walked into the livery and found that Abraham was keeping the children busy shining the leather on Laticia's buggy.

221

"You keep this thing looking like new, Abraham," Pop told him.

"Thank ya, Sheriff Winslow. Miss Laticia's mighty paticlar 'bout her buggy."

"Care if I sit a spell?"

Abraham hurried to pull up a crate. "Here ya are. You jist make yoresef ta home."

Holly helped Pop seat himself as Brody took his crutches, held up one leg, and tried to walk with them. He fell face-first into the hay.

"Hold on there, son," Pop said, laughing.

"How do you do this?" Brody asked, jumping to his feet.

"Just hope you never have to learn," Pop replied with a grunt.

Taking the crutches from Brody, Holly handed them to Pop. "Better put these up before Brody breaks it. He's bad that way."

Missy hopped over on one foot. "Can I twy?"

Pop pulled her onto his lap. "Those sticks are too long for a little'un like you." He retrieved a piece of peppermint from his pocket and pretended to pull it out of her ear. "Well, look what I found—this must belong to you."

Will pulled on his ear. "Do I got one, too?"

Pop motioned for him to join them. "I'll just bet you have." A mint magically appeared from Will's ear; then Pop flipped Holly and Brody each a piece. "You'd better not eat it until after Glori-Lee feeds you dinner, or we'll all have to answer to Zoe. Go on, now—Glori-Lee's expectin' ya."

The children pocketed the candy and skipped up the street to the café.

Pop turned to Abraham, his demeanor sobering. "Zoe's done good by them."

"Yes'sa, Miz Bradshaw's a fine woman...fine woman."

"She wants to keep them, you know."

"Yes'sa, I knows that." Abraham spit on his rag and rubbed hard on a spot of dirt on the buggy seat.

"I hear Laticia is set on taking them home with her."

"Yes'sa, I knows that, too." He slapped the rag against the wheel spokes.

"What do you think about it?"

"Don't reckin I have a say in it, Sheriff."

Pop smiled. "Oh, I reckin you have a lot of say in things, Abraham."

Abraham grinned back, his teeth flashing white in his mahogany face. "Ways I see it, them young'uns need a ma and a pa. Miz Laticia's too old ta be lookin' fer a man, but Miz Bradshaw—" He rolled his dark eyes toward Pop. "She ain't too old a'tall."

"What're you tryin' to say? If Zoe were to marry, Laticia might consider letting her adopt the children?"

"Seems likely—if'n it was the right man."

Pop's fingers smoothed his mustache thoughtfully. "Hmmm—you know, Abraham, you may be right. Perry Drake has an eye for Zoe. Now he'd make a good—"

"I sez—if'n it was the *right* man. Miz Laticia mighty paticlar 'bout who be a papa to her nephew's chil'un."

"She couldn't find fault with Perry. Why, he's the town banker; they'd not want for anything—"

"Sure 'nuff, Sheriff, but Mr. Drake be jist one more fish in the pond. He not blood kin."

"Then who? Cade?"

Abraham slowed the rag and wiped in small circles. "Well, now, he *ain't* jist one more fish, now is he?"

Pop shook his head. "Zoe wouldn't have him. She makes no bones about being out of sorts with him. They fuss all the time—"

Abraham chuckled. "Yes'sa, jist like married folk."

"She wants the kids...he don't want her to raise 'em alone..." Pop stopped and thought a moment. "'Course, if they were to marry each other, that would solve the matter. But that'd sure take some doin'." He slapped his knee. "Abraham! By doggies, that's it."

Abraham shook the dust from his rag. "I knowed a smart man like you'd think o' somethin'."

Pop grabbed hold of Abraham's arm and pulled himself up. "Hand me my crutches, my good man. I've got to call a town meetin'."

Abraham glanced up. "Right now?"

"Right now," Pop said. "The sooner, the better."

Abraham went on polishing. "Now if'n the buggy wheel was to break, it would take me a little while to fix." He paused, scratching his head. "Might take—oh, much as four, five hours to get the job done."

"Broken buggy wheel?" Pop mused. "That'd be a shame—delayin' Laticia's trip home and all."

"Sure 'nuff, Sheriff, sure 'nuff." He grinned.

"Well, now, Abraham, you best go tell Miss Laticia yore shore sorry, but her buggy wheel jist broke."

"Yes, sir, I'll do that, Sheriff. Don't 'spect she'll take kindly to it, but cain't be helped. These things jist happen."

Pop laughed at Abraham's saintly smile. "See you later. I got a meetin' to call."

"Quieten down, now! Let's have some order here!" Pop banged the gavel on the table, shooting Edna Mews a warning look. "Edna, can't you and May exchange those blasted pork chop recipes later?"

"Don't tell me to quieten down! I want to fix pork for supper tomorrow night," Edna complained.

"Walt ain't gonna die if he don't have pork chops for supper tomorrow night. Everyone sit down!"

Chair legs scraped noisily against the wooden floor as the citizens of Winterborn took their seats. The meeting room of the town hall was jam-packed; everyone had dropped what they were doing to attend.

"This better not be a waste of my time," Frank Lovell complained.

Sam Pritchard took hold of Frank's arm. "Sit down, Frank. You ain't got no place to go. At least you ain't got gout."

225

"Shut up about your dadburned gout, Sam," Frank grumbled.

"Now then." Pop laid the gavel aside once the room simmered down. "I've got news."

Glori-Lee stood up. "What kind of news?"

"We ain't got the fever; we got the measles."

A stunned silence fell over the crowd as the information sank in. "Are you certain?" Walt Mews asked.

Pop nodded. "Doc's got 'em, so does Ida, Bruce, Bonnie, Clyde Abbott and his boy, Saul and Belle, and now Cade."

"Well, I'll be darned." Roy Baker burst out laughing. Others joined in with relief.

"Seems Seth's younger boy had them a few weeks back," Pop said. "He must've started the epidemic."

Edna stood up. "Seth and Bonnie've always brought the young'uns to the Saturday night dance. Now that I think about it, Jimmy wasn't feeling good a few weeks back. I remember he asked me for four or five cups of punch that night. His eyes were bright as marbles. He must've been runnin' a fever then."

"Well, he's shore enough passed it around," Pop said.

"Would the measles make a body that sick?" May Wilks asked.

"Doc said they affect adults harder than children. Fever, sore muscles, headache, and eye irritation can fell a grown man." Pop scratched his head. "The patients have gone home, but I'd suggest anyone in here that hasn't had rubella, stay clear of the ill for the time being."

The townspeople talked among themselves, expressing their relief.

"Are we gonna start up the Saturday dances again, now that we know it isn't the fever?" Harry Miller asked.

Pop gave him the evil eye. "We got far more important things to discuss right now, Harry."

"What's that?"

"Laticia Wiseman."

Silence fell over the room. Sawyer stood up. "That witch? The woman's a pain in the...neck! All she knows to do is beat folks with her cane and stir up trouble. I'd be more than happy to run the old harpy out of town." Sawyer rubbed his shoulder. "I owe her one."

"That won't be necessary," Pop said. "I got a plan." He walked to the back of the room and closed the doors for privacy. As he returned to the podium, he motioned for Abraham. "Come on up here."

Abraham stepped back. "No'sa, Sheriff. I's got nothin' ta say."

"You've got plenty to say. Now get on up here, we're wasting time."

Abraham followed Pop to the front of the room. All eyes were focused on the black man with the snow-white hair as he stood next to the sheriff, nervously twisting his battered straw hat in his hands.

"Tell the people what we discussed in the livery earlier this evening."

"I's don't think—"

"Abraham thinks Laticia might back off

about takin' the children if Zoe Bradshaw was to marry."

"Marry who?" Woodall Thompson asked, looking at his watch.

Abraham hung his head, whispering under his breath. "Miz Laticia will strip my hide if she hears I'm over here talkin' 'bout her."

"She ain't gonna hear a word about it," Pop promised. "And you ain't talkin' against her. You're doin' her and the town a service."

Abraham nodded his head. "Yes'sa, I's only thinkin' 'bout Miz Laticia's welfare. She's a good woman."

Shelby Moore stood up near the back. "What's the purpose of this meeting, Pop? Git on with it. I've got to git on home and milk before dark."

"Calm down, Shelby. Here's the problem. We all know what's been going on the last few days: Addy and John died and Cade came back."

The back door opened, and Seth Brighton entered the room.

"Sit down, Seth. I was just gettin' ready to mention you," Pop said.

Frowning, Seth took a seat next to Shelby.

"Like I was saying, Cade and Zoe are at each other's throats over who'll take the kids."

Glori-Lee joined in. "Thought Addy left that up to Cade."

"She did," Pop conceded. "But Zoe wants them."

Seth spoke up. "Me and Bonnie are takin' the kids."

"Why would Zoe want them? She's a woman

228

alone," Hank Farnsworth pointed out.

Gracie was on her feet in a flash. "Because she loves those children as if they were her own flesh and blood! Who better to see after them? I don't know why Addy didn't leave them to her in the first place."

"Why should she? Cade is their uncle," Walt called.

"Cade doesn't know the kids," Willa Baker argued. "He never bothered to come back to visit all those years. Why should he be the one to decide their welfare?"

Lawrence Willis waded into the fray. "Because he's the children's blood kin!"

Pop held up his hands for order. "People, people. This is the problem! We can go on all night about who should or shouldn't have them. No one in this room would dispute that the guardianship of those kids belongs to either Zoe or Cade, but there's a new cog in the wheel."

"What's that?"

"Laticia Wiseman. She wants them."

The women gasped. Beulah Tetherton began to fan herself.

"Isn't that her right?" Perry Drake interceded. "Miss Wiseman is the children's only other living relative. Why shouldn't she assume custody?"

"Laticia is too old to raise four young children!" Gracie declared. "And those kids are scared to death of that woman. I've seen the way they hide from her and shake all over when she comes near them."

Pop nodded. "Tell *her* that. She wants to take

the kids home with her. Come hell or high water, if Cade don't take custody of those kids, she will."

Roy Baker looked agitated. "How can Cade take custody of 'em? He's on the road—he can't be a father to four children."

"Wouldn't it be better if family raised them?" Perry insisted. "Laticia can hire proper help. She has the funds."

Seth stood up. "Bonnie and me are takin' the kids. Bonnie will be over the measles in a few days, and in another week or so I'll have that extra room finished. I don't see what all the fuss is about."

Pop banged the gavel as the room erupted in a noisy debate. "People!" He looked at Seth. "No one would argue that you and Bonnie would make a good home for Addy's children, but who among us don't think that Cade and Zoe are the likeliest ones to raise them? Lord knows the kids love those two as much as they did their ma and pa."

Silence cloaked the room. The crowd stared back at Pop. Beulah Tetherton fanned harder.

Pop nodded at Abraham. "Abraham?"

Clearing his throat, the old man said softly, "I's know it's none'a my business, but I's agreein' with Pop 'bout there bein' a sensible solution. Now, Miz Laticia ain't gonna back off this matter easily—believe me. She won't stand for Mista Kolby to give away her flesh and blood. No'sa, she won't stand fer that a'tall. But now, the sheriff done come up with a good idee. If'n there was some way we could get Mista Kolby and Miz Bradshaw married—well, then, there'd be no question who'd get them."

The townsfolk stared in awkward silence.

"'Course," Abraham chuckled, "gettin' those two together ain't gonna be easy."

"This is ludicrous." Perry got to his feet. "Zoe shouldn't be forced into marriage."

Pop waved him down. "Sit, Perry. We all know you're sweet on her, but this town's a family, and circumstances dictate that we lay aside our own interests and think of what's best for the children."

"Then I'll pursue my intentions. I'll marry Zoe."

Pop groaned and beat his fist on the table. "Are you blood kin to Addy's children?"

Perry frowned. "You know I'm not."

"Then I can't see how that will solve the problem."

Walt Mews cleared his throat. "Getting Cade to marry Zoe seems pretty far-fetched. How are we supposed accomplish such a feat? Those two mix like oil and water. What if they catch on to what we're doing?"

"It's up to us to make sure they don't catch on—leastways until we get 'em married."

"They're sensible adults. How do you think you can pull off something of this enormity?" Perry snapped.

"Yeah, how are you even gonna git them to carry on a decent conversation?" Sawyer grunted.

Edna Mews rose to her feet. "I would love to see Zoe married. Since Jim died she's had it real hard, trying to run the store and make ends meet. And Cade isn't so bad—he was raised proper. Senda and Mac Kolby were the finest people on earth. But if Cade married Zoe, wouldn't that be inviting all sorts of riffraff into town?"

"It would!" Jake Bledso spoke up. "I don't want to worry about having one of my children killed by a stray bullet from some wanted man's gun."

Voices of dissent swelled through the crowd.

"I don't have anything against Cade; he's a fine boy," Roy Baker said. "But Edna's right. We don't want trouble here in Winterborn."

Complaints rose louder.

"Listen now! Quieten down!" Protests momentarily diminished as Pop took command. "What you're saying is all reasonable concerns. And there's problems you haven't even thought about. What about Cade? If we were to trick him into marrying Zoe, what about his safety?"

Expressions in the crowd sobered.

"What about his safety?" Pop repeated. "Cade has enemies—dangerous enemies. We all know he's a good boy. Maybe his occupation isn't to our liking, but—Roy? Have you forgotten the time you were about to lose your farm, and Cade sent money through Mac to pay it off?"

Roy hung his head.

"And Walt? Have you forgotten the time that storm blew out the front window of the barbershop, and you didn't have the money to replace it? Who was it that sent that twenty-five-dollar wire a month later?"

"Cade," Walt acknowledged. "Addy always kept him informed of the town's doin's."

Pop's gaze moved around the room. "Don't none of us like the way Cade makes his money, but we don't seem to have any objection to spending it. May Wilks!"

May glanced up.

"What about the time your mother broke her hip, and Cade sent the money to pay her doctor bill?"

Ralph Otis chimed in. "Or the time my heifer died during the winter, and my kids didn't have fresh milk. When Cade got wind of it, he had Mac buy another cow and bring it over that same week."

Pop lowered his voice. "That's what I'm saying. Cade is one of our own, and he needs our help. He just don't know it. We all know he loved Addy. He's got to be torn by the decision to stay or go, who to give the kids to, or to keep them himself. I say we're his family. We need to help him out."

"But how?" Lucy Ellen Black asked.

"Well, that's where my plan comes in." He briefly explained what he had in mind, and all but Perry and Jake Bledso nodded.

"If we go through with this cockamamie plan, we'll have to protect Cade's back," Walt warned.

A few of the men in the crowd seconded the suggestion.

"I'm a pretty good shot, if I do say so myself," May Wilks said.

"I can outshoot any man in this room," Lucy Ellen declared.

"It'll take every last one of us." Pop's face sobered. "And there's no assurance we can pull this off, but if we're going to keep Laticia from taking the children, we'll have to act now. Seth, for the good of Cade and Zoe, you and Bonnie will have to go along with the plan. I know you want the children, but I think you'll agree that Zoe will make them a good ma."

Seth nodded. "Bonnie will be disappointed, but what you say is true. Zoe does a fine job with those kids. Bonnie and I only want what's best for them."

"It's not that Miz Laticia wouldn't treat the chil'un good," Abraham said. "She'd see to 'em real good, but kiddies need young folk to raise 'em. 'Fraid neither me or Miz Laticia got the energy any more."

"Then it's settled," Pop declared. "I'll put the plan into action. As soon as the fever breaks, Cade'll pop out with the measles. It's not likely he'll make a handsome groom, but I doubt Zoe will notice." Pop chuckled. "Hate to do it to those two, but who knows—they might take to marriage. Stranger things have happened."

"The plan is insane," Perry said. "Cade hasn't the fortitude to stick around, or to be a husband and father. There must be another way."

"There ain't no other way." Pop banged the gavel and dismissed the meeting. "I've got work t'do."

Chapter 14

"**I** don't want soup! I want a *meal*," Cade demanded.

"It's not soup, it's broth!" Zoe took a deep breath, then tipped the sheet from under him. He landed with a bounce on the bare mattress, glaring at her.

"Broth is not soup!" she repeated. "And stop complaining. Since everyone's gone home, you have the bunk now, not some uncomfortable floor pallet."

"Broth is *broth*. It's runny, flavored water, even worse than *soup*. Soup has something in it—meat, potatoes. A man can't live on runny water, or in this miserable bunk."

"Runny water is all you have. You'll have to eat it or go hungry."

Cade sat up on the bunk and scratched. He picked up the bowl of broth and looked at it. "I'll eat it *and* go hungry." He took a sip, frowning. "How do I know this is measles?"

"It only makes sense. You tended the sick, and you were out at the Brightons' place. Did you have the measles when you were little?"

He shook his head. "No. I think I'd remember something this annoying—and I sure don't remember Ma starving me to death."

Zoe plumped a pillow. "You are the worst patient on earth. All you've done is complain."

He shoved the bowl of broth aside and lay back. "I want out of here."

"'Here' meaning the jail? Or 'here' meaning Winterborn?" She knew the answer without asking. He wanted out of Winterborn—away from the measles, from Laticia Wiseman, from her. He sat up, reaching for the broth. Tasting another spoonful, he made a face.

"It needs salt."

"It's *too* salty."

"You're trying to starve me."

"Starving would be too slow, too humane." She paused. Putting her finger on her temple as if devising a sinister plan for his death and leaning closer to his ear, she whispered, "Perhaps I've poisoned the broth—yes—or, perhaps I'll pick some poison mushrooms and have Glori-Lee slip them into your food tonight—even better. Poison mushrooms. A rather nasty death, but then you're not going anywhere for a few days. You've got time to die slowly, agonizingly slowly. Yes, I must find a mushroom that will cause drooling, foaming at the mouth, maybe nausea, difficulty in swallowing, bloating—severe bloating is always a nice touch. Then there's the hope of delirium, hallucinations, eyes bulging, fatigue, fainting—"

Cade gave up on the broth and lay back again. "I want a steak—a big, juicy one with potatoes swimming in gravy."

"Don't we all?" She picked up the dirty linen and left the cell.

"Get me another pillow," he called after her.

"Get it yourself."

"Come on. My head hurts."

"There's an extra pillow right beside you."

"My water's tepid. I need cool water. My mouth's dry."

"You should have drunk the broth. It's wet."

Zoe glanced up as someone entered the jail. "Hi, Pop. How's the leg this morning?"

"Stiff as a poker." Pop limped to the desk and lowered his bulk into the chair. Propping his crutches against the desk, he sat for a moment, looking around. "I've missed this place."

"No reason you can't resume your normal duties." She folded a blanket and laid it over a chair. "You've had the measles, haven't you?"

"Had 'em when I was a young'un." He glanced at Cade. "Why you got your face covered with a pillow?"

His answer was muffled. "I feel like hell."

Pop chuckled. "Sounds like he's gettin' better."

"He must be. He's cranky as an old bear. The pillow over his face is his not-too-subtle way of blocking me out."

Zoe tidied up, stacking blankets and pillows in a pile. "Gracie said you called a meeting at the town hall last night. What about?"

"Gracie didn't tell you?"

"Only that you announced the sickness was measles instead of the fever."

"That's about the sum of it. I thought it'd be easier to get the town together than send someone from house to house."

"I'm sure everyone's relieved to hear it isn't the fever." She carried a stack of blankets past the cell and stored them on the shelf just outside it.

"They seemed to be."

"Anything else going on?"

"Folks are up in arms about Laticia. Don't want her comin' 'round to cause trouble. You know how she can be."

Zoe knew exactly how Laticia was. She'd been at the jail twice in the past twenty-four hours, harassing Cade. But due to Gracie's hospitality and unequaled pot roast, Laticia was comfortable in her quarters and likely to stay past her welcome.

"Well," said Zoe, "in a few days Cade will be well enough to settle his business with Bonnie and Seth." It wasn't a pleasant thought, but a realistic one. She had to face reality. Without the children, she just might sell the store, maybe do seamstress work for Mrs. Penscott. She'd tried to hold onto Jim's heritage, but she was just too tired to fight anymore.

The front door opened, and Seth walked in. Pop smiled. "Morning, Seth. How's Bonnie?"

Seth took off his hat. "She's feelin' much better."

"Stay for a cup of coffee?"

"No, can't socialize. Came to talk to Cade."

Pop nodded toward the bunk. "You'll need to take the pillow off his face so he can hear you."

Seth stepped into the cell. Bending over, he lifted the pillow. "Kolby?"

Cade blinked.

"Got some bad news."

Zoe winced when she heard the gravity in Seth's voice. Was there anything *but* bad news in Winterborn?

"What?" Cade asked.

"Me and Bonnie can't take the kids. We had a long talk last night, and we decided we need to have a couple more young'uns of our own to fill that extra room I'm building."

Cade swung his feet to the side of the bunk and sat up. "What?"

"I know it's disappointing, but me and the wife don't think we ought to take on the children right now."

"But the kids would make you a good family," Cade argued.

"Four more would likely put me under, Kolby."

Cade got up from the bunk and started to pace. Zoe could see the worry in his eyes. "I was counting on you, Seth."

She swallowed a leap of anticipation when she realized Cade was slowly running out of options. Surely Seth's decision would make him realize he *had* to give the kids to her.

Seth reached out to shake hands. "I hope you don't hold it agin me, but I thought you'd want to know now rather than later."

Cade shook hands, nodding. "Sorry it didn't work out."

Seth put his hat on. "Hope you're feelin' better soon. When the rash comes, a little bakin' sody on those spots will help the itchin'."

Seth left the jail, closing the door behind him. Zoe could have heard a pin drop as Cade sank down on the bunk and put his head in his hands.

239

Pop sat at the desk, running his forefinger and thumb through his mustache. Outside, Seth whistled to his team, and a moment later the old buckboard rattled off.

"Well, now." Pop lowered his splintered leg to the floor. "Who wants a cup of coffee?"

"Zoe," Cade called, "get me a steak from Glori-Lee's."

"Glori-Lee's right in the middle of cooking dinner. You'll have to wait."

"I'm not waiting. I'm hungry. I need to get out of here and get my business taken care of. What was the name of that Amish family you mentioned, Pop—over near Saline? I'll ride out there after dinner."

"You're not riding anywhere," Zoe scolded. "You'd scare a body to death, white as a sheet, shaky-legged and wild-eyed, talkin' crazy with fever. Get back on that bunk!"

"I've got four kids who need a home. They're not going to get one with me lying around here." Cade stood up and reached for his hat, holding on to the bunk rail for support. "If you won't go after that steak, I will."

Zoe blocked his exit from the cell. "Over my dead body."

Cade towered above her, his features hard. "I'd prefer to do this peaceful, but I am bigger than you."

She lifted her chin. "You're not leaving this cell."

"Step aside, Red."

"No." She crossed her arms and planted her weight. "This could be easily settled if you would only listen to common sense. Bonnie and Seth can't take the children. Everyone else has children, or doesn't want more. That only leaves me—me, who is ready and willing to take them, so you can get on with whatever it is you're in such an all-fired hurry to get on with!"

"Get out of my way, Zoe."

"I have your gun." Her chin motioned to the gun cabinet. "You're not going anywhere." His dark look didn't shake her.

"You think I'd let you disarm me?"

"I did, didn't I?"

Leaning down, he slipped a small pistol from his boot. The weapon dangled from his forefinger by the trigger guard. "Oops."

Insolence did not deter her, nor did his cocky attitude. "When you're sleeping, I'll get that, too."

"I said, get out of my way."

She swallowed, holding him at arm's length when he tried to push past her. "Pop! Help!"

Pop got up from the desk and hobbled to the cell. He stopped suddenly, his eyes focusing on a corner near the bunk. "Is that Bonnie's ear-bob?"

Zoe's gaze swung to the floor of the cell. "Where?"

"Right there, beneath the bunk. That sparkly gizbob. She'll be wantin' that, won't she?"

Pushing past Cade, Zoe walked into the cell, dropped to her knees, and peered under the bunk. "Where? I don't see anything."

"Show her, Cade." Pop pointed with one crutch. "It's right there."

Cade knelt beside Zoe. "I don't see anything, either."

Her head shot up and banged against his when she heard the door of the cell clang shut.

Cade stood and whirled around. "What in the hell are you doing?"

Pop turned the key in the lock, a big smile on his face. "I'm doing you a favor, son. You two ain't comin' out 'til you decide who's gonna take those kids—you or her. You got the whole dadburned town in a uproar tryin' to figure this thing out! And now Laticia's breathing down our necks. Some of us need relief!"

"Pop! Have you lost your mind?" Zoe ran to the cell door, clasping the bars. "Open this door immediately! The children need—"

"I'll look after the children," Pop said. "You just get your business in order."

"I have ironing sprinkled down—it will mildew!"

"That's a mighty good incentive to get this over with as quick as possible, don't you think?"

"Pop, open this door," Cade demanded. "I haven't got time to play games."

Pop hung the key over a hook in the far corner of the room. "Sorry—I can't hear nothin' but Ben Pointer's hammer hittin' against the anvil."

"Pop!" Zoe and Cade chorused loudly.

Pop limped back to the cell. "You two can stay in there 'til you're old and gray, or you can sit down and talk this thing out like sensible adults. It's your choice, but you ain't leavin' 'til you've worked it out. When you come

242

out of that cell, the arguments will be over, and those kids better have a good home."

Zoe stared at him.

Pop stared back just as hard. "Your pa would whip you for actin' this way."

"This isn't fair. Cade already has his mind made up. For his own selfish, impractical, improbable reasons, he won't let me have the children—"

Cade's jaw firmed. "She's not getting them."

"See? He'll never consent to give me the children."

"Never," Cade concurred. "So stop wasting our time, Pop."

"That's too bad. You're talkin' like you're going to be in there a long time. But I have faith in you. If you think about this long and hard enough, the answer will come to you." He leaned closer to the bars. "I'll give you a hint: the answer's right there in front of your noses. Has been all along."

Cade rattled the bars. "Why don't you just tell us what you have in mind and spare us a lot of argument?"

"Nope. That's your job."

Turning, he thumped out the front door and closed it behind him.

"Sawyer!"

Sawyer stood up, spitting. "Yeah, Pop?"

"Still got that credible stuff?"

"Yep."

"Don't let anyone come in 'cept Glori-Lee with the food."

Sawyer grinned, patting his badge. "Yes, sir."

Nodding, Pop hobbled across the street.

Zoe looked at the clock on the wall. For four hours they'd sat, not speaking. How long could they keep up this silence?

She glared at Cade resentfully. There he lay, hat over his face, ignoring her.

"Cade."

"What?"

"This is crazy. If we're ever going to get out of here, we have to talk."

He rolled off the bunk and walked to the bars. "We can talk until doomsday, but I won't change my mind. I'm not giving the kids to you."

Measles or no measles, he needed a good throttling, Zoe decided. "Fine, but soon it's going to be out of both our hands."

Cade turned to look at her, his eyes bright with fever. "Pop can lock us up, but the decision is still mine to make."

"Laticia says she's taking the kids home with her. If we're both locked behind bars, she'll do what she wants."

He returned to sit beside her on the bunk.

Zoe reached over to feel his forehead. "You better lie down. You look sick."

"Isn't that how most starved men look?"

"Stop complaining."

"My head hurts—and it's from not eating."

"You'll be fine in a day or two, as soon as the spots appear."

"That's all I need. Spots."

"Spots are the least of our worries." She sighed, resting her head against the wall. "If I were to get on my hands and knees and beg you, would that convince you to let me have the kids? Wouldn't that make more sense than handing them over to Laticia?"

"Am I mumbling my words? No—I said, no. Scoot over. I'm lying down." She scooted, and Cade wadded the pillow under his head and stretched out.

"Am I so incompetent that you don't trust me with their welfare?"

"I know you'd be a good mother."

Picking up the other pillow, she whacked him across the head. "You stubborn mule!"

He grabbed the pillow out of her hands and pitched it to the floor. "You won't give up, will you?"

"No." She crossed her arms.

Sitting up, he took a long breath and released it slowly. "All right. I didn't want you to know this, but there's someone out to kill me—Hart McGill."

Her hand flew to her throat, and she suddenly felt sick to her stomach. Kill him? That wasn't surprising, not in view of his vocation, but he made it sound as if McGill had made it a personal vendetta. "What does that have to do with the kids?"

"McGill's out for revenge. He's already killed my best friend. He'll kill anything or anyone connected to me."

"He'd kill children?" She couldn't imagine what kind of animal would kill innocent children.

"He'll kill anyone close to me. When we meet up the next time, only one of us will walk away."

She sat for a moment, trying to understand. Her hand crept over to cover his as the silence continued.

"Why would he hate you so?"

"I killed his brother."

"Cade. For money?"

"In self-defense. I was taking the son of a bitch in when he turned on me. It was either me or him, Red. I chose me."

"Does McGill know where you are?"

"I hope not. I'm banking on his thinking I'm on my way to Saint Louis, but he's no fool. I have to get the kids settled and move on before he realizes he's been tricked."

"That's why you're so eager to leave? Because you think you're endangering the children's lives?"

"McGill will come to Winterborn." Cade made her look at him. "I won't put the children, or you, in his path."

"I'll move."

"No. I have to place them with someone who has no connection to me. You and I go way back. It would be insane to leave them with you, and I'm not just thinking about the kids—I'm thinking of your safety, too. I always have been."

Finding her voice, she said, "You're right, of course." Her words were barely a whisper. "The children must come first." She slid off the bunk and paced the small cell. "But Laticia. Letting her have them isn't the answer. McGill could easily come after her, too."

"Not a chance. One look at her, and he'd run like the yellow bastard he is."

She smiled, aware that he was trying to lighten the mood. "The kids would be miserable with Laticia. Cade, please. I'll do anything to keep them with me. I'll move, change our names—anything."

"Red." He reached an arm out to her, and she went willingly. Lying across his chest, his arms wrapped tightly around her, she felt protected from the McGills of the world. "I can't let you move and change your name. This is your home," he said.

She jerked back. He knew nothing about her—nothing. She'd kept the truth bundled up so long, she was about to burst. "If those kids are taken away from me, I'll have nothing." The only weapon she had left was the truth, as painful as it was. She didn't want his sympathy, but she wanted Brody, Will, Missy, and Holly badly enough to risk it all. "I'll never have children of my own."

"Of course you will—"

"I can't, Cade. I'm barren."

"Barren?"

"Yes, barren." She watched as his eyes darkened, and pain crossed his face. He gently pulled her back to him. She laid her head against his chest, choking back tears.

"Are you certain?"

"Years ago, I—" It was hard. She had kept the awful secret hidden for so very long, she couldn't find the words or the heart to bare her soul.

"You could be mistaken. Maybe your husband—"

"It wasn't Jim's fault."

"Did he talk to Doc Whitney?"

"He didn't have to."

Cade nodded. "Pride. But if he wanted—"

"Jim wanted kids as much as I did—darn you, Cade!" She sat up, fumbling for his handkerchief. "You owe me Addy's kids!"

He stared back at her. "I owe you Addy's kids?"

"Yes." She sniffed, dabbing the handkerchief at the corners of her eyes.

"Are you going to tell me why, or are we playing guessing games?"

She sniffed again. "How could you be so blind?" He couldn't know the can of worms he was opening, he couldn't—but maybe it was time he did. It wouldn't change an iota of their lives, but he should know.

"Cade." Her hand caressed his cheek. He was so hot with fever. "I...don't know how to say this. Addy wanted to tell you, but I wouldn't let her. I had such bitterness in my heart." There was no kind way to say it, no way to spare his feelings. "I was carrying your child when you left seventeen years ago."

The words sounded like a cannon shot in the quiet cell.

He stared at her. "What?"

"Shhh—just listen." Dredging up the past reopened the hurt and pain. "At first I was ecstatic. We were going to have a baby—you and I had created a tiny human being. I couldn't wait for you to come home so I could tell you."

He shook his head, disappointment in his eyes. "Why? Why didn't you let me know?"

She bit her lower lip. "When you didn't come home—a few months later—I got scared. I certainly couldn't tell Papa. I had no one to tell—except Addy. I cried constantly. Then the bleeding started—all that blood." She choked on a sob.

He reached for her hand, but she jerked away. "Don't—" She felt driven to tell it, to relieve the awful hurt. "Addy found me the night I lost the baby. If it weren't for her, I would have died. She nursed me back to health and never told my secret."

Cade pulled her into his arms and held her tightly. "If I had known—I'm sorry."

She sobbed harder. "I'm sorry, too. Sorry we never got to see our baby."

"Did Ma know?"

Zoe pushed away, wiping her eyes. "Senda? Goodness, no. If she'd known, she would have come after you and dragged you back by the ear."

"Someone should have."

"I didn't want you to be dragged back. I wanted you to come of your own accord."

He held her, stroking her hair. She felt peace for the first time in years. "I don't hate you, Cade. I thought I did at the time, but that's over now."

"I should have been with you."

"Addy knew the doctor had told me I could never have children after that, yet she left her children to you, not me, despite how much I love them."

Their gazes clung for a long moment before Cade asked, "Was our baby a boy or a girl?"

"I don't know. I hoped for a boy." She looked away. "I was going to name him Cade."

He smiled. "After his pa."

Reaching for a damp cloth, she sighed. "What are we going to do about Laticia?"

"I don't know." He leaned back, closing his eyes as she applied the cloth to his forehead. "She isn't going to rest until the kids are with family."

"Well..." Zoe bit her lip, trying to work up the courage to suggest a plan—a dangerous one, and not without pitfalls. "I have a solution."

"Go ahead. I'm listening."

"We could get married."

"To whom?"

She swatted him. "Each other, Cade."

Cade shifted his weight, then pulled the cloth off his face. "Didn't you hear a word I said about Hart McGill?"

"Hear me out. It's crazy, but it will work. We marry; the children will be mine. You leave, disappear, and write to them on birthdays and holidays. If you must engage in this ridiculous game of revenge, you can deal with Hart McGill outside Winterborn. He'll never know about the kids or me."

"McGill would know. It would never work." He got up and paced the floor.

"I'll do anything to keep the kids. It's the only way it can happen. We have to make Laticia think the marriage is genuine."

"No. I'd be putting not only the kids in jeopardy, but you, too. If McGill knew I had a wife and—"

"He won't. You'll be gone. Hart McGill will be tracking you again. Everything will appear normal." She felt surreal, uninhibited. There'd been a time when she would have given her life to be Cade's wife; now she was asking him to give his.

He stopped pacing, turning to look at her. "I don't know, Zoe—"

"Call me Red."

He looked at her seriously, but the beginning of a smile gave him away.

"Please, Cade. It's the only solution. We'll get Laticia out of everyone's hair. She can't argue that the children aren't with family. You're family, and if you marry me, I'll be family."

"And what happens when I leave? I don't want to disappoint them. They've been hurt enough, and so have you."

How would the children feel when he left? Exactly as she would. Sickened. Heartbroken. They would be losing yet another loved one. And the children certainly loved him. But did she? She admitted she had stronger feelings for him than she wanted—but love?

She looked at him for a long while. "As I said, I'll move—I'll go where McGill can never find us. I'll change my name, and the children's."

She would miss Winterborn, but she would have the children. She would find solace in them. Why, then, did she feel the weight of the world on her shoulders when she thought of life without him?

"There's got to be a better way," Cade said, rubbing the back of his neck.

"There isn't, and time is running out. Abraham can't stall Laticia forever. She'll be leaving—with the children, if we don't do something."

"I can't get married. I've got the measles."

"There's no law that says a marriage isn't legal just because the groom has measles. Reverend Munson could officiate at the door so he wouldn't be exposed." Zoe was warming to the idea. There was nothing left for her to lose. She'd lost it all seventeen years ago. She lowered her eyes teasingly. "Is the big, bad bounty hunter scared of a little round wedding ring?"

Cade snorted. "Real scared." He pulled her to him, his lips a breath away from hers.

"You can't kiss me; you've got the measles," she protested.

"Watch me. "

His lips were hot with fever, which only intensified the impact of his embrace on her. It was not a ravaging kiss; it was tender and gentle, igniting a yearning deep inside her. Her mouth remembered him, his taste, his feel. Tongue touched tongue. Her hands felt his muscles bunch beneath her touch. Her fingers eased upward to cradle his face; the short stubble of unshaven skin tickled her palms. She closed her eyes weakly, trying to ward off his power over her.

Cade pulled back. "Marriage. To you." His fingers laced through strands of her hair, pulling her closer. She shuddered with need before gently pushing away.

"I'll do whatever it takes to keep the children," she said.

"What kind of marriage would it be?" he whispered.

Hot waves swept through her belly at his sensual tone. "Short." Still shaken from his kiss, she tried to make light of the situation. "Does this mean you accept my proposal?"

He sank to the bunk, reaching for the pillow. The long wait before he spoke was maddening.

"I don't think I've got the strength to make it to the church."

"You don't have to. I'll take care of everything."

"Hell. Call the reverend." He laid his head on the pillow.

Zoe grinned when she saw she'd won. Jumping to her feet, she grabbed a tin cup and dragged it back and forth across the bars. "Pop, bring the preacher! There's going to be a wedding!"

Chapter 15

As the jail door closed behind Zoe, Cade got up and left the cell. Pop came in, grinning. Scratching a red spot on his face, Cade peered at his image in the cracked mirror. "I'm going to make a hell of a sorry-looking groom, Pop."

"You and Red gettin' married? Never thought of that."

"Not until I get my steak." Cade sat down and propped his boots on the desk.

Pop chuckled. "I'll tell Glori-Lee to fry you one the size of Kansas."

"Texas," Cade corrected. "Make it the size of Texas, and a potato the size of New York. I'm marrying the redhead. I may need strength."

"Maybe I ought to get Zoe one, too." Pop sat down, lacing his fingers behind his neck. "We got to keep this marriage on an equal footing."

When Pop left for the café, Cade sank lower in the chair, tipping his hat over his eyes. So. He and Red were finally getting married. He smiled, then quickly sobered. She was right; marriage was the only way to outfox Laticia. Laticia was hardheaded but not senile. If the kids had a good home, she wouldn't fight him for custody. Red could give them a good home.

But if he was putting her life at risk...He couldn't live with that.

The mental image of her laughing eyes made him smile. "A marriage of convenience." Even the words disturbed him. He'd once thought that if he ever married Zoe, it would be for always, but she didn't feel the same about him now as she had years ago. And he didn't blame her. She'd been in his thoughts every day since he'd left, and even more since he'd returned. What he felt for her had grown stronger through the years, but she'd made it clear she resented him for leaving her and would never get over it.

After she'd told him about the baby, her feelings had begun to make more sense. He'd never dreamed she'd been carrying his child. If he'd known, he would have come back. If Addy had sent word, he would have returned immediately and married Zoe. Addy and Zoe thought they knew him so well, but this showed they didn't know him at all. Could Addy's request, that he see to the children's welfare, be her way of making him come home and finish what had started between him and Zoe all those years ago?

The news that he'd lost a child pained him deeply, even though it had happened a long time ago. He might have come home to find a grown son or daughter. Would she have lost the child if he'd been there with her? So many questions, so many emotions—how did he sort them out?

The door banged open, and he looked up. He could smell his steak a mile away. "It's about time."

Glori-Lee followed Pop inside and set the sizzling steak platter on the desk. "Think this is enough to get you through a wedding night?"

"You might want to bring one more. They've tried their damnedest to starve me to death."

"Pop thought I ought to bring one for Zoe." Glori-Lee chuckled as she left the room.

Pop motioned toward the platter. "You don't have much time, boy. Eat up."

Cade sat down in front of his food. "I guess this will be a far cry from when Zoe married Jim."

Pop eyed his steak and potato. "Well, a

little. How'd you feel when you got the news?"

"A week's drunk, and a month of resentment later, I swallowed my pride and admitted she had every right to marry another man."

She'd married Jim, but he'd had to work long and hard to even think of another woman. The marriage had been a bitter pill to swallow, even though Cade had known he was being irrational. Why he'd thought she'd wait for him forever, he didn't know.

Putting on a clean shirt, Pop shook his head. "Don't know why you two took so long to see what's right in front of your noses."

Cade pretended to misunderstand. "Yeah, Glori-Lee cooks a mean steak."

"It ain't the damn steak, Kolby. I'm talking about this marriage bein' the smartest thing you've ever done."

He laughed. "Smart? I gain a wife and four kids with one 'I do.' You call that smart?"

"Don't you be runnin' down matrimony. You might really take to it. Me and my missus, God rest her soul, had a good life, and if you'd give that little woman of yours half a chance, you'd have one, too."

"Doris didn't have Red's temper."

"Well, explain that to my horse. I spent my fair share of nights in the barn." Pop jerked his string tie into place. "Seriously, son, I don't want you hurtin' that little gal. She's a good woman, and everybody's fond of her. Your hide won't be worth a plugged nickel if you do her wrong."

Cade almost choked on the piece of meat he was chewing. "I have no intention of hurting Zoe, but you know the reason we're getting married. Zoe doesn't love me."

Picking up his boots from the floor, Pop spat on them and polished the toes. "Well, I don't know about that. I figured she had her eye on you since she was a young'un. Wouldn't be surprised if she still did."

Zoe hurried across the street with a hundred thoughts racing through her mind. She would have to quickly press her good blue silk, while Holly helped Will and Missy into their Sunday best. Brody had eaten so many biscuits lately; she hoped he could button his knickers.

She couldn't wait to tell them about the wedding. It might not be an ideal solution, but the children would be hers. Hers! Excitement bubbled in her throat. And she would be married to Cade, and who knew? Maybe he would like married life so well he would—

Whoa. Zoe paused, drawing a deep breath. This was exactly the sort of irrational thinking she would have done seventeen years ago. *Just press your good blue silk and be satisfied you no longer have to fear Laticia.*

"Zoe! Wait a minute. I want to talk to you."

She turned to see Perry Drake stepping out of the bank. "No time right now, Perry," she called. "I'm in a hurry."

He caught up with her and took her arm to slow her down. "What's the rush? Is there a fire?"

"No, of course not." She didn't know how

to tell him she was getting married. He'd read far more into their friendship over the years than she had. Still, she knew he would be upset when he heard she was marrying Cade. "There's no easy way to say this, Perry. I'm getting married."

His face drained of color. "You mean they talked you into that ridiculous plan?"

"What plan?"

"The town's plan—you don't know?" He shook his head as if the irony was too much.

She frowned. "I don't know what you're talking about."

"Pop came up with the idea, and the whole town went along with it—except me and a couple others who had better sense."

She snorted. "I can assure you, this is entirely my idea. I want the children, Perry, and the only way to get them is for Cade and me to marry."

"This is insane. Come to your senses!" He took her arm, attempting to steer her toward the bank. "Come to my office and let's talk about it. If it's a husband you want—"

Jerking free of his grasp, she stood her ground. "Laticia said that only family could raise the children. If Cade and I marry, I'll be family and there will be nothing she can do about it."

"My dear." She resented the pained sufferance in his voice. "I know you feel obligated to those children because of your close friendship with Addy, but think of the advantages they would have living with Laticia. She's well-off enough to hire all the help she needs to raise them. They would have the best education—"

"Perry, I love those children and they love me. I know my money is tight, but I'll find a way to give them what they need."

His eyes were grave. "I can't believe you're actually going through with this nonsense."

"It's the only solution, Perry. Please try to understand."

"If you're intent on this madness, I'll stand by you. I'm aware that this marriage is nothing but a sham. Once Cade leaves, I'll help you have the matter discreetly taken care of."

She couldn't believe Perry had said that. She knew the marriage wouldn't be real, but he made it sound so sordid, almost cheap. Once, she would have thought the same thing. Vows taken between a man and woman in the sight of God were not to be taken lightly, and Cade *would* ride away and never come back. But that wouldn't make her devotion to him or the children any less sincere.

She glanced toward the jail. "Perry, we'll have to talk about this later. I have to get the children, and—"

As if she hadn't said anything, he went on. "Those children will be grown and gone in a few years. You'll need companionship. It's no secret how I feel about you."

She was feeling more and more uncomfortable with the conversation. Perry was a confidant, a friend, but it was becoming increasingly clear that he only wanted her— not the children.

"There's something you need to understand, Perry. I will *always* have those children. Even when they grow up and marry, they will still be mine. Their children will be my grandchildren."

"Of course, my dear. I didn't mean to imply that you should just forget them. I meant, we could have a nice life together after they're grown—just you and me. I've always wanted to travel. We could go back East—"

Zoe shook her head, finding the irony of the situation almost laughable. Yesterday she had had no husband; today she had two men ready to marry her. It was almost funny, except there was only one man she wanted. The one she couldn't keep.

"We'll talk later," Perry called as she ran up the front steps to the store entrance.

"Kids!" She hurried past the counter, down the aisle of canned goods. "Get cleaned up and into your best clothes—" She looked around the kitchen. Holly, Missy, and Will sat at the table, long-faced. "What's wrong?"

Will's bottom lip jutted out. "Brody's runnin' away and I want to go with him, but he took all the biscuits."

"Run away? Biscuits? What's this all about?"

Holly got up and put her arms around Zoe's waist, leaning into her. "Brody wrapped Glori-Lee's leftover biscuits in a napkin and said he was running away to California."

Zoe gave Holly a consoling pat. "Where is your big brother?"

Missy pointed to the bedroom. "He's puttin' his clothes in a tow sack."

"Biscuits, too," Will added. "He took Glori-Lee's napkin. I told him he'd get in trouble, runnin' away with Glori-Lee's napkin, but he said he didn't have time to listen to a six-year-old whiner." He teared up. "I ain't a *whiner*. She said he could have the *biscuits*, nothing about keepin' the nap—"

"Okay, Will, that's enough. I'll wash the napkin, and Brody can return it to Glori-Lee."

Will rose and clung to her other side. "Brody won't let me go with him."

Zoe squeezed the two children tightly against her. "No one is going anywhere."

Missy laid her head down and began to weep. "We don't want to go with Aunt Waticia."

Holly turned dark eyes on Zoe, eyes far more mature than her eight years. "Please don't make us go with her."

"Is that what all the running away is about?" Zoe was relieved when all three nodded. "Well, I have good news for you. Your Uncle Cade and I are getting married. That means no one is going anywhere. You're going to live with me."

The squealing and leaping was so loud, Zoe had to cover her ears. "Children, please!"

Brody appeared in the bedroom doorway, a sack over his shoulder, munching on a biscuit. "You really going to be our ma?"

Zoe held out her arms, and all four children came to her. "Your ma will always be your ma, but you'll be my very own children now. We'll be a real family." She blinked back tears of joy. "I'll be the best mama I can be."

"Is Uncle Cwade ouw pa now?" Missy asked, her innocent blue eyes twinkling up at Zoe.

Zoe nodded. The children looked so happy, she couldn't tell them Cade wouldn't be staying. She wouldn't spoil their day—her day, her wedding day.

"I'm going to call him Uncle Pa," Will announced, his tone serious.

Missy giggled, then covered her mouth. "Me, too."

Zoe laughed with her. "Get cleaned up while I press my blue dress." She glanced at Brody. "I hope you didn't crumple your Sunday clothes into that bag, Mr. Wiseman. I don't have time to iron them. Your Uncle Pa is waiting at the jail for us to get married."

Missy started to hop up and down. "We'we going to get mawwied, we'we going to get mawwied!"

Sawyer stuffed a chew into his jaw and called to Susan and Judy, who were trying to look in the jail window. "Go on now. Git. Cade is gettin' married, and Zoe ain't goin' to take kindly to you hangin' 'round gawkin' at him."

The young girls grumbled but stepped back into the crowd.

"Make a path, everyone," Sawyer instructed. "The bride-to-be and her brood's comin' through—did you hear me, Sam? I *said*, step aside."

"Shut your dadburned mouth, Sawyer. I'm movin' fast as I can. I got gout, you know."

Zoe felt proud as a peacock as she and the kids marched into the jail. Edna Mews handed her a nosegay of black-eyed Susans she had picked from her garden.

Pop had put on a clean shirt for his role as best man, and Zoe had never seen Gracie, her matron of honor, look any prettier.

Gracie patted her pale green dress. "I'm as nervous as if it were my own wedding day."

Zoe flashed her a smile, then quickly wiped Will's nose and straightened Brody's shirt collar. The children were a beautiful sight to behold. Her heart beat with anticipation. They would soon belong to her—her and Cade.

Nearly everyone in town had turned out for the event, and Zoe noticed for the first time that something wasn't quite right. She didn't think so much about Pop's wearing a gun and holster, but Gracie looked downright strange with a derringer tucked into her cummerbund. Zoe turned, her gaze scanning the assembled crowd. Half the onlookers were toting weapons. She frowned. Did they think Cade would back out, and they had brought the means to make him change his mind?

"Should the kids be near me?" Cade asked.

She felt his forehead. He was much cooler, and she noticed a couple of red dots on his cheek. "I think the crisis is over. You're breaking out."

Doc stepped over to examine the red marks. "Yep, you got the measles all right. Should start feeling better now."

The children stood between her and Cade,

joining hands. Missy wore a permanent grin on her face and couldn't take her eyes off Uncle Pa. "Awe you glad we'we mawwying you, Uncle Cwade?"

Zoe's heart swelled when she saw Cade smile back at Missy, then give her a wink. They were family. Even if it was for a short time, they were family. She tightened the sky-blue sash on her dress, aware of the way Cade's eyes lingered on her. Pulling her to one side, he put his mouth close to her ear.

"You look pretty," he whispered, and lifted her locket to his lips to press a kiss against the small golden bauble.

"So do you—not pretty," she amended, flushing. "Handsome." She took the locket from his fingers and kissed it, too.

Cade patted Zoe's bottom as he stepped around her to take his place. She discreetly grabbed his impudent hand and bent his thumb back.

Though she knew the terms of the marriage, she couldn't help feeling excited. Mrs. Cade Kolby, mother to the Wisemans. Mother. It had a nice ring to it. Ring!

She quickly turned to Cade. "We don't have a ring."

Cade looked blank for a moment, then turned to Pop. "No ring."

Pop motioned for Ben Pointer and whispered in his ear. Ben nodded, then hurried out the door. He was back shortly with a ring he'd fashioned out of copper. Zoe had never felt so much pride in the townspeople as she did today.

Judging by the looks on their faces, they were thrilled to be here. Little did they know that it was nothing more than a marriage of convenience.

But why all the guns? She had never seen Ben Pointer carry a rifle, and his boys had those shotguns over their shoulders—and at a wedding, no less!

She watched Brody pull a biscuit from his shirt pocket and hand it to Cade, smiling up at his uncle. Cade grinned, waving the child's offering aside.

Reverend Munson arrived, and the crowd surrounded him, all smiling and nodding.

"Dearly beloved, we are gathered together in this house of—" He paused, clearing his throat. "—in this place, to witness the joining of Cade Kolby and Zoe Bradshaw in holy matrimony—"

"Git on with it, Preacher," Roy Baker yelled, "before he changes his mind."

Reverend Munson cleared his throat, then recited the vows.

Reaching for Zoe's hand, Cade stared deeply into her eyes. She swallowed, her gaze locked with his. Her stomach twisted into knots as he spoke his vows with firm conviction. She was grateful for his compassion. No one would guess by the sincerity in his voice that he was marrying her only to give her the children.

The vows were exchanged and witnessed. Reverend Munson closed the Bible and pronounced, "You are man and wife."

Everyone expressed their good wishes.

Kisses were showered on the children, who dutifully returned kiss for kiss.

Cade lifted Zoe's hand and raised it to his lips. "May I kiss the bride?"

Touched by the gesture, she raised his hand to her mouth. "Only if I'm permitted to kiss the groom."

Smiling, he pulled her to him.

"Kiss her, Uncle Pa," Will urged.

Missy giggled, and Holly looked embarrassed.

Brody finished off his last biscuit. "I ain't never gonna kiss a girl," he declared.

Cade grinned at Zoe. "You'll change your mind one of these days, son. Girls can be real nice to kiss."

His tone was soft and seductive, and Zoe felt herself leaning into him, welcoming his embrace.

Their lips had barely brushed together when a clamor came from outside the jail.

"Step aside! I'm coming through!" The swish of Laticia Wiseman's cane whipping the air caused the townspeople to quickly move back and give her the right-of-way.

Laticia's glare pinned Zoe to the wall. "What do you think you are doing?"

Missy stepped forward, wrinkled her nose, and stepped back. "We got mawwied, Aunt Waticia."

"Married!"

Cade pulled Zoe closer. "Laticia, Zoe and I were just married." He smiled. "She's family now."

"Why wasn't I told of this?"

"It was decided rather quickly..." Zoe ventured timidly.

"Abraham!"

"Yes'm?"

Laticia jabbed the air with her walking stick. "You know about this?"

"Jist got wind'a it," he said, coming up behind her. "'Bout ta come tell ya, but got a spell with my belly—"

"You and your *belly*. We're going home where we can get something decent to eat." She whirled and poked Cade in the stomach with the tip of her cane. "I don't know what you're up to, but if I hear that these children are living with anyone but you and Zoe, I'll have your hide hung from the tallest tree. You hear me?"

"Yes, ma'am," Cade said. He glanced at the children and winked. "Better run along. Wouldn't want you coming down with the measles."

"Nonsense. Never been sick a day in my life. Don't intend to start now." She bent down to Holly, who shrank back when her aunt came face-to-face with her. "You children ever need anything, you just let your Aunt Laticia know."

They all nodded, their eyes bulging.

"Abraham! Hitch the buggy. We're going home."

The spinster left in as much of a flurry as she had come in.

"Whew," Edna whispered to May Wilks. "She

needs some of my soap to cover that unfortunate smell she's cursed with."

While Cade talked with Pop, Zoe and the children ran home and hurriedly tidied the living quarters. The children assumed the marriage was the same as their ma and pa's, so it was useless to think Cade would sleep on the settee.

The thought of their first night together preyed on her mind. She felt like a schoolgirl on her first date.

"Uncle Pa is comin'," Will announced, looking out the kitchen window.

Missy pushed open the screen door and ran out to meet him. Zoe watched her leap up and wrap her legs around his waist, planting kisses all over his face.

"Now that's worth coming home for," he said as he walked in carrying the little girl. He looked at Zoe. "Next?"

Zoe felt her face flush. "Have you seen yourself?"

"No. Why? Do I need a shave?"

She pushed him toward the mirror near the sink. "That, too, but—"

Cade put Missy down, then looked into the mirror and groaned. "Do I look like this all over?"

"Do you itch all over?"

"Yes."

"I believe that answers your question." She stifled a giggle. "I'll get the baking soda paste, and you can put it on."

"I'll do it fow you," Missy said.

Cade's eyes met Zoe's. "Thanks, honey, but I think maybe your new ma should do it."

Zoe narrowed her eyes at him. "Go in the bedroom. I'll bring you the paste."

He wrinkled his nose at Missy. "She sure knows how to take the fun out of measles."

Later that night, when the children were asleep, Zoe brought cups of tea into the parlor. Cade was stretched out on the settee reading a journal.

"Feeling better?" she asked.

He took a cup from her. "Better, thanks." After taking a sip of tea, he moved his feet to the floor and patted the seat beside him. "Sit down. I want to talk to you."

She sat down and studied her cup. "The children are so happy—we did the right thing, Cade."

"Did we?"

She looked up. "Don't you think so?"

"I admit I've fallen in love with those kids."

Smiling, she said, "Easy to do." Their eyes searched each other's. "Not so easy to undo, huh?"

"Not so easy, but you know what I have to do. I'll stay another week or so, until Laticia is satisfied the marriage is binding."

"Is it safe for you to stay?"

He didn't answer her question. "If I could stay forever, I would. I don't want to go, Red. The kids—you."

Her gaze darted up to meet his. "Me?"

"It's not going to be easy, raising four children on your own."

She smiled, leaning back. "You've made me very happy. I can't complain."

"Are the children enough for you?"

She thought for a long moment. Was it enough? No, she wanted him. She never thought she would wish this on anyone, but she wanted Hart McGill dead. "It'll have to be. I know that."

The mantel clock struck midnight, and Zoe knew the awkward moment had arrived. "It's late."

"Do you want me to sleep here?"

"No, the children would wonder why we weren't sleeping together like their ma and pa. I put Missy on the pallet with Holly."

Cade ran his fingers through his hair. "I don't know, Red. I'm not sure I can sleep in the same bed with you and not—"

"Of course you can. I'll make it easy for you." Whether the vows were spoken in earnest or in need, they were no less married. It wouldn't be so hard to sleep with him, to know he was lying next to her, to pretend he would always be there.

"We could—"

"Don't say it." She was having the same aching want, but she was strong. She would not consummate a marriage that wasn't going to last more than a week or two.

Zoe undressed first and crawled under the covers. Cade joined her a few minutes later and lay stiffly beside her.

"Good night," she whispered.

"What's good about it?"

She stuffed the corner of the blanket in her mouth to keep from giggling. Eventually, she heard his even breathing and she relaxed, relieved he wasn't going to make an issue of the marriage bed.

Toward morning, she felt a hand on her bottom. "Cade!" she hissed.

"Huh?" Cade sat up sleepily. "What's wrong?"

They turned to look at each other, but their view was blocked as a yawning Missy sat up between them and asked innocently, "Is it mowning yet?"

A brisk wind whipped the sheets on the line Monday morning. Cade rounded the corner of the building and came to a dead stop when he saw his wife. The sight of her trim bottom poking up as she leaned over, up to her elbows in fresh laundry, sent blood rushing to his most sensitive extremity. Four or five clothespins were stuck in her mouth, and her slight weight was buffeted by the wind as she pinned up a long row of petticoats. The starched muslin snapped briskly in the stiff breeze, which turned her hair topsy-turvy. It was as if Cade were fifteen again, spying on her at the swimming hole. Once, she'd stripped out of her clothes and waded in, loosening her long red hair to float freely on the shimmering water. Today his blood was racing exactly the way it had at his first sight of her bare breasts.

Coming from behind, he reached around

her and held the garments to the line so she could move easily. "Are we running a boarding house?" he asked.

She smiled, accepting his help. "No, why?"

His gaze scanned the lengthy stretch of clothes. Overalls, long johns, women's dresses, and children's garments filled the billowing rows. "An orphanage laundry?"

"No."

"Confederate army?"

She pinned up another skirt. "No, silly, we just have a lot of wash."

He shook his head. "No one on earth is this dirty."

"There's a stack of clean blankets in the kitchen. Will you take them over to the jail for me?"

"Sure. I just want to kiss my wife first."

"Silly you. Now, what do you really want?"

"Baking soda." He scratched an angry blotch. "I'm itching like blue blazes."

She made a sympathetic face. "It must be awful."

The itching couldn't hold a candle to the tightness in his groin. Being married in name only was worse than beating himself senseless with a rock. "Where are the kids?"

"Playing at the livery."

"I thought Abraham left."

"He did. They like Ben. He gives them apples."

"*I* give them apples."

"You spoil them rotten, and you have to stop. They're beginning to expect all the licorice

272

and gum balls you generously dole out from the candy jar."

"A little candy never hurt anyone."

"I mean it, Cade. Stop being so permissive with them. They're crazy about you, and it's only going to make it harder when you leave."

"All right." He handed her a petticoat that looked too big for her. "I'll make it a point to be as mean and cranky as you are—"

She threw the wet petticoat at him, and it hit him in the face.

Leaning over, he calmly plucked up a pair of bloomers and flung them at her.

A full-blown laundry war erupted, and they fought it out until the last clean sheet lay dirty and trampled under their feet.

His stomach tightened at the sight of her hair falling loose and unfettered over her shoulders, her face flushed with exertion. He wanted to pick her up and carry her to that damn bed. With Missy not around to protect her, he'd show her no mercy. Hours of no mercy. Days of no mercy.

Grinning, she scooped up the laundry basket. "I opened a new box of baking soda this morning. It's on the kitchen cabinet." Walking toward the washtub, she called over her shoulder, "Will you be home for supper?"

He shouldn't be. If he was smart, he'd be riding out about now. "What are you having?"

"Rabbit and dumplings."

Rabbit and dumplings. His mouth watered just thinking about it. He winked, smiling when she blushed. "Try keeping me away."

He opened the back screen and stepped into the kitchen. It was quiet without the kids' chatter. He wondered what it would be like to be ten years old and have no responsibility other than to keep out of trouble. Moving to the mirror, he dabbed the soda mixture on his face. A fine-looking groom he made. Measles. At his age. It would be humiliating if McGill caught him in this predicament.

His gaze moved to the gold locket lying next to the dishpan. Red's.

Bending closer to the mirror, he frowned. The stubble of beard felt familiar, but it itched as much as the rest of his body did. Rubbing his chin, he looked at himself and was disgusted with what he saw.

You like this idea of marriage, don't you? Get over it, son. Don't get comfortable with family life. It's not for you—not now, not ever. The feel of Zoe lying soft and warm against you, drifting off to sleep with the smell of her hair instead of the smell of wood smoke. Her soft breathing, so different from the lonely call of a coyote.

Shoving the images aside, he brushed his hair into place, then settled his hat on his head.

Crossing the street a few moments later, he dropped the blankets by the jail, then headed for the mayor's house. Knocking on the door, he waited until Gracie answered. Her face split in a wide grin when she saw him.

"Lordy, if you don't look a sight."

"Can I come in? I'm not contagious, just ugly."

Gracie opened the door wider. "You looking

for Lawrence? He's over at the town hall. He and—"

"Actually, I want to talk to you."

"Oh?" Gracie closed the door and shooed him into the parlor. "I'll make coffee."

"That's not necessary; I won't take up your time. I wanted to talk to you about a personal matter."

Gracie patted her bun, her face reddening. "Well..."

"About Zoe."

"Oh?" She looked puzzled. "Personal?"

"I know you and Zoe are close. That's why I came to you. I'd rather no one else knew about this conversation."

"Certainly." Gracie's features sobered. "It sounds serious. What's wrong?"

"I'm not sure, but I have a hunch Zoe's having money problems."

"Oh." Gracie folded her hands, seemingly uneasy with the subject.

"She's in trouble, isn't she?"

Her uneasy gaze darted about the room. It landed on a mussed sofa pillow, and she stood up to fluff it. "Did Zoe say something to you?"

"No."

Sitting down again, Gracie busied herself picking at a thread on the cuff of her sleeve. "I didn't think she would talk to you about that."

"Then *you* talk to me about it. Is she taking in washing and ironing for extra money?"

"Well...what do you think?"

He thought about the loaded clothesline—

not just this morning, but every morning since he'd arrived. "I think no one's that dirty."

Smiling, Gracie looked up. "She'd have my hide if she knew I was telling her problems, but, yes, she's been washing and ironing for other people for some time now. She's been in financial trouble since Jim died. He left her a stack of unpaid bills, and the store books carried a lot of credit that somehow never got paid. She's had to take in extra work to make ends meet."

Cade's jaw tightened. "I knew it."

"Zoe's a proud woman, Cade. She doesn't want others knowing her problems. I wouldn't know about them if I wasn't with her every day to see the worry lines around her eyes. She works herself near to death, and now that she has four extra mouths to feed, she's working even harder."

"What debts does she have?"

"She'd never tell me, but I do know the bank payment seems to be the hardest for her to meet. Jim borrowed heavily during the last year of his life. Lawrence and I have encouraged her to sell the store, but she won't hear of it. The store has been in the Bradshaw family for years, and she feels she can't let it go."

Cade felt his anger growing. Why hadn't Zoe told him about her situation? He'd offered money for the children's keep, but she had refused it. Why? Because it was his money? Blood money? Was pride overriding her common sense? She couldn't lose the store. It was all she had.

Cade rose to his feet. "Thank you, Gracie. I appreciate your honesty."

Gracie sighed. "If Zoe were to find out—"

"She won't." He smiled. "And you can trust me on that."

"I do trust you, Cade. You're the best thing that ever happened to Zoe. I hope you don't have to go off on your bounty-hunting any time soon."

"Me, too, Gracie." He slipped on his hat and pulled it low. "Say hello to Lawrence for me."

Perry Drake was bent over a ledger when Cade appeared in his office doorway. Perry frowned. "Where's Mary Beth?"

"She wasn't at her desk."

"Sorry. I'm busy." The banker went on with his work.

Cade walked over to the desk and closed the ledger. He met Perry's angry stare. "You just got unbusy."

"What do you want, Cade?"

"I'm here to pay off Zoe's note."

Perry paused in thought, then motioned toward a chair. "Sit down."

Cade removed his hat and took the seat opposite the desk.

"I understand congratulations are in order."

"Yes. Zoe and I were married yesterday."

Perry didn't look happy about the turn of events. Cade knew the man wanted Zoe for himself, but he wasn't there to argue the point.

The banker steepled his fingers. "I'm surprised the town pulled the ruse off so easily."

"What ruse?"

"Tricking Zoe into marrying you."

Cade kept his temper in check. Drake was a sore loser. He expected that. "Zoe wasn't tricked into anything."

Perry pushed back from the desk and crossed his legs. "I understand it's a temporary arrangement. Zoe feels Laticia Wiseman is too old to rear the children. That isn't my thought, but it's Zoe's."

Cade lifted a brow. "Who said the marriage is temporary?"

Drake's smile was as cold as a January wind. "Come now, you're not implying the union is born from undying love?"

"I'm not implying anything. What are *you* trying to imply, Perry?"

"Only that I'll go along with the arrangement—for now."

Cade looked away, fighting the urge to wipe the smirk off Drake's face with the back of his hand.

"I'm aware Zoe has a good heart," Perry went on. "She's concerned about your sister's orphans, and her strong sense of responsibility won't permit her to see them go to strangers."

"Really." Cade leaned back and looked at the pompous banker. "I get the impression she loves the kids."

Perry opened a walnut box on his desk and took out a cigar. He inclined his head. "Smoke?"

Cade shook his head.

"Pity." He studied the length of the imported cigar. "I purchase them in Boston. They're very good, actually."

Cade got back to the point of the visit. "How much does Zoe owe the bank?"

Perry held a match to the tip of the cigar, puffing. "Sorry. That's privileged information."

"Not for her husband."

Fanning the match out, Perry grinned. "You're not her husband, Kolby. You're nothing more than a temporary fix to an impossible situation."

Cade's eyes narrowed. "How much does she owe the bank?"

"I said that's privileged information."

"Not if I'm paying it off."

Perry's feet hit the floor, and he scooted back to the desk. "You can't do that."

"My money isn't good here?"

"Of course it's good....It's just—"

"The note, Drake. I'm paying it off." Cade stood up and stared at the banker. "Now."

Perry pushed back and got up. "We'll see about that. I'll have Mary Beth get Zoe, and we'll settle this—"

Cade watched the color drain from Perry's face when he blocked his way. "Get the damn note, Drake."

He'd like to think he was intimidating the contemptuous runt, but he knew his present limitations. He might have a Colt strapped to his thigh, but a man with baking soda smeared on his face carried little authority. Still,

Drake ran a bank, and if a man was offered good money, Drake couldn't afford to turn it down.

Straightening, Perry walked to the door to summon his secretary. "Please bring Mrs. Bradshaw's complete file."

"Mrs. Kolby's," Cade corrected.

Perry cleared his throat. "The file, Mary Beth."

Cade sat in silence as he and Drake waited. Within a few minutes, Mary Beth returned and laid a sheaf of papers on the desk. "This is Mrs. Bradshaw's full accounting, Mr. Drake."

"Thank you." He nodded for her to leave them in privacy.

Perry scanned the long columns. "Are you aware of what you're doing? This is a goodly sum."

"Just tell me how much."

The banker handed the document to him, and Cade read it. "I'll wire my bank in Wichita. You'll have the full amount soon."

"If that's your decision." Perry inclined his head, gritting his teeth.

Cade got up to leave. "One other thing, Drake." He settled his hat low. Perry looked put out, refusing to glance up or respond. "I don't want Zoe to know where the money came from."

Perry lifted his gaze. "What am I to tell her? Her fairy godmother came to her rescue?"

Cade winked. "Tell her you paid it off. It'll strengthen your position in my wife's eyes."

Chapter 16

The front door of the Bradshaw General Store opened and the Kolby family emerged, all dressed in their Sunday best. Cade, Brody, and Will wore suits and ties. The dresses that Zoe, Holly, and Missy wore rivaled the patch of colorful wildflowers blooming next to the porch.

It was hard for Zoe to believe the week had passed so quickly; even harder to believe Cade had agreed to go to church. If she didn't let herself think about McGill, she could picture them as a real family. Not one argument had occurred this week; they were making progress.

Missy paused to preen for Cade. Turning in a wide circle, she held out her arms. "Do you like my dress, Uncle Cwade?"

"It's unusually pretty, Missy."

The little girl's eyes suddenly clouded. "My ma made it fow me."

Kneeling beside her, Cade pulled her close and held her. "Your ma was a real good seamstress. You must be very proud of such a pretty dress." He drew Holly to his side as well. "And might I say, I'll have to beat the boys away with a club this morning because you look so fetching."

The tender scene touched Zoe's heart. She hadn't known he had such a soft spot.

"Did you love my ma, Uncle Cwade?"

"I loved her a lot, Missy. Your ma was my sister—the way Holly is your sister."

281

Missy's tears dissolved, and Zoe laughed when the little girl gazed at him slyly, as if he'd said something very amusing but not quite credible.

Cade grinned. "Once, your ma and I were little, just like you and Will and Brody and Holly. We played together, ate our meals together, lived in the same house, got switchings from our ma and pa."

Missy pushed against his chest. "You did not! Ma's too big to get switchings!"

"Missy, stop asking your uncle so many questions." Zoe opened her parasol and studied the sky. "I'm afraid we're in for another rain."

Picking Missy up in his arms, Cade squeezed her affectionately, then set her in the buggy he'd gotten from John and Addy's barn. "It won't rain for awhile."

"We awe weally going to have fun, Uncle Cwade." Missy tightened her hold on Cade's neck. "We'll go to Sunday mowning meeting and thennnn...we'll go on a family picnic."

Cade glanced at Zoe and grinned. "I can't think of anything more fun. Can you?"

Zoe laughed. "Sounds like fun to me." She straightened her bonnet, nervous about being seen with Cade at church for the first time as newlyweds. The townspeople would look for signs of marital bliss, and all they would see would be signs of sleepless nights. It had been a long time since a man had been in her bed. The old saying "two's company, three's a crowd" came to mind. She was relieved that a simple wedding band wasn't going to interfere with Missy's sleeping preference.

Zoe bit back a smile, thinking how nice it would be if the marriage were real. It was torture having Cade's warm body so close, but so inaccessible. She wondered how John and Addy had managed, then smiled when she realized that finding intimate time obviously hadn't been a problem. Brody, Will, Holly, and Missy were living proof of their passion.

Cade glanced in her direction. "Something funny?"

"No." She pulled on her gloves, then drew a steadying breath. "We'd best hurry or we'll be late for the service."

The bell in the steeple tolled the Sabbath as the newly formed family arrived. Buggies and carriages filled the field next to the Good Shepherd Baptist Church. The Kolby family filed in and came to a sudden stop inside the front door.

Brody looked at Zoe. "Where do we sit?"

Zoe glanced down the long rows of wooden benches. The Kolby pew was on the right; the Bradshaw pew, on the left near the front. The Wiseman pew was closest to the back.

Will polished the toes of his shoes on the back of his pantlegs. "Where do we sit now? Are we a Kolby, a Wiseman, or a Bradshaw?"

Zoe glanced at Cade expectantly.

"Yeah, Uncle Cwade. What are we?"

Taking Missy's hand, he held Zoe's with his other and led them down the aisle. The other children followed. Pausing at an empty row near the front, he ushered the family in.

"Oh," Missy said. "We'we a new family—just us!"

Cade slid into the seat beside Zoe and pulled Missy onto his lap. "That's right. We're our own family now."

"Oh, goodie!"

Zoe settled back in the pew, aware that all eyes were on them. She felt Gracie's beaming consent and Edna's glowing approval. Though she shouldn't, she felt proud sitting next to her handsome husband. The red splotches on his face had faded and were barely noticeable. In her estimation, he was the most handsome man in the room.

Cade shifted in the pew, leaning closer to whisper, "Why is everyone staring?"

Pretending to scrunch lower in her seat, Zoe looked at the ceiling.

"What's wrong?" Cade's gaze followed hers. He stared at the open rafters.

"We're all afraid the roof's going to fall in," she said in a low voice.

His eyes scanned the sturdy beams. "Looks strong enough. Have you been having trouble with it?"

"No, but you're in church this morning."

He gave her a sour look as Edna Mews got up from her seat and came over to them.

"Hello, dears. My, don't you make a fine-looking family. Addy and John would be so happy."

Zoe tried not to show her bliss. "Thank you, Edna."

When Reverend Munson took his place at the pulpit, Edna slipped back to her pew, and Zoe picked up a hymnal. Cade flipped noisily through the songbook, looking for the right page. Zoe reached over and turned to "What a Friend We Have in Jesus." as Lorraine Munson took her place at the organ and started to play.

Cade's deep baritone blended melodiously with Zoe's alto as they sang the first of the morning's selected hymns. Zoe was taken back twenty years to when they had sung together as children in the same church.

The congregation sat down as the music died away, and Reverend Munson approached the podium with his Bible under his arm.

Turning his benevolent eyes on the newlyweds, he said, "Good morning, friends."

"Good morning, Reverend," the congregation chorused.

"And what a glorious morning it is. I see the Kolby family is with us today." He inclined his head toward Cade and Zoe. "No better place to be than in the house of the Lord."

The minister opened his Bible, and Zoe did a double take when she saw the outline of a six-shooter beneath his suit coat.

Cade leaned closer. "Is that a gun?"

She put her finger to her lips and nodded, afraid someone would hear him. Her eyes widened when she noticed the blunderbuss lying across old Bess Harris's lap.

"Reverend Munson carries a *gun*?" Cade asked.

She elbowed him to be quiet.

"The Scripture this morning is about love. The Good Book tells us from the beginning of creation, God made them man and woman. For this cause, a man shall leave father and mother, and likewise shall a woman leave her parents, and the two shall become one. Consequently, they are no longer two, but one, flesh." The minister paused, clearing his throat. "Where God has joined two together, let no man come between."

Reverend Munson closed the Bible and grasped the sides of the pulpit, leaning toward the congregation. He paused for a moment as if in deep thought. "Marriage is a covenant between a man and a woman and God."

When Cade squirmed beside her, Zoe acted as if she didn't notice. Why Reverend Munson had picked this morning to preach on the sanctity of marriage, she didn't know. Did he guess their marriage was for improper and self-serving reasons? Guilt nagged her. A week ago, the children had seemed a viable and sane reason to marry. This morning, the minister's words reminded her that marriage was a sacred union not to be entered into lightly, and she felt a twinge of conscience.

What would God have had her do? Turn the children over to Laticia, and watch the fear in their eyes as they went off to be reared by a woman who would make a more appropriate great-grandmother? Perhaps marriage wasn't the right answer, but it was the only one they had had at their disposal.

Cade fidgeted in his seat, occasionally glancing at her. Did he feel the pressure, the focused eyes, the consenting nods in the congregation? Zoe suddenly felt too warm.

"A woman should cleave to her husband and

he to his wife, forsaking all others," the reverend said. "That's what the Good Book tells us."

Fanning herself with a hanky, Zoe blew a lock of hair off her forehead. *Was he looking at her and Cade?* Thirty-five minutes of preaching felt like a month. She hadn't realized she was as rigid as a board until she saw Woodall Thompson checking his pocket watch, signaling that the service was coming to an end.

She fanned harder when the reverend focused on Cade. "This morning I want to close this service in Cade and Zoe Kolby's honor with the message found in First Corinthians."

Zoe bit her lip, trying to control her emotions. The solemnity of the moment had silenced all in the room. Not a whisper sounded or a head turned.

The reverend spoke now from memory, choosing words everyone in the room could understand. "If I had the gift of being able to speak in other languages without learning them, and could thus speak in every language there is on both heaven and earth, but I didn't love others, I would be talking only to hear myself talk. If I had the gift of knowing everything that will happen in the future, and knew everything about everything, but didn't love others, what good would it do? Even if I had the gift of faith so that I could speak to a mountain and make it move, I would still be worth nothing at all without love."

Reverend Munson lowered his voice. "Love

is patient and kind, never jealous or envious, never boastful or proud, never haughty or selfish or rude. Love does not demand or seek its own way. It is not irritable or touchy; it doesn't hold grudges and will hardly notice when others do it wrong. It is never glad about injustice, but rejoices whenever truth wins out. Love does not rejoice in unrighteousness, but rejoices in the truth; bears all things, believes all things; hopes all things; endures all things."

Zoe swallowed back tears, wanting to believe. Was everlasting, unselfish love between a man and woman possible? Across the aisle she saw Gracie and Lawrence holding hands. Their union had stood the test for more than forty years.

Edna and Walt sat together, Edna dabbing her eyes with her handkerchief as Walt patted her knee. Thirty-seven years ago, they'd started life together.

Everywhere Zoe looked in the church, she saw couples who had taken vows and held them sacred. Yet she had taken vows she never intended to keep. How could she presume to judge Cade when her own life needed a good housecleaning?

Reverend Munson stepped down from the podium. "In closing, the Good Book tells us: faith, hope, and love abide—and the greatest of these is love." He looked at the congregation. "I hope each and every one of you in this room will remember these words and apply them to your own marriages." His gaze rested on Cade. "For until a man finds his purpose, he will not find happiness."

After the service, Cade made his way out of the church, pausing to visit with well-wishers. Now that the children were settled, Zoe knew their days together as a family were over. Reverend Munson's sermon had been poignant, but they'd come too far to abandon reason.

Cade had promised to make the parting brief and unemotional. He'd tell the children that something had come up and he had to leave. He just wouldn't tell them he wasn't coming back. In time she would have to find the words to explain why he hadn't returned.

As Zoe watched him shake hands, admired his smile, and warmed to the deep timbre of his voice, she knew she'd miss him even more this time. Her newly formed family would never be the same once he was gone. He'd leave a void big enough to throw Herschel Mallard's dead bull through, but that was the bargain they'd struck. Endless lonely days and cold nights was the price she had to pay.

Reverend Munson's message had hit its mark. If she'd had any thoughts of dissolving the marriage, they were gone now. How could she break her vows when she'd spent most of her life wishing Cade was her husband?

As the crowd started to disperse, Cade took hold of Will's hand. Zoe noticed Missy playing nearby in a mud puddle and sighed. "She'll ruin her dress," she told Cade.

"It'll wash, won't it?"

She called for Missy to come to her, fishing a handkerchief out of her handbag. As Missy ran up, she handed Cade her purse and begin to wipe at the muddy stains.

"Missy, you know better than to play in the dirt."

Cade playfully draped Zoe's reticule over his arm and began twirling it primly around his wrist in an attempt to make Missy laugh. She favored him with a toothless grin.

Holly giggled. "Uncle Cade, you're silly."

"And he makes a pitifully homely woman," Zoe teased, joining in the nonsense.

Cade straightened, pretending to take offense. "I beg your pardon?"

Zoe handed him the soiled hanky, and he daintily shook it loosely in the air and executed several graceful pirouettes as the girls' laughter grew louder.

Encouraged by their reaction, he twirled again on one foot—and landed in front of Shelby Moore, who was just coming down the church steps.

Moore did a double take of comical disbelief.

The hanky in Cade's hand sagged. "Morning, Shelby."

Shelby pushed past him, muttering something under his breath that sounded like "sissy bounty hunter."

Cade grinned as Shelby stalked off. "Shut up, Moore, or I'll hit you with my handbag."

• • •

Gracie and Lawrence paused to watch Zoe and her family climb into their buggy, then they turned to speak to Edna, Walt, and Sawyer. Pop joined them, and the six visited for a few minutes.

Gracie's eyes followed Cade's and Zoe's buggy as it rattled out of the churchyard. "They make a fine-looking family, don't they?"

Pop nodded. "Cade is sure stickin' 'round a long time. Thought he'd have headed out by now. Must be takin' to family life better than he thought he would."

Sawyer bit off a wad of chew and stuck it in his jaw. "He's jist stickin' 'round to keep that old crone off his back. My guess is he'll be movin' on before long."

"Don't call it rain before you're wet," Pop said. "I have a feelin' those two will be together for a long, long time."

"Well," Gracie said, "I don't think theirs is a marriage in the biblical sense."

Edna frowned. "You mean what I think you mean?"

Gracie nodded.

"Did Zoe tell you that?"

"Of course not, Edna. A lady wouldn't tell tales out of school, but..." Gracie hesitated a moment, glancing at the men. "Missy mentioned that she sleeps between them at night."

"Now, that's a shame," Walt said. "Those two need some time alone."

Sawyer spat. "That marriage needs some of that credible stuff."

"It sure does," Pop said. "Anyone in the mood for a shivaree?"

"A shivaree?" Gracie patted her handkerchief to her bosom. "Aren't we a little late? They've already been married a week."

Pop cackled. "All the better. They won't be expectin' it."

As they entered the store, Zoe pulled off her bonnet and called over her shoulder, "Get your clothes changed, children, while I make the sandwiches." She walked through the store tying an apron around her waist. There were a dozen and one things she should be doing, but when Cade had mentioned a picnic, she'd known she was outnumbered.

"Can I help?" Cade took off his coat and draped it over the back of a kitchen chair.

"Thanks—here." She handed him an apron. "Don't get your shirt dirty."

"You mean Jim's shirt."

She looked away. She'd meant to dispose of Jim's clothes, but she'd been busy. Cade's broad shoulders strained the fabric across his back. The arms were tight, and the buttonholes stretched to their limits, accentuating his larger build.

When she looked back, Cade was holding up the apron, trying to figure out which end was top and which was bottom. She imagined he wasn't too happy about wearing it.

"How do women get into these contraptions?"

Zoe glanced over her shoulder as she sliced bread. "Need some help?"

He nodded, holding the apron out to her. She slipped the neckpiece over his head, then reached around his waist to tie the sash.

"Thanks."

"You're welcome." She continued to slice the bread, feeling warm beneath his perusal as he watched her perform the mundane task. "Something wrong?"

"I was just wondering what the hell hit me."

"What do you mean?"

"How did I get into this predicament? Until a couple of weeks ago, I had only myself to worry about. Now I'm in an apron about to have a picnic with my wife and four kids."

Smiling, she ignored the rush of sentiment his confession provoked. "And?"

"It's not a fair fight." His voice dropped to a husky timbre. "Five against one."

Over her shoulder she said, "Are you going to help or not?"

"What do you want me to do?"

Be a husband and a father. Love me, stay with me. If you loved us, you'd find a way to make it work.

"Get the picnic basket from the back porch and pack a jar of relish. Oh, and wrap up a few cookies—not too many. Brody will eat them 'til they're gone."

Cade was listening, but half his mind was on the way her hands delicately placed thick slices of ham on the bread. He turned away, unable to keep his eyes off her breasts as she stretched up to reach something on the top shelf. Lust wasn't his only emotion; he admired her—admired the way she handled the kids and her life, and how hard she worked to keep everything going. The bare nape of her neck, so white and vulnerable, had such an arousing effect on him that he completely lost his train of thought.

"Cade!" She put her hands on her hips. "What is the matter with you? You put a jar of tomatoes in the basket. I said relish. And get the leftover chicken out of the icebox."

"Sorry," he murmured. She was domesticating him. Making him wear aprons, wash up before supper, and shave every day. Today in church, the preacher had read the "love" verses from the Bible. The worst thing was, he'd liked it.

"We can't take our clothes off in front of the boys," Holly complained as the children emerged from the bedroom. "Brody said he has to go in his long johns 'cause he can't find his everyday britches."

"Oh, poo!" Missy said, wrinkling her nose. "Bwody has a hole in the seat of his long johns."

Zoe untied her apron and laid it on the back of a chair. "No one is going to a picnic in his underwear. Cade, if you'll finish wrapping sandwiches, I'll find the elusive britches. Hurry along, girls, and change your clothes."

Cade stacked the sandwiches on a piece of butcher paper and wrapped up the package, then stuck it into the basket, next to the plates and utensils. Then he wrapped and packed the chicken. He found himself whistling under his breath. His hands paused, and he smiled, thinking about the time he'd snuck up on Zoe and Addy at the swimming hole one sunny afternoon years back. Their clothes had been hanging on a branch, begging to be taken, so he'd obliged. If he hadn't laughed so loud, they would never have caught him. The look on Zoe's face when she'd waded out of the water, naked as a bluejay and spoiling for a fight, had been worth getting the switching of his life from Mama when Addy told on him.

"Anybody here?"

Cade glanced up to see Shelby Moore standing at the screen door. "Come on in, Shelby."

"Hate to bother you on Sunday, but—" Shelby eyed Cade. "Pop still laid up?"

"Yeah. What can I do for you? Found any more dead bulls?"

"No, it's my chickens this time, but—uh—it can wait. I see you're busy—"

Cade looked down, then jerked off the apron. "Just getting ready for a picnic."

"I think I'll wait for Pop to get back to sheriffin'."

"I can take care of it, Shelby."

"No disrespect, Kolby, but Pop can handle it later."

Shelby left as Cade absently reached up and scratched an itch. Hell. He knew Shelby was thinking he was a big sissy.

With a full belly, and the kids off swimming in the creek, Cade lay down on the blanket beside Zoe, who'd dozed off. He rolled to his side and gazed at her. She deserved the well-earned rest. He'd never known a woman who worked as hard as Red did. He lifted a lock of her hair and let it slide between his fingers. The brownish tress smelled of soap and sunshine. Snapping off a blade of grass, he ran it lightly under her nose.

Murmuring, she brushed her chin.

He lowered the blade, tickling her jawline, then along her forehead, in soft, fluttery strokes.

Her hand grazed her nose and she squirmed, opening her eyes.

Tenderly he brushed hair from her cheek. He caught her hand and held it against his face. Her gaze was soft; her skin, warm. The scent of wildflowers wafted on the air, reminding him how sweet she was.

"Stop it."

"Why don't you make me?" He scooted closer, determined not to let her go. It was past time she admitted her feelings for him. They were nose-to-nose. Her breathing quickened, confirming she wasn't as immune to his advances as she claimed.

"Cade, the children will see us—"

"So? They know we're married." He caught the tip of her ear in his mouth and tugged playfully. A small gasp escaped her lips, and he smiled. As her hands pushed against his chest, he felt her tremble and knew she didn't want him to stop.

Shoving him aside, she sat up. "Behave yourself."

"When you're around, I can think of only one thing." He watched a blush brighten her cheeks. She was beautiful, and he wanted her with a passion he'd never known was possible, a passion that had grown over the years, smoldering and intensifying like a fire in his soul.

"Cade," she warned, narrowing her eyes. "You're impossible."

He casually ran the blade of grass along the swells of her breasts and neckline, wishing he could push the fabric aside. It had been so long since he'd seen her undressed or run his hands over her smooth skin. He'd been little more than a boy back then, and now he wanted to love her like a man, slow and easy, with all the passion and tenderness he'd saved only for her.

"Do you know, I used to think about you every night just before I went to sleep?"

"You did not."

"I did, Red." He tilted her chin with his finger and admitted in a low voice, "Every night I imagined your smile, and the way your left cheek dimples when you laugh." His finger moved across her lips, down her neck, then tugged on the tuft of lace at the neckline between her breasts. "Want to know what else I imagined?"

"No."

"Coward." His fingers toyed with her bodice, trying to pull it a bit lower, but it seemed as stubborn as the woman who wore it. What would it take to convince her he loved her? It wasn't fair to love her, then to

297

leave her, but he couldn't help himself. He wanted this woman more than life itself, yet it was her life he had to protect.

"You're terrible, you know it?" She lay back down on her stomach.

"Give me an opportunity to redeem myself." He slipped his arm around her waist and pulled her back to face him. She looked as young as she had the day he'd left—the same beautiful smile, the same fiery red hair, the same tiny waist—but she filled out the top of her dress like a woman instead of the young girl he'd left behind.

Her gaze softened as he twisted a lock of her hair around his finger. He'd be a happy man if she always looked at him the way she was doing at this moment. "What did I do to put the twinkle back in those lovely eyes?"

"You gave me the children."

That wasn't the answer he'd hoped for, but it was a start. As he lowered his head to kiss her, she didn't pull away. His lips closed over hers, and his tongue teased until she parted her mouth and let him explore her warm, familiar sweetness. She tasted so very good, responding to his kiss with a fervor that drove all rational thought from his mind, waking his masculine needs. If he didn't stop kissing her, he'd embarrass himself in front of the children. Reluctantly he pulled back and stared into her glazed eyes.

"I'll be forever grateful, Cade." She touched his cheek. "I'll be the best mother to our children that I know how to be."

"*Our* children, Red? They're yours now."

"No," she said, her fingers tracing his nose, his eyebrows, his cheeks. "No matter what happens, they're ours." She threaded her fingers through his hair and sighed. "I'll write you often, and the children will write, too. Maybe someday, when they're older, you can come visit."

"No. When I ride out, it will be for good." Her eyes filled with pain, and he squeezed her hand. This was the pain he didn't want to put her through, the hurt he didn't want to face. "No letters, no visits. It has to be that way, Red."

"You don't want a letter from me? Or from the children?"

The anguish in her voice tore at his heart. It wasn't what he wanted, but he had no choice. "No. If they found one of your letters they'd come after you, Red. I can't risk that."

"Then don't leave."

"Do you want me to stay?" Silence hung between them like a heavy, dark shroud.

Zoe sighed. "Would you stay if I asked?"

"How-do, folks!"

Cade and Zoe broke apart to see Ben Pointer's two sons coming through the clearing, shotguns over their shoulders.

Cade frowned. The first meaningful conversation he and Zoe had had since they'd been married, and these two yokels had to interrupt them. "What are you doing out here? Hunting?"

"Er—that's right," said one.

"Yeah, huntin'," said the other.

They stood as still as church mice except

for their eyes, which were rolling back and forth, scanning the area. Cade knew they weren't hunting. They had no bag to carry their game, and both of them were hanging together instead of scouting the area. They were definitely not hunting.

"Looking for squirrels?" Zoe asked.

"Yeah...yeah, squirrels—"

"Quail."

"Well, which is it?" Cade asked.

"Quail."

"Squirrels."

The older boy pushed the other, then tipped his hat to Zoe. "Nice seeing you, ma'am. Looks like there ain't no trouble here. We'll be moseying along now."

Cade nodded. "Be careful going home."

When they were out of earshot, Zoe looked at Cade. "What was that all about?"

He shook his head. "Have you noticed that everyone in town is suddenly carrying a gun—even Gracie?"

"And Reverend Munson," Zoe said. "I've never known him to carry a gun, ever, but he had one stuck in his belt this morning."

"Pointer's boys weren't hunting squirrels *or* quail." Instinct told him something was wrong. He glanced around, his hand resting on his Colt.

"What is it? Do you hear something?" Zoe asked.

A clap of thunder disrupted the conversation. "Damn," Cade said, putting on his hat. "It's going to rain."

Zoe grabbed up the basket and gathered the

corners of the blanket just as the first drops fell.

Taking her hand, Cade called the children out of the water. "Run for the buggy!"

The kids scrambled onto the bank, enthralled by the sudden rain shower. "Can we play in the rain?" Brody asked, holding his face toward the sky with his mouth open to catch the drops.

"Can we?" Will yelled, mimicking his brother's action. The boys danced and jumped around, snatching water from the air.

Cade laughed. "Why not? Don't drown yourselves!"

"You're silly, Uncle Pa," Will said, running in exuberant circles.

The girls picked up big globs of mud and flung them at their brothers.

"Uncle Pa," Cade repeated as he and Zoe made a dash for the buggy. "Do I look like an Uncle Pa?"

"You look like every Uncle Pa I've ever seen."

They fell onto the buggy seat in a fit of laughter. With a couple of yanks, and Zoe's help, Cade raised the leather top into place.

"We might as well have played in the rain with the kids," Zoe said, collapsing breathlessly against the back of the seat. "We're just as wet."

"I don't want to play with the kids," he said, pulling the blanket around her. "I want to play with you." He felt her shiver as he snuggled up against her and slipped his arm around her shoulders. "You're cold."

"Not with you beside me."

His other hand found its way inside the blanket to her waist, then higher to cover one breast. She swatted him away and he couldn't stop the grin that tugged at his mouth.

"Is that all you think about?" she asked.

"When I'm with you." He groaned and let his hand wander again. She swatted him harder this time, and he laughed. Rain pattered against the top of the buggy. It seemed as if they were alone in a very small, very damp cocoon. He'd never been more aware of her as a woman—her scent, her soft curves, her warm breath. With the tip of his finger, he turned her chin toward him. "Hello, Mrs. Kolby."

She blushed and batted her lashes seductively. If he'd known calling her Mrs. Kolby would have such an effect on her, he would have called her that sooner. He could tell by the way she turned her head that she wanted to hide the pleasure she took in his advances. When she opened her mouth to protest, he kissed her—a long, sweet kiss that reminded him of the carefree days of their youth. A kiss that was fast getting out of control, at least on his part. He lifted his mouth and brushed a lock of wet hair from her forehead. "I've missed you."

"I don't want to hear it."

"I think you do." He nuzzled her ear. "The trail is a lonely place. It gives a man a lot of time to think. Of what he's had, and what he's lost." His lips found her earlobe, and he nibbled and kissed until she moaned. "I never knew how lonely I was until now." He traced the outline of her ear with his tongue. "Can I kiss you again?"

Her silence said no, but her soft amber gaze told him yes. He knew that look and wasn't about to let the opportunity slide. He captured her mouth hungrily, refusing to pull back even when she pushed hard against him. He lifted her onto his lap so she could feel the evidence of his need.

She moaned again, and his hand found the front of her bodice. One by one he unfastened the buttons, groaning when she deepened the kiss. Finally she was responding to him. Maybe soon she'd share her bed as his wife. Without a child between them, without past hatreds.

"Zoe?" Brody yelled.

At the sound of his voice, Cade felt Zoe stiffen in his arms. The next sound he heard was the flat of her hand against his cheek. The pain of the slap wasn't nearly as bad as the pain of rejection.

"Can I have another piece of chicken?" Brody asked.

Zoe slid off Cade's lap, taking the blanket with her. "In the hamper," she murmured, turning her back and quickly buttoning her bodice.

Cade laughed to himself as she straightened her appearance, her cheeks as red as beets. As much as he cared for the children, they sure didn't help his love life.

"Look what you've done, Cade Kolby."

Her voice had taken on a stiff air of authority that hadn't been there a moment ago.

"What have I done?"

"You've embarrassed me and the children. Don't ever do that again!"

"Brody is more than happy with his chicken, and I was more than happy with mine."

"Chicken? Me?" Zoe tilted her chin and looked down her nose at him. "Someone needs to remember the terms of this marriage."

"You're afraid, Red. Admit it." The way she squinted her eyes and pursed her lips made him laugh. She was afraid of him, and she had every right to be, but it didn't stop him from wanting to make love to his wife. It was past time they consummated the marriage.

Chapter 17

The sudden cloudburst gave way to a gentle shower as Zoe and Cade sat silently in the buggy. But the peacefulness of the countryside was abruptly shattered by a loud blast.

"What in—" Zoe peered out, trying to locate the source. Someone was beating a drum, the regular rhythm vying with the blare of a tuba.

The children screamed as cowbells clanged and shotguns blustered.

"Is it a circus?" Zoe asked.

Cade jumped out of the buggy, reaching for his gun.

Zoe's hands flew to her cheeks. "Oh, dear—

Cade! Don't shoot! It's Walt and Lawrence...
firing in the air."

As Cade lifted her down, she caught sight
of a strange procession coming into the
clearing. Was that Walt Mews playing the
tuba? And why was Gracie grinning like a
Cheshire cat?

Sawyer approached the buggy, ringing a cow-
bell. Edna Mews banged on a kettle with a
wooden spoon, while May Wilks burst into a
zealous rendition of "Oh, My Darling Clemen-
tine," substituting Zoe's name for Clemen-
tine's.

The children, wet and muddy, joined in the
gleeful melee. They clasped hands and skipped
around in a circle, singing along at the top of
their lungs.

Cade turned to Zoe.

She shook her head, feeling her face drain
of color. "I think it's a shivaree."

"Oh, hell."

She took hold of his arm for support.
"What are they thinking—"

Her words were cut short when Gracie
and Edna grabbed her by both arms. "Stop
this," Zoe hissed, trying to break free as they
pulled her along to a waiting carriage. Cade
reached out for her but was stopped by Walt
and Lawrence.

"Hold him, men!" Sawyer shouted.

Zoe squirmed when she caught sight of
Pop cackling on the sidelines, jabbing a
crutch in the air. "By doggies!" he said. "Surprised ya, didn't we?"

"Surprised" was putting it mildly, Zoe thought as she was shoved into a buggy. "Gracie, have you lost your mind?"

"Not at all, my dear. Just relax. You're in for the time of your life."

Edna picked up the reins and slapped them against the horse's rump.

"Where are you taking me?" she yelled above the commotion.

"Can't tell you," Edna yelled back. "It's a surprise!"

"What about the children?" Concern overwhelmed her as she looked back. Walt and Lawrence were on either side of Cade, holding on tight.

Gracie patted her hand. "Don't worry about your young'uns. May's taking them home with her for the night." With a laugh, she added, "Gonna teach them to cheat at checkers."

It dawned on Zoe that her friend's intentions were well-meant but disastrous. "Gracie, I'll not stand for this."

Edna giggled. "If things go right, you won't be doing much standing a'tall, girl."

"Edna!" Gracie chastised.

"Well," the older woman said with a sniff, "she won't."

Glori-Lee was waiting in front of the café, hailing them with a wave of her chubby arm. "Pull up to the side entrance. I got my best room all fixed up!"

Gracie and Edna got out and brought Zoe with them. All the balking in the world couldn't match the strength of the two older women. Zoe finally gave in, jerked her dress into place, and climbed the side staircase on her own accord in lieu of being bodily dragged.

As they walked down the hall toward the bedroom, Zoe could smell the scent of gardenias. Pausing before a closed door, she waited with pained tolerance as Gracie opened it. When the door swung wide, she gasped. Heavy green drapes covered the windows. The room was lit with flickering candles, and the bed had more ruffles on the ecru canopy and spread than Zoe had ever seen. Puffy, colorful pillows were scattered across the bed and around the floor. Two glasses and a bottle of wine had been placed on the bedside table. Pale green silk scarves adorned the backs of a chair and matching settee. Why...it looked like a sheik's den of iniquity!

Zoe's gaze came to rest on the tub in the middle of the room, filled with sudsy water. The familiar scent of Edna's homemade soap rose from the hot water. Her hand stopped Glori-Lee's when the woman began to unbutton her dress. "What do you think you're—"

"This won't hurt a bit," Glori-Lee said, a big grin on her face. "You just get in that tub and soak a spell in Edna's perfumy bubbles. Once you're all pink and pretty, you can slip into this lovely soft nightie."

Gracie held up the flimsy, pale blue, off-the-shoulder satin gown for Zoe's inspection. The white ribbon laced through the tatting around the neckline and tied in a bow looked sweet. The ends of the ribbon trailed down to the hemline. The gown was beautiful and, under other circumstances, Zoe would have been delighted to wear it.

"Girls, I know you mean well, but I can't—I won't—"

Edna snatched the gown out of Glori-Lee's hands. "Law, a girl can't get into trouble wearing a gown like that." She produced a sheer, wispy creation that made every woman in the room blush. "Now, *this* is a gown."

"Absolutely not!" Zoe declared, turning from the sight. "Why, it's...disgraceful. I might as well be naked."

Edna raised one eyebrow. "That's the point."

Gracie took the gown, and she and Glori-Lee admired it.

"My," Glori-Lee whispered, "that's just about the prettiest thing I've ever seen. Where did you get such a wicked thing, Edna Mews!"

"Walt bought it for me when he went to Kansas City a few years back."

Intrigued, Zoe leaned over to look. The gown was exquisite, sinfully gorgeous. The angelic-looking fabric resembled spun-sugar candy.

"Cade's going to love this," Gracie mused, fingering the gossamer material.

"Wouldn't any man?" Edna seconded.

Zoe leaned closer. "It is lovely, but the straps—won't they be a little uncomfortable...stop this!" she demanded when she realized she was going along with their lunacy.

"Shush." Gracie pushed her toward the

tub, where Edna stripped her camisole and pantaloons off before helping her into the bath. She scooped up a small pail of water and poured it over Zoe's head.

"You're drowning me!" Zoe protested, covering her bare breasts with her arms.

The older woman rubbed a bar of sweet-smelling soap over Zoe's hair, working up a mountain of lavish suds, while Glori-Lee lifted one of her legs, then the other, running a washcloth back and forth. Zoe had to admit the attention felt good. She slid deeper into the hot water as Gracie reached for an arm to lather.

"That's it—don't fight it, dear. We have to get you pretty and smelling sweet for your anxious groom."

"Now, son," Pop said, "if you hadn't put up such a fuss, we wouldn't have had to tie your hands."

Cade sat in a tub at Walt's bathhouse, trussed up like a Christmas turkey. "Pop, when I get loose—"

Pop chuckled. "You'll be too busy to retaliate."

"Never saw anyone who hated a bath like you do," Walt said, adding a kettle of hot water to the tub.

"Owwww! Watch where you're pouring that!"

"Yeah, take it easy," Pop said. "You don't want to scald parts he may be aneedin' later tonight."

Sawyer doubled over with laughter.

"Wouldn't want that now, would ya, Cade?"

Cade tried to get out of the tub, but Pop pushed him back down with a crutch. Walt dunked his head under the water. He came up, sputtering and cussing.

"The only part of my body I intend to use is my foot—to kick your butts from here to kingdom come!"

"Now, now, calm down," Walt said. "Ain't much of a marriage without a wedding night. Don't 'spect you and Zoe have had much time alone with all those young'uns around."

Lawrence lifted Cade's foot out of the water and scrubbed it hard with a brush. Cade jerked it back under the suds.

"Ticklish?" Lawrence asked. "Never would have thought it."

"Don't do that."

Lawrence snickered, trying to grab his foot. Cade snatched it away.

"You *are* ticklish!"

"I'm not ticklish. I'm just particular about who washes my feet."

"No time to be bashful." Pop sat on a keg, propped his splinted leg on a box, and watched the antics.

Cade lifted his bound wrists and slapped them back down on the water, splashing the onlookers.

"Now look what ya did," Lawrence said, pointing to the front of his drenched trousers. "The wife'll skin me."

"Let me out of this tub!"

"Pipe down. They can hear you in the next county," Lawrence said, rubbing a towel over

Cade's head. "Okay, Walt, he's all yours. Get his hair combed up real pretty-like—want him to look nice for his missus."

Sawyer held up Cade's clothes. "Don't 'spect he'll be needin' these. I'll just take them home with me."

Cade's protests fell on the closed door. He turned to Pop. "Get me out of here."

Pop shook his head. "They got their hearts set on a shivaree. Best just ride it out, son."

Walt finished combing Cade's hair. "Now comes the tricky part." He pulled out a straight razor. "I can shave you with you sitting real still, or you can wriggle like you've been doing and take your chances."

Cade froze in place as Walt slid the sharp instrument over the lower part of his face in several swipes until his skin was smooth. The sting of lotion being slapped on his cheeks brought him to life. He put his elbows on the sides of the tub and lifted himself up.

Pop stepped back, away from the splash. "Whee doggies!" he said, eyeing Cade up and down. "The missus is gonna be real pleased."

Cade glared at him. "Winslow, you're a dead man."

Laughing, Pop and Walt slapped each other on the backs.

"Get my clothes!"

Pop laughed again and held up a white cotton garment and matching hat with a tassel. "Oops. Ain't got nothin' but this here nightshirt. Guess it'll have to do."

"I am not wearing a nightshirt," Cade

warned through clenched teeth. He stepped out of the tub, and Walt began to towel him dry while Cade tried to smack his hands away.

"Suit yourself," Pop said, tossing the garment aside. "But," he added, giving Cade the once-over again, "can't say Zoe will be too thrilled when you walk in buck naked. She might take offense."

Walt folded the towel and laid it on the counter. "From the looks of this place, you'd think we gave a polecat a bath. More water on the floor than in the tub."

Cade looked around. "Serves you right. Now get my clothes."

"Put the nightshirt on, son. You're not getting your clothes 'til mornin'." Pop laughed. "Come on, Walt, let's get this 'polecat' over to Glori-Lee's."

Walt looked Cade in the eye. "What'll it be? We untie you so you can put on the nightshirt, or you stay tied and walk naked as a jaybird through town?"

Scrubbed, rinsed, and buffed, Zoe felt like a baby as Gracie and Edna rubbed her down with a large fluffy towel. When they finished, Glori-Lee handed her Edna's scandalous gown. She giggled, holding up the filmy material for inspection. "It'll be big on you, but I figure you won't be in it long enough to worry about the size."

Zoe reached for her clothes, but they had mysteriously disappeared. She quickly crossed one arm over her chest; the other reached down to cover her lower region. "Very funny, ladies, but now I have to go home. The children—"

"Oh, no, you don't." Gracie held her back. "The fun has only begun."

"*Now* who's being crass?" Edna asked, stifling her own giggle.

Gracie swatted Edna. "I didn't mean that!"

Glori-Lee cackled. "Now, Gracie, don't try to tell us you don't still have a little fun with Lawrence every now and then."

"Well, I—," Gracie sputtered.

"What about you, Edna?" Glori-Lee asked. "I saw the way you and Walt looked at each other when the preacher was talkin' this morning about love and all that stuff."

Edna ran a brush through Zoe's hair. "Walt and I have our moments."

Glori-Lee turned to the mirror and patted her hair into place. "I'll tell you something, girls. There may be snow on the rooftop, but there's still fire in this old furnace. If the right man was to come along—"

Zoe took the brush from Edna and tossed it on the table. "I think we can adjourn this meeting."

"Not quite," Edna said, looking at her pin watch. "You best put on that gown. You should be getting a visitor—"There was a loud knock on the door. "—about now."

As Gracie reached to open the door, Zoe quickly jerked the gown over her head and stood frozen in place as Edna tied her hair back with a pink silk ribbon.

Pop shoved Cade into the room, and she bit her lip to keep from laughing. He was wearing a ridiculous nightshirt and a cap with a fuzzy tassel that hung just below his left ear. The nightshirt struck him midway between his ankles and knees. Barefoot and hairy-legged, he looked about as amorous as she felt.

Tipping his hat, Pop kept his head turned as the older women filed out. "Sleep tight," he said, and closed the door.

A moment later it opened again, and a pair of boxing gloves sailed into the room. "Little gift from Sawyer. He don't use these anymore. Thought they might come in handy tonight."

As the lock clicked into place, Cade stripped out of the ungainly nightshirt and pitched it to the floor. "I'm not sleeping in this damn thing."

Zoe's mouth dropped open; he stood before her as naked as a newborn baby. She averted her eyes, but she'd seen more than she should have. Or had she seen exactly what she wanted? Since she was half naked herself, it was hard to look disinterested about his present state of undress. Her eyes drifted back as he stalked to the washstand, grabbed a towel and wrapped it around his waist. How could she ignore anything that blatantly male? He put every man she'd ever known to shame. That was the problem. She'd compared every man to him, and none had stood the test.

Jim, God rest his soul, had been a good and honorable man. He'd given her his love and support, but even Jim had known that Cade was in her heart, and he'd accepted it. Now

Jim was gone. She was married to Cade and stuck in this bedroom with him. Alone.

"I hope you know how to pick locks," she said.

He stepped to the door and rattled the handle. It refused to budge. "I think Pop is getting senile."

"I think the entire town is out of its mind." She got into bed, lay back, and trailed her fingers lightly over the pillow. "We'll just have to make the best of it until morning."

"No."

"Does the big, fierce bounty hunter not like the idea that he's at someone else's mercy?" Zoe couldn't help but laugh at the disgruntled look on his face. "You're pretty bossy for a man wearing nothing but a towel."

"It's not funny, Red."

"Really?" She covered her mouth with her hand to hide her giggles. "I think you look quite charming." When his eyes darkened to a challenging hue, she shrank deeper under the covers. He lifted a sardonic brow at her and gritted his teeth.

"Want to fight?" he challenged.

She knew better than to taunt him when he was in this mood. In her most innocuous voice, she answered, "No. Why would you think that?"

He walked to the bed and jerked back the covers. Scrambling to the opposite side, she glared at him, conscious that his gaze was glued to the gown. "Don't you touch me!"

"What happened to the woman who kissed me in the buggy? You wanted me to touch you;

you enjoyed my kisses. You wanted more, and I know it, Red."

"Ooooh!" She threw a pillow at him. "You're crazy."

"Am I? Why don't you be honest for once and say you want me?"

Zoe supressed the urge to scream, holding her breath instead. He crossed his arms over his chest and stared at her with that smug look he got every time he thought he was right.

"Want you? Never!" she declared.

"You've had a burr under your saddle since the day I rode into Winterborn. When you came out of the store, you were mad enough to shoot me." He laughed. "Good thing you hate guns." He picked up the boxing gloves from the floor and threw them at her. "Put 'em on, Red. You want a fight, I'll give you a fight."

She threw the gloves back at him. He caught them against his chest and laughed.

Of all the nerve! she thought, furious. First he kissed her, then he wanted to fight. Well, she wasn't about to give him the satisfaction of either. She lay facedown, pulled the covers over her head, and screamed into the mattress.

No sooner had her scream ended than she felt a rush of cool air hit her backside. He had yanked the covers off. His hands found her waist, and she felt herself being lifted from the bed.

"Put me down!"

"No. It's time we settled this."

Her face flamed beneath his arrogant perusal as he forced her to stand. She turned her back on him, realizing she'd just afforded him a wonderful view of her practically bare backside. "Stop looking at me. Have you no shame?" Judging by his reflection in the mirror, his bold gaze caressing her derriere, he didn't.

"I have nothing to be ashamed of," he said. "I'm looking at my wife. There's no law against that."

"I'm not your wife, and you know it."

"That must mean the good reverend doesn't have the power to marry people." He chuckled. "What will people say when they learn every married couple in the county is living in sin?"

"You know what I mean." She tried to cover her breasts with her arms and turned to face him, pretending a confidence she didn't feel.

"No, I don't." He was a breath away from her now. "Admit it, Red. You want me to make love to you." He pulled her to his chest. "Say it."

She pushed him back and glared, full of frustration. Nothing she did intimidated him. He stood with a bedroom grin on his face as if he considered this situation little more than juvenile amusement.

"I don't desire you, and stop playing silly games with me."

"All right," he said, picking up the boxing gloves, "let's fight." He grabbed her right wrist and shoved a glove on her hand.

"Stop this," she said, trying to hide her left hand from him. He reached behind her, forced her hand to the front, and pushed the other glove on. After tying both laces, he took a step back to assess her with a sardonic grin. She watched in trepidation as he reached out with his left fist and tapped her on the chin.

"Come on, Red. Fight." He grinned, grazing her chin again. "If we can't make love, then we'll do what we do best: fight."

With a flourish, she rested the gloves on her hips. "You're acting like a child."

"Am I? You're the one who blushes and pulls away every time I touch you."

"I never agreed to kissing and touching. Our deal was to marry for the kids, and you know it."

"I don't make deals. I agreed to marry the woman I care about so she could have what she wanted: the children."

She took a deep breath. "Care about? I'm not a fool, Cade. You married me because Laticia pushed you into a corner."

"That's it, get mad. Let it all out, Red. Let me have it." He stepped closer, pointing to his chin. "What are you waiting for? Come on, hit me!"

"Don't be asinine."

He tapped her on the jaw. "Cat got your tongue? Since when have you been reluctant to tell me what you think?"

She shook her head, refusing to appease him.

He reached out and boxed her shoulder. "Let's duke this out, man to man."

"No!"

"You'd like nothing better than to get rid of all that anger that's been eating at you for years. Here's your chance. I'm offering you a way out. We're not going to settle anything between us until you make me pay for walking out on you."

Zoe crossed her arms, refusing to rise to his bait.

"We're locked in here until morning. We can make it either pleasant or nasty. It's your choice."

The challenge in his voice said he was dead serious, and the dark, dangerous look in his eyes meant business. She squealed when he lightly boxed her jaw with his bare knuckle. "Stop it."

He tapped her again. "Come on, fight me."

"Leave me alone!"

Cade jabbed at her shoulder, forcing her to take a step back. The man had lost his mind! He was nothing more than an overgrown child, taunting her into this madness.

"Come on, fight me!" With the flat of his hand, he pushed her shoulder. "Get rid of the resentment, Red. I was a thoughtless bastard— *say* it."

"Why? So *you* can feel better?" If he wanted absolution, he'd come to the wrong place.

"No, so *you* can. Brrrkkk, brrrkkk."

Zoe's eyes widened as she watched him tuck his thumbs into his armpits and flap his elbows. He strutted around the room like a chicken, making obnoxious clucking sounds. If she hadn't known better, she'd have sworn he'd been drinking. "Stop acting like an ass!"

"You're worse off than I thought if you can't tell an ass from a chicken!"

"Ooooh!" She hauled back and landed a center punch to his stomach. He stepped back and put both hands where she'd made contact. She socked him in the jaw, smiling when she heard a groan. "Is that what you want?"

"Maybe not that hard, but you got the idea." He cocked a brow. "Give me another shot."

"Leave me alone, Cade. I don't get mad like I used to." She swallowed hard, trying to control her temper. "You can continue this childish taunting, but I'm going to sleep."

She threw herself onto the bed, landing stomach-down on the overstuffed boxing gloves, silently cursing the clumsy gloves, the lock on the door, Pop, and Gracie, but most of all Cade—the one who'd hurt her, the one who wanted to fight, the one who would leave her again. Tears burned her lids as years of frustration screamed for release.

Rolling out of bed, she walked to him and unleashed everything she had in one blow after another until he finally fell backward, tripping over the nightshirt he'd left in a pile.

The towel around his waist slipped to the floor.

It served him right, she thought, her eyes drawn to his raw masculinity, her body betraying her mind. Her cheeks burned, and she turned her back on him.

"That's more like it." Cade stood, picked

up the towel, and resecured it around his waist.

"You snake!" She rushed at him with a flurry of punches.

"Hell, I thought you didn't get mad anymore." He held his arms out to the side. "Harder, Red. Punish me the way you've always wanted to."

She hit him over and over again, unable to stop now. "At first, I wondered what happened to you, not knowing if you were dead or alive. I thought I'd lost you *and* the baby." She punched him soundly in the midsection.

"I didn't know about the baby, dammit! I was wrong, I admit it. But you were wrong for not telling me!"

She flailed at his chest. "Why didn't you come back, Cade? Why didn't you love me enough?"

"I was young and foolish." He blocked a direct hit to his nose. "I'm sorry, Red. I never meant to hurt you."

"Really? I suppose you thought leaving me here, alone, was supposed to make me happy? I gave you my virginity, Cade!" She punched him in the stomach. "I loved you, and all I got in return was a few short letters, a box of smashed chocolates, and a broken doll!" She slammed her gloved hand into him three more times, one for each of his gifts. A lone tear rolled down her cheek, and she shivered as he lowered his head and kissed it away.

He picked up the locket around her neck and let it lie across his fingers. "I'm glad you've always worn this." He brushed another tear from her face with the back of his hand.

She bowed her head, unable to meet his gaze. There was so much he'd never know or understand. She held out her hands. "I'm finished now."

Cade untied the strings and pulled the gloves from her hands. "Are you sure you're finished?"

"I'm finished."

He threaded his fingers through her hair. "Are you ready to forgive me?"

"Maybe, if I knew why you didn't come back." She felt tears well and blinked them back.

"A million reasons—none of them good enough." He pulled her to his chest. "I wish I knew, Red. One day turned into a week, then a few months, then years. After a while, I realized you were better off without me."

She pushed back. When she tried to walk away, he grabbed the front of her gown.

"Let go," she said.

"I did that once. I have no intention of letting go now."

She eased back, his grip on the gown straining the thin fabric. "You'll be leaving me again, and I have no intention of putting myself through the same agony. Now, let go." His hand held the garment firm, and she felt her anger rise. "Cade!" She twisted and jumped back, and the gown ripped. A gasp escaped her throat when she saw him staring with a smirk on his face, what was left of the flimsy fabric still in his hands.

"You animal!" She threw herself on the bed, scrambling for the covers.

"Don't hide from me." He rolled her onto her back and pinned both of her wrists to the mattress. "You're beautiful." He bent and kissed her neck, inching his way lower. When he reached the tip of her breast, he stopped and looked up at her. "Let's not fight anymore. Let me love you."

Her breathing was ragged, and butterflies danced in her stomach. His piercing blue gaze raked her naked body. She wanted him to love her, but could she accept such pleasure for one night only, and live the rest of her life without him? His hands splayed across her abdomen, caressing her skin as they worked their way toward her breasts. She moaned.

"Red?"

"Hmmm?"

"Will you allow me to love you?"

"Loving you was never the problem." She studied his intense, questioning look. "Forgetting is what's difficult."

Her hand found the thick mat of hair on his chest, his muscles firm beneath her touch. Sanity fled when he pushed her hand lower, his devilish chuckle fueling her desire.

"You never forgot me," he said, nibbling her earlobe.

"You've been with me every night of my life since the first time we made love."

His tongue traced a line to her lips and then entered her mouth, taking her with a hungry passion. His tender but demanding kiss fueled the fires that had lain dormant, bringing them to life in ways she'd never felt before.

"I've missed you, Red," he murmured. He laid a trail of kisses under her chin and down her chest to the tip of her breastbone, then back up. "God, how I've missed you."

Placing her hands on his cheeks, she guided him to her lips. She kissed him the way she'd dreamed of so many times over the years; but this was real: his bare chest against her breasts, his stomach against hers. Then she felt him pull the towel away, and his need pressed against her, drowning her in the exquisite sensations she longed for. She desired every inch of his delicious body like a child craves candy, and she feared, like the child, she'd never get enough.

"Cade." His name rolled off her lips before she knew she'd said it, and tears rolled down her cheeks.

"What's wrong, sweetheart?"

"You're going to leave me again, and I don't think I can bear it. Oh, Cade, I can't..."

He placed his fingertips on her lips. "Shhh. Let me love you. Let me know you as my wife. Give me this memory."

Her heart drummed beneath her ribs as his hands explored her body, slowly, not missing one inch of her bare flesh. His touch set her on fire, and she thought she'd die when his mouth closed over her breast, his tongue teasing and tasting. He was the man she loved, had always loved, and his touch seemed so right. She needed his love in every way.

What he said was true. They were husband and wife in the eyes of God and in the legal sense, so why not share what they both wanted? His mouth worked its way down her stomach, and she remembered their young love, which couldn't compare to this. They'd both been shy, inexperienced, sharing hours of rushed intimacy, afraid someone would find them. Now they had the right to be together, and his tender kisses said he loved her. That was all she needed to know.

Slipping his hand between her thighs, he moaned, and she felt the muscles of his back tighten beneath her fingertips. He lifted his head when she whispered his name, and his eyes filled with emotion as he lowered his mouth to take hers again.

"Oh, Red. I've never wanted you more. You're the reason I came back."

"No, Cade. It was because of the children." He'd always hidden his true feelings behind a tough demeanor, but now he was showing her a side of himself she'd known existed, yet never thought she'd see.

He caressed her cheek with his hand and kissed the tip of her nose. "I won't deny that the children played a part in my decision, but it was you I was desperate to see. The children brought us together. They forced us to face our past, and they made me see how much I love you, how much I've always loved you."

Tears streamed unchecked down her face. His admission unleashed the flood of emotions she'd denied, thoughts she hadn't dared admit, even to herself. Somehow she'd always known he loved her, but hearing the words made her surrender complete, her forgiveness easy. Whatever problems lay between them held no meaning; every threat to their happiness melted away. Only the love she felt mattered, only the man in her arms: her one and only love.

His mouth covered hers with a tender urgency; his kiss asked forgiveness and confirmed his love. She'd waited for this moment, hoped and dreamed through countless tear-filled nights to have him in her arms, to have his love. He pressed for entry, and she could deny him nothing. She'd always belonged to him, always would.

As she felt the heat and urgency rise to unbearable heights, he slipped inside her, claiming his rights as she wanted him to, slow and easy, hot and demanding. Her body began to move in rhythm with his as he buried his hands in her hair, and his thirsty kiss asked more and took all she could give. The years of separation had only fueled the fires of their suppressed emotion, making this moment more beautiful than the dream.

His thrusts quickened and his breathing became ragged, driving her wild, pushing her harder to become one with him, to become his wife. Her hands roamed the well-muscled planes of his shoulders. She met his fervid gaze, memorizing every ruggedly handsome feature of his face.

She could no longer think, was barely able to catch her breath as waves of pleasure coursed through her body. He held her powerless, filling her with his exquisite virility, claiming every bit of her womanhood. Sweat beaded on his brow as he moved faster, demanded more, and gave her all of himself. The room began to spin as he took her higher, consuming her very soul. Her body shook as waves of delight gripped and pulsed, turning the dull light of the room into blinding brightness.

His movements turned into a frenzy, and she clutched his shoulders as he found his release. She stroked his arms as he slowed to a gentle rhythm. He lowered his head to give her one last tender kiss before he rolled off her to lie by her side. Zoe turned to face him and smiled.

Smiling back, Cade traced her jaw with one finger. "Thank you, my love. You've given me more than I deserve."

"We both deserve to be happy, Cade." She averted her eyes. "I'm afraid you've stayed too long. I'm afraid Hart McG—"

He silenced her words with his mouth. "Tonight is for us, and there's still a lot of night left." His hand closed over her breast.

"Cade!"

"As my wife, it's your duty to please your husband."

"Maybe I should put the boxing gloves back on." She let out a shriek when he pulled her on top of him and pushed her into a sitting position, his gaze locked with hers.

"What I have in mind won't require gloves."

"You really don't have any shame, do you?"

Cade shook his head and chuckled, his hands moving down her stomach, touching the part of her that still ached from the feel of him.

He grinned when she reached toward the floor where the boxing gloves lay. Pulling her back, he laughed. "Let's see your other talents."

She bent down and nibbled his neck. "I think you've seen them all." She shivered when a slow, seductive smile crossed his lips.

"Then it's time I taught you new ones."

Chapter 18

"Gracie, I haven't got time to play checkers tonight," Zoe said. "Get Hallie Morgan to play in my place." Zoe reluctantly allowed Gracie to hurry her along the Willises' flagstone walk.

"Nonsense, a body needs a rest. You've been working your fingers to the bone; you can't keep up this pace. That handsome new husband of yours can do without you for an hour or two." Opening the screen door, Gracie shooed her into the house. As Zoe stepped into the foyer, a shout went up.

"Surprise! Happy birthday!" May Wilks held a birthday cake covered with candles, as Willa Baker and Edna Mews beamed.

Startled, Zoe's hand came up to her throat.

"Did you forget it was your birthday?" May asked.

Catching her breath, Zoe patted her chest, her eyes moist with joy. With so much happening, it had completely slipped her mind that today was her birthday.

"Girls...I don't know what to say. Thank you."

"Rum cake!" May Wilks rolled her eyes. "My favorite."

Confusion broke out as Gracie flew into the kitchen for coffee. May set the cake on the table and insisted Zoe blow out the candles.

When Gracie returned, Zoe closed her eyes, made a wish, then blew. Thirty-six candles went out; the thirty-seventh sputtered in protest. Drawing another deep breath, Zoe put it out.

The women clapped. "Speech!"

"No, really..."

"Speech!" they chorused again.

Keeping a steady but warm eye contact, Zoe said, "Thank you. The greatest gift I have is friends like you."

They waited, smiling.

"Is that all?" Gracie prompted. "With the week you've had, I'd think there'd be other things you'd want to mention."

"Of course." Zoe studied her friends' earnest faces, thinking how lucky she was to have them. "It has been an interesting two weeks," she admitted. "Laticia's departure, my sudden marriage to Cade, the children being truly mine, and all those cases of measles!"

Gracie laughed. "It's been a time you won't soon forget."

Zoe laughed with her. "Not likely."

"Let's cut the cake!" May sliced thick wedges of rum cake as Gracie handed Zoe an envelope. "Perry dropped this off earlier. He said to tell you happy birthday, and he hopes things will be brighter for you next year."

"What'd he mean by that?"

"I don't know—I thought you would."

"Perry remembered my birthday?" Zoe opened the white envelope, and her smile gradually faded as she read the legal document. Refolding it, she put it in her pocket.

"Well?" Gracie looked at her expectantly. "What is it?"

"The note to the store."

"The note...to your store?"

"Paid in full."

The women *ahhh*ed.

"Oh, my," May breathed.

"I knew Perry thought that you and he— but now that you're married to Cade..." Gracie swelled with indignation. "Why do you suppose he'd do a thing like that?"

"I don't know. Of course, I can't accept it."

Edna's eyes were as round as pancakes behind her thick glasses. "If it's already done, what can you do about it?"

"I...I'm not sure, but I can't let Perry pay off my debts."

"Well, he certainly knows how to shop for a woman. Wish Lawrence would take lessons from him." Gracie reached for one of the gaily wrapped packages that were stacked in a neat pile on the table. "Here's my present."

"Oh, Gracie, you shouldn't have."

"It's not much—just a doily I crocheted for your kitchen table."

"Like the one you have on yours!"

Gracie nodded. "You've always been so taken by it; I thought you'd enjoy having one of your own."

"Thank you." Zoe's eyes danced as she examined the delicate pineapple pattern. "It's wonderful."

May handed her a small parcel. "I made you one of those necklaces you like so much."

"Those pretty glass beads?" Zoe smiled jauntily. "May, you shouldn't have."

May's face flushed with happiness. "I hope you like green. I thought it would look good with your hair."

"Oh, it's marvelous." Zoe got up and went to May, who fastened the necklace around her neck.

Zoe straightened. "How does it look?"

"Good, even if I made it myself."

"Well, my gift looks pretty puny next to the others," Edna apologized. "I painted you a winter scene." She brushed the front of her dress, looking embarrassed. "Ain't much, but I think it turned out right nice."

Zoe unwrapped the watercolor, and they *ooooh*ed and *ahhh*ed over it. "It will look perfect in the parlor. Thank you all. I love every one of my gifts."

"Can't none of them hold a candle to Perry's." The women laughed, agreeing that was impossible.

May slapped her knees, then got up. "I say

we have another piece of cake and play checkers."

The checkerboards were brought out, and the games began. Zoe felt her thoughts drifting to Cade and the children. When she'd left, Holly had been making taffy. Missy had made Cade promise he'd oversee a family pull. She dreaded the sticky mess that would probably await her when she got home.

"May Wilks! I saw that!"

May stared at Edna. "Saw what?"

"I saw you slip one of your black pieces in place of a red."

May gasped. "Why, I did not!"

"You did so!"

"You did, too, May. I saw you," Willa said, taking a bite of cake.

"Saw me," May scoffed. "You can't see your hand in front of your face."

"Can too. I'm wearing my glasses tonight."

Zoe eyed her own red checkers.

"So, how is married life?" Edna asked Zoe as she studied her next move. She reached over and swatted May's wandering hand.

"I've been married before, Edna," Zoe reminded her quietly.

"But not to Cade Kolby," Willa interjected. "He's some man. All that muscle. He could fairly break a woman in half if he held her tight enough." Willa peered at Zoe over the rims of her glasses.

Smiling, Zoe changed the subject. "How is Walt, Edna?"

"He's got a touch of bursitis in his left

arm, but with business off because of the town being quarantined for those few days, he didn't have to close up shop."

"That's good."

Gracie paused, looking at Willa. "Why are you fidgeting? Is the rum in that cake going to your head already?"

"No." Willa pretended interest in the board, but a moment later she was twisting in her seat again.

"Willa," Gracie snapped. "Stop moving around. You'll slosh coffee on my good lace tablecloth."

"Sorry."

"What's wrong with you?"

"I got something on my mind."

"Something I ought to know?"

"No." Willa's gaze swiveled to Zoe.

Zoe lifted her brows, swallowing a piece of cake. "Something *I* ought to know?"

"You ought to know it, but you're not going to want to know it."

Zoe's fingers rested lightly on a king. Her eyes searched Willa's, and the concern she saw there made the small hairs on the back of her neck stand up. She immediately thought of Cade. "What is it, Willa?"

Willa wrung her hands. "I hate to ruin the festivities, but I just have to say it. Roy had business in Suffox County this morning. While he was there, he said he heard several men talking about Hart McGill."

At the mention of McGill, Zoe went cold. She licked her suddenly dry lips, ignoring the tremor in her hand. Pushing her cake aside, she dabbed her mouth with a napkin. "What about him?"

"McGill's in Suffox County."

The news was so shocking that no one could speak for a moment.

Gracie leaned over and laid her hand on Willa's arm. "Willa...is Roy sure?"

Willa nodded. "He says McGill is bragging how he's coming after—well, just bragging. You know how men are."

Zoe pushed back her chair and got up. "Excuse me—I need some fresh air." She ran into the kitchen.

"I'll come with you," Gracie called after her. A moment later, the screen door banged shut behind them.

Zoe was holding her stomach, pacing the side porch when Gracie came up beside her.

"Are you all right?"

"Why is it anytime I find a tiny shred of happiness, it's taken away from me?" Her voice disintegrated into a childish whimper.

Gracie sighed and put her arms around her. The two women swayed, patting each other affectionately. "Go ahead and cry. You have reason to feel sorry for yourself."

Zoe buried her face in her friend's shoulder and bawled. A dull, empty ache gnawed at her soul. Pettiness didn't become her, but neither did widowhood.

"Life can get tedious." Gracie rocked her back and forth until her tears subsided.

Wiping her nose, Zoe drew back, ashamed of the outburst.

Gracie reached into her pocket, took out a clean handkerchief, and handed it to Zoe. "There's something else you ought to know."

Zoe gave a half-laugh, half-cry. "More?"

"I suppose you've noticed everyone in town's toting guns."

Zoe nodded.

"It's for Cade's benefit. When Pop hatched up this plan to get you and Cade married—"

"*What?*"

"Well, nobody here could stand the thought of Laticia taking those kids, so Pop called a town meeting, and we all decided the only way to make certain you got the kids was to have you and Cade get married."

Zoe was dumbfounded. "Perry said something to that effect, but *I* was the one who suggested we get married."

"But that wouldn't have happened if Pop hadn't locked you and Cade in jail and made you think."

"Gracie." Zoe sank down on the porch swing. "I feel like an utter fool."

"Don't know why you should. The plan accomplished the purpose, didn't it? Laticia's gone home, and the children are legally yours."

Zoe shook her head, sick at heart. Her purpose was achieved, but at what price? Cade's safety? McGill was breathing down his neck, all because he'd stayed too long in Winterborn to appease her. After last Sunday night at Glori-Lee's, he was finding it even more difficult to leave—and she found it impossible to let him go.

"So why is everyone wearing a gun?" she asked.

"To protect Cade."

Gracie's words brought tears to Zoe's eyes.

"Why should it surprise you? He's Mac's and Senda's boy—he's one of our own. We do what we can for our own, you ought to know that."

"How could any of you possibly hope to protect Cade from McGill?" The thought that eighty-year-old Bess Harris could protect anyone was ludicrous, yet Zoe recalled the blunderbuss resting on her lap during services Sunday morning.

"Oh, Gracie." Zoe's whisper sounded more like a desperate prayer. "What am I going to do?"

"You're gonna go home, sit down, and tell your husband whatever is in your heart." Gracie's eyes softened. "It shouldn't be so hard. He told Lawrence he was gettin' real attached to those kids and...can I say it?"

"Please...don't."

"I'm going to say it anyway. A blind man can see the way he looks at you. He doesn't want to leave, Zoe. He's come home. A man has a right to come home. The town will accept his past if he's willing to stay."

"Cade would never knowingly endanger the town."

"Even for you?"

"Especially for me," she whispered. "I wouldn't let him."

"Then go to him, now. Tell him McGill is here. Let him make the decision."

"He'll be gone by morning." The words were like bitter gall in Zoe's mouth.

"You can stop him from leaving. You need him, Zoe; he needs you."

"I can't, Gracie." Zoe lifted her hand to her mouth, biting her knuckles. "I don't want him killed."

"Is he going to spend the rest of his life running from this outlaw McGill, this disease on society?"

"He's not running from McGill. He just doesn't want the confrontation to take place here in Winterborn, in front of the children. Once they meet, only one will walk away."

Gracie supported the small of her back as she studied the sky.

Zoe could only think of Cade and how unfair it was that the same stars were shining on McGill, crouched somewhere like a hungry predator in the blackness, waiting to pounce.

"I'm going home, Gracie."

Gracie nodded, still looking up. "I'll say your good-byes for you and bring your gifts later. Now go, girl...see to your man."

Zoe trudged home feeling as if the world were anchored to her shoulders. She had to tell Cade about McGill, and that would mean he'd leave immediately. She'd known it was bound to happen, but she wasn't prepared for it. Not after Sunday night. And the children—how could she tell the children? They loved him as much as she did.

A dim light shone from within when she

reached her back door. All was quiet. Maybe the children were in bed, and she wouldn't have to cope with telling them tonight. She would busy herself cleaning up the candy mess she knew would be left from the taffy pull. Smiling wearily, she thought about Cade's lack of domesticity. In the kitchen, he was like a bull in a china cabinet.

The screen door closed behind her, and her gaze fell on the table. It was adorned with her best lace tablecloth, china, candles, and a bottle of wine. She turned around to survey the entire room. It was spotless. The boys were sound asleep in the corner, and she could hear Holly's and Missy's breathing coming from the bedroom.

Tears sprang to her eyes. They had cleaned up their candy mess, and Cade had obviously put them all to bed. This was her family, and this wonderful, blissful feeling would be reduced to despair, all because of Hart McGill. How she hated him for ruining her life.

"Back so early?"

She turned to see Cade standing beside the ironing board in the corner. Her mouth dropped open at the sight. He was ironing.

Glancing up from the board, he grinned and gestured toward an overflowing basket. "There was such a big pile, I thought you needed help."

She wanted to cry when he held up Brody's best Sunday shirt with a scorched iron imprint up the side. Guilt flashed across his face. "I'm not very good at this—"

She was so overcome with gratitude, with love, it took a moment before she found her voice. "You're doing fine...thank you."

He set the iron on the stove and came to her. Bowing, he gallantly kissed the back of her hand before handing her a small gift tied with a huge pink bow. "Happy birthday, Red."

She was dumbfounded. "How did you, of all people, remember my birthday when I didn't?"

He grinned. "Surprise."

Her breath caught as she opened the package and found a small music box with a heart etched on top, in which "C.K. loves Z.K." was engraved in script.

Zoe sank down on a chair, face in her hands, and burst out crying.

He dropped to his knees beside her and put his arm around her shoulder. "What's wrong? I thought you'd like it."

She pulled away and stood up, handing the gift back. "This is the worst day of my life. And now I come home and find you...drunk!"

"*Drunk*? I'm not drunk. I might have had a little wine, but I'm not drunk."

Tears clouded her vision, and she could barely make out his features in the candlelight. "Then why would you be giving me a present—and ironing?"

He turned his head, then looked back at her. "It's your birthday!"

"But you've never given me anything for my birthday!"

"I never was around before. I am now, and I wanted to give my wife something special. Why make a big deal out of it?"

"Oh, Cade!" Her tears flowed more heavily. "Willa told me that Roy heard McGill is in Suffox County."

The silence was suddenly deafening. Getting slowly to his feet, Cade set the music box on the table. Then he stuck his hands in his back pockets and moved to the window.

"Is he sure?"

She nodded, choking on a sob. "McGill's... here." A moment later she felt his arms slide around her waist and pull her against him. He buried his face in her hair. His warm breath brushed her temples.

"We knew this was possible."

"No," she whispered. "It's too soon...."

Turning her around, he held her tightly and let her cry herself out. When her sobs subsided, he helped her wipe her eyes.

"Better?" he asked.

She shook her head. She would never be better, not as long as McGill threatened them.

"Here." He pulled a piece of taffy from his shirt pocket. "Eat this. I think the kids and I quite possibly made the best darn taffy this side of the Missouri River."

She looked at his satisfied grin and broke into a smile. Come what may, she had to face it. Besides who but Cade would think of candy at a time like this? She removed the brown paper from the homemade confection and put it in her mouth. "Did you and the children have a good time?"

He laughed. "It took a considerable amount of elbow grease to get the mess cleaned up. Will can pull taffy faster than any kid I know—and get it stuck in more places."

"Must take after his Uncle Pa." She chewed, grinning through her tears.

He exchanged a sympathetic look with her. "What about you? Did you have fun at the party?"

"Hmmm, up to a point—I received a surprising gift."

"Oh?"

She swallowed the last of the candy. "You're right. This is *very* good."

He lowered his mouth to hers and caught the sweetness on his tongue. "Hell, it can't get any better."

Pulling back, she tried to organize her thoughts. Being so close to him made it impossible. "The gift was from Perry."

"Really?" Cade wiped his hands on a cloth.

"He gave me my bank note marked 'paid in full.'"

Cade crossed his arms and leaned back against the table. "He paid off the loan?"

"Apparently."

"Why would he do that?"

Was that jealousy in his voice? Her heart jumped at the thought. "Naturally, I can't accept it."

"Why not?"

Zoe took the cloth from him and wiped the stickiness off her fingers. "Would you want me to accept a gift of that magnitude from Perry Drake?"

"Why not? What difference does it make who paid the bill? You're out of debt, aren't you?"

"Yes, but that isn't the point. I don't think Perry can comfortably afford this, and I frankly don't want to feel obligated to him when—" She paused.

"When what?"

She took a deep breath. "When you're gone. I don't want him to think I would—"

"Marry him?" Cade laughed.

She turned, eyeing him sourly. "What's so funny?"

"You." He leaned over and whispered, "You're too much woman for Perry Drake. Don't look a gift horse in the mouth. Take the windfall and run."

"I wouldn't think of it. I don't have feelings for Perry Drake. I never have, and I never will." She straightened a stack of linens. "This is one birthday I'll not soon forget."

Cade smiled. "And it's not over yet."

When she looked at him, he pretended innocence. "Maddy hasn't given you her gift yet."

"Maddy?"

"That horse has good taste; I have to hand her that. If you'll follow me to the livery—"

"Oh, no, you don't." She knew that look, and she wasn't that gullible.

"Why not?"

"I don't trust you, that's why." She recalled the silly boxing game that had ended with her in his arms, a place she tended to be a lot lately. She hated to think about the seductive potential of the fragrant hay in the dark loft. Her face sobered. "What about McGill?"

"I don't want to talk about McGill. Come on. Maddy wants to give you her present. After that, we'll come back, have a nice midnight, candlelight dinner, then, who knows?"

She didn't trust herself with him, but her curiosity was piqued, and the idea of spending a few minutes alone in the barn was too enticing to resist. "All right, I'll go to the barn—but none of your funny business. Understand?"

Cade held up his hands, pleading innocence. "Trust me, my love. My business will not be funny."

Maddy whinnied softly as Zoe stepped inside her stall. The night air was chilly, and she pulled her shawl tighter around her shoulders. The scents of hay and kerosene from the lamp permeated the barn.

Cade patted Maddy's neck and moved her to one side of the stall.

"I hear you have a birthday present for me, Maddy." Zoe jumped back, laughing, when the horse nudged her roughly. She turned to Cade. "I think she's anxious to give it to me."

He put his arm around her waist. "So am I."

"Cade," she warned.

"I mean, I'm anxious to see what she got you."

She leaned against him, relaxing. Actually, she didn't care if he had tricked her. It wasn't hard to put her troubles aside and just be with him. "I know exactly what you meant."

"Then you shouldn't be surprised when I do this." He scooped her up in his arms and swung her over his head. Maddy shied, trying to move away and bumping the side of the stall.

"Put me down!"

"You need to eat more birthday cake! You're light as a feather!"

"You wouldn't like me if I was fat."

He let her slide down his length until their faces were inches apart, then kissed her lightly. "I'd like you if you were as big as Maddy and as mean as Laticia."

"Liar. Now put me down. Where's this so-called present Maddy has for me?"

"You don't believe she has one, do you?"

"No, I think you've lured me into this barn for your own self-serving purposes."

She giggled when he tickled her ribs. "You're a woman of little faith." He set her on her feet and turned to pull a small box from the saddlebag hanging near the stall door.

She watched his grin fade, and his face revealed tenderness for her. He'd become a loving husband and father, and her reliance on him scared her.

"Maddy will die of a broken heart if you don't accept this small token of her appreciation."

She carefully opened the velvet box. Inside she found a tiny gold wedding band. Her eyes misted as she studied his expectant expression. "When did you—"

"There's a jeweler in Suffox County who makes rings and watches." He winked. "When Maddy saw this one, she thought of you."

Upon closer examination, she saw two hearts locked together with a "Z" in the middle of one heart and a "C" in the other. It reminded her of the time he had carved their initials in the old oak tree on the hill. "Oh, Cade, it's beautiful." She kissed his cheek. "I never knew you could be so sentimental, so sweet."

"It's Maddy, remember?" He smiled. "Maddy says when you're particularly lonely, look at this ring and think of me."

She giggled. "Think of a horse?"

"Think of me, because I'll be thinking of you."

His voice was as soft as a whisper as he leaned toward her, touching his nose to hers. She kissed him, holding nothing back. Finding the right words was still hard at times, but they didn't always need words.

With a moan, he lifted her in his arms and carried her to an empty stall, where they fell into the sweet-smelling hay in a tangle of limbs. "I'm such easy prey for you," she murmured as his fingers loosened the buttons down the front of her dress.

"I'm glad."

Moonlight streamed through a crack in the roof, allowing a sliver of light to shine on his handsome face. She couldn't stop touching him. Her hands explored the lines of his face, wanting to burn them into her memory forever.

She wanted him, needed him so badly it hurt—despite that loving him would only make parting unbearable. Her very being reached out to him, craving the feel of his touch, the sound of his voice, and the tenderness of his kiss. Her resolve had fled the night of the shivaree, and she never wanted to find it again if it meant shutting him out of her life.

"Cade." She cradled his face in her hands. "Thank you for making this birthday so very special."

Raising himself on one elbow, he gazed at her. "You are special." His lips slid to her collarbone, where he kissed every exposed inch.

It felt like their first kiss, magnified a hundred times. "Why do I always believe your sweet talk?" His chuckle sounded devious, but her thoughts were lost as he slipped his tongue between her lips ever so lightly.

"Because you're the only woman I ever loved."

His fingers tugged the cotton fabric from her shoulders. Before she knew it, he was unlacing her camisole and pushing it aside. She smiled as he admired her breasts with insatiable eyes, his hands working to free her waistband. He pulled her skirt free and groaned at the layers of petticoats.

"Why do you wear so many clothes?"

"I like making you work for what you want." Her heart raced as he freed her petticoats and tossed them aside before tugging at the drawstring of her pantaloons. "And what *do* you want, Cade Kolby?"

"You, Red."

She lifted her hips, and he peeled the last garment from her body. She loved the way he looked at her, the way he made her stomach tingle with anticipation. Tears welled in her eyes when she realized it would be their last time together.

When he stood and backed away from her, her eyes widened. He kicked off his boots; then, with slow deliberation, he removed his shirt and laid it across the wooden partition. His hands moved to his belt, but his gaze never left her. When had he became such a master of seduction?

"You could hurry," she accused, watching him ease down his jeans and long johns together, one inch at a time.

"Anxious?" He smiled. "I want this to be the night when you want me as badly as I want you."

"Oh, Cade, I do." Her body, as well as her heart, ached for him. He made her feel wanted, the way every woman dreamed of being wanted. As he shed his clothes, the sight of his erection sent shivers down her spine. He lowered himself on top of her, his lips brushing hers as bare skin met bare skin.

Her hand splayed across the mat of dark hair on his chest, as he nibbled along her bottom lip until she thought she would go mad with longing. She shuddered when his mouth moved to her breast. Desire, hot and unchecked, hummed through her veins.

Murmuring his name, she opened to him. She memorized his spicy scent, his rough caress, the pressure of him deep inside her. It was all she'd have once he was gone. These precious moments would have to last a lifetime.

Though the night was cool, beads of sweat dotted his upper lip. His mouth devoured hers, and she adored his salty taste. He teased her, pulling out of her, then starting to enter, then pulling back again. He had become an expert of sweet torture, deliciously sensual, able to elicit her passion with ease. They had come so far, forgiving and learning to love. Now they were about to say good-bye, and her soul cried for mercy. It wasn't fair to find lost love only to have it ripped away again.

She gasped when he thrust fully inside her and began his artful rhythm. Her hands slid to his buttocks, her fingers kneading his firm flesh. She wanted to hold on to him, to their love, to the moment—to stop the inevitable. He'd become her life, and she'd never again be complete without him.

Closing her eyes, she clung to him as he took her higher and higher into the special world of love they'd found and cherished. Tears escaped, though she clenched her lids tighter. She couldn't let him go. The pain of the past was still too fresh; the old wounds had barely healed, yet she was being forced to reopen them. She whispered his name and held on tighter than she ever had before. To let him go was to lose him, but she was lost in his love.

Everything around her faded. All she could see, feel, touch, or smell was him: his rugged masculine body pressed against her; the hair on his chest tickled her breasts as he moved, pushing her higher toward the unreachable star. In an instant, the heavens opened around her in a million blinding lights. She heard him groan as he joined her in the ultimate union of their love.

His arms shook beneath her hands; his strength was drained. He moved over to lie in the hay, his hand on her stomach, gently drawing circles on her skin. She moved to face him, to savor every last detail of his magnificent body.

"How soon do you have to go?" she asked at last.

"Shhh," he said.

She threaded her fingers in his hair and fought back tears, but it was no use. She couldn't help the way she felt. Tears fell uncontrollably, and she began to sob. "It...it isn't fair. I just got you back!"

"Don't cry...please...don't cry, Red." He took her hand, twisting the ring around her finger.

How could she stop? The way he touched her wedding band expressed what words never could. A part of him would always be with her. It was his silent promise, but it wasn't enough. She wanted him here, as her husband, as her lover.

"Oh, Cade, I...I..." Her voice wouldn't cooperate, and her body began to tremble.

"Please don't cry." He wiped tears from her cheeks.

Determination was written on his face, the tenderness he'd shown while making love replaced with the tough facade of a bounty hunter. She silently cursed his profession. "We could go with you, me and the kids—"

"No, I've told you. When I leave, it's over."

She turned away from him and wrapped herself in her discarded petticoats. Suddenly she felt chilled and alone, the familiar ache beginning in her heart. The tears wouldn't stop, and she didn't care. His hand found her shoulder, his touch warm on her cold skin.

"I'll miss you."

"Oh, Cade." She rolled to face him. "I know what it's like to miss you. I spent years missing you. Isn't that enough for one lifetime?" She tried to catch her breath between sobs. "Please...don't leave me."

He pulled her to his chest, but the warmth of his body only made her cry harder.

Chapter 19

A rooster strutted through the barn, lifted his beak and crowed at the rising sun that shone through cracks in the door. Cade looped the girth under Maddy, kneeing her sharply when the horse puffed her belly. "Don't give me any trouble, girl. I've got enough woman problems." After cinching the strap tight, he stepped back and smacked the horse on its flanks. "Just because you got a pretty face, don't think you can work me."

Zoe entered the barn holding a cup of steaming hot coffee. Standing on tiptoe, she kissed Cade good morning. Their eyes held for a moment. "You do have a time with your women. I'm going back to the store. Don't leave without having breakfast."

Cade glanced up as Pop tottered in.

"There you are, Cade—oh, mornin', Zoe. You're out and about early this morning."

Cade put his arm around Zoe's waist when he saw that Pop's sudden appearance embarrassed her. "I'll be in to say good-bye in a few minutes," he told her.

She nodded and kissed him again before slipping around Pop and out the door.

Cade adjusted the stirrup leathers, then led Maddy out of the barn. Pop trailed behind him.

"Guess you heard the news?" Pop asked.

"How long have you known McGill was getting close?"

"A day or two."

A muscle in Cade's jaw worked. "Why didn't you tell me?"

Pop caught up, catching hold of his shirtsleeve. "Hold up. We need to talk."

Shrugging Pop's hand away, Cade grabbed Maddy by the bridle and led her down the street to the general store.

Pop hurried to keep pace as fast as his crutches would allow. "No use getting bent out of shape. I didn't tell ya because I knew the town had ya covered."

Cade stopped in his tracks. "The town what?"

Pop paused to catch his breath. "I said, the town has ya covered. No one's gonna let McGill get ya."

Cade's face hardened. "I take care of my own back, Pop."

351

"That might be, but now you got a little help."

Looping the reins around the hitching rail, Cade stepped back, lifted his hat, then settled it low on his forehead.

"You haven't noticed the guns the townspeople been totin'?" Pop met his even gaze.

"I've noticed—guess they've got a right to carry guns if they want."

"They're protectin' ya!"

"Me?"

Pop nodded. "We took a vote, and it was unanimous in your favor."

"Why in the world would the town think they'd need to protect me?"

"Because..." The old man paused, glancing toward the store entrance. "We figure it was the least we could do, seeing as how we forced you to marry Zoe."

Shaking his head, Cade smiled. "I don't know what the hell you're talking about. Go over to Glori-Lee's and get your breakfast. She'll be taking biscuits out of the oven about now."

"Okay, bury your head in the sand like a dad-burned ostrich, but it's the truth!" Pop shook a crutch at him. "If it weren't for the town, you wouldn't be ridin' outta here today, confident your nieces and nephews have a good home."

Pausing on the lowest step, Cade braced his hand on one of the porch posts. "All right. What's this all about?"

"You ready to listen?"

"Depends on what you're going to say."

"When we—the town—realized that you and

Zoe couldn't do anything except butt heads, we decided to take matters into our own hands. John's and Addy's kids were likely to suffer if we didn't do something, so we called a town meeting and decided we had to get you and Zoe together, or the kids would go to Laticia."

"The kids are my responsibility—"

"A responsibility you weren't living up to."

"Pop, you're talking crazy. You, or the town, didn't have anything to do with me marrying Red."

"Oh, no? Who locked you in the jail?"

"Zoe came up with the idea of marriage—"

Pop shook his head, his tongue pushing out his lower lip.

"She—"

"Suggested it, like we hoped she would," Pop said. "Or like we hoped you would, if you ever stopped hagglin' long enough."

Cade's hands fisted at his sides. "Did Zoe know anything about this so-called plan?"

"Nope. Didn't tell her a thing. She'd never have gone along with it if she had."

Slapping the post, Cade stepped up on the porch.

"No use doing something foolish," Pop warned. "What's done is done. The kids are where they belong, and there's no reason you can't stay around and be a husband to Zoe and a pa to those children. Let McGill come after you. Bring this thing to a head, and get it over with. The town's willing to stand and fight beside you. What more could you want?"

"I'm leaving, Pop. I'm saying good-bye to the kids and Red, and I'm going."

"Don't be a fool. There's nothing out there for you." Pop limped up the steps, trying to block Cade's path to the inside. The old man's faded blue eyes pinned Cade with a long, silent scrutiny. "Listen to me. You're like my own boy. Give it up, son. You got everything you ever wanted right here. Reach out and take it. Take what you've wanted ever since you rode out of here seventeen years ago. Can't you see, your sister's giving you another chance? Don't be a fool and let it pass."

Cade reached for the door handle, and Pop rapped his hand with a crutch. Cade cursed as he looked at the red welt on the back of his knuckles.

"*Listen* to me. Stay here and fight McGill. When it's over, you'll have Zoe and the kids. You ain't lived no life that cain't be changed with a little effort."

Cade's shoulders slumped as the weight of Pop's words washed over him. "I wish it was that easy, Pop."

"It *is* that easy. You're the one making it hard, you stubborn fool. Is it the money?"

"It was never the money."

"Then stay. Until a man finds his purpose, he's never goin' to be happy. Isn't that what Reverend Munson said? You've found your purpose; now stay with it."

Cade nudged him aside and reached again for the door handle.

"Listen to me, knucklehead!" Pop shouted. "If you *was* my boy, I'd turn you over my knee, no matter how big you are. Maybe you've found your purpose, and you're just not man enough to know it!"

Cade entered the store and slammed the door behind him.

Zoe was in the kitchen when the slamming front door made her drop the pan she was holding. She ran into the store. "Cade?"

"Get the kids up."

"What? What's the—"

"Get the kids up, Red. I haven't got time to argue. I want to tell them good-bye."

The look in her eyes cut him to the bone. He knew he was hurting her and the kids. It couldn't be helped if he were to keep them safe. His one regret was that she would never forgive him. How could she?

"God forgive me," he mumbled as he grabbed a handful of jerky and tossed it into a knapsack. He walked through the store, stuffing other dried and nonperishable food into the bag. Zoe turned and hurried into the living quarters.

He glanced up a moment later to find four tousled-haired children watching him pack.

Missy's lower lip jutted out. "What's wong, Uncle Cwade? Are you mad 'bout something?"

"I'm not mad, Sunflower. Something's come up, and I have to leave." The little girl's eyes followed him as he moved about the store.

Zoe reached out and put her arm around Brody. Cade refused to look at them. He'd never thought leaving them would be this hard.

Hell, yes, Pop. Stay around, raise the kids, be a husband. Easy to say; damned hard to do.

Stay, and McGill would always hold the winning hand. Even if he outdrew the bastard, there were more brothers, more kin, looking to settle the score. Pop accused him of not being man enough to stay, but he was man enough to walk out and give Red and the kids a chance at a normal life.

"Don't go away, Uncle Cade." Brody's lower lip trembled. "You ain't taught me how to shoot a pistol yet."

"Sorry, son." Cade turned his back. "Ask one of the Pointer boys to teach you."

Missy started to cry, holding onto Zoe's skirt. Holly reached over and took her sister's hand. "Don't cry, Missy."

"Uncle Cwade is leaving," she sobbed. "I don't want him to leave." Missy's tear-rimmed eyes implored Zoe. "Make him stay, Zoe, make him stay!"

Zoe drew the child closer, quietly soothing her.

"Are you tired of being a pa already?" Will asked. "'Cause we could be better. I won't make such a mess next time we pull taffy."

Cade closed his eyes. The boy tore at his heart as badly as Zoe's silence did. Leaving was the most difficult, painful thing he'd ever done.

Zoe left the children and came to be by his side. "You'll need sugar and coffee." She reached for the items, helping him sack them. Their eyes met and darted away. As she edged past him, she laid her hand on his shoulder and squeezed. "You'll need warm clothing.

It'll be getting cold soon. I'll pack a few of Jim's things."

The knot in his throat tightened. "I don't want your husband's clothes."

"Don't be foolish, Cade. It's good, warm clothing. Jim would want you to have them." She disappeared into the back rooms. The children hadn't moved from the doorway.

"Are you really going?" Brody asked.

"Yes, son." Cade wanted to take the boy in his arms and tell him the truth. Ten was old enough to understand that life didn't necessarily deal from the top of the deck, and there were worse things than being a coward. A coward could be tempted to stay and subject his family to his enemies, but a man ran hard and fast to protect the ones he loved.

"It ain't fair!"

"Brody, don't raise your voice to me," Cade warned.

"I hate you! You shoulda never come back. Ma said you'd stay. She said once you got here, you'd love us enough to stay and keep us. She said you'd marry Zoe 'cause you was always sweet on her, but Ma lied! You ain't gonna stay. You're gonna run away and never come back, just like you always do!"

Brody's words stung deep. Addy had promised innocent children that he'd come back for good? Why would she do that? Why? Hell, he knew why. She could read him like a book. Pop was right. She was giving him a way back, but she'd failed to take his life into consideration. He wasn't the callow youth who'd ridden out of here looking for adventure. He'd found a bushel basket of it, enough to sicken him. He'd gone at life like a kid eating too many green apples because no one was there to stop him. Now he was paying the price.

Oh, Addy. Why did you promise something I can't give? Don't you think I would stay if I could? Don't you think I know you loved me enough to give Red back to me? Don't you know how it hurts—

The front door slammed shut, and he glanced up to see that Brody was gone. "Brody!"

"I'm going with my brother!" Will shouted. "We don't want to live here anymore! You're mean!" He raced out the door before Cade could get around the counter.

Missy dashed after them. He reached out and snagged the hem of her nightgown. "Zoe!"

Zoe appeared in the doorway. "What's wrong?"

"The kids are running off."

"The kids are *what*?"

"Running away, dammit!" He glanced at Missy, who was kicking and squirming on the floor. "What are you doing, Missy?"

"I'm having a big ol' fit so you won't go!"

Leaving the girls to Zoe, he walked to the door and jerked it open. "I'm going after Brody and Will."

"Cade," Zoe called out, running to him. "You have to leave; I'll go after the boys." She paused in the doorway, her eyes begging him. "Go on—I'll go after them."

He reached out, touching her lips with his

finger. "I can't go knowing there's a couple of little boys out there crying their hearts out, thinking I don't give a damn about them."

Her eyes were grave. "Hart McGill is a county away. I thought we agreed the children's safety came first."

"That was before I knew what an Uncle Pa was."

She caught him close. "I can't keep up this facade. It's tearing me apart to let you go," she whispered.

Drawing her to him tightly, he rocked her in his arms. "Say it," he whispered harshly.

"I can't—"

"*Say* it, Red."

"I *love* you—"

She wrapped her arms around his neck and buried her face in his shoulder. "I love you."

After kissing her roughly, he set her aside. "Fix breakfast. I'm going after our boys."

Cade knelt beside the trunk of an oak tree, watching the boys. Overhead, a songbird trilled to its nearby mate.

Brody and Will were on their knees at their parents' graveside. Dirty tear-streaks smudged their faces and, as usual, Will's nose needed wiping.

Rising, Cade walked over and handed the boy a handkerchief. "Blow hard."

Will jerked away, wiping his sleeve across his nose. "Don't have to do nothin' you say— you don't care 'bout us anymore."

Cade knelt between the two boys, and Brody jumped up and ran to his grandparents' tombstone. "Look," Cade said, "I don't want you to think I don't care about you. I do—a lot. Now come on. Let's go back home. Zoe's worried—"

Brody kicked a clump of dirt. "Why should we do what you say? You're not our pa. Our pa is there." He pointed to John's grave.

Will sat back on his haunches. "We come to say good-bye to Ma and Pa. Then me and Brody's gonna be bounty hunters. We're going to shoot people, just like you."

Cade looked away. Bounty hunters. When had he ever encouraged that? "And where do you plan to do this bounty-hunting?"

"Wichita," Will answered.

"And how do you plan on getting to Wichita?"

"Brody knows the way—he knows lots of stuff."

Cade looked over at Brody, who was staring at his bare feet. "That right, Brody? You going to Wichita? In your nightshirt?"

"Maybe even California." Brody refused to look at him. "What do you care?"

"Well, you may not believe it, but I do care. I can see why you'd be mad at me, but why Zoe? Do you want to hurt her?"

"You did," Brody spat out. "Ma said you hurt her real bad once."

"Yeah," Will agreed. "But she said the good in you would come through someday, and you'd come back and make it up to her."

Cade picked up a rock and threw it. Addy

again. He was at a loss to explain why she'd filled their heads with empty dreams.

Brody smacked his hand against a tombstone. "You ain't got no good in you. You came back just to hurt everyone again."

"I think it's time we had a talk." Cade motioned for them to sit down. "You're both old enough to know the truth."

"I don't want to know any ol' truth," Brody said.

"That's too bad, because you're going to hear it. *Sit down.*"

Brody kicked the dirt a couple more times before he dragged himself over to where Will sat. Cade pointed to a spot beside Will, and Brody plopped down, propping his chin on his hands.

Sorting his thoughts, Cade took a moment. "First of all, being a bounty hunter is not what you want to do."

"You're one," Brody said.

"And if I had it to do over again, I'd have made a smarter choice."

"Like what?" Will peered up at him.

"Like farming, or running a livery—or a thousand and one other jobs that would be a better way to make a living."

He sat down between them, putting his arms around their shoulders. "I'd like to be your pa. I just can't."

"Why not?" Will asked. "Don't no one tell *you* what to do; I hear you tell Zoe that all the time."

"This is different."

"Uncle Pa." Will's eyes pinned him. "If

you didn't have to chase that bad guy, would you stay here and be our pa?"

"I would, Will. I'd like that."

"Then stay."

Appeal to his reasoning. Cade thought. "There's this man—his name is Hart McGill. He's looking for me."

Will leaned into Cade's embrace. "You can hide under Zoe's bed. That's where I hide from Holly when—"

"You don't understand, son. McGill is one of the bad guys. He wants to kill me." Cade wasn't sure if the boys understood. "I can't put you and your sisters and Zoe in danger. I have to go far away from Winterborn so McGill will never know about my family."

Will squirmed. "He might shooted you dead?"

Cade nodded. "That's what he'd like to do."

Brody leaned back on his elbows. "I could shoot him dead, I'll betcha."

"Yeah," Will seconded. "Brody says he's gonna learn hisself how to shoot."

Cade shook his head. "Guns aren't the answer, boys. A man doesn't learn to shoot so he can kill another person. He respects a gun and the harm it can do. You shoot a shotgun so you can hunt rabbits. You fire a rifle to kill deer to put meat on the table. The only time you shoot another person is to protect those you love."

"Is that why you like shootin' bad guys?" Will asked. "To protect people?"

Cade ruffled the boy's hair. "I don't like shooting anyone, but I wouldn't stand by

and let an outlaw run roughshod over innocent people. That's why I hunt the 'bad guy'
and turn him over to the law."

"Or shoot him," Brody reminded.

"Occasionally I shoot, but not unless he
forces me to."

Brody stood and walked around them. "If
you showed me how to shoot a pistol, I could
scare McGill so bad he'd run away and never
come back."

Cade laughed. "I guess you could, but
you're not going to."

"I could try!"

Will threw his arms around Cade's neck and
hung on for dear life. "I don't want you to be
dead. Please, Uncle Pa, don't let that bad guy
shooted you. Brody and I will help you put
him in jail."

Cade stood, lifting Will with him. The boy
wrapped his legs around Cade's waist and held
on tight as Cade extended his hand to Brody.
"Come on. We'll do a little target-shooting
before I leave." He should be riding out right
now, but when he looked at their faces, he knew
he couldn't go—not yet.

He drew a steadying breath, cupping the back
of Brody's head with his hand and pulling him
tightly against him. "Brody, you're the man
now. When I leave, I want to know I can
count on you to see to the household. Keep
Zoe and your brother and sisters safe."

Brody nodded solemnly. "You teach me
to shoot a gun, and I'll protect 'em."

"That means you won't be able to go to California to be a bounty hunter."

Brody stuck his chest out. "No, sir. I'll take real good care of your family, Uncle Cade."

Will yanked on Cade's sleeve. "Does that mean he's my boss now?"

"Red's the boss, but Brody's your big brother. He'll take good care of you. That right, Brody?"

"You mean if somebody at school wants to beat up Will, I can sock 'em in the nose?

Cade chuckled. "I'd try talking it out first—" He paused, then conceded, "But if reason fails, then sock them in the nose."

The three males walked back to town in silence, except for an occasional sniff from Will to staunch his runny nose. Cade offered his handkerchief again. This time, Will took it. After using it, the boy handed it back, then fell into step with Cade, trying to match his stride. Cade smiled, realizing there'd never been anyone who'd wanted to be like him. He'd have to be blind not to see how the boys looked up to him. He walked beside their short bodies, watching them kick dirt. He'd like to be around to see them grow to manhood. And the girls—he'd give an eyetooth to be there when suitors came courting, to make sure they were worthy of such beauties.

He shook away the thought. For someone who knew nothing about kids, he was taking his role as Uncle Pa awfully seriously.

"Hey, Ben!" he called as they approached the livery.

The blacksmith looked up from his anvil. "Hey!"

"Me and the boys are going to do a little target-shooting behind the building."

"How come the boys are still in their night-shirts?" Ben called.

"They left the house in a hurry this morning."

Waving his consent, Ben continued to shape a horseshoe.

Cade set up a row of empty bottles on a bale of hay several yards away from the livery.

"Will, you watch while Brody shoots first." Cade emptied all but one bullet from the chamber of his Colt and handed it to Brody. "If it's too heavy to hold steady with one hand, you can use both."

Brody lifted the pistol, his arm quivering from its weight. Cade guided the boy's other hand to the grip. "Hold it still, and look down the barrel until the bottle you're aiming at is in the sight." Cade kept his voice low and even. "When you've got your aim where you want it, squeeze the trigger real easy. Don't jerk; squeeze, real easy-like."

A loud blast split the silence. Brody's arm shot straight up, and he fell backward against Cade.

Cade laughed at the boy's startled expression. "Got a little kick to it, huh? You okay?"

Brody nodded. "Did I break a bottle?"

"No, but you scared a couple birds off the fence." Cade took the pistol from Brody and put another bullet into the chamber. "Want to try again?"

The smile on Brody's face assured him he'd have it no other way. "This time, relax, but keep your arm straight." Cade stood behind the boy and put his large hand over Brody's smaller ones. "See the bottle at the end of the barrel?"

Brody nodded.

"Get it in your sight and...squeeze."

Another blast, but this time, with Cade's help, Brody stayed upright and the bottle shattered.

"I did it!" Brody jumped up and down. "I did it, Uncle Cade." He turned in circles. "Did you see it, Will? I did it!"

"My turn now," Will said, his voice excited. "I bet I can shooted two bottles!"

Cade instructed Will in the same concise manner he had Brody, and after several attempts and a sore hand, Will finally broke a bottle. The little boy puffed up like a peacock, and Cade could barely control Will's enthusiasm long enough to teach him how to reload.

"I want to try one more time, Uncle Cade," Brody said.

"Your arm will hurt so bad in the morning, you won't be able to lift it."

"I don't care!" His eyes shone with pride.

"Once more; then we go home." He'd stayed too long already.

"What's all the racket back here?"

The three turned to see Pop, on his crutches, round the corner of the livery.

Will ran to meet him. "Uncle Pa showed me and Brody how to shoot! I shot a bottle a hunnert miles in the air!"

Pop let out a belly laugh. "A hunnert miles? Now that's a long ways, boy. How'd you do that?"

Will shaped his hand in the form of a gun, his finger pointing toward the bale of hay. "Ka-pow! Ka-pow!"

"That'd do it," Pop said, then raised his eyebrows to Cade. "Thought you were gone."

"I am. I had this one last thing to do for the boys."

Pop looked at the youngsters. "How'd you do, Brody? Your bottle go *two* hunnert miles?"

Brody beamed. "Almost. Look how many times I shot." He proudly displayed the redness on his right hand, which was beginning to swell.

They turned as a carriage pulled up beside the livery. Cade hurriedly reloaded the Colt, relieved when he saw who climbed out of the buggy.

"Abraham!" Will squealed. "I shooted a bottle!"

A big smile split the old man's face "A bottle? Now ain't that somethin'."

Brody ran to meet him. "I shot a bunch of 'em."

"I see a bottle ain't safe in this town no mo'."

Pop hopped over to the buggy. "What're you doin' back in town?"

Abraham wrapped the reins around the brake and got down. "Miz Laticia wanted me to bring this here big box o' clothes for the young'uns. Said no kin o' hers was goin' 'round lookin' like ragamuffins."

"Sounds like Laticia," Pop said, his gaze running over the big wooden box. "She musta bought out half of Wichita. This crate's big enough to bury one of Mallard's bulls in." He pounded his fist on top of the crate. "Sturdy as they come."

"She sure 'nuff bought out half the mercantile," Abraham said, "jist afore she come down wif a bunch o' them red spots."

Cade slipped the Colt back into his holster. "Laticia has the measles?"

Abraham grinned. "Doctor says she be laid up a few days, then she be her ol' sef agin."

Pop slapped the black man on the back. "And you thought you'd get outta town before she's her old self again."

Grinning, Abraham shook his head. "Now, Sheriff. I ain't sayin' nuthin' bad 'bout Miz Laticia."

"You never do, Abraham," Pop agreed. "She's a lucky woman to have you to look after her."

"No'sa. I's the lucky one. Owes a lot to Miz Laticia. Taught me how ta read 'n write when she jist a young girl. Back then, wern't looked on too favorable for a black man ta read." He let out a hearty laugh. "Miz Laticia paid no mind ta what others said. Said she wern't gonna have some ignernt soul drivin' her 'round. So ever'day she drummed them numbers and letters inta my head 'til I learned 'em."

Cade glanced at the boys. "Help Abraham get the box of clothes unloaded, and make sure you send a proper thank-you to Aunt Laticia."

The boys jumped up into the buggy, pulled open the box, and rifled through the contents.

Brody wrinkled his nose when he held up a boy's blue velvet coat. "Sissy clothes," he complained.

Will pulled out a pair of shoes his size with silver buckles on the toes. He frowned, holding them up for Cade's inspection. "Do I have ta?"

"Miz Laticia don't know much 'bout what young'uns likes ta wear," Abraham apologized.

"The clothes are much appreciated," Cade said. "Zoe can alter whatever needs to be fixed. She's handy with a needle and thread."

"You ain't goin' to try to haul that box, are ya?" Pop asked, glancing at Cade.

"Hell, three of us can't move that box. We'll have to empty it and carry the clothes to the store. Abraham can keep the box."

"Don't know what'd I'd do with such a big ol' box." Abraham scratched his head.

Pop smacked a crutch across the top of the crate. "Might come in handy for somethin'."

Chapter 20

Grim faces stared back at Zoe at the breakfast table. Feeling plenty grim herself, she avoided Cade's gaze as she took a pan of biscuits from the oven. The scent of rain was heavy in the air as Missy dished up fried potatoes and Holly poured Cade's coffee. Thunder rolled in the distance.

Cade glanced at Missy and Holly and smiled. "Thank you, girls."

Despite the girls' red eyes and the slight

quiver in their chins, Zoe thought they had accepted Cade's decision to leave.

Latching onto Missy's skirt, he tugged playfully. "Cat got your tongue this morning?"

Zoe shook her head warningly when Missy started to tear up.

Cade changed the subject. "Sounds like rain's moving in."

"We can always use rain," Zoe said, taking her seat at the table. She reached for Holly's hand, and the family formed a circle. "Brody, will you bless the food, please?" She bowed her head as Brody said grace. When the amen was pronounced, she forced her mind to go blank. If she allowed herself to think, she would start crying, and that's the last thing she wanted to do.

Cade picked up a knife and buttered a biscuit for Missy, then glanced at Brody. "Haven't you got something you want to tell Zoe?"

"Cade taught me how to shoot a pistol!" Brody's eyes were bright with excitement.

"Me, too," Will announced.

Zoe picked up a bowl of gravy and started it around.

Cade smiled, his glance bouncing back and forth between her and the boys.

"Is that so?" she responded.

He reached under the table and gave her thigh a reassuring squeeze. "A boy needs to know these things. Doesn't mean he'll be a bounty hunter."

Her lips drew into a tight smile. "I suppose that spending your last hours with the children taking a nice walk would have been much too ordinary," she commented.

"That's what we figured, wasn't it, men?"

The boys nodded, stuffing scrambled eggs into their mouths. "It was fun," Will exclaimed. "I hit a bottle a hunnert miles in the air!"

"I hit mine two hunnert!" Brody said.

Cade took a bite, winking at Holly. "I thought the girls could help me tie my bedroll to the back of Maddy's saddle. What do you say, Holly? Would you do that?"

Holly nodded halfheartedly.

Zoe passed the butter. "Eat your breakfast, Missy."

"I'm not hungwy."

"Of course you're hungry." Cade lifted her fork and tempted her with some of the eggs. "Come on, sweetheart, it's good."

Shaking her head, the little girl looked at Zoe, her eyes brimming over with tears.

"It's all right if you want to leave the table. I'll keep your food warm in the oven."

Missy got up and ran into the bedroom. The family ate in silence except for the occasional ping of a fork scraping a plate, a noisy swallow of milk, or the clunk of a glass being set down.

Zoe choked down her food as the clock chimed eight, sounding like a dirge.

When somebody banged suddenly on the back screen door, she jumped as if she'd been shot, and was relieved to see one of Brody's playmates standing there. "Brody is eating his breakfast, Freddy. You'll have to come back later."

"Pop said come and get Cade quick," the ten-year-old blurted out.

"Cade is eating—"

"Hart McGill is in town." Freddy Henderson jumped on one foot, then the other. "Pop said Cade's got to come right *now*!"

The mouthful Zoe had just swallowed soured in her stomach. "Dear God," she whispered.

Brody scraped his chair back from the table, tipping over his glass of milk.

Zoe's heart pounded so loudly she was sure Cade could hear it. Nausea coursed through her in violent waves. She closed her eyes, taking deep breaths.

Cade slowly laid his fork aside and got up.

Her hand came out to stop him. "No..." The word was a pitiful cry, that of a wounded animal in need of help.

He squeezed her hand before reaching for his gun belt and fastening it around his hips. Tying the leather strap to his right leg, he looked at Brody. "You remember what we talked about this morning?"

Brody nodded, his face as white as the stream of milk running off the table.

"You take the others and keep them in the bedroom until someone tells you to come out."

Brody's eyes widened.

"It's all right, son. You're the man of the house now."

"You gotta mind me, Will." Brody herded Will, Holly and Zoe toward the bedroom. Zoe turned and looked at Cade, praying this was a nightmare and she would wake up soon.

"Go on," he said. "The kids need you."

"I can't let you leave—not like this..." She felt light-headed, powerless. The room spun, and she lifted her hand to her forehead, trying to orient herself. She couldn't fall to pieces now; she had to think of the children.

Squaring her shoulders, she took a deep breath. "All right...all right. The children will be fine...I'll be fine. Do what you have to do." The words tasted bitter in her throat.

Suddenly Cade was there, his firm shoulder supporting her. His familiar scent filled her senses, and she reeled with fear.

"Listen to me, Red." He gripped her arm. "If anything happens to me, you and the kids go somewhere safe outside Winterborn. Do you understand what I'm saying? McGill will come after you if you stay."

She nodded, swallowing. "Yes...I'll leave with the children—but I have no place to go...."

"Pop will help you."

Cade moved her toward the bedroom where she could hear Missy's hysterical crying. She needed to calm the child. *Please, God, give me the strength to see this through.* She patted Cade's hand. "I'll be fine, I'll be fine...I just need a minute." Her knees buckled, and she fell against him for one blissful, comforting moment. Her arms wound around his neck, and she buried her face in his shoulder, then kissed his cheeks, his eyes, anywhere she could blindly touch. He matched her kisses, nearly crushing her in his hold.

"My prayers go with you," she whispered, knowing the need in her voice for him to run, and not look back, belied her outward calm.

"Listen to me, Red." His expression was so tender it nearly took her breath away. "Because of you and the children, I didn't leave. I couldn't. Now my past has caught up with me. McGill is here. I can't run anymore." He wiped a tear from her cheek. "Can you understand?"

"Oh, Cade, I can't bear it if...."

"Shhh." He laid his fingertips across her lips. "Do you remember why I gave you the name Red?"

"Because of my hair." She touched his whisker-roughened cheek, needing to absorb his every essence.

"That's what I told you, but it was because you had the temper and strength of a man, and I admired that." He smiled. "Find that strength, Red. Be the woman I know you are. Be brave for the children."

She started to laugh and didn't know why. "It wasn't my hair?" Her laughter turned to quiet sobs, wracking her body as he kissed her before he turned to leave.

"Go into the bedroom, Red."

Blindly, she released the clasp on her locket and put the chain around his neck. "I want you to have this. I want a part of me to be with you out there."

He pulled her to him and kissed her so hard she could barely breathe. Then he left.

Brody emerged from the bedroom and took her gently by the hand. "It's all right, Zoe. I'll take care of you."

The boy led her into the bedroom. Outside the window, the faint sounds of men's shouts came to her. It sounded as if Main Street were being cleared of horses and buggies. Lifting her head, she saw the children crying, their young faces full of fear. She took a handkerchief and wiped Will's runny nose as she heard another yell. Her heart raced.

Gathering the children to her bosom, she searched for words to allay their fear. The apprehension in their eyes made her want to cry harder, but instead she dried her eyes.

Taking another deep breath and sitting, she smiled at Brody. "Have I ever told you the story about Cade and Pop going coon-hunting when Cade was just about your age?"

Brody shook his head, his face pale with worry.

"My," she said, patting the bed beside her in an invitation for the children to join her, "were those two ever a sight. They took off for the woods, guns over their shoulders, ol' Blue on the trail of something. The other dogs joined in all that baying, not having the slightest idea what they were howling about..."

Her eyes moved to the window; the commotion outside was getting louder. Lifting her voice, she spoke over the noise. "The preacher said they were just all imitating ol' Blue, but that old dog sure knew how to spot a coon..."

Pop waved a crutch in the air and yelled at the crowd gathering on the corner. "Git off the street!" When the flock didn't move, he yelled louder. "Go on home, now; there's gonna be a shoot-out!" Hobbling across the street, he motioned for horses to be untied and buggies moved. "Get these animals out of here!"

Several men released the horses and sent them galloping with a brisk swat to the hindquarters. Buckboards and buggies rattled toward the livery.

At the north end of town, Hart McGill's silhouette loomed as storm clouds moved in. A sharp crack of thunder split the dark morning sky, and Cade rounded the corner of the general store. Pop hobbled across the street to meet him.

Main Street cleared. Onlookers, fearing for their safety, ducked into nearby businesses and jerked the shades down.

Cade lifted his hat, ran his fingers through his hair, then settled it low. Glancing to the north end of town, he said, "Looks like I stayed a day too long."

Pop's weathered face looked older than Cade had ever seen it. "You don't have to do this, son. Let me run the no-good out of town, tell him to move on."

Cade studied McGill's outline. The image of Owen Cantrell's widow seared his mind. Owen had been shot down in the prime of his life by this cold-hearted bastard, and Cade pondered the certain knowledge that were McGill to find out he'd married Zoe, she would never be safe again. No, he had to fight.

"Jest concentrate on what you're doin', son."

"Get out of here, Pop. This is my fight."

"This is *my* town."

Cade took a money clip out of his pocket and handed it to Pop. "If this doesn't turn out the way I want, see that Red gets this. Make sure she leaves Winterborn tonight. She'll argue with you, but don't listen to her. If I lose, McGill will come after her and the kids next. Tell her to buy a place out of state—somewhere far away, where she and the kids will be safe."

Pop waved the money aside. "Don't need that. I got a piece of land in Missouri so remote, mosquitoes cain't find it. I'll take care of your family if anything happens."

"Thanks, Pop."

"The only thanks I want is for you to come out of this alive." He put his hand on Cade's shoulder. "You keep a steady hand. You can take him. There ain't a better gun around than Cade Kolby's."

Cade smiled. "Tell my family I was thinking of them."

Pop nodded. "You need to tell 'em, not me. It's not over 'til it's over. Now, git out there and do what you gotta do." He limped on across the street.

Dark clouds hovered overhead, turning daylight into dark. Thunder rolled as the storm moved in. Settling his hat lower, Cade stepped into the middle of Main Street, his mind cleared of all thoughts but one. McGill. His hand rested loosely at his side, his gaze focused on the man who stood at the other end of Main Street—a man who had haunted his dreams and ruled his life.

He took his stance, one he'd taken more times than he cared to think about, but it felt awkward and unnatural today. Main Street was empty, except for a lone mutt who ambled along in front of the bank.

Dust swirled off the rooftops and settled on the street as he stared McGill down. More thunder rumbled overhead, and gusts of wind whipped at his clothing. Bits of debris stung his face, and he blinked against the gale.

The bearded outlaw hawked up a wad and spit to one side. "Finally showed your cowardly face, huh, Kolby?"

Cade's hand hovered just over his holster. "What took you so long, McGill?"

McGill advanced, his sinister eyes glaring at Cade through the whirling dust. "You shoulda knowed better than to try to hide from a McGill. You're a dead man, Kolby."

"We all have to go one time or the other."

"And you're going today." McGill's fingers flexed loosely at his sides.

They each took a step closer, then two. Lightning crackled, and rain poured from the heavens.

Cade swore when he saw Pop out the corner of his eye, leaning against the side of the jailhouse, hand on his gun. Ahead of him, Cade saw faces of various citizens of Winterborn begin to appear behind store columns and peeking around the corners of buildings. The barrel of a gun protruded from the partially open door of Walt's barbershop.

Cade took another step, then another. McGill's eyes narrowed. "Heard you took yourself a right purty wife. Too bad she's gonna be widowed again. Twice couldn't be much fun—but don't you worry none. Ol' Hart will see to the little woman's needs." He laughed. "Got me a hankerin' for those red-headed women—they got a lot of fire in the bedroom, if you know what I mean."

Cade stiffened. Pop's whispered words reached him. "Don't let him rile ya, son."

"Steady as it goes, boy." He heard Walt whisper.

Cade's eyes never left McGill's right hand. He took a deep breath, blinking against rain starting to pepper down.

"Yep, heard wifey is real purty. 'Spect she'll be real lonely after yore dead—" McGill's hand flew to his gun.

Cade dropped to one knee and fired. The Colt exploded with a deafening roar at the same time McGill's Buntline Special blasted, the gunfire overpowering a clap of thunder.

Hot lead grazed Cade's left arm. Blood seeped through his shirt, crimson against the blue, rain-soaked fabric, and he fell to the ground. His hat landed next to him.

"You filthy son of a bitch!" yelled McGill. The Peacemaker had caught the desperado in the groin, dropping him. McGill sat up, gripping his thigh and moaning in agony as he got off another round. The slug seared a hole through Cade's hat, knocking it several feet in the air.

Taking slow and deliberate aim, Cade rose on one elbow and fired again, then fell back as a staccato volley of bullets sent Hart McGill into a dance of death, as silence descended. When he looked up, McGill lay in the dirt, staring sightlessly into the whistling wind. Rain pelted onto the road, splattering mud across the dead man's face.

The men of Winterborn calmly blew the smoke from their gun barrels and moved back into the shadows.

Rolling to his side, Cade yanked loose his bandanna and tied it around his bleeding arm. "Dammit."

Pop quickly hobbled over and shoved him back to the ground. "Oh, merciful heavens, Cade's dead!" he cried.

"Pop!" Cade protested, trying to get up. "I'm not dead."

Pop planted a boot in the center of Cade's chest. "Oh, yes, you are. Stay!" he ordered.

Cade rolled onto his back and clamped his eyes shut, gritting his teeth against the stinging ache in his left arm.

"Don't move a muscle," Pop repeated, then turned and hobbled over to where McGill lay sprawled. He counted the holes in the outlaw's chest and he whistled under his breath. "Nine. Shoulda been ten. Walt Mews couldn't hit the side of a *barn*." He hurried back to Cade. "You okay, son?"

"Okay, just grazed. What in the hell is

going on? Who told those men to get involved? This was my fight."

"Not necessarily. The town likes to protect its interests, and keeping you alive happens to be one of our main interests right now." Pop looked around. "We gotta act fast."

Already the townspeople were pouring out of doors and alleyways. Lawrence, Roy, Walt, Ben and Woodall passed Gracie, May, and Edna on the run. Frank Lovell hurried along beside Bess Harris. Doc came running with his black bag. He leaned down and put his ear to Cade's chest. "He's alive. Lay still, son. Let me look at that wound."

Pop pushed the doctor away. "You're wrong. He's dead. Stay back—ever' last one of you—and act like you're grievin'."

"What?" Walt frowned. "You gone off your rocker, Pop?"

Motioning for the crowd to gather round, Pop bent low. "Now listen to me. We ain't got time for chitchat. No telling who's watching these goings-on. We got to unite and put on the act of our lives."

"What'd you mean?" Roy Baker whispered. "It's over—McGill won't be botherin' no one no more."

Edna turned to look at Cade. "Yeah, with McGill dead there's no reason Cade can't stay now, be a husband and father to Zoe and the kids."

Pop kept his voice low. "And because we don't want no other vengeful outlaws comin' after him and stopping that from happening, here's what we're gonna do. We're gonna have a funeral the likes of which this town ain't never seen, and we're gonna have it this afternoon."

Roy looked puzzled. "Who died—that we care about?"

Pop smiled. "Why, Cade died."

The crowd turned to stare at Cade, who still lay in the middle of the street. He lifted a finger and waved back.

"What are you talkin' about?" Gracie demanded. "Cade's as alive as we are—"

"Hush up, woman!" Pop straightened and motioned for Roy and Ben to come forward. "We need two good strong men to carry the deceased to their restin' places."

"Carry McGill to his grave? I wouldn't waste the time or the effort," Ben declared.

Pop shot him a peeved look. "Listen to me, you knuckleheads. *Hear* what I'm sayin'. Pretend you got some learnin! *Two* men were killed in a gunfight here today. *Two*. Cade Kolby and Hart McGill. Get it?"

The crowd stared at him, their expressions blank.

"Cade, rest his soul, is dead. *Comprende*?"

Slowly but surely, what Pop was trying to convey sank in. One by one, heads began to nod in the crowd.

"Kolby's dead," Walt said. "Bit the dust, a goner."

Enthusiasm for the ruse began to spread throughout the crowd until every last one was in on it.

Hope flared in Cade when he caught the significance of Pop's statement, but it quickly died. "No," he said, still lying there. "It'll never work."

Pop glanced down the street. "Hell, it won't. Don't move a muscle. You're dead, boy. Dead as a doornail."

"How is this going to help anything?" Cade muttered. "I can't come back to Winterborn."

"Kolby cain't come back, but now, his cousin in the Arizona Territory, who looks an awful lot like him, could sure ride in here any day, couldn't he?"

The townsfolk looked confused.

"Couldn't he?" Pop prompted. "Think about it, people."

May glanced at Cade. "You ain't got no cousin in the Arizona Territory."

Gracie punched her, and May's expression turned peevish. "Well, he ain't. I'd know a thing like that. Senda never said a thing about a cousin—"

"Of *course* he has, May," Gracie patiently explained. "Don't you remember? Cade and...and...Tray...Williams, Senda Kolby's sister's boy, looked so much alike when they were young'uns, Senda said she and her sister could hardly tell them apart. Why, I'll bet Tray so strongly resembles Cade that if, say, Cade had been able to grow a beard and put on a few pounds before he died, why, it'd be hard for anyone to tell Cade and Tray apart. Don't you suppose?"

"Cade *hasn't*—oh." May stopped short. "Oh." She grinned. "Well, yes, seems I *do* recall Senda saying how much those two babies favored each other. Goodness, someone needs to wire Tray immediately that his cousin Cade is deceased, and he needs to come and see to his widow's needs."

"It will never work," Cade predicted in low undertones.

The town disagreed, everyone suddenly remembering cousin Tray. Walt winked at Cade. "Nice fellow. Not as wild as Cade, as I recollect."

Roy scratched his head. "Yeah, more settled. Always told my wife that Cade's cousin Tray would be more likely to take a shine to family life than him. Tray and Zoe jest might hit it off real good, don't you think?"

Lawrence smiled. "Why, no telling. Zoe could end up marrying Cade's cousin, and the two of them could live right here in Winterborn and raise Addy's kids. Tray might have a strong head for business—might even get the general store back on solid footing."

Sawyer spit. "Wouldn't that be somethin'?"

"Shore would." Ben grinned. "Stranger things have happened. Walt? Want to help me get the bodies into the stable? It's wet out here."

When a rap sounded at the back door, Zoe felt faint. She willed her legs to move. Taking a deep breath, she opened the back door and saw Pop. The grim look on his face confirmed that her worst fear had been realized.

"No," she whispered.

"No," Pop repeated. "He's alive, Zoe."

Her knees buckled, and Pop reached out to catch her.

"Come on, girl, don't give out on me now." He moved her to a chair and sat her down.

"Where's Cade?" She looked at Pop, tears running down her cheeks.

"Fit as a fiddle—with the exception of a little crease in his left arm. Doc will see to that after the funeral. Cade's about to get laid out. You up to attendin'?"

By now she was so busy laughing through her tears that she was aware of only one thing: Cade was alive. "What?"

As Pop quickly explained the town's plan, Zoe's eyes widened in surprise and gratitude.

"Now," Pop continued, "I want you to leave this house with a long face and wearin' widow's weeds, you hear? No matter how relieved you are, if we're gonna keep your man around, you're gonna have to act like you've got the weight of the world on your shoulders."

Zoe jumped up, nearly taking Pop to his knees with an exuberant hug. "Thank you, Pop, thank you!"

The children heard the commotion and came running out of the bedroom.

"Cade's alive," Zoe announced.

"Oh, boy!" Missy danced around the floor, latching onto Holly. "Oh, boy, oh, boy!"

Brody and Will beamed.

"Honest?" Brody asked.

"Honest," Pop said. "But we're all gonna have to playact for a little while." Pop explained what had happened, described the hastily devised plan, and outlined the roles they had to assume to pull it off.

"I can act *real* sad," Brody said.

"Me, too." Will nodded, screwing up his face.

"I can cwy any time you want," Missy offered. "Weal, *weeeal* loud."

Pop gathered Cade's family to him and smiled as he patted Zoe, who was still sniffling, on the back. "Well, now, ain't this nice. Family helpin' family." He nodded. "Now that's how it should be."

"You in here, Abraham?" Pop was breathless as he entered the dimly lit livery a few minutes later. Maddy whinnied in her stall.

"I's here, Sheriff."

"Did you do what I told ya?"

"Yes'sa. I's got the buryin' box ready."

"We gotta work quick. You think a body will fit in there?"

"Don'cha worry. That box big enough to hold five men. You was right, Sheriff. It shore come in handy."

"Well, fill it with rocks and nail the lid shut real tight, Abraham. Then take a rock and scratch 'Cade Kolby' 'cross the top."

"Yes'sa." Abraham grinned. "Miz Laticia be real proud ta know I's usin' my learnin' ta write. Might make up for her having them red spots. Oh, lordy, Sheriff. The wrath o' the devil hisself descended on the house when she come down wid da fever. Blamin' that 'no-good Cade Kolby.'" Abraham chuckled and hammered the last nail into the makeshift coffin. "Yes'sa, that 'no good Cade Kolby,' may he rest in peace."

Pop put his hat on. "We'll bury McGill in a whiskey barrel. He ought ta like that. And Abraham? This is between me and you and the town. As far as anyone knows, Cade Kolby and Hart McGill killed each other in a shoot-out."

"Yes'sa. This ol' black man don't know nuthin' 'bout nuthin'."

Pop adjusted his crutches under his arm. "Things should settle down around here now. I got a wire this mornin' from the sheriff of Wizard County. Seems the Nelson gang is behind bars. They won't be causing no more trouble and McGill's dead." Pop took a deep breath. "All in all, I'd say it's been a pretty good day."

"It is, indeed, a sad occasion that brings us together here today." Rain sluiced down on the Reverend Munson's head as, late that afternoon, he stood before two open graves.

Zoe wept silently beneath the umbrella, holding the kids close beside her as she surreptitiously searched the crowd. Where was Cade? She wouldn't be surprised to see him standing nearby, witnessing his own funeral. Her body convulsed with happiness and she swallowed, trying to maintain a somber demeanor. When she saw him, she was going to kill him herself—with love.

She lifted her head and stared straight ahead. The whole town was present, weeping, crying, carrying on. Her gaze suddenly focused on a tall figure standing near the back, dressed in a black poncho, hat pulled low over his face.

The man crossed his eyes and stuck out his tongue at her.

Her mouth dropped open, and she quickly looked away. Cade! He *was* here! The man who'd never arrived in time for a funeral in his whole life!

The makeshift coffins stood beside the open graves as the reverend read from the Bible, intoning "Ashes to ashes, dust to dust."

Gracie and Edna fell upon each other's shoulders, sobbing.

"Gracie, did you eat *onions* for supper?" Edna hissed.

"Quiet down, Edna Mews. I wasn't sure I could cry on cue, so I got an onion hidden in my hanky." She raised it to her face until fresh tears welled.

"Whew! I'd do anything for Zoe—even stand out here in the pouring rain at a funeral service for a man who isn't even dead—but I can cry on my own, thank you very much, and I have no intention of smelling like a stew pot!"

Just then, Reverend Munson closed the Bible, and Missy stepped forward holding Bud's jar close to the wooden box. "Bud wants to say good-bye, Uncle Cwade." She laid her baby face against the coffin. "Bet you wish Bud could stay with you, huh, Uncle Cwade?" She grinned.

Several hours later, another knock sounded at Zoe's back door. She raced to answer it and threw herself into Cade's arms. "I was so worried about you."

"Oh, hell, I'm fine. Exceptionally fine for a soaking wet dead man." He shrugged out of the wet poncho and kicked the door shut with his boot, then kissed her long and hard and with the assurance that nothing would ever separate them again.

"Where have you been?"

"Lying low on the outskirts of town. I sneaked in the back way so I wouldn't be seen."

"Oh, Cade, do you think what the town is trying to do will work?"

"At first I didn't, but I'm willing to try anything, Red, for us to be together. I'll have to stay out of sight for a few weeks. Then my so-called cousin will arrive from the Arizona Territory to take my place with my wife and my kids..."

She giggled at the absurdity. "Are you really willing to give up so much for me and the children—even to the point of becoming someone else?"

Her face sobered. "I'd give up anything for you and the kids. It won't be easy—it's not easy now, faking my own death."

Now that he was here, safe and sound, she couldn't resist making him squirm a little. The woman in her needed him to tell her *exactly* what he'd do for her love. "Tell me what you'd give up for me if you had to," she goaded.

"I'd give up my life for you. My reputation as a bounty hunter. My identity—God, woman, you've brought me to my knees."

As he bent to kiss her, she caught his head in her hands. "Would you repeat that?"

"I've given up bounty-hunting, living on the trail, the single life, all for you. Is that what you want to hear?"

"Partly. Repeat the part about bringing you to your knees. That idea makes me very happy."

His eyes shone with such love, the sight stole her breath away. "You win."

She smiled. "It was never a *game* between us, but that's what I want to hear."

"Yeah?" He kissed her again. "I suppose you also want a decent proposal, too?"

She nodded again. "It would be nice."

His eyes softened. "You know I've never stopped loving you."

"In my heart, I'd hoped that."

"Know it." He drew her closer. "Will you marry me?"

"Who's speaking?"

"Oh, hell." He thought for a minute. "Tray somebody."

She cocked her head with a warning look. "I need you to be a little more specific."

"Okay. Tray Williams. Picture me twenty pounds heavier and with a beard."

She lightly brushed his cheek with her fingers. "I think a beard would look very handsome."

"You didn't the day I rode in."

She grinned. "You weren't Tray Williams the day you rode in."

He caught her hand, stilling it. Looking deep into her eyes, he whispered, "Red, will you marry Tray Williams and make him the happiest man on earth?"

Touching her mouth lightly to his, she luxuriated in the warmth of his love. "Of course I'll marry him."

"Reverend Munson doesn't need to be here to make it official first, does he?"

"What's your big hurry?"

"I have a strong need to make love to my wife. Now."

She kissed him, murmuring against his lips, "Strange...your wife has the same urge...."

Gazing into her eyes, he whispered, "I, Tray Williams, take you, Zoe Kolby, to be my lawfully wedded wife. To have and to hold, in my arms and in my bed—"

"Cade."

"—from this day forward, 'til the day I die. I promise to love you more each day, and I promise never to leave you—or ever pretend I'm dead—again."

Zoe laughed and wiped tears with her sleeve. "I, Zoe Kolby, take you, Tray Williams, to be my lawfully wedded husband. I promise to let you hold me in your arms and in our bed from this day forward, 'til the day I die."

He smiled. "There's one more thing."

She knew what she'd left out, what she hadn't told him, what was in her heart.

"If you don't say the words, I'll have to make love to you until you do."

"That's intended to frighten me?"

His hold tightened. "You're a hungry wench, aren't you?"

Her eyes met his intimately. "Only for you."

The passion in his gaze made her weak in

the knees. "It better be 'only for me.'" He grinned. "I don't want Perry Drake hanging around, trying to..."

"Pay my debts?" She eyed him knowingly. "You paid off that note, didn't you?"

"Me? Why would you think that?"

"Wipe that grin off your face. I put two and two together a long time ago. If Perry was inclined to do such a thing, he would have told me up front. You, on the other hand, are sneaky, conniving, underhanded—"

He touched her lips with his finger. "Say it."

"All right, all right. I *love* you. I've always loved you, and I always will."

His kiss stopped her, and she was lost in love. Nothing had ever felt more right, more welcome. He pulled her so tight against him she could barely catch her breath. For the first time, she found security in his embrace and knew it would last forever.

Gently, sweetly he ended the kiss. Her head swam with a million things she wanted to say, questions she wanted to ask, but being in his arms was enough. He nuzzled her ear with his nose, and he whispered what he wanted to do.

"Cade!"

"I told you, I *need* to make love to my wife."

"You're going to have to wait, Mr. Williams. I have to wake the children. They'll want to see you, to know that you're truly all right."

Cade picked her up in his arms and started toward the parlor. "In a minute. Right now I'm a man possessed. I want you now, Mrs.—

tell me again what our name's going to be?"

"Williams," she said, laying her head on his chest. His kiss was so masterful she would have agreed to anything he asked. Wiggling closer, she succumbed to her husband's ardor.

"Uncle Cwade!" Missy suddenly latched onto Cade's thigh. "You'we home!"

Zoe stepped back to let the other children between them as well.

Cade caught her arm and pulled her back. "I'm not through with you."

She smiled. "Better explain things to the kids, first."

Brody shoved his way in front of Will. "I cried real hard at your funeral, Uncle Cade. I pinched my arm so I could make real tears."

"He pinched my arm, too," Will said, sulking. "Made me cry out loud. Then Holly thumped me on the head."

"You were making a scene," Holly said, acting very grown-up.

Cade smiled and drew them all into his embrace. "You all did good. Even I was convinced I was in that coffin." He bowed down and kissed each one. "I've got something to say. We're family and always will be, but Cade Kolby is dead and buried. I'm Tray Williams now, and when I come back in a few weeks we'll all get married again. We'll be the Williams family."

Missy ran from the room and was back in seconds, thrusting Bud's jar toward Cade's face. "Bud, this is Tway. He looks like Uncle Cwade, but his name is Tway Williams. He's going to be youw daddy."

Zoe smiled.

"Tell Bud you love him, Tway Williams," Missy urged.

Cade stared into the jar. Beady eyes stared back. He cleared his throat and shifted nervously, turning toward Zoe for help. She nodded for him to comply. Taking a deep breath, he muttered, "I...I love you, Bud."

Zoe ushered the children toward the bedroom. "I think it's time you all kissed Tray good night."

After smothering Cade with enthusiastic hugs and kisses, the children scampered out of the room. Cade pulled Zoe back into his arms. "I can't believe I just told a damn tarantula I loved him."

"I thought it was very touching. Cade would have never been so sentimental, but Tray...I think I'm really going to like that man."

His lips found hers, gentle but possessive. The future lay before them, uncertain, exciting, with the promise of love. Zoe tilted her head back, gazed into the heavens, and whispered, "Thanks."

Above the driving rain still falling outside the window, she could have sworn she heard Addy say, "You're welcome. What are friends for?"